INHERENT TRUTH

BLOOD SECRETS ✦ BOOK 1

ALICIA ANTHONY

ISBN: 978-1-7333624-1-2 (Print)

ISBN: 978-1-7333624-0-5 (Ebook)

Published by Drury Lane Books, USA.

Keep up with Alicia online for up-to-the-minute news and reader extras at:

www.AliciaAnthonyBooks.com

Cover Art by Paper and Sage. www.PaperandSage.com

For Grandmother

*Thank you for teaching me what creativity can do for the soul.
I only wish I'd thought to ask more questions.*

PROLOGUE
LIV

I was ten when I watched my cousin die. Granted, at the time I didn't know the kid I'd seen through a light blue haze was a member of my family. To me, he was just a stranger, like all the rest. A specter sent from the depths of my brain to wake me up in the middle of the night. I still remember like it was yesterday.

The dream sent our household into a sleep deprived frenzy. Me, screaming for my parents to turn on the lights, tears running in rivers down flushed cheeks. My dad, sitting on the edge of the bed, rubbed his hand in circles across my shoulders, consoling me. It took a long distance phone call the following morning for my mom and dad to understand that the dream had been more than a figment of my overactive imagination.

"How did it happen?" My mother's voice was tight, wobbly as she spoke into the kitchen telephone receiver. It was the only one in the house that was still corded. I watched from the living room couch as she twisted the stretched curlicues of cord around her index finger.

When she slid into a chair at the kitchen table with her

hand planted firmly over her lips, heaviness descended on the room, blanketing the air with cold finality. To this day I remember the lead weight in my chest, the struggle for breath. Maybe that's what he'd felt in his last moments. My mother was still holding the phone in one hand when she turned to stare at me. Eyes wide with some emotion I couldn't yet interpret. Now, sixteen years later, I can tell you for certain it was terror.

My sixteen-year-old cousin, Curt, had been killed racing home from a party to make curfew. I'd seen it all. Told my parents every detail. The skid on the damp roadway. The slam into a poorly placed telephone pole. Even the good Samaritans who'd stopped in the dead of night to try to dig him out of the twisted wreckage. Smoke filtered up from the heap of metal before I saw him, standing on the other side of the car, smiling at me.

"Tell Mom, I'm sorry," he'd said. His voice cut short by the wail of a siren.

It's funny. I can still picture that dream in lifelike detail. But now, instead of terror, there's a peaceful comfort attached to the memory. I think that's how it works for me. The visions can't hold any power over me once I work them out–figure out how to help.

In those early days, I'd been scared senseless. I'd wake up in a cold sweat, flailing to turn a light on, to familiarize myself with reality again. For a while I slept with the bedside lamp on, hoping the luminescence would create some kind of barrier between this world and the next. It was my grandmother who helped me realize it was useless, of course. The dreams were a part of reality–my reality, anyway.

But that awareness of what my dreams were–what that made me–changed everything. The energy in our household sparked with frustration. My mother and father argued. Family outings trickled to a rare occurrence. My life consisted of school, home, homework, and bed, praying to whatever god would listen to let me sleep through the night. Every once in a while some deity would listen, most times, not. I learned to keep what I saw to myself. Wash, rinse, repeat.

Within two years, my mother had run through all the psychiatrists and magic pills she could find to make me normal again. By the time I was twelve, I was spending the majority of my time at my grandparents' farm, away from the family I'd disgraced and the marriage I'd destroyed. At least, that's how it seemed to twelve-year-old me.

"I will not allow my daughter to be a freak." My mother's words after a particularly heated exchange with my father regarding my condition are what drove me to become the Liv Sullivan I am today.

The "f" word, as I'd taken to calling it, hummed in my skull now, just as it had when I was a girl. Hunkered down on the steps of my parents' home, eavesdropping through tears, the people I loved arguing about an affliction I didn't fully understand and over which I had no control.

Of course, if it wasn't for all of that, I might never have learned I had two choices in life–remain the small-town freak or reinvent myself as a big city fraud. I chose the latter, finding out pretty quick that the best place to hide was in plain sight.

I grabbed my headset off the chair and slid into position in front of my laptop, fresh cup of coffee in hand. Rays of early January sun filtered through the sliding glass door of my studio apartment.

"Liv, you free?" A clipped note of anxiety in Celeste's voice crackled through the earpiece. Cee and I had worked together for almost two years now and although we'd never met in person, she was the closest thing I had to a friend. She worked from headquarters, dispatching calls, and always passed the most challenging cases off to me. But more calls meant more money. I glanced at the stack of unpaid bills on the corner of my desk. At this point, I'd take just about any loon she threw my way.

"I'm here, Cee. What's the story?"

"Won't say. Came in on the direct line. Asked for you by name."

"Gotta be a regular. Patch him through." The musical *ding* from my headset signaled the transfer. I waited for the line to click open before launching into the script. "Thank you for calling Celestial Spirit, my name is..."

"Olivia." My name on his voice split my mind in half, emptying my lungs and echoing with an all too familiar surge of electricity. I cleared my throat, fighting the haze that pulled me in, raking over my skin like fingers of an unseen being. My scalp prickled against the force. He kept talking, unaware I had no breath to respond.

"They routed me through two other people before you, *Gabriella*." He dragged the pseudonym out, letting it roll over his tongue. I shivered, a snake of fear crawling down my spine. "You should use your real name. They already know where you are."

I sucked in a breath, forcing air into my lungs and squeezing my eyes shut against the onslaught of memory that wasn't my own.

"I'm sorry, do we know each other?" I fought to infuse my voice with some sense of normal.

"Not yet," he said.

There was a pregnant stillness before the image slammed into me. I squinted against the hum in my skull, focusing on the yellow smiley face mug on my desk. Bright colors sometimes helped stave off the visions. But the image tightened its grip, seeped into my consciousness and blocked out the comfortable reality of my studio apartment.

Blue eyes, frightened and wide, stared at me–a moving image clawing its way into my consciousness, refusing to let go. Long honey-blonde hair swept crossways over pale skin. A gust of wind sent her locks flying, twisting them over her face and obscuring her features.

She turned to run, a yelp of fear filling the wooded space around her. Thunder broke the silence, followed closely by a bolt of lightning that lit the entire woods– a woods I knew.

"It's taken them a while to find you," the caller said, his voice cutting through the buzz, grounding me in reality.

I shook my head, the image dissolving from vibrant hues into shadows surrounded by blue haze. I picked up the mug of coffee from my desk, thumbing the hard smoothness of the ceramic handle, anything to maintain connection to the real world. As I brought it to my lips, my hand trembled, sloshing a bit of the black liquid onto the papers below. I covered the headset mic and forced an exhaled, "Just get this over with."

"Tell me what question urged you to call today, and my spirit guides and I will help uncover the answers you seek." Somehow, I managed to deliver the line without a hint of wobble in my voice. Although, the scripted nonsense still made my stomach twist.

It was bad enough when I had to say it to random hotline callers, the ones who wanted to know if they should take that job offer or if the guy they met on the train was "the one." But callers like this? Thank God these guys didn't call often.

"You see her, don't you?" His breath hitched in the line between us. I caught the hint of an accent. Born somewhere else but raised in the States?

I replaced the mug on my desk and closed my eyes, allowing the blue haze to trickle in, like smoke under a doorway. The image flooded back, the panic behind her eyes punched through the fog as the image widened. She turned away, long pale legs beneath cut-off shorts pumping as she ran. Large hands reached for her. Tree branches stretched gnarled fingers, slashing the soft, exposed flesh on her face and arms.

"She's your sister." Somehow, I knew. The same way I knew he wasn't lying when he said they knew where I was. If only I could figure out who "they" was. "She's missing."

I clenched my jaw as the image shifted. The haze intensified, the hum along my jawbone sending a slice of pain through my temple. She tripped. A panicked scream ripped from her lungs. Her attacker lunged. She faced him, scrambling, crab-style backward. Another bolt of lightning split the sky. And I saw it. The familiar boat house at the edge of my grandparent's farm, two thousand miles away in Cascade Hills, Ohio.

"Who are you?" I managed into the headset through clenched teeth. "Where are you calling from?"

There was only breath on the other end. The open-air silence of satisfaction. Of someone who'd accomplished what he'd set out to do.

Large hands gripped the girl's throat. Not girl exactly—a few years younger than me—twenty, twenty-two maybe?

"Don't do this. Please don't do this." Her voice was small, constricted by the hands wrapped around her throat. Her attacker squeezed, pulling her forward and thrusting her back with the force of a jackhammer. She dug dirty, chewed fingernails into the back of his hands, his arms. But he was too strong, she too fragile. Words became gasps. Widened eyes. Silent fish gulps of air. One last thrust sent her tumbling backward. Her limp body landing with a crunch against the leaf-strewn ground of Sullivan woods—my woods.

I squinted against the scene. My own muscles trembling in response to the force. A rollercoaster of terror roared through my gut. I jerked the headset from my head and bent to the side, over the trash can, waiting for the dry heaves to subside.

Breathe, I coached. Pushing out breath and pulling it in to ease the panic constricting my chest. The heat of a tear against my cheek completed the familiar cycle, evaporating the image and pulling me back from the brink of someone else's reality.

"Are you there?" His voice was small and tinny from the headset speaker. I shoved the earpieces back onto my ears.

"I'm here," I assured. Apologizing, I adjusted the mic so that my irregular breathing didn't overpower our conversation.

"How long has she been gone?" I asked. Silence on the other end of the line.

"You'll be next, Olivia," he finally said, his voice dark, clotted with emotion.

I ignored the warning, jotting notes on the pad of paper in front of me. *Girl, missing, blue eyes, strangled, Sullivan Farm.* My fingers hesitated over the last words, a trickle of guilt joining the ranks of second-hand terror.

The corner of the script I was supposed to be using peeked out from under the short stack of mail on the edge of my desk. I tugged it free. *Stick to the script this time, Olivia.*

"Have you called the police?" I asked, flipping through the tabs, searching for the label marked, Illegal Acts.

My boss's latest warning came just two days ago. Her bracelets jangled like rings of bells cuffing both wrists. She'd warned me more than once not to veer from the accepted attorney-vetted script. It seemed psychic call centers were less connections to the otherworld and more well-oiled money machines. Go figure. No one, not even my boss, thought I actually possessed psychic abilities. Little known fact, the more you claim to have them, the less people believe you.

"It's too late, Olivia. The police don't care about people like us."

I closed my eyes, pulling the emotion from his voice. Anxiety. Hurt. Frustration. But deep down, a sensation I didn't expect—honesty. The energy thumped, pulsing against my eardrums.

"She trusted them. You saw how that turned out."

I pushed the script away. Screw protocol. "How do you know who I am?"

The heat of his frustration singed my ears as he responded. "Don't push us away, Olivia. They want you back in Cascade Hills, and they'll find a way to make it happen."

The familiar *beep* of the ten-minute warning cut through the silence between us.

"You deserved to be warned. You're the only one with the power to stop them. Please, Olivia. We need you."

1

———

LIV

My grandmother's voice pierced the haze of sleep. *"It's time, Olivia."* Her spoken words transformed into the melodic chorus of "Danny Boy," a song I'd heard countless times over lazy summer days spent at my grandparents' farm. Perfectly in tune, and full of my grandmother's usual warmth, only the intense melancholy in her voice signaled that life was about to change.

I roused as the shroud of sleep fell away—not completely awake, but somewhere in that in-between state that exists only in dreams. That fine line between reality and the whims of the subconscious. I knew the space too well.

My grandmother was not really here, not in my tiny apartment in Southern California. Yet this was more than just a dream, a fabrication of the typical sleeping mind. Walking the line of the normal subconscious would have been a blessing. But no, as usual, I'd gone beyond, straddling this world and the next.

I rubbed my eyes and turned toward her voice. She stood at

the kitchen sink, not my own nondescript stainless steel version, but the old porcelain apron-front atop the aged wood cabinetry in the Sullivan farmhouse. I sat up on the edge of my bed and listened as she digressed from singing and began to hum the remaining stanzas of the classic Irish tune. A red and white gingham dishtowel flicked expertly around a bright floral-patterned dish, finally coming to rest across her shoulder.

She turned toward me, and the breath caught in my lungs. No matter how many visions I had, I never seemed prepared. Her apparition as real as if she'd landed that afternoon at LAX. More fully-formed than the intense grip of daytime visions, the nighttime images were easier to immerse myself in. I forced a breath and took in the full vision of my grandmother. She winked at me as she made her way from the kitchen toward the antique dining table that had materialized in my living room. All that remained of my studio apartment was the bed on which I sat. My familiar walls and décor slid away into the foggy abyss that framed the vision in front of me.

Grandma's pale blue dressing gown fluttered gently against sun-starved legs. How many Saturday mornings had I come downstairs to the kitchen at Sullivan farm to see exactly this image? For anyone else, that's what this would be—a memory-induced dream, a creation of the subconscious. But not for me.

The blue of her gown, coupled with the stream of light filtering through an imaginary window, added a shimmer to her eyes. My grandmother had the most beautiful eyes. Rich pools of pale cornflower blue that twinkled when she laughed. A knot rose in my throat. How I longed to hear that laugh.

"Do you remember this one, Liv?" She looked at me. Her gaze pulling like the fingers of some unseen force, coaxing me to join her at the table. I worked my toes into the carpet beneath my feet and I stood from the side of the bed, shuffling toward the vignette in front of me. She pushed a grainy photo-

graph across well-worn oak as I slid into the chair opposite her. The spindles of the oak chair pressing into my spine were the only proof I'd moved from my perch on the bed.

"I took that when he was on a weekend leave in Germany. Can you believe I flew all the way over there just for a weekend with your grandfather?" A light chuckle, like a breeze through well-tuned wind chimes, escaped her lips.

I smiled at the mischievous glint in my grandma's watery blue eyes. "I bet he was glad you made the effort."

She reached her hand to cover mine and gave a squeeze. The warmth of her touch spiraled a note of helplessness down my spine as I battled the nugget of comprehension that explained her appearance. I clenched my jaw against the tears pricking at the backs of my eyes, determined to focus on the smiling faces of my young grandparents, primitively colorized in the photograph in front of me. They'd looked so happy.

"It's time." Playfulness evaporated from her voice. *"You ignored the warning, but you can't ignore your legacy."*

My stomach tightened as she took the photograph from my hand and replaced it in the leather-bound photo album I remembered seeing at the farm.

"This is about the girl in the woods, isn't it?" My voice rose above the tentative whisper I usually used with visiting spirits. The call had come a couple months ago, just after New Year's, but there wasn't a day that slipped by it didn't weigh on me.

Every time I closed my eyes, I saw her. Fearful, wide, blue eyes, freckles sprinkled across the bridge of her nose, but what haunted me the most were the familiar trees, the boat house where I'd played hide-n-seek as a child. The gentle lap of water against the nearby shore. All tarnished now. I once knew every square foot of that woods. But that seemed like a lifetime ago. The last time I'd been at Sullivan Farm was over three years ago when we'd moved my grandmother into an assisted living center.

"I expect you'll take good care of these." She ignored my question and patted the cover of the album gently, running both hands over it as if she didn't want to let it go. *"There's something I need you to find, Liv."*

Before I could respond, my grandmother turned, ushering a little girl from the bluish fog behind her. I shoved away the flash of blue eyes that pricked from my memory. This wasn't the missing girl from that mysterious call, the color and shape of her eyes was proof enough for me. I waited for her to speak, but she remained mute. Rosebud lips pressed in a hard line. She just stared at me with enormous deep green eyes.

Her strawberry blonde hair was arranged in pigtail braids and tied with blue satin ribbons, one of which was dirty, the bow bedraggled. She wore a pale yellow dress with short sleeves, the hem draping just above the dimples of her knees. Tiny blue embroidered flowers danced in rows across the smocked bodice. A pair of matching socks and well-worn Stride Rite Mary Janes completed the look. She was cute. Haunting, but adorable.

I shrugged off the eerie familiarity. Images of family photos flew like microfiche files through my brain. I searched each one for someone who could match the girl's description but came up empty. One thought nagged. I shoved against it, but it persisted—she looked like me.

"Who is she?" My voice a whisper, a waver in the silence.

"The answers rest with her. Come home, Liv." My grandmother's voice hung like an echo as the vision faded, dissipating like sun-burned fog. I searched Grandma's eyes. The knot in my throat thickened with the understanding that I'd never again see their sparkle in the light of day. She raised her long, thin fingers to her lips and blew me a kiss.

EARLY MORNING SUNLIGHT streamed from my balcony window. The heat of it warmed my face as I blinked my eyes open. The dining table was gone. The ghostly farmhouse kitchen replaced with my own Formica breakfast bar. I lay in bed, my fingers still pressed to my lips, an unrealized effort to return my grandmother's goodbye. I'd learned through the years how to speak to the visitors when they came. I could even touch them if the conditions were right. But I'd yet to master the ability to create lasting physical movement.

I pulled myself upright in bed. A sense of déjà vu washed over me as I lowered my feet to the floor. I paused, staring at the blue polish on my toes, ignoring the first trill of my cell ringtone, giving the remaining fuzziness time to release its grip. I coughed through the knot in my throat, the only tangible reminder of my grandmother's visit, and snatched my phone off the nightstand, ignoring the caller ID.

A soft-spoken nurse from New Horizon's Retirement Community asked for me by name. "I'm sorry to have to call, Miss Sullivan. It's your grandmother, Grace. She passed away this morning, just a couple hours ago."

I'd known on some level, of course. The dream was proof of that but hearing the words from another's lips made it real.

"Grace asked that you be notified first. It's my understanding you have a bit of a journey ahead to get here."

I nodded as if the nurse could see me.

"We'll call Foster's Mortuary. Have her taken there until you can arrive to confirm her arrangements. Okay?"

"Yes," I squeaked out. The suck of grief pulled at my gut, twisting until I thought I might be sick. Clarity hit with sudden force. "My mother. Have you notified Beth Sullivan?"

"Not yet. Would you like us to take care of that for you?"

"Please," I managed. The first word I'd spoken with any kind of conviction since the call came in. I thanked the nurse again and hung up, staring at the phone in my hand. Most of the horrors that peppered these visions were manageable—strangers I could distance myself from. But no amount of ignoring or suffusing the situation would change the fact that the one person I'd always been able to count on, the woman who helped me make it to adulthood, was dead.

A draft ruffled the curtain at the open sliding glass door leading onto my tiny balcony. I sucked in a breath of the cool morning air. Nothing like the pure country breeze that filtered through my bedroom window at my grandparents' farm. L.A. held a different mystique, the distinct rubber and gas of traffic mixed with the spice-infused aroma of the nearby Korean restaurant. I closed my eyes, inhaling the familiar scent of my current surroundings, anything to keep me grounded.

I stared out the balcony window. The Hollywood sign peeked just above the array of low-slung buildings. I tossed my phone onto the bedspread and stood up, forcing truth aside long enough to grab my laptop off the desk and search for the cheapest flight home to Cascade Hills, Ohio.

2

LIV

The room at the Holiday Inn was pitch black. The faint glow of streetlights filtered in around the edges of closed curtains as I peered through the darkness. Switching on the reading lamp above the bed, I grabbed the journal I'd learned to keep handy.

Come home, I scrawled, for the second time. My grandmother's words. The same ones that hung in the air after her first visit two nights ago were haunting me now.

"Well, Grandma, I'm here. Now what?" I whispered into the darkness. My fingers skimmed over the blank page in my lap, arcs of graphite morphing into the face of a little girl as I sketched. Her familiarity was haunting. She couldn't be more than five-years-old. Wide eyes and thin-pressed lips.

I finished my drawing, flipping back a few pages to the image of the young woman. A connection was there, I was sure. But no matter how hard I tried, I couldn't find it. Did I know her? Had we been friends? I sighed. What did it matter anyway? Grandma was dead, and like every other vision I had, so was she.

I replaced the pencil and notebook on the nightstand, hunkering down under the thick hotel bedspread. The distant scream of a siren, blaring its way toward some emergency colored my futile attempt at sleep.

I tossed under the weight of the duvet. My mind shuffling between images of my grandmother and a ghostly little girl, the terror-stricken eyes of an innocent young woman, and the inherent expectations of this journey back to Cascade Hills. No train of thought allowed my brain the peace it needed to find sleep. I sighed in the silence of the room. If I was going to find out what my grandmother needed from me, there was only one place to start–Sullivan farm.

In one swift movement, I flung the covers off and rose from the bed. I skipped the shower and dressed in the dark–the fluorescence of the bathroom lights too much for my overworked and jet-lagged brain. I opted for jeans and an old Cascade Hills High School sweatshirt that should have been retired a decade ago. Refusing to neglect my gums, I squeezed a dollop of Crest onto my toothbrush and watched my reflection in the mirror, wondering, not for the first time, why a scared little girl still stared back at me today.

THE CLOCK on the dashboard of my rental read just after three A.M. when I pulled onto Sullivan Road. Empty corn and soybean fields flanked both sides of the car. A smile tickled the corners of my lips, a familiar peacefulness rising in my chest.

I loved coming to my grandparents' farm. Through the school year I spent every weekend here, and in the summer I might as well have changed my address. Mom and Dad went about their normal small-town lives–my father, a successful attorney turned town politician, my mother, the respected phil-anthropic socialite.

We lived near Sullivan farm, in the town of Cascade Hills, but I always felt caught somewhere in between when the three of us were together. Out here at the farm, though, I was free. Free to be who I wanted, do what I wanted, and most impor-tantly, dream without fear of judgement. That absence of judgement was only present at the farm. Staying here was liber-ating on so many levels.

I slowed to pull into the long driveway. 7667 glinted back at me, the headlights of the rental catching the reflective numbers on the mailbox post. The final seven leaned at an odd angle, a reminder of the emptiness that awaited me at the end of the drive. I breathed a long sigh, an effort to tamp down the unjustified squeeze of excitement in my chest.

I knew the house was empty...cold...lifeless. Had been since my mother convinced my grandmother to live at New Hori-zon's. The house was too big. Too much for my grandmother to take care of alone. And now, even the room at the retirement home was empty. Regardless of reality, the exhilaration of being home sucked the air from my lungs.

The old Victorian farmhouse came into view, looming like an eerie shadow. I maneuvered the car in the overgrown gravel of the barn lot, parking perpendicular to the sidewalk, ensuring the headlights would illuminate the front door. Part of me half-expected my grandmother to open the screen door and step out onto the wrap-around porch. She would wipe her hands on her apron before spreading her arms wide, enveloping me in a bear hug. I shook the threat of the tearful memory away and focused on the darkened residence.

The massive brick façade was now partially obscured by decades of ivy growth creeping along its face and climbing each of its three chimneys. Grandpa had done his best to keep it at bay, knowing the damage it could cause, but Grandma took a liking to it, and after his death she'd let it grow unfettered.

I could see vegetation beginning to lay claim to parts of the porch that had previously been free. The dark windows and mossy brick sent a chill down my spine, prickling the hairs at the back of my neck and dampening the euphoria that had been building since pulling onto Sullivan Road. I'd always known I'd have to give this place up eventually, but how do you say goodbye to the one place you felt safe?

I shifted the Civic into park, making sure to keep the key on accessory mode so that the headlamps would continue to shine. I'd worry about a dead battery later, if it came to that.

"I'm here, Grandma," I whispered into the frigid night. "Help me find what you need."

My breath rose in a cloud of vapor as I lifted myself from the car and closed the door behind me. I cleared my throat, coughing through a clot of tears, and picked my way up the cracked cement walk. I glanced eastward, realizing too late that the only flashlight I had was a tiny LED on the end of my apartment keychain. *Stupid*, I muttered under my breath, scolding myself for being completely unprepared as I returned to the car to dig the light out of the bottom of my purse.

Three deteriorating steps led onto the generous porch. Ivy doused everything in darkness, even the headlamps fighting to pierce the veil seemed dim and insignificant. I angled sideways, a fruitless attempt to allow the Civic's beams to shine through. Headlights or not, the porch remained swaddled in a blanket of black.

I squeezed the keychain LED on and stepped carefully toward the front door. My fingers slid along the trim of the entryway, searching for the handle of the storm door I'd swung open countless times before. Cold metal found my palm and I gripped the handle, yanking it toward me. With a groan of hesitation, the door gave way.

Propping the storm with my foot, I pushed against the lever action knob on the leaded glass door. Locked. As it should be. I aimed the tiny beam toward the lower right casing. Fashioned by Grandpa more than fifteen years ago, the tiny box chiseled into the trim held the only spare key I knew about.

My lungs squeezed with the memory of my Grandpa, hunkered down over the doorframe, drilling and chiseling while I cried in Grandma's arms. They'd been gone, playing cards with some friends, when a fight with my parents sent me running. I'd hitched a ride from town, not the most intelligent move for a thirteen-year-old girl, but desperation does funny things to a person. I'd been alone on the porch for a couple hours before they got home and found me there. After that, the key was always tucked away, just for me.

I held my breath and closed my eyes in silent prayer. The cover shifted beneath my fingertips, eventually breaking the seal of time and shimmying free. The glint of metal in the beam of LED was my reward. The pull of a smile on my lips followed me as I withdrew the key from its hiding place and turned it in the tarnished lock.

The entry door gave way to a wake of thick, musty air, deadening the dregs of excitement that had somehow held on. The tiny pinpoint of light penetrated only a foot or two before dissipating into the murky atmosphere. I coughed through the dust and waved it away from my face.

Even though I'd known the house was empty, I was not prepared for this. The familiar smells of vanilla and lavender, mixed with a hint of Pine-Sol, were long gone, replaced by the unmistakable scent of emptiness. I checked my watch, hoping that, somehow, I'd travelled through time and ended up closer to dawn than I really was. No such luck.

I peered into the blackness toward what was once my grandmother's living room. I could make out the couch, still situated in front of the fireplace across the room. To my left would be my grandfather's study and the staircase. To my right, the dining room and hall to the kitchen. Navigating these rooms would not be a problem. How often had I snuck down the stairs, through the parlor, and out the kitchen in the middle of the night without anyone noticing? More than I cared to admit, that's for sure.

I walked blindly through the foyer, into the parlor and toward the kitchen hall. Grandma had been in the kitchen when she came to me. It was as good a place to start as any. The last time I'd seen my grandmother's photo albums they'd been tucked safely in the pie safe at the edge of kitchen counter. I was hoping to find the haunted eyes of a little girl staring out from one of the yellowed pages. But besides that, the kitchen was on the east side of the house. It would get light before any of the other rooms did. And right now, light was in desperately short supply.

I reached into the darkness around me, grasping at familiar furnishings to get my bearings. My fingers slid along the back of the couch. Covered with a sheet, it sat like a ghost in front of the gaping black mouth of the wood-burning fireplace.

I palmed the wall beside the living room fireplace with my left hand. The plaster was cold and hard, leaving a film of grime on my skin as I pushed forward. I imagined my handprint on the wall, my fingers displacing three years of dust. Grandma would be devastated to see her home this way.

Why Mom couldn't have spent some of Dad's money to hire a company to clean the place once a month was a mystery. I flicked the light switch at the corner a few times, out of habit more than anything else. Mom never would have kept the electric on out here.

I shuffled around the corner and into the hallway. My feet thumped against something, halting my forward movement. From memory, nothing should have been here crowding the hall to the kitchen. I kicked gently with the toe of my tennis shoe. Whatever it was gave way against my feet, sliding an inch or two across the hardwood. I aimed my LED toward the floor, squinting at the object–a cardboard box, ragged and unclosed. The LED beam waned, and I squeezed harder. A dark shape spilled from the open flaps of weathered corrugation–still unidentifiable.

The tiny beam flickered twice and died just as I summoned the courage to take a closer look.

3

———

LIV

"Stupid tiny little button-cell batteries." I said it as if I'd get a response, shaking the keychain and pushing the dime-sized button even harder. As if more pressure would force energy into the dead battery. I pocketed the useless keychain and kneeled blindly in front of the box, hoping whatever was sticking out of the top would be identifiable in the darkness.

I felt from side to side until something tickled my palm. Soft. Fabric. I ventured a touch –gliding the material between my fingers. Not cotton. The cloth was too slippery. My fingernails over its surface made a light *shhh* sound, tugging a memory loose from my childhood. An evening spent under the stars with my dad, the cool *shhh-shhh* of my arms against the exterior of a sleeping bag. That was it. I suddenly didn't care where it had come from. If there was a sleeping bag, surely the possibility of a flashlight being stuffed in beside it existed.

A flash in the hall mirror stopped me cold, my arm poised in mid-search. A darkened silhouette, backlit by two cars in the driveway, climbed the porch stairs, feet from the open entryway door. I froze, my eyes glued to the reflection, working to make out details. Someone I knew? I hadn't told anyone I was coming out here, not even Cee knew I was in Cascade Hills.

Heavy-soled shoes echoed against the boards of the porch floor, reverberating through my chest, mimicking the pounding in my ears.

I pressed myself against the opposite wall, closing my eyes to breathe through the wave of panic that clutched me. Forcing air in and out of petrified lungs proved a challenge as I worked to tamp down the growing knot in my stomach. I slid silently to the floor, the mysterious box my last line of defense. What was I going to do, fling a sleeping bag over him? Old episodes of Scooby Doo flitted with the edges of my memory. It always turned out okay for them. I forced my eyes open, tracking the reverse image of the figure in the mirror. Tall. Broad-shouldered.

The front door gave a familiar groan. *It's too dark. He can't see you.* The rational part of my brain reasoned with my fear receptors, but fear disputed. *Your car is out there, dummy. He knows someone is here.*

I flattened against the wall, working to coach my heart into a serviceable rhythm. I watched what I could through the mirror. One glance away and back again...gone. I risked a glance toward the front window, creeping my fingers along the plaster wall until a beam of light aimed my direction.

"Cascade Hills Police! Anybody in here?" A man's voice penetrated the darkness.

My heart pounded in my ears. The hairs on the back of my neck stood at attention. I had two choices—answer him or continue to hide in the shadows. If the rental hadn't been outside, I definitely would've stayed hidden. Although, the fact suddenly occurred to me, I was Grace Sullivan's granddaughter. I had every right to be here.

I gathered my wits, ready to step forward into the waiting beam of his flashlight. But before I could, a distinct *bang* ricocheted through the silence of the empty house–the unmistakable percussion of the back door slamming closed. I'd recognize it anywhere.

Thick *thumps* on the wooden risers of the patio stairs echoed into the night. The officer's flashlight followed my own line of sight, swinging away from the hall and toward the sound, shrouding me again in total blackness.

My mind raced, processing possibilities. The house was empty. The idea that someone would hole up in a vacant house in the country wasn't far-fetched. But my skin crawled with the thought that I'd been in here, alone, with whoever was willing to spend the remainder of the wee morning hours running from the Cascade Hills Police.

The officer turned on his heel, exiting the same way he'd entered. I stepped out of the hall, my legs jellified. He disappeared around the corner of the house, taking off at a sprint toward the rear patio and apparent escapee.

By the time I found enough strength to force my legs into motion, he was standing about twenty feet from the corner of the house. He swept the high-powered beam of his flashlight across the overgrown yard. I tracked the arc of light across the backyard. Nothing. Just the breeze in the tall grass and faint ripples of lake water washing onto the shore. He didn't have to spend summers here like I did to know there were a thousand places to hide between the house and lake, not to mention the outlet Cascade Lake itself offered.

His voice was calm as he called for backup. I waited until he'd pocketed his cell before clearing my throat. The wariness in my voice surprised even myself. "Did you see who it was?"

He spun around. The blinding beam of light sent a pulsing ache to the back of my eyes.

"Hands up where I can see them."

I shoved my hands toward the sky, squinting against the brightness, forcing my eyes to stay open. I couldn't make out any features. He was nothing but a dark shadow, no longer distracted by a rogue trespasser, and now wholly focused on me. His silhouette advanced toward me, arms extended, closing the distance between us.

My body reacted before my mind could process that the extension of his right hand was a gun. My heart kicked up a beat, thrumming against the inside of my chest. I should have stayed inside, hidden in the shadows. I sucked in a jagged breath. Reminding myself that I belonged here.

"I'm not armed." It was barely a whisper. I said it again, louder this time. Wasn't that what I was supposed to say? Images recently raked across the news media indicated it didn't much matter. But he did stop his advance. Gun still poised.

"What's your name?"

"Olivia..." Another whisper. I cleared my throat. "Olivia Sullivan." The words felt like sandpaper on my tongue.

He took a step back, relaxed his stance. "Who ran out the back door?"

I shook my head. "I don't know. I thought I was alone."

He swept me up and down in the beam of his light. I exhaled as he holstered his gun. Squinting, I lowered one arm, shielding my light-starved eyes from the painful glare. Still, all I could make out was his outline.

Tall and broad shouldered was true enough. And he wore a jacket—what looked like a leather jacket. No hat. Did cops even wear hats anymore? I checked beyond him, the reeds near the lakeshore swayed gently in the breeze. How easy it would be to hide there. A sudden surge of panic tightened its grip around my lungs.

"This is private property, ma'am." His voice distracted me from the shoreline. "What business do you have here?"

I strained to get a better look at the man attached to the voice. Searching for proof that he was who he claimed to be.

"I'm sorry..." I hesitated before adding an uncertain, "...Officer. This is...*was*... my grandmother's home." I could hear my words wavering in the air between us. *Pull it together, Olivia.* Cold air pricked at the bare skin on my neck and face.

The man removed the flashlight beam from my face long enough to scan the area around us once more. With help from the halogen glow of headlights, I started to make out some of his features. He had a square jaw line. Dark hair cropped shorter on the sides than on the top. The angle of his nose a silhouette in the ambient glow. My eyes dropped lower. His right hand still rested on his sidearm.

A nervous flicker shimmied down my spine. He fixed the beam on my face, blinding me again. On instinct, I lifted my hand against the invasive shaft of light. He stepped forward, making a point to aim the flashlight off to the side. It still lit up my face, but at least I could look at him without squinting.

"She passed away yesterday." My breath caught. It felt wrong when I said it.

"But she hasn't lived here for several years. She's been in a nursing home. I've been out of state." I caught myself. *Verbal diarrhea.* That's what Cee used to call it when we had callers that gave us more information than we needed.

"We got a call about a possible intruder at this residence. Do you have any identification on you?"

"Um... of course... it's in the car. I'll get it."

He nodded. Lighting a path and following me toward the rental. "The electric is turned off here, I assume?"

"Yes."

"So, you were in there in the dark, then?" Suspicion added an edge to his voice.

I held up my tiny keychain.

"It just went out." I couldn't help but flash a smile at the officer. It was a horrible nervous habit that had gotten me in trouble more than once over the years. I knew it looked a bit off, someone prowling around a deserted house at four o'clock in the morning with nothing but a broken LED keychain to light their way. I scolded myself again for forgetting to bring a proper flashlight. The seed of panic took root in my gut, tipping the corners of my nervous smile into a frown. Someone *had* been out here, doing God knows what. And I'd been in there with them.

I could feel the officer watch me as I walked. Sparking an involuntary pulse of attraction, followed by a flicker of uneasiness.

"You don't have a cell phone?" he asked, voice ripe with skepticism. He hesitated before adding, "There's an app for that, you know."

I cringed at my stupidity. Of course, there is. What idiot forgets that? I stuffed away the embarrassment of not using my cell phone flashlight and popped open the driver's side door. The interior light bathed his face in a mild glow for the first time. Light eyes danced in the low light. He studied me a beat before letting a reserved chuckle slip out, his eyes landing on the tiny keychain again.

The sound of his laugh sent a cascade of calm to counteract my churning insides. I liked the sound of it—real, warm. He wasn't making fun, just enjoying the absurdity of it all.

I reached into the front seat for my purse. The corners of my lips pulled up into a smile once my back was turned. He was handsome. Had a great smile (what I saw of it anyway), one of those relaxed grins that puts everyone at ease. I might have even noticed a dimple or two. *Are you freaking serious, Liv? Focus.*

I struggled with my wallet, working to shimmy my license from its place between the filmy plastic window and a plethora of other rarely used cards. My eyes had finally adjusted to the lack of light. Blessedly, unobscured by the dusty atmosphere of the house. The muscle in his jaw tensed when he saw my California license.

"California?" he asked.

"I grew up here, but I've lived there since college." Why was I explaining myself? I had every right to be here. I pulled myself up as tall as my five-foot-three frame would allow.

"Why were you here?" he asked, stepping away and narrowing the beam of flashlight toward my face again.

"My grandmother's funeral is in a couple days. I wanted to find her photo album so we could use a few pictures for the service." It wasn't a flat out lie.

"At four in the morning?"

"I couldn't sleep," I admitted. No lie there.

He stood, surveying me and my license. The muscle in his jaw ticked.

"I'm sorry for your loss, but I'm sure you understand, I'll need to do some checking before I can allow you back in the house. There's a car on the way. We need to find out who was inside and why." His eyes roamed back to the house. "How'd you get in anyway?"

I hesitated before admitting, "I know where the spare key is."

"So, the door was locked when you got here?"

"It was." I realized then that whoever was out here had to have broken in some way. A window? The back door? The cellar? My key? There were a hundred different ways someone could get in an old house like this. I followed the officer's gaze to the looming exterior and scanned the darkness around us. Farm fields edged the property to the north and west, woods to the south, and Cascade Lake to the east. There wasn't another house within miles. Who would have reported an intruder?

The heat of the officer's stare broke through my thoughts as he continued, "Right. Well, I'll need a local address and phone number... in case we have questions later."

I met his eyes for the first time. A wave of panic crashed over me. The intensity of his gaze stripping me bare. It was as though he could see inside me, read my thoughts. I shook the ridiculous idea away and gave him my cell number. He scrawled it into a palm-sized notebook. I watched in fascination while the muscle in his jaw worked as he copied my license information underneath my cell number.

"Here's my card... in case you need to get in touch with me." He quickly printed a phone number on the back of the card. "I'm Ridge McCaffrey. My cell is on the back. I'll call you once I've checked you out..." He hesitated, clearing his throat and clicking the ballpoint pen a couple times in rapid succession, a dimple appearing in his left cheek. "Once I've *verified* your information."

I smiled. Nice to know I wasn't the only one struggling with composure.

"Will you let me know when it's safe to come back? There are some things I need to take care of out here." I lifted my head to study his face again. The contrast between dark eyebrows and vibrant eyes was riveting. He held my gaze as he handed my license back. Our fingertips brushed. Heat rose into my cheeks as a surge of electricity passed between us. *Jesus.* I looked away. *What the hell was wrong with me?*

"Of course. I'll let you know what we find out."

The wail of approaching sirens sounded from the state route. At least maybe they'd figure out who'd been holing up in my grandmother's house. I doubted they'd find the culprit before dawn, though. A chill wormed its way down my spine as the next question crept into my mind. *How long had the intruder been here?*

"Drive safe," he offered, his voice deep and smooth, a trait I hadn't noticed yet. He strode back to his own car and picked up a radio, mumbling something I couldn't hear. His eyes met mine as I slipped into my own car and watched him through the side view mirror as he slid into the driver's seat of an unmarked black Mustang.

A niggle of worry crept in. Was he really an officer with the Cascade Hills Police Department? I never asked to see a badge. *Stupid.* Wasn't that Personal Safety 101? I kept watching as he backed up, allowing space for me to execute a three-point turn before he killed the growl of the Mustang and headed back into the house. I glanced repeatedly through the rear-view mirror for as long as possible before rounding the bend in the drive, pushing the house and car out of sight.

I focused on the crunch of gravel beneath the tires of my rental. By the time I made it at my snail's pace to the end of the drive, two Cascade Hills cruisers were pulling in, putting to rest the twinge of suspicion. *You should stay,* my inner critic chimed in. I squashed her demand for answers and pulled onto Sullivan Road.

Answers weren't likely in the dark hours of morning with a thousand places for a criminal to hide. They had a job to do, and I'd only be in the way. I sucked in a deep breath and stepped on the gas, speeding away from the tickle of warmth wrapping itself around my insides.

Had he flirted with me? I had to physically shake my head and exhale loudly to make myself stop. That was ridiculous. So, what if he had? He struck me as the type who didn't have any trouble landing a girl. I was sure he'd had plenty of practice.

Haunted eyes slid into memory, a grim reminder I didn't have time for extracurricular activities. There were too many other pressing matters to take care of. It took me a moment to recall them all–the little girl with Grandma, the woman in the woods. And now an intruder in my grandmother's empty house. Besides, no matter how much I wanted the warm togetherness of a relationship, I had too many secrets of my own. Secrets that were better off tucked away in the shadows.

4

———

RIDGE

Ridge McCaffrey watched from the driver's seat of his Mustang as the taillights of Liv Sullivan's rental disappeared, morphing into the halogen glare of a Cascade Hills PD cruiser. He ran the pad of his thumb over the tips of his fingers, still tingly from her touch. Ridge shook away the sinking feeling in his gut and drug himself from the cocoon of his car, motioning to Adam Miller, the officer who'd pulled to a stop in the barn lot.

"We've got patrol parked up the road a bit," Adam started. "They can give us eyes if the perp tries to haul ass out of that end of the lake."

"The granddaughter was in here alone," Ridge explained the situation as he led Adam into the house.

Adam gloved his hand before flipping a switch on the wall inside the front door.

"There's no electric. Perp exited out the back door."

The two men swept the scene in beams of their flashlights, moving toward the hall.

"What was she doing here?" Adam asked.

"Looking for a photo album. They're preparing for her grandmother's funeral." Ridge shrugged in the darkness. "I imagine grief was a driving force behind the dead of night escapade."

Adam let out a chuckle, examining the cardboard box at the mouth of the hallway. "Sleeping bag, lighter, flashlight. Someone's made themselves at home it looks like." Adam pulled a zippered bag from the corner of the box, dangling it between them before unzipping it and pulling out a plastic bag of marijuana, followed by packets of white pills.

"I'll call BCI and request a team. We'll tape it off for now. Nothing we can do without more light."

Adam agreed and followed Ridge from the hall toward the back door. Nothing appeared out of place except the door. Once locked, the intruder had used brunt force to break free, splintering the wood in the frame around the lock. The door now swung crooked, no longer able to seal itself.

The two men trotted down the wooden risers into the overgrown yard. Headlights from the patrol car pierced the darkness on the neighboring side of the lake. The surface of Cascade Lake remained mirror-smooth. No evidence of a boat or person breaking the calm. Ridge wished he felt that same calm in his gut right about now.

"This is a nice place. Too bad they've let it get like this." Adam's small talk infused the silence with an air of normalcy, and Ridge sucked it in. Exhaling an agreement as they taped off the scene.

By the time they returned to Adam's cruiser to log their findings, the crime scene unit team was pulling in. Ridge excused himself from Sullivan Farm as the sun peeked over the tree line, leaving the investigation in Adam's capable hands.

Ridge's supervisor, Special Agent in Charge, Marcus Sowards, had called for a meeting and there was no way Ridge could chance being late. With the end of his most recent assignment came an opportunity for promotion. Which was exactly what Ridge was hoping for–a way out of this undercover post in Cascade Hills and back to DC, where the real action was.

SOWARDS WAS WAITING when Ridge pulled into one of the parking spaces at Glen Helen Nature Preserve. Ridge checked his watch. 8:58. Right on time. On the rare occasions Ridge met with Sowards, it was usually at the Bureau's Cincinnati Field Station. Once he'd trekked to the Columbus Field Station. But never had he met Sowards in a public park. The hairs on the back of his neck rose a bit, his own personal "something's not right" radar. He couldn't remember the last time that internal early warning system led him astray.

Ridge killed the engine of his Mustang and lifted himself from the bucket seat. He slammed the door and looked both ways before crossing the lot, trotting to catch up to his superior. Almost as tall as Ridge's 6'2", Marcus Sowards was an intimidating man–solidly built with steely gray hair and a perpetual scowl on his face. Dressed in khakis, topped off by a pressed shirt and blazer, he looked completely out of place among the civilians out for a morning hike at the neighborhood park.

For March, the weather was nice. Sun shone through light cloud-cover in a whitish-grey sky–typical of Ohio winters. But the weather report indicated it would last less than twenty-four hours, a winter storm warning already issued for the western counties.

Sowards tipped his jaw to the side, acknowledging Ridge. "There's a bench about thirty yards up the trail," Sowards said as Ridge fell in step beside him.

"Why'd you want to meet here?"

Sowards scanned the area before answering. "This is off-the-record business, McCaffrey. I needed somewhere without eyes and ears."

Ridge nodded. Sure now that the promotion he'd been hoping for was not coming. At least, not today. He brushed a rogue branch out of the way as they approached the empty bench in a small clearing.

"I want to thank you for your reports on Grace Sullivan. They were very thorough."

"Hope they were of some help to you." Ridge wasn't sure how helpful the senile ramblings of a dying old woman could be, but that's what the Bureau had asked for, so that's what he'd given them.

"They were." Sowards attempted to clear the ever-present rasp from his voice. "She trusted you. Your talks with her provided exactly what we hoped. Which is why we're reassigning you."

A squeeze of anxiety took hold in Ridge's chest. This wasn't the reassignment he'd been hoping for. "I'm guessing DC is out of the question."

"We've got some loose ends in Cascade Hills. One in particular." Sowards pulled a file from his shoulder bag and handed it to Ridge.

Green eyes stared back at him from the open file folder. His breath hung, unexpelled, in his lungs.

"Olivia Sullivan is back in town for her grandmother's funeral. We need you to keep her here."

"Why?" He wasn't normally one to question authority. Two tours in the Marines had trained that out of him. But it seemed better than the alternative of telling Sowards they'd already met. At least until he knew more details.

"You remember all those conversations with Grace, the abilities she attempted to breed into her own granddaughter."

Ridge didn't try to stifle the laugh. "Come on, Marc, you can't be serious." But one look at his supervisor gave him all the evidence he needed.

Sowards sighed. "Grace was on Bureau payroll. The government's been utilizing her program for intelligence purposes for over two decades. Everything you need to know is in the file."

"You're telling me the US Government employs psychics to gather intel now?" Ridge smiled, but his supervisor's silence was enough to kill the ribbon of playfulness.

Ridge breathed through a growing knot of skepticism in his chest. "So, what do you want with the granddaughter?" The memory of Olivia Sullivan's eyes burned a hole in the back of Ridge's mind. The way his skin warmed under her fingertips. He thumbed the pads of his fingers. It had just been an instant, but the spark was there.

"We need to know how much she knows about her grandmother's business dealings. Make sure nothing ..." Sowards searched for the right word. "... sensitive comes to light as Grace's estate is distributed. We need to know if Olivia is aware of her grandmother's involvement with the Bureau. Does she know about the other assets?"

"There are others?"

Sowards' chin dipped, a silent affirmation. "Read the file, Ridge. This is a highly classified operation. Everything I'm at liberty to say is in there."

Ridge flipped through the thin stack of papers clipped into the folder, some of which were heavily redacted. This was his test—a way to see if he could play with the big dogs in DC before they decided on reassignment.

"Assuming I believe that any of this could be true," which he didn't. Ridge ran a hand through his hair. "Is she psychic?"

Sowards shrugged. "That's what you're going to find out for us."

"So, I'm just supposed to ask her if she sees ghosts? If she's psychic, won't she know we're trailing her?" Ridge couldn't keep the sarcasm from infiltrating his voice. "I didn't sign up for some X-Files bullshit, Marc. That's not me and you know it."

Sowards' flinty eyes shone all business. "That's why you're the perfect agent for this job, Ridge. You can be objective. Read the file. Your cover remains the same. But find out what she knows."

"What if she doesn't want anything to do with us, or this operation?"

"You're a very persuasive man, McCaffrey. Convince her. Better us than the alternative." Sowards stood, pulling his car keys from the pocket of his khakis. "No official reports on this one. Call me with anything you have."

Sowards was about ten feet away when the reality of this assignment started sinking in. "Marc?"

Sowards turned.

"What's the nature of the threat?"

Sowards shrugged, his eyes scanning the empty trails as he approached Ridge. "If she is what Grace claims? Someone out there wants her dead."

5

LIV

I stood in the cramped hotel room shower at the Holiday Inn allowing rivulets of water to warm my chilled skin. Images flip-flopped through my mind. Taut skin around scared blue eyes, rough hands gripping delicate skin, pushing a stranger against an earth I knew too well. The slam of the back door at Sullivan Farm, a dark shadow sprinting toward Cascade Lake. The green eyes of a little girl that looked too much like my own. The scenes fought for attention. I shoved at them both, allowing the memory of the officer to gain some purchase, his touch that sparked an electric response. Gooseflesh rose over my bare skin. Each image delivered a fresh wave of emotion–fear? Grief and confusion? Hope? The last was a sensation I hadn't encountered in quite some time.

The girl in the woods took precedence. I'd already waited too long, should've returned to Cascade Hills after that call. I could've been here when Grandma died. There was no salvation for the girl in the woods, but I could've saved Grandma from dying alone.

I squeezed a half-dollar of shampoo into my hands and

worked it through my hair. I'd call the officer later, maybe even visit the precinct, find out if he knew who'd broken in, and how. I toyed with the idea of asking about unsolved missing persons cases in the area. Maybe then I'd have a field of possibilities as I searched for answers to questions I wasn't sure how to ask.

I stood under the stream of water, rinsing shampoo foam from my hair. The officer's card tucked securely in my wallet. And I couldn't help but repeat his name in my mind, finally giving in and lending it voice in the privacy of the shower. "Ridge McCaffrey..." A whisper silenced by the rush of water. The memory of it on my lips lingered, though. The feel of it soft and beckoning, like the comfort of a favorite blanket.

I turned the faucet off and wrapped a towel around my midsection. I was dressed and out the door within twenty minutes, the memory of Officer McCaffrey relegated to a life raft I'd undoubtedly need for this meeting with my mother.

I'd avoided her since landing in Columbus late yesterday evening, but this morning we had business to attend to. And I refused to let her disappointment and my own feelings of inadequacy mar the plans for my grandmother's funeral.

Foster's Mortuary and Funeral Services sat on the corner of Main Street in the middle of Cascade Hills. A turn of the century Victorian, it was destined to become either a small-town bed and breakfast or the town's staple funeral home. When Richard Foster bought and converted the place back in the early 1970's, the fate of the home was secured.

I could count on one hand the number of times I'd been there. I was pretty good at staying as far away from death and the recently deceased as possible. It was just good strategy for someone like me. Getting too close thinned the veil that kept unwelcome visions at bay. Outsiders thought it was selfish. I preferred to think of it as self-preservation.

My mother, dressed to the nines, skirt and jacket perfectly

pressed was already there. Her chestnut hair neatly coiffed and makeup flawlessly applied to porcelain skin. She'd always been a beautiful woman. But I hadn't expected her to bring a guest.

The stranger sat next to her as I entered through the office door, held open for me by Matthew Foster, Richard's son and heir to the mortuary business in Cascade Hills. We'd graduated together, and it was hard for me to see him as anyone other than the kid who puked on the slide at recess one sunny spring day in third grade.

"Good to see you, Liv. My condolences on the loss of your grandmother. She was a wonderful woman."

"Yes, she was, thank you." The lump I'd managed to avoid most of the morning surged to the back of my throat as Matt led me to the empty chair beside my mother.

"I thought you'd call," my mother whispered while Matt maneuvered his way to the other side of a gargantuan desk that spanned the entire wall, making the low-ceilinged basement room appear even smaller.

I muttered the expected apology. A game we'd played since I moved to Los Angeles nearly a decade ago. She'd pretend to care, and I'd pretend to believe she did. It worked. At least it had until now, until news of this man stroking my mother's hand had gone unreported. Of course, how can you report news to someone who rarely calls? Guilt crept in alongside irritation.

"As you know," Matt began, "Grace was an immaculate planner. She's already taken care of most everything. Just a few odds and ends to tie up here today. Dates, times, that sort of thing."

Matt droned on. Flowers. Songs. Scripture. We interjected our opinions when a line had been left blank, a T uncrossed, or an I undotted on the form in front of him. I'd known for years that her entire service was already planned, bought, and paid for. *"Not fair to leave those decisions to grieving relatives,"* she'd said one day as I helped her weed the garden at Sullivan Farm. The memory of her voice wound around my throat, constricting my vocal cords.

"We'll take care of all the remaining arrangements, Mrs. Sullivan," Matt nodded to my mother, who returned the gesture. "Do any of you have any questions or concerns before the ceremony tomorrow?"

The room was silent.

"I'll be back with the final paperwork. Make yourselves comfortable. I'll only be a moment."

All three of us—Mom, me, and the stranger—watched Matt jog up the nearby staircase.

"I'm sorry." I didn't want to be the one to break the silence. But I couldn't sit there anymore ignoring the man with a too familiar grip on my mom's right hand. "I'm sorry. I don't believe we've met."

In my mind the words were delicate, careful. But contact with the air twisted them, turning them into a hateful outburst from a poorly adjusted daughter.

"Olivia," my mother shot at me, shifting away from her friend to deliver a melt-iron stare she'd be disappointed to know no longer had the effect it used to.

"I do apologize for being an unwelcome guest today. Your mother asked me to come. I should have thought better of it. Olivia, right?" He stood, hand outstretched, waiting for me to reciprocate.

"Liv," I said out of habit more than anything else, taking his hand. There was a lilt in his voice I recognized from trips to Ireland with my grandmother. Tall and slim, salt and pepper hair graying solidly at the temples, he was, by most accounts, a handsome man.

"Lyle Hunt."

He shook my hand, one pump and I pulled away. Brushing the unwelcome buzz of energy off on my jeans.

"I own The Hunter Grille here in town. I'd love to take you ladies to brunch when we're done here. Would you have the time, Liv?"

I glanced at my mother, looking for some response, but the expression on her face was foreign to me. She gazed up at the man next to her, a tiny smile turning the corner of her perfectly lipsticked mouth. Affection, I realized. A swirl in my gut–like someone let the plunger out of a full tub, churned through me.

"Actually, I have a few things I need to take care of this afternoon, but thank you, Lyle." I managed to respond before the knot in my chest choked me. Matt, tromping back down the steps with a wad of papers in his hands, saved me from further conversation.

"Here you go ladies. I look forward to seeing you both here tomorrow morning for visitation and then, of course, the funeral and interment will follow."

My mother rose and followed Matt to the door. Lyle's hand on the small of her back was, for reasons I couldn't explain, unsettling. *Get a grip, Liv. Dad's been gone eight years. You're not a little girl anymore.* I suddenly felt like a jilted kid, one who'd had to leave a store without the promised toy, straggling behind mom and dad with her lip puffed out in protest. Living in L.A. had allowed me much needed distance from this place, these people, maybe even myself.

"Please join us," the voice of my mother as we approached the parking lot. Her hand slid down my arm. Comfort. A memory, like a bolt of lightning through the sky, sliced into me. Breakfasts–just Mom, Dad, and me–laughing over pancakes made to look like smiley faces. Sometimes I forgot that there had been good times. Before my cousin's death, before everyone started judging me as either a freak or a liar. "Please," she whispered, "for me."

I nodded, incapable of speech, and followed my mother to the black SUV parked two spots from my rental. Lyle opened the rear passenger door and smiled. His grey eyes twinkled as I slid into the back seat. Coming back to Cascade Hills was going to test every last ounce of my adulting skills.

6

———

LIV

The Hunter Grille sat on a corner in a newer section of Cascade Hills. It was a beautiful building. Large plate glass windows lined the front and side, over-looking a creek that wound its way through the slender path of woods separating high-end stores and shops from a neighboring sprawl of million-dollar homes backing onto a golf course. It was hard not to be impressed.

White linen tablecloths and waiters and waitresses in immaculate black dress topped off the effect. We were the only ones there, and it was clear the restaurant wasn't yet open for the day to the general public.

"How long have you owned The Hunter?" I ventured after the waiter completed his service of tea and coffee.

"It's been just about four years now. Ever since I moved to Cascade Hills."

"I recognize your accent. Irish, right? What part of Ireland are you from?" I brought the porcelain teacup to my lips.

Lyle sat back in his chair, his eyes darting to my mother, glinting with a hint of surprise.

"Aye. You've a good ear. All over, really. Grew up in County Wicklow. Then culinary school in Dublin. Opened a small pub just south of Dublin City with some friends–in a little town called Greystones, if you know it. I managed the pub nearly twenty years before venturing out on my own."

"I hope you don't mind my asking, but why Cascade Hills?" Cascade Hills was a great little town, but the operative word was "little." Seemed a strange choice for someone in the restaurant business.

"You're not the first to ask." He smiled again, the skin at the corners of his eyes crinkling. "I'd always wanted to open something a little more upscale. Didn't have the funds to do it in a big city. The overhead alone would have ruined me. The Irish economy was taking a dive, so, a chance meeting with a lad I'd gone to university with led me to take a look at Cascade Hills." Lyle paused, breathing in the atmosphere and resituating his napkin. "When you were younger, this place was called Sebastian's, I believe. Do you recall?"

Lyle waited for a response. His grey eyes seared into me, sending a prickle down my spine. I stirred my tea. I remembered Sebastian's. The overabundance of silverware arranged meticulously on the table, my father sitting across from me, his laugh filling the space between us while a waiter scraped crumbs from the tablecloth with a small silver blade. I nodded to Lyle. "I remember."

"I've changed the place up a bit. It was in bad shape when I bought it. Nearly falling down. But you can't beat the location. Took about a year to rebuild. It was a risk, but the opportunity was too good to pass up."

"Well, it looks like the gamble has paid off for you."

"It certainly has..." He hesitated, squeezing my mother's hand as an aproned waiter brought us our food–eggs benedict, perfectly crisp bacon, muffins and toast, complete with an array of fruity jams and preserves in silver serving dishes.

My mother patted the top of my leg as we began to eat. Between bites, she leaned over. "I'm glad you two are finally getting a chance to meet. I wasn't sure how to tell you about him. So, thank you."

I nodded at her. A woman I hadn't expected to see on this trip. Sweet, caring, all the emotions I remembered lacking in my last years in Cascade Hills were now wholly apparent.

Memory is a funny thing. I now understood why eyewitnesses so often got the details wrong. Why did I only remember the awful words, harsh looks? The constant disappointment?

"So, Liv, what about you? I can't get anything out of Beth here." He smiled at my mother, his grin shifting his demeanor from well-dressed businessman to fun-loving class clown. "You live in Los Angeles, right? What is it you do?"

The question was innocent enough. I just didn't know how to answer.

"I work in customer service." Mom shoveled a bite of toast into her mouth, looking untroubled. So, I decided to dive in. I'd either come up cleansed of the secrets I'd been keeping or resurface into the world I remembered. "I worked for a company called Celestial Spirit. It's a psychic call center actually."

An uncomfortable silence passed around the table. My mother's pleasant expression turned unsettled. I leaned toward her, "I guess we both were keeping a few secrets."

Lyle was the first to break the silence. "How interesting. Pardon my foolishness, but if you don't mind my asking, how exactly does that work–a psychic hotline?"

"It's a matter of close observation, really. I listen. Make

educated guesses. I took a couple psychology courses in college, so I think that helps. I like the idea that I'm helping people feel better about themselves, even if in a very small way. The company is downsizing, so I'll be looking for something else when I head back."

My mother was staring at me now. "Liv, can I speak to you a moment... alone?" Her voice was stern.

We exited the dining room, cutting a path toward the ladies' room. "How could you embarrass me like that?" She looked almost panicked.

"Mom, this is not a reflection on you. He asked me what I did for a living. What would you have me do... lie to him? If you two are so close, don't you think he might find out eventually?"

"I don't expect you'll stay long enough for him to find out anything." Mom spat the words as if they tasted bad.

"I don't plan to stay any longer than I have to."

My mother's hazel eyes bored into me. "I swear, if you start talking about any of your...your..." She got hung up on the word.

"Dreams?" I supplied. It's what we'd always called them. The word just had a different meaning for my family than most. "Do you really think I would bring that up with someone I barely know? I don't bring it up around you, why would I suddenly begin spouting about it around Lyle? Believe it or not, you've trained me well."

Mom shook her head, sinking onto the couch in the lounge area of the bathroom. The Hunter's women's restroom rivaled the square footage of my studio apartment. Nice. A familiar knot took hold in my chest, the squeeze of disappointment filling my lungs.

"I'm sorry, Olivia. It's just...you could have been so much more. You had so many opportunities. If you could just forget about all that psychic nonsense you could have a wonderful life."

I lowered onto the sofa next to her. "Mom, I'm sorry I never told you what I did before. But hiding in plain sight works. It's what I do. Well... did. But I can't turn the dreams off. I would if I could, trust me. But, like it or not, it's part of who I am."

"It doesn't have to be that way, Olivia. I've done some checking and therapies have come a long way. If it's the money, I'll help you. I just want..." Her voice wavered.

"You want me to be normal. I get it. But it's not that simple, Mom." I picked at the cuticles of my nails, pretending to study my hands. Tears I swore I wouldn't shed pricked at the backs of my eyes. Memories of doctor appointments and drug combinations sprang to mind. Some succeeded in making them fuzzy—dulling them. But none of them forced the visions away completely, no matter how much money my mother spent, or how hard she hoped for the perfect outcome. "We should get back, Mom. Lyle will think something's wrong."

Mom nodded, taking a moment to pat away the tears that skimmed thin streaks through her makeup.

"Liv," she stopped, her hand on my forearm. "I'm sorry. I told myself I wouldn't let our past get in the way while you're here. Is it too late for a fresh start?"

Her eyes locked on mine and an unfamiliar pulse of gratitude slipped over me like a warm blanket. "It's never too late." For the first time in my life, I meant it.

7

___

LIV

The day of my grandmother's funeral was bitterly cold. It was snowing. Not big, white fluffy flakes perfect for catching on your tongue, but small pebble-like shards that pelted those unfortunate enough to be outdoors. There always seemed to be some type of precipitation on the day of funerals, at least the ones I'd experienced.

Memories of my father's service crept in as I dressed. It hadn't been cold, but the rain had poured from the sky in buckets, inspiring a rather short graveside ceremony in his honor. It seemed fitting to have a snowy day decorate his mother's interment.

I stared into the mirror, tucking the green silk blouse around my waist and smoothing the black pencil skirt down my thighs. This had been Grandma's favorite blouse on me. The last time I'd worn it was eight years ago, at my father's funeral. I could still remember dressing in front of the mirror in my room at the farm. She'd come in with a strand of pearls and fastened the clasp at the back of my neck, telling me the blouse brought out my eyes.

"They are as green as the hills of Éire," she'd said.

I gazed into the green irises that stared back at me from the mirror. I'd never been a huge fan of makeup, but I figured a little mascara and eye shadow couldn't hurt. I added just enough powder to mask the freckles that sprinkled over the bridge of my nose, before running a brush through my auburn hair. Thick sections cascaded past my shoulders as the brush went through, pulling unruly curls out into soft waves.

The California sun kept the natural highlights vibrant, the streaks of strawberry a stark contrast for dreary Ohio March. Satisfied, I stooped to put on the black heels that I hoped would give my petite frame leverage against taller friends and relatives.

One last deep cleansing breath. "This is for you, Grandma."

I slipped into my coat and snatched my purse and umbrella off the desk before pulling open the hotel room door.

THE LOT of Foster's Funeral Home was already full, and I struggled to find a decent parking space. Grace Sullivan had been well liked and respected in Cascade Hills and beyond. She had lots of hobbies, many of which she'd shared with me. I'd spent more than a few Saturdays at painting or quilting classes, learning right alongside my grandmother.

She'd also been active with several area philanthropic organizations. All of which earned her friends from all walks of life. Even though she hadn't been able to get out and about the past few years, the packed parking lot was proof that she'd not been forgotten. I'd never been prouder to be her granddaughter.

I slipped through the back entrance of the facility, once a large Victorian home, now seemingly stuck in time in an effort to preserve the memories of loved ones passed. I wasn't a fan of funerals, but I despised the obligatory calling hours even more. I hated looking at the faces of people I had rarely, if ever, seen and accepting their sad sympathies with a manufactured hug or handshake.

Don't get me wrong, it wasn't that I didn't appreciate them taking the time to show their love for my grandmother... I did, very much. But I always got hung up on their stares, their eyes. The same eyes that judged me when I became the town freak, now stood in a slow-moving line, waiting to dredge up all those old memories. Small town gossip never dies.

My mother reached for my hand as the procession began. She pulled me up next to her at the front of the room. I glanced at the ornate box my grandma had chosen to hold her remains. The Sullivans had never been a family of mourners. No open-casket viewing. No final good-bye. Both my father and grandfather had been cremated, buried in the Sullivan plot at the local cemetery. Grandma was following suit. I used to resent it, the fact I never got a last look at their face, never got that closure I so desperately needed. But that was before. Before I realized how truly temporary our bodies really are. Funny what perspective can do for a person.

The line of strangers ebbed and flowed. Some stayed after dawdling through the line, taking their seats to wait for the funeral to follow, but most just came and went. I was about to breathe a sigh of relief for the fact that none of my old friends or classmates had ventured out, when a familiar face appeared in the doorway.

Even at a distance, through the expanse of room, he was unmistakable. Stocky, only standing about three inches taller than me, his hair was the same golden brown that I remembered, streaked like mine by the California sun. As he got closer, gooseflesh rose on my arms and legs. The line crawled like a snake, the end slithering closer, heightening the panic that slid down my spine. When he finally reached me, his voice was soft and sincere. Just as I remembered.

"Hi, Liv. I'm so sorry about your grandmother."

"Thanks, Jason," I choked out. "Did you come all the way from California?"

"I've actually been in Columbus for about a year now—on business." He took my hand. The stuck breath in my lungs suffocated me. I exhaled the air in a tight line, the warmth of his hand conjuring up memories I'd just as soon keep sealed in the pressure cooker of my mind. "I thought maybe we could talk later... if you get a minute."

"Sure." I nodded as he smiled at me. The left corner of his mouth curling first, followed by the right—the same smile that enchanted me when we'd first met. I clenched my jaw to resist the surge of familiar feelings, picking out the hurt from among the ashes of my memory. I'd give him a minute of my time, he deserved that for showing up here today. But not a nanosecond more.

Jason sidestepped toward my mother, offering her the same syrupy smile. Her eyes grew wide and a grin cracked her face. His charms had always worked on her. She opened her arms to him as I averted my gaze, trying, without success, to infuse disgust into the range of emotion that washed through me.

I tried desperately not to think of him during the funeral service, but he was there, lurking in my subconscious. When I noticed him follow us out to the cemetery for the graveside service, a hint of trepidation settled over me. It was in the lull after the service that unwelcome memories crept into the recesses of my mind.

Shards of ice pelted my face as I studied the jagged rows of headstones that rolled up one side of the hill and down another. Each one a vacant memory. I remembered sitting in Jason's dorm room like it was yesterday. Me, on his roommate's bed with a couple other friends at the University of Southern California. Jason across from us on his own bed, playing Hotel California on a cream-colored Fender Stratocaster for a growing crowd of fresh faced co-eds.

The passers-by were drawn in as easily as I had been. They'd pop in and out just taking in the magic of his gift. But I was the one who'd been entranced, the one who fell under his spell.

The words had fallen so easily out of my mouth. *"So, do you give lessons?"*

"Well, no, I never have..."

"Would you consider it?"

His intense, heavy-lidded stare was enough of an answer and successfully emptied the room of other curious observers.

"For you?" he'd asked, once the room had cleared.

We were inseparable for nearly two years. I never learned how to play the guitar–imagine that–but I'd gained something far more valuable. Love. College was halfway over when he asked me to marry him. But relationships can't hinge on love alone. There was one secret I'd kept even from him.

After we moved into an off-campus apartment together, I knew I couldn't keep up the charade. I told him in bed one night. At first, he'd seemed fine with it. Looking back, he didn't even act surprised. Maybe he never completely understood, but I had to give him points for trying.

He slipped away gradually, dissolving like sand under the repeated crash of ocean waves. I wish it had been quicker. It's like ripping off a Band-Aid. Quicker is always better.

My father died that winter and I dropped out of college a semester later to my mother's furious chagrin, unable to take the stares and whispers that followed me all over campus. I never anticipated that he'd tell other people. To me, it was a secret between us. To him it was an anomaly to be shared. I considered enrolling somewhere else, but my heart wasn't in it. My future no longer held promise.

I brushed a layer of ice from the top of the nearest monument. Each headstone in the cemetery represented a truth never told. I knew that from the visions. No ghost came without secrets. Sometimes they wanted them exposed–like my cousin, Curt, and his apology to his mom. Other times they wanted them buried more deeply than they were able to manage in life. Their secrets might not make them a freak, like mine did, but all of us had regrets.

I knew coming back to Cascade Hills would open a scab. I'd already disappointed my mother. Had been reminded too many times of my father. I couldn't decipher why some strange little girl was hanging out with my dead grandmother, and what any of that had to do with an obscure phone call from a stranger who prompted a vision of a dead girl in the woods at Sullivan Farm. Regurgitated memories of a relationship I thought I'd healed from was the last thing I needed.

Jason was nowhere to be found by the time I left the cemetery. Heading back toward Mom's house, I knew there'd be another group of family and friends to deal with. I'd take that party over Jason any day of the week and twice on Sundays.

Mom's house was full of family and friends. My grandmother's brother and sister, both just a bit younger than her and with the same pale blue eyes, worked wonders in bringing my focus back where it belonged.

They had endless stories to tell about my grandmother, and I shared some photographs I'd taken of Grandma on my last visit home. It helped my mood to hear everyone speak about Grandma with the same affection I felt. The world had lost a wonderful, gracious woman. "Irreplaceable" was a word that floated in the air like an unpoppable bubble. And each time I heard it, my heart gave a little leap followed by a wrenching sadness that settled in the pit of my stomach. Maybe this was what true loneliness felt like.

I'd been at Mom's for a couple of hours before sneaking off for a moment of solitude. I stood in front of one of my mother's antique armoires on the lower level of her house, working to unseat some sadness while fingering the array of family photographs spread in frames at eye level.

When steps echoed off the travertine tiles behind me, I jumped. My finger caught the corner of a particularly elaborate enamel frame, knocking it to the floor and scattering shards of floral inlay across the tiles.

"I didn't mean to startle you. You doing okay?"

"Fine." I crouched, gathering the pieces in my palm. Irritation crept up my spine as he squatted next to me, picking at the few that I'd missed. "I didn't realize you were here."

I placed the pieces on top of the armoire. What could I possibly have to say to Jason? The venom-tongued comebacks I'd concocted after he left me had long since disappeared from my stored vocabulary. After six years, my acute hurt and anger had morphed into regret spliced with the dull ache of rejection.

"I didn't want to interfere with family time." He motioned up the stairs. Voices trickled down from the kitchen. "I've been outside. Was hoping we might get a chance to catch up a bit. We never really talked about what happened...between us."

"That was a long time ago, Jason." I was proud of myself for sounding so detached after spending most of the afternoon reminiscing moments I thought I'd forgotten.

He reached out a tanned forearm, brushing my hair over my shoulder with the strong hands of a guitar player. "You look good, Liv."

"Thanks," I muttered, refusing to return the favor as a tickle of regret shot through my system.

His hand lingered on my shoulder a beat too long, his thumb working small circles into the hollow beneath my collarbone. My breath caught in my throat before I managed to shrug away.

"I know I messed things up. But if you ever want to talk... I'm a pretty good listener."

Memories of nights spent curled together on our hand-me-down couch, talking about the minutiae of our days flickered through my mind. It had been a long time since anyone had listened–really listened.

My voice sounded far away to my own ears as I answered, "Thanks, Jason. I'll think about it."

"There's a little place down the road, Flanagan's. I'll be there at nine. I hope you'll join me."

I stared as he walked away, shaking the fog from my brain. It took a full ten minutes for me to gather my wits enough to rejoin the safety of the group upstairs.

8

LIV

Jason's invitation wove its way into the back of my mind as I rode the elevator to the fourth floor of the Holiday Inn. What could it hurt? My grandmother's voice nudged from the depths of distant memory.

You need to get out more, Liv. Go places. Don't let what others think dictate your self-worth, my dear. Be proud of who you are.

My imagination toyed with the idea. Jason already knew about the visions. If he was interested now, he must have made peace with it. Of course, the logical side of my brain interjected the fact that he probably figured me for an easy lay after the death of my grandmother. That side had a very good point. But did I care? I was a consenting adult. How long had it been since I'd been with a man?

I started to do the math before giving up, disgusted with myself and a lifestyle that could rival a hermit. Grandma certainly would never approve of a grief-induced affair with the man who'd broken my heart into shards even super glue couldn't fix. Chilling blue eyes framed by dark lashes sneaked from the depths of my mind. I sighed through the bubble of anxiety that filled my chest.

Alone in my hotel room, I unloaded my dressy purse back into the one I carried every day. As I shifted my iPhone into the other bag, I noticed a missed call and voicemail message. I held the phone to my ear and shimmied out of the skirt. Expecting Jason's voice from the unknown number on the other end, I pulled my pantyhose off with one hand while listening to the message.

The voice stopped me mid-tug. An involuntary thrill spawned in the pit of my stomach—a flooding warmth. I sank onto the edge of the mattress, one leg still entangled in a mess of nylon and Lycra.

"Miss Sullivan, this is Ridge McCaffrey, with the Cascade Hills PD. I hoped to be able to talk to you in person, but... I wanted to fill you in on what happened at your grandmother's farm the other night. You are cleared to go back. I'd recommend replacing the locks as soon as possible." There was a pause, his voice lower when it came back on the line. "Take a flashlight next time." Another pause, his voice returning to all business. "I'll be at the precinct tomorrow. Feel free to give me a call."

I replayed the message again. Searching for a hint of interest hiding in his voice. Secretly hoping it wasn't there. I was over-analyzing, as usual, and a knot of disappointment lodged in my gut. Regret over not taking the call personally. I checked the time. It was after nine, too late to call under the guise of official business.

One more surge of loneliness trickled through me before I pulled myself from the bed. I wadded the pantyhose into a ball and stuffed them into my open suitcase. At home, in my own apartment, I could have handled this. I could occupy myself with photography or books—work, even. But here... I stared blankly at the four silent walls closing in on me before snatching my purse and coat and heading out the door.

I pulled into the parking lot of a non-descript strip mall just down the road from the Holiday Inn. I could say one thing. It was certainly convenient. If I'd known it was so close, I would have walked. The glowing marquee read Flanagan's in script, with a four-leaf clover used as the apostrophe.

It was an average pool bar, like one of the many I'd frequented during my stint with Jason. Green felted pool tables lined the right-hand wall. A light wood bar stood off to the left, dotted with uncomfortable looking stools, none of which were vacant. I searched the crowded bar for Jason, realizing too late that an Irish bar the day before St. Patrick's Day was a bad idea.

A couple of the unfamiliar faces turned my way, scanning me up and down like tigers locking in on their prey. A shiver shimmied down my spine. I was too out of practice for this. I turned away as guy number one jutted his chin in my direction, a move that could only be the precursor to some cheesy pick up line.

Finally, the sandy hue of Jason's hair caught my attention from the other side of the room. He stood with a group of three guys, chalking his cue near the farthest pool table.

"Liv," he called out. His face brightened, and he waved in my direction, replacing the cue in the rack on the wall.

I returned the wave with a short semi-salute.

"I didn't think you were going to come," Jason said. "I'm glad you did."

I hazarded a look into his eyes. The flecks of green and gold were just like I remembered. My muscles tensed involuntarily as he draped his arm around my shoulder, leading me toward a stool at the back of the bar. As we sat, I couldn't help but imagine the bright blue eyes of Ridge McCaffrey studying me instead.

Jason ordered our drinks, a Corona for himself and a Guinness for me. At least he remembered what I drank. I nursed the bottle as he talked, alternating my train of thought between why any self-respecting Irish pub didn't have Guinness on draught, and why I'd decided to come.

He leaned forward, the hint of lime hanging on his breath, and told me how good it was to see me. His fingertips brushed my thigh, tickling through my jeans. I stared down in shock for a moment as his hand came to rest on my knee. How long had it been since I'd felt the warmth of his hands on me? Had it really been six years? Time evaporated.

The familiarity of his touch sent flickers of longing through my core. The caress of guitar-calloused hands invaded my memory. This was the man I thought I'd have children with, experience life with, grow old with. Anxiety mounted as I wondered if I'd have the will to say no. Relief replaced the growing seed of panic when he pulled his hand away.

"What brought you to Cascade Hills?" I asked, an attempt to distance myself from the sexual tension.

"We've got a client in Columbus," Jason said, flicking his hand to the side. "I'm a consultant." He'd had enough of this conversation. Jason studied filmmaking at USC, but I knew that wasn't the direction he'd gone after graduation.

"What kind of consulting?" I asked, focused on topics that wouldn't bring up the past. His eyes never met mine, almost as if he was ashamed of the new career choice. I knew that feeling.

"Um..." He squinted, narrowing his eyes at me as if I'd asked why he refused to spay and neuter a pet. "Why do you want to know?"

I shrugged. "Just making small talk, Jason."

"You're right. Sorry. I assess security needs for a variety of corporations." He picked at the napkin under his drink. "Computer stuff. It's pretty boring, actually. What about you?"

"I'm a photographer," I lied. But I liked the way it felt on my tongue. The last thing I wanted was to bring up the very thing that separated us in the first place. I wasn't trying to impress him, but I didn't need his pity, either.

"Good." He seemed pleased. "You always took incredible pictures, Liv. I still have the one from Santa Monica Pier. You know, with the sunset filtering through the spokes on the Ferris wheel."

"Yeah, I remember that one." I also recalled what happened later that evening on the floor of an unlocked lifeguard hut, but I wasn't about to bring that up now.

He smiled that lopsided grin before signaling the waiter for his third Corona. "You need another?"

I shook my head. There was no way I could let my brain get foggy around Jason. We had too much history. It would be too easy to fall back into old patterns, too easy to let loneliness take over. *But isn't that why you came?* My inner critic scolded as the image of suffocatingly silent hotel walls flooded back.

"Why did you ask me here tonight?"

He stared at me a minute before answering. "I've missed you." He said it as though it was the most ridiculous question he'd ever heard. "I wanted to talk to you... see if there's any chance..."

Was he really doing this?

"I thought maybe we could give it another try, you know?" He took a swig of his Corona.

"You left me, remember?" A remnant of hurt from the night he'd walked out niggled its way into my core.

"That was a mistake. I'll be heading back to L.A. soon, and I'd really like to give us another shot."

I studied his face. His soft eyes combed over me, but they didn't have the inebriating effect they used to. There was no doubt I was yearning for intimacy, someone to talk to, a warm body to be with. I needed someone, that was true. But I didn't need it to be him. It may have taken six years, but I'd done it. This was my moment. I was ready to leave Jason in the past, where he belonged. A warm balloon of pride bloomed within me.

"I think maybe *this* was a mistake," I said. I dug in my purse for some cash and laid it on the bar. Stepping down from the stool, I slipped into my coat.

"Liv, wait... don't go." He reached out for my shoulder, but I managed to step away before his fingers could take hold.

I never looked back as I fought my way through the maze of people toward the door of the crowded pub. The pelting snow had stopped, but cold night air bit at my skin. I inhaled a deep lungful. This was what success must feel like.

Heading toward my car at the other end of the parking lot, still basking in the glow of victory, I didn't see him approach from behind. His hand reached around my midsection, grabbing my coat and spinning me around, shoving me against the side of a nearby van.

His hands were strong. Always had been. I didn't fight as he pressed into me, his grip on my wrists tightening.

"Jason, what we had... It's over." The words were quiet. Panic sapping strength from my lungs.

"Then why did you come?" His words were a bit too loud, a product of the alcohol buzzing through his veins.

"I was lonely," I admitted, twisting against his grasp. With a jerk, I pulled one hand free, shoving him away. "Go back to California, Jason. There's nothing for you here."

9

RIDGE

Ridge popped open the door of his Shelby. Eyes laser focused on the couple pressed against the Econoline van less than fifty feet away. It took everything Ridge had not to wrap his hands around the throat of the man forcing himself on his newest target.

"The lady's not interested." Ridge's voice cut through the night like a blade, startling to even his own ears. And loud enough to get the jerk to step away, loosening his grip on Olivia's wrist so that she could twist away.

"Mind your own damn business." The expected retort.

Ridge edged himself between Olivia and her attacker. The guy's eyes widened as Ridge grabbed him by the shoulder, shoving toward the pub. He made a point to stop midway to the door, allow the drunken idiot to gain some perspective, before he peeled back the bottom of his jacket to expose his sidearm and badge.

"Assault *is* my business."

The asshole's arms went up in the air. "Alright, alright.

Whatever. We were just having a conversation." He backed toward the entrance to the bar.

Ridge had to give the guy credit for only stumbling twice. "Looks to me like the conversation's over."

"You won't get this chance again, Liv. Ever." He threw the final word over his shoulder, turning toward the door and reaching for the handle.

Music blared from inside and went quiet again. Blanketing the parking lot in semi-silence, a background track of passing cars. The white-hot streak of anger roiling Ridge's insides calmed to a simmer.

"You okay?" Ridge asked, turning to face Olivia. She stood just a few feet away, rubbing her wrist.

"Fine...what are you doing here?"

Ridge nodded toward the strip of businesses. Next to the pool bar sat a mom and pop convenience store. Lucky for him it was still open. "I was visiting a friend. Thought I'd grab a gallon of milk before I head home."

He waited for her to process his lie. Her eyes were still wide, the product of an adrenalin rush. But it was her bottom lip, the corner tucked in a soft bite, that he couldn't take his eyes off of. "Olivia, right?"

She cleared her throat and held out her hand in greeting. "It's Liv, actually." A one-shouldered shrug. "Everyone calls me Liv."

Ridge took her hand and pumped once. There it was again, that spark of electricity running along soft, smooth skin. He hadn't imagined it after all. He smiled at the woman in front of him.

"Did you know that creep?"

"Jason? Yes, you could say that."

Ridge took a step back, maybe he'd misinterpreted. "Boyfriend?"

Liv laughed, a nervous giggle. "Uh, no. Not for a long time, anyway. Thanks for stepping in, but I had it under control."

"I could see that." And he could. She'd handled herself well, quiet, but assertive. It was time to change the subject. "I called earlier. Did you get my message?"

Relief washed over Liv's face. "I did. I wanted to call you back, but it was late."

"It's never any trouble. You can call my cell anytime. I don't have very regular hours and I don't sleep much."

"Right." She crossed her arms over her chest and glanced toward her car.

Shit. He'd made her uncomfortable.

"Did you find anything? At the farm, I mean?"

This was the opening he'd been hoping for. "Come by the station tomorrow. I can fill you in on the details. Maybe you can help us identify a few things. We didn't find the intruder, if that's what you're wondering."

Liv nodded. Right now, the farm was his link to her, the ace up his sleeve. But he couldn't help wondering how much she knew. If the stories Grace Sullivan had told him were true, Liv was the real deal. But he wasn't sure what that meant exactly, or why it was so damn important to the Bureau.

"Any chance you can clear me to go back?" Liv asked.

"Soon. We've gathered all the evidence, just trying to put the pieces together."

Ridge had dealt with would-be psychics before. Could Liv predict the future–gaze into her crystal ball for missing children or lottery numbers? The image nearly made him laugh out loud. Liv was an opposite pendulum swing from the boardwalk fortune tellers that peppered cases now and again with their woeful tales of missing children that had yet to be reported, and oddly enough, never were.

"I'll see you tomorrow then," Liv said, heading back toward the Civic. "Thanks again."

Ridge waved, raking his eyes over the woman in front of him as she walked away. Fortune-teller seemed unlikely considering the course of tonight's events. Maybe she could read his thoughts. He hoped not, despite not being entirely truthful about his intentions, not all of the notions running through his mind had been G rated. Maybe she was one of those new age psychics that read auras. Ridge shook his head and slid into his Mustang, watching Liv drive away.

Whatever her skills were, two things were for certain. She was the petite, girl-next-door type that could get him in trouble. And he had a shit ton of research ahead of him if he was going to make this operation quick and get out of Cascade Hills and back to his dad in Virginia.

10

LIV

Cops liked doughnuts, right? Although Officer McCaffrey didn't look like he'd ever stood in the same room as one, let alone eaten it. I waited at the counter at the local bakery deciding between a dozen basic glazed sourdough or the more elaborate jelly and cream-filled concoctions. I placed my order and slid to the side, allowing the next person in line to ogle the array of caloric delicacies.

The Cascade Hills Police Department was housed in a short, squat brick in the shadow of the county's gargantuan court house. I'd only been there once before, with my dad when he'd applied for his last concealed carry permit, two weeks before his death. I balanced the large pink doughnut box on one arm and swung the plate glass door open.

The counter was just feet away, the uniformed officer behind it shielded by another layer of glass.

"Can I help you?" she asked as I righted the box that started to topple from my balancing act.

"I'm here to see Ridge McCaffrey." Saying his name sent an uncontrolled tickle of heat through my core.

She looked me up and down, tossing, "McCaffrey here yet?" over her shoulder to a man standing at a nearby filing cabinet. Another officer, I could tell by the sidearm and badge attached to his belt but dressed in street clothes. He leaned around for a closer look, a slow smile spreading across his face.

"Yeah, he's here. I'll take her back."

The female officer continued to glare at me even as I thanked her. The second officer pushed open the thick wooden door that separated the lobby from the inner workings of the station, extending a hand to me as the door slammed with a defiant click.

"If you're here to see McCaffrey that must make you Olivia Sullivan."

I nodded. So he'd talked about me.

"Adam, Adam Miller. I'm Ridge's partner. Whatcha got in the box?"

His brown eyes gleamed as I opened the box and let him choose the first sugary confection. He pinched the long john between his thumb and forefinger and nodded toward the back of the station. "Ridge is back in records. We've spent our morning poring over paperwork. You know, the glamorous life of a police detective." He shot another friendly smile at me before hollering toward an open hallway. "Ridge, you got company." He shoved a bite of doughnut into his mouth before nodding toward a nearby desk. "Have a seat, he'll be out in a minute. Can I get you some coffee?"

"Sure, that would be great," I said. A bubble of nervousness built in my chest. I slid the box of doughnuts onto the desk in front of me, glancing down at the jeans and grey sweater I'd chosen that morning. I sighed, I'd been going for the "cute but not trying too hard" look that other women my age seemed to pull off effortlessly with their messy buns and yoga pants. I wasn't sure I'd hit the mark, but there was nothing I could do about it now.

His shadow cast across a hallway wall before I ever saw him. His dark washed jeans hugged the muscle in his thighs but weren't too tight. A light blue button-down shirt opened conservatively to the second button. He seemed engrossed in the file he carried. It was the first time I'd seen him in full light, and I had to swallow to stop the sharp intake of air.

Even in the harsh fluorescent lighting of the police station he was undeniably attractive. I was right about his hair, wavy, and just long enough to wind through my fingers. He was taller than I'd gauged in the dark, though, standing at least six feet.

He glanced up from the open file, doing a double take before stopping a few feet from the desk where I sat. His desk, I realized. I hopped up, the heat of embarrassment warming my cheeks.

"Sorry," I started. "I'm early. But I brought doughnuts." I gestured toward the box on his desk. *Stupid,* my inner critic chimed in. He still had yet to speak.

"There he is," Adam's voice cut through the awkward silence. He handed me a steaming cup of black liquid and piled a handful of creamer containers and sugar packets on the corner of Ridge's desk. "I didn't know how you took your coffee. Fair warning, though, station coffee has a tendency to be strong."

I thanked Adam, realizing that Ridge had yet to take his eyes off me. "Thanks for walking her back, Adam."

Adam gave Ridge a quick salute and headed off down the hall toward the front of the station where I'd found him. "Holler if you need anything."

Ridge waited until Adam was out of earshot before he spoke. "It's nice to finally see you in the daylight."

"Likewise." I tried to stifle the nervous giggle that rose up through my chest, but it was too late. When I looked back at Ridge, he wore an amused grin, complete with dimples and day-old stubble intact. I realized then, he'd be just as suited for an underwear ad as he was walking around a station house with a gun on his hip. Again, heat flared in my face.

"I came early because I'm on my way to my mom's. She had out of town company all day yesterday, so I thought I could help her clean up today."

"Right. Well, this won't take long. I just want to ask if you recognize a few things."

He gestured for me to sit at his desk, giving me the comfy leather office armchair, while he pulled an orange plastic chair alongside. As he settled next to me, I caught the trace of cologne. A hint of spice mingling with shower-freshness. A surge of heat invaded my core. The ridiculous urge to trail my lips up his neck, inhaling whatever aftershave he wore as I went, overpowered my senses. *Christ, Liv. Get a grip.*

He tucked the file he'd been carrying under a pile on his desk and flipped open the folder on the top of the stack. He arranged some photographs in an array in front of me.

"These are some items we found at the farmhouse that seemed out of place. I was hoping you might be able to confirm if you've seen any of them before. Do you know if they belonged to your grandparents?"

The first picture was of the box I'd tripped over in the hall. In the photograph, it sat on the floor, next to the wall in the hallway, just where I'd seen it. But of the rest of the photos, items taken from the box—flashlight, lantern, sleeping bag, matches, pocket knife—only one was something I'd seen before.

"I've seen this sleeping bag. My dad and I used to go camping in the woods out there. I'm pretty sure that's one of our old sleeping bags."

Ridge jotted a note in a small notebook. "Do you know

where it was stored before it showed up in that box?"

"The barn maybe? I really don't know. I haven't seen it in years."

Ridge gathered those pictures and laid a new spread out in front of me. One look, and my skin started to crawl. Small baggies of white pills, others of a powdery substance, a flame singed spoon, and worst of all, a prescription pill container labeled with my grandmother's name. I could feel Ridge's eyes boring into me.

"Any of this look familiar?"

A clutch of panic took hold of my chest, inhibiting speech. I shook my head instead. The threat of tears at the back of my eyes gained momentum.

Ridge didn't push, and I took a moment to compose myself while he gathered the photographs and replaced them in the folder.

"How long have they been out there, can you tell?" It was little more than a whisper, but he heard me.

"Hard to say. Vacant houses are an open invitation for vagrants, especially out in the country like that. We've even seen it in other areas of town. Really, it's lucky you went out there that night. If you hadn't, I'm sure whoever packed that box would still be there." His voice had turned to velvet, soothing nerves worn raw by the photographs and cutting loose the tears I'd been holding back. The first one landed with a splat on the faux wood top of Ridge's desk. I wiped it away with my fist, hoping he hadn't noticed.

"Liv, I didn't call you out here to upset you. I know this is hard. It's okay. We've had surveillance stationed out there since Wednesday. Whoever was there, hasn't been back."

Ridge reached toward my shoulder, as if to brush my hair away from my face, but he pulled away at the last minute, leaving me wanting his touch—some proof that I wasn't completely alone in this. Instead, he reached for the Kleenex and handed me a tissue. I allowed anger to seep in and take over, anything to stem the flood of tears in front of a stranger. Except, Ridge didn't feel like a stranger.

"So, that's it? We just hope they don't come back?"

Ridge shrugged. "There's just not a lot we can do at this point. He didn't steal, didn't damage any property."

"How would you know?" The bite in my words, although unintentional, forced Ridge back a step.

He scanned the room, sliding the cup of undrinkable coffee from my hands, his voice a conspiratorial whisper. "Mind if I walk you out?"

So, that was that. So much for getting answers. My insides churned as I followed Ridge. He wove his way through the maze of desks toward an exit at the side of the building, walking me all the way to my car on the other side of the lot before stopping. He ran one hand through his hair while I unlocked the doors with the keychain fob.

"I'm sorry I couldn't give you the answers you're looking for. Really, I am."

A flutter in the pit of my stomach settled the churn when he spoke. He was trying, I had to give him credit for that.

"When can I go back?" I'd given up asking anything about a missing woman. They'd already put this case on the back burner, and I had no proof. What was I supposed to say? *I think a girl was murdered at Sullivan Farm.* I'd learned my lesson when it came to law enforcement and psychic phenomenon. The two did not play well together.

He lowered his head. "Give me until tomorrow. I'll make sure it's ready for you."

"I appreciate that."

His eyes met mine as I started to turn toward the Civic, rooting me in place. The urge to reach up, soothe the worried scrunch between his brows, elicit that dimpled laugh, choked out the frustration.

"Liv, I don't know how long you plan to stay, and I know this is the worst timing, but..." His voice dipped. "I'd like to take you out to dinner sometime. If you're interested."

The flurry in the pit of my stomach grew as his words registered. Every fiber of my being wanted to scream, *Yes!* Leave it to my brain, however, to question the why of it all. Did he have more evidence than he'd shared? Was he still investigating? Trying to work his way into our family? Did he know about me? I squashed the last thought. He didn't grow up in this town. To him, what happened ten years ago would've been nothing more than a blip on the news. Besides, thanks to my dad, any record of that night was sealed. In spite of the springboard of thoughts polluting the moment, it only took one more look at Ridge, the pain behind those eyes, for three monosyllabic words to silence the laundry list of disapproval.

"I'd like that."

Ridge's dimpled grin was my reward, and I smiled back. Meeting his gaze for a moment before casting my eyes downward to the pebble-based blacktop.

"Tonight? I could pick you up at seven." His statement was a question.

I agreed and popped open the door of my rental. He pulled the door open wide, the air between us electrified. My fingers tingled with an unfamiliar sensation as I slid inside, waiting for him to close the door.

I suddenly felt like Lauren Bacall in an old black and white Bogart movie, the kind I used to watch with my grandmother—except for the age difference, of course. This kind of thing didn't happen to me—hadn't happened since... I suppressed thoughts of Jason, disgust from the previous night quelling the remaining fuzz of electricity.

11

RIDGE

Adam was waiting for Ridge when he came back from walking Liv to her car.

"Good doughnuts." His partner held up what was left of his second long john. "You should have one."

Ridge shook his head and lowered himself into his desk chair. He slid his hands along the armrests on instinct. Strawberries and cream. He could almost still smell her.

"I found what you were looking for," Adam said, propping himself on the corner of his desk. "We've got some newspaper articles that mention Liv. The most recent was her grandmother's obituary of course, nothing earth-shattering there. Her dad died about eight years ago. Suicide."

Ridge was listening, but his mind was spinning. Sowards' mandate to press Liv, find out how much she knew about her grandmother's involvement in the Bureau weighed on him. He wanted to know more, yearned to know everything about her. But he could care less about some crazy Bureau experiment. His urge was primal, not intellectual.

"But here's the most interesting part," Adam continued. "She's got a juvenile record."

That got Ridge's attention. "For what?"

Adam shrugged. "Don't know yet. It's sealed. I'll see what I can–"

"Jesus," Ridge scrubbed a hand down his face. "I asked her out."

Adam stopped mid-sentence. "You what?"

Ridge shot a look at his partner. What else could he do? He was sick of half-truths. Adam was holed up in this one-horse town the same way Ridge was–placed undercover by the Bureau. But now, Sowards was excluding the one confidante Ridge had, and the job he was charged with was getting more difficult by the day.

"What aren't you telling me?" Adam was perceptive, Ridge gave him credit for that. Ridge fingered the pen on his desk, weighing his options, *click-click-click-click*. Adam slid into his chair, checking over his shoulder for the eavesdropping ears of the Cascade Hills PD.

"You've talked to Sowards." Adam guessed.

Ridge's silence was the answer he needed.

"Already been reassigned? Christ. What now? To her?" Adam jutted his chin toward the exit, fire blazing from his eyes.

Screw Sowards and his dictate. Adam was on a need to know basis, according to his SAC, and as far as Ridge was concerned, Adam needed to know that Liv was his newest assignment, especially if she had a record.

"So, what... we keep tabs on her like we did Grace?"

"Protection detail. Sowards claims Grace's involvement with the Bureau could've put a target on Liv's back."

"Why? That crazy program she told you about?"

"Evidently, not so crazy." Ridge wasn't looking forward to the fallout of this discussion. But the two men went silent, exchanging understanding glances as precinct Captain Frank Wallace rounded the corner toward their workstation.

"Got a problem at the old Sullivan place, thought you two should get out there and check it out."

Ridge stood, slung his jacket over his shoulder and headed toward the parking lot. Adam fell in step behind him, beating Ridge to the unmarked cruiser at the edge of the lot.

THE FRONT DOOR of the farmhouse hung open when Adam and Ridge arrived. The scent of urine hung heavy in the air, prompting the men to pull their shirts up over their noses. Not that it did much good. Whoever had been here wasn't happy that their stash had been confiscated.

Ridge sidled up next to one of the uniforms surveying the scene.

"Early morning, had to be. Perp must've slipped in when we changed shifts." The young officer looked at Ridge, obviously at a loss for a decent explanation. "The place was covered all night."

Ridge stepped carefully through the rooms. Overturned furniture, an entire secretary full of paperwork, tipped and scattered in the foyer, created a carpet of papers beneath his feet. Profanity spray painted across the living room wall. This would've taken longer than the few minutes of a shift change. Ridge clenched his jaw to keep the frustration of accusation at bay.

How would he ever tell Liv about this? The image of her head tipped downward, tears dripping onto his desk, flooded back, tugging at his heart. This place held her childhood memories. He may not know much about her, but that much was clear. And those tears had seared into him like drops of lava, scarring his core. He'd do whatever it took to keep her from shedding any more.

"McCaffrey, Miller! You're going to want to see this."

Ridge followed the voice to the back porch, where a tech was already photographing an array of old magazines spread to the edges of a glass-topped coffee table.

Finger painted words filled the top of the table. Ridge read the blood red scrawl twice: *She's not who you think she is.*

"Is it blood?" One of the officers asked what every one of them had been thinking. No one replied, allowing the *click-click* of the camera to provide a soundtrack for the moment.

"BCI just pulled in," Adam said, tilting his head toward the driveway beyond the patio exit.

"Tell them we'll need them out here," Ridge said, backing away from the table. "And if it is, get me a rush on the DNA."

12

LIV

"You look great," Ridge said, standing at my hotel door at seven o'clock. His eyes swept me from head to toe. Every inch of me warming under his gaze.

I checked my too-dressy-for-the-occasion blue dress I'd slipped into for the date. It was one of those dresses that you buy on a whim, but then never wear because, let's face it, you never go anywhere where jeans aren't standard. I smoothed the dress and grabbed my jacket, hoping the heat flooding my cheeks wasn't too obvious.

"You're not too hard on the eyes yourself, Detective McCaffrey." This comment earned me a short laugh as Ridge offered his arm.

He'd showered and shaved since this morning's meeting. Trading the blue button-down for green, the tail poking out from beneath his black leather jacket. I caught a whiff of his aftershave as we turned the corner in the hall. A tickle in the pit of my stomach sent a spike of anxiety up my spine. *What the hell was I doing?*

Ridge led me to the parking lot where he opened the passenger door of the shiny black Mustang Shelby.

We were on the road when I broke the silence. "Nice car. 550 horses must get you where you need to go pretty fast."

Ridge's shock was apparent.

"It does," he chuckled. "How is it you know about cars?"

"My grandpa was a mechanic. I spent a lot of time with him. His pride and joy was a 1965 Shelby GT350."

"Wow. Now that's a piece of art. My dad had a couple classic cars. A '57 Chevy and a '62 Impala. He wasn't a mechanic, but he enjoyed tinkering. I think that's probably where I get my fascination with them. I don't work on them though. They wouldn't run if I did."

He shot a smile in my direction. And there was that laugh again. Something deep inside me stirred each time I heard it. Wrapping me in warmth, like a favorite blanket.

I was a girl who appreciated a moderate dose of American muscle, but I hadn't talked to anyone about cars since high school. It felt good to bring it up, like I was emancipating a little piece of myself that had been held captive for far too long. There were so many fragments of me still holed up somewhere deep inside. I couldn't imagine ever setting all of them free.

Ridge drove carefully toward the other end of Cascade Hills. For most of the day, the weather had threatened to unleash another ice storm. Right now, it was dry, but the roads were still shiny and slick from yesterday's ice. While he focused on the highway I asked, "So, where are you taking me tonight?"

"I've got a buddy that owns a little bar, just on the outskirts of town–Murphy's. I thought we'd go there. They've got great food, pub style. That sound okay with you?"

"Pub style works for me."

Our conversation flowed, from classic cars to how the community of Cascade Hills had been changing. Questions I should be asking about the investigation and the all-but-forgotten image of a wide-eyed girl, gasping for breath in the woods at Sullivan farm, danced on the periphery. *We'll get there.* I promised them.

In no time we were pulling into a small parking lot situated along the back of a stone building. The lot overflowed. Cars lined the street and along a split board fence that ran the perimeter of a gravel lot.

I may have grown up in this town, but I'd never been here before. I pegged it for a newer development, although, the façade screamed anything but. Music poured from the doors of the traditional Irish pub. Appearing as though it had been transplanted stone by stone from Ireland herself, it was the polar opposite of Flanagan's.

Murphy's exterior was understated, but the interior was striking—full of dark wood and comfortable well-worn booths placed in nooks and crannies throughout the pub. The bar was magnificent. Bottles of every size and hue lined the mirrored back wall, the Guinness logo proudly displayed in bold lettering across the front of the tap. The rich wood of the bar glistened under a layer of lacquer. Now, this was my idea of the perfect pub.

Ridge nodded to the hostess and we sat ourselves in the only open booth, away from the live band, as I absorbed my surroundings. A huge stone fireplace separated us from the commotion of the bar. People wearing goofy green hats and shamrock glasses crammed themselves together on that side of the pub. In that moment, idiocy found me and planted itself firmly in my lap.

"St. Patrick's Day," I said. Embarrassment washed away the last hints of satisfaction lingering from the car ride over.

Ridge smiled at me, crystalline eyes twinkling. "I should have reminded you."

The moment only got worse when a cute blonde waitress bounded up to the table bearing a grin that belonged on a Colgate commercial.

"Ridge! I didn't expect to see you here tonight," she gushed before noticing me sitting across the table. Her grin collapsed.

"Melanie, this is Liv Sullivan. Liv, Melanie Murphy," Ridge introduced.

"It's nice to meet you... Murphy... is this your pub?"

Melanie shook her head, her blonde locks cascading in waves around her shoulders. I suddenly felt a pang of envy for this young woman, a few years younger, and who seemed to be pretty familiar with Ridge.

"Melanie is the owner's little sister. My friend, Brian, owns the place," Ridge explained.

I nodded and forced a smile at Melanie. I could feel her sizing me up, judging me.

"You're not wearing green." She nodded my direction.

"I know," I admitted. The horror of my faux pas crashed in on me. "It's been a week. I sort of forgot what day it was."

"Well, you know what that means, don't you?"

I raised my eyebrows in anticipation, glancing at Ridge before he stopped Mel.

"She's new here, Mel. She doesn't know. Just put it on my tab, okay?"

"Whatever you say." Melanie shrugged, her perfect lips curving back into that sparkling smile. "What can I get you two to drink, then? You want the usual, Ridge?" Her eyes never left him.

"Yeah. The usual. What about you, Liv? What's your poison?"

"I haven't had a Guinness on tap since I was in Ireland. There's no way I can pass that up."

"Sure. I'll get those right out." I could swear the girl winked at Ridge as she left the table.

I watched Melanie bounce to the bar, ringing a brass bell before hollering to the crowd, "Round of drinks courtesy of the girl at table 23!"

A chorus of merriment erupted from the mob around the bar. Pint glasses raised in the air and eyes focused in our direction. I slid lower in the seat, hoping to distance myself from the horde of cheering people.

"I had you pegged as a Bud Light kind of girl," Ridge said, ignoring the mob and guiding my attention back to him.

"Guinness is the only beer I can stand. I got a taste for it when I went to Ireland about six years ago. I have a hard time finding it on draught at home, though." I glanced back at the crowd. "You're not really going to have to pay for all those drinks, are you?"

Ridge laughed. "Knowing Brian, probably."

"Sorry," I managed, but Ridge just smiled.

"So, what took you to Ireland? I've always wanted to go, track down some family heritage maybe."

"My grandmother. She actually owns... owned... several properties over there. She loved it...went at least twice a year. I got to see the town where her family lived before coming to the United States during the famine. Even met some distant relatives. It was the trip of a lifetime." I hesitated, grief creeping up on me. "I could live there. I don't think there's anywhere else outside of the US I'd want to live, but there, I definitely could."

Too much information, my inner critic chided. But when I looked up, Ridge actually looked interested.

"So where are the Sullivans from?"

"Tipperary. They were farmers before the famine."

Ridge was silent, his eyes boring into me. A tingle started in the tips of my fingers. I rubbed them against the fabric on my thighs, but the friction only heightened the already uncomfortable sensation.

"What?" I asked, suddenly self-conscious.

Before he could answer, Melanie flirted up to the table with two pints of Guinness on a serving tray.

"Can I get you anything to eat tonight, or are you just drinking?"

"We're going to eat." Ridge glanced down at the menus that neither of us had opened. "What's the special tonight, Mel?"

"Tonight we have the Irish pork loin with a whiskey-honey glaze, served with savoy salad, carrots and champ."

Ridge looked at me for approval, one perfect eyebrow arched in a question mark.

"That sounds delicious," I assured.

"We'll each have the special then. Thanks, Mel."

That flutter began again in the pit of my stomach as he dismissed her, turning his attention back to me. Melanie lingered just a moment before stalking back to the kitchen. She was going to spit in my food, I was certain of it.

"That makes sense, then," Ridge said.

"What does?"

"Your family owning almost 400 acres around here."

I looked down at the table, fiddling self-consciously with the napkin beneath my drink. "I didn't know there was still that much left. I know they sold some off over the years."

"You know, you should have told me that the house was in your name when I found you there the other night. I wouldn't have been so hard on you."

I stared at Ridge, shocked.

"It's not in my name," I said haltingly. "It was my grandmother's."

Ridge shrugged and sat back in the booth.

"She must have put it in your name before she passed." He

took a sip of his drink. "It's not uncommon. Saves you the hassle of taking it through probate." His eyes darkened, curiosity taking over. "You didn't know?"

I shook my head. "I didn't." I took a long sip of my own Guinness.

"Sorry, did I say something I shouldn't have?"

"No, it's just... my mom has talked about it. I think she has a realtor lined up already. She wants to sell."

"Well," Ridge chuckled, "she certainly can't do it without you. Does she know it's in your name?"

I shrugged. Ridge backed off, shifted gears.

"Speaking of the farm...I should have called this afternoon." Ridge spun his pint glass between his thumb and forefinger. His smile evaporated. "There was another break-in. I didn't want to tell you on the phone."

"Is it bad?" I asked.

"They wrecked the place pretty good this time. Nothing some deep cleaning and paint won't fix, though."

He brought his eyes up to meet mine. There was pain there. A hurt I didn't quite understand. But this news wasn't anything I didn't expect.

"After I saw the pictures this morning, I figured it would happen. No druggie leaves their stash without coming back for it."

"You're not upset?"

"At the jerk who used my grandmother's home as his personal motel? Yes. But I can understand why you didn't call. I kind of went off the deep end this morning. I'm sorry."

I watched the tension in Ridge's body drain away.

"That place means a lot to you. I know you want to get back out there. Techs have gathered some evidence. This break-in might turn out to be just the break we need. We'll know more in a couple days."

Ridge slid his hand across the table, looping his index finger around mine, his thumb sweeping arcs over the back of my hand. There it was. The buzz I'd first felt the night we met. I swallowed against it. Biting back the urge to pull away.

"Don't go out there alone, okay? Let me go with you. Until we figure out who's doing this, it's not safe."

The butterflies in my gut launched into flight. I pulled my hand away and smiled. "I could use the company." *What? Did I really just say that?*

Melanie sidled up to the table with our meals just as the line of concern in Ridge's brow dissolved into a smile. She cleared her throat a little too loudly, announcing our selections and placing them in front of us. Ridge never took his eyes off of me. The intensity of his gaze burned into me. I couldn't help but look away, tucking my lower lip behind my front teeth to try to hide the nervous desire that seeped to the surface and heated my cheeks.

"Thanks, Mel. I think we're good for a while," Ridge said, his stare searing into my bitten lip. "So, Liv, tell me about yourself."

"What do you want to know?"

"Well, let's see, I know you're Judge Stephen Sullivan's daughter. People still talk about what a great man he was. Well-respected from what I gather. That takes care of some of the background, but I want to know about you. You've been gone from Cascade Hills for a while, right? What is it you do?"

Here we go, faced with the question I hated more than any other. Should I lie? Probably not such a great idea considering his profession. I took a deep breath, keeping my eyes lowered onto my food.

"I left for the University of Southern California after high school. Never really came back after that. Except for visits."

"What do you do out there?" He asked again, not letting me

get by with the diversion. "Customer Service. I work from home for a call center."

"Really? What company?" he probed, not missing a beat.

"I'm guessing you already know the answer to that question." The words slipped out before I could second guess myself. I glanced at him, gauging a response. One corner of his lip curled in a satisfied smile. He knew.

"Fair enough. You looking to stay in customer service?"

I chomped against the giggle that rose with his decision to stick with "customer service." I shook my head, "No. I never thought I'd be spending my life that way."

Ridge looked as if he wanted to ask something else. Probably whether or not I really was a psychic. If there was one lie I was sure I would tell, it was that one. I prepared for the inevitable, but he changed course.

"Now we're getting somewhere!" Ridge smiled, the dimple reappearing in his left cheek. "What is your dream, Liv Sullivan?"

"Photography." The word popped out without hesitation. *See?* My inner critic chimed in. "I always thought I'd like to open a photography studio."

"Ah, the artsy type. Guess I figured you more as a sorority girl."

"Didn't anyone ever tell you that you shouldn't judge a book by its cover? First light beer, now sorority chick? What other myths can I bust for you this evening?"

"I'm sorry. You're right. I have a bad habit of making assumptions. A product of my profession, I guess. Usually, I'm a pretty good judge of people."

"Well, you may need to recalibrate your receptors, Detective McCaffrey." I smiled at him to take the sting out of my words, but his eyes were dark, distant.

"Your turn," I said.

"What?"

"Your turn to tell me about you. And just remember, I don't have the luxury of police department resources at my disposal."

He chuckled. Shoveling in a bite of pork, he shrugged as he chewed. "Not much to know. I've been with Cascade Hills PD for about six years now."

"Hobbies?"

"Not much time for anything else."

"Okay." I hesitated before going in for the kill. "Do you always ask out alleged trespassers?"

He eyed me carefully, one corner of his mouth tipped up.

"No. I have to admit this is a first."

"So," I prompted. "Why start now?"

I locked eyes with Ridge, refusing to let him gloss over this one. He held my gaze. "Let's just say, you intrigue me, Liv Sullivan." He smiled, any hint of darkness gone. "Next question, counselor," he teased, eyes sparkling.

I laughed. "Did you grow up around here? I don't remember you from school." I took a chance, desperately hoping he wasn't someone I *should* know.

"No. I was born and raised outside of Wytheville, Virginia. A tiny town called Bishop's Hollow. We came to Ohio for work about ten years ago."

My stomach flipped. "We?"

Ridge's ocean eyes met mine. I knew what was behind the expression. I'd seen it countless times when I looked in the mirror–heartache.

"My wife and I...ex." He held my gaze throughout the explanation, "She was with an advertising firm in Columbus, so we moved there. Later, I was transferred to Cascade Hills." He paused and looked down. His knife sawed needlessly through the fork-tender pork. "It didn't exactly work out."

A pause strung like taffy between us.

"Well... Whatever happened, I'm glad you decided to stay," I said quietly.

"Me, too." He sounded shocked at his own comment. "My grandpa used to say that everything happens for a reason." He crinkled his nose. "That's cliché, isn't it?"

"Not at all." I smiled. "Yeah, well, a little."

I wanted to ask more about his wife. What happened between them? Divorced, obviously, but for how long? Possibilities flitted through my brain. Fortunately, our continuing conversation was enough to satiate me for the time being. It was far too early to ask those questions, I decided.

Besides, I planned to be back in L.A. by the end of the week. This was nothing more than an excuse to get away from the four walls of my hotel room, I tried to convince myself.

"Can I ask you a question? It's about work."

"Sure," he shrugged. "About the farm?"

"You could say that." I swallowed the fear that crept into my chest. "Have there ever been any other reports of crimes out there? Break-ins? Disappearances?" The last word was not much more than a whisper, nervousness taking control. I shoveled a forkful of salad into my mouth, focusing on its crunch.

He watched me. The concerned line reappearing between his brows. "I'd have to look to be sure, but I don't recall anything." He hesitated. "What do you mean by disappearances?"

My skin prickled. I couldn't do this. If I wanted answers I'd have to find them on my own.

The trill of Ridge's ringtone saved me from answering, so I went back to my food while he excused himself. I'd worried that it would be a struggle to act natural, be *normal* around Ridge, but until I'd asked that stupid question, it had been easy.

Our conversation flowed like water, obscuring the fact that I'd known him a little more than forty-eight hours. That fact kept my inner voice prodding from the recesses of my mind, *this will never work, you'll never be able to let him know who you really are.* Yet, I already felt like he knew me better than anyone else had in a very long time.

"Liv, I'm sorry. We're going to have to cut this short. It's work."

I could see it in his eyes, though. Uncertainty. "Something happened at the farm, didn't it?"

He slid back into the booth. "They uncovered some evidence we didn't see this afternoon. They want me to take a look."

"Take me with you."

"Liv, please ..."

"You said it yourself. It's my house, right? Don't I have a right to know what you found?"

Ridge's chest rose and fell with a resigned sigh. The hint of a smile crept onto his lips. He wanted me to come. Ridge stuck his hand in the air to get Melanie's attention, and nodded at me.

"You do intrigue me, Liv Sullivan." He said after Melanie flitted away with his payment. He reached for my hand to help me out of the booth.

"Just so we're clear," I said, standing. "The feeling is mutual, Detective."

13

LIV

I don't know what I expected when Ridge pulled up to the Sullivan farmhouse that night. Electric was still off, so the team from BCI had set up high powered lights on tripods to aid in the search. Ridge had been pretty quiet on the way in. His command not to touch anything as he opened the passenger door for me, was the first he'd spoken since the glow of town dissolved into the blackness of countryside. Nerves. Not nervousness exactly, but anxiety.

A suck of breath seized my lungs when he led me inside. Overturned furniture–the foyer carpeted with a layer of letters and papers spilled from the secretary now face-down on the entryway floor. I blocked the urge to kneel down and start scooping them up.

Ridge gave my hand a squeeze. "It's okay if you want to wait outside."

I tossed that option around while my eyes drifted to the profane scrawls etched in paint across the plaster walls of the living room. *Bitch. Whore.* Tags directed at me. Whoever had been in the house had seen me. At the very least, knew I was a woman. I swallowed the weight of that epiphany.

"McCaffrey, we're back here." A female voice echoed against the walls of the empty house.

Ridge released my hand and headed toward the back of the house. "Watch your step."

I followed a few paces behind him down the hall, through the kitchen, and out onto the back porch. With each step the air grew colder. The only heat produced by the tripod lights emitting their warm, Do Not Touch, hum. Frigid March air seeped freely through the open porch door, permeating the rest of the house.

A group of four officers and technicians huddled around the old trunk my grandparents used as a coffee table. I'd never seen it open, but it was tonight. A photographer snapped pictures while another tech dusted for prints. A third held the bluish light by which they could see. Only one of them looked up as Ridge entered. She gave me a quick once-over, her eyes returning to Ridge with a silent warning.

"Liv Sullivan?" Her tone told me she already knew.

I nodded. The sudden motion jostled loose the wall that held back a familiar scene. I could smell the decay of autumn leaves. Feel the pressure of hands around my throat. I backed away from the scene as blue eyes blazed into memory.

The officer stepped forward, placing herself between me and the trunk. She removed a glove and extended her hand. "Shana Collins, I work with Ridge at the precinct. Sorry I interrupted your evening." She shifted her attention to Ridge. "Most of the damage was focused on the front rooms, until we brought out the luminol. ME is on the way."

I backed into the kitchen, hoping for some relief from the vignette playing out in my mind.

The two techs closest to Ridge parted to allow him through.

"*Jesus.*" The tension in Ridge's voice was enough to force me away. The following "Take her outside," was overkill. Shana joined me as I backed into the middle of the kitchen, tucking myself into the shadow of the hallway.

She shoved the wadded glove into her jacket pocket. "Come on, let's get some fresh air." She laid a hand on my shoulder and smiled warmly. The warm pools of her chocolate eyes provided enough tenderness to chase away the assaulting images.

Once on the front porch, she dusted the seat and back of the peeling wicker rockers that had always been a mainstay at my grandparents' farm. She sat and sighed, inviting me to do the same. "It's really beautiful out here. Did you spend much time here growing up?"

I couldn't figure out how Shana managed to look so comfortable in the arctic blast with the remains of a dead girl thirty feet away. I tugged my parka closer around my neck. The temperate California climate had definitely thinned my blood.

"Every summer." I worked to focus on the conversation. Anything to stay rooted. "More often when I could think of a good enough reason."

Her laugh tinkled like bells, filling the ivy ensconced space of the porch. "I know that feeling. Let me guess, rift between mom and dad?" She looked over at me, continuing a steady rocking cadence back and forth, back and forth.

"Something like that."

She smiled, reaching over to pat my hand. Her skin was the color of mocha. Her voice deep and sincere. "When was the last time you were here?"

Tight curls of hair escaped from underneath a police-issue baseball cap. She was so likable I almost didn't realize she was interrogating me.

"Two days ago. I came out Friday morning to find a photo

album for my grandmother's funeral service. It's where I met Ridge."

Shana's lips curled into a moonlit smile. "We'll figure out who was here, you know. It's just a matter of time."

Silence stretched between us. "What you found in there, it's bad, isn't it?"

"I'll defer that to Detective McCaffrey. This is an open investigation, Liv. Until we have more answers, I'm afraid I'm not at liberty to say."

The veil of uncertainty clouding her eyes was the proof I needed.

THE RIDE HOME was worse than the ride out. The quiet drone of road noise weighted the air. Ridge's brain on overdrive while mine tried to make sense of what instinct told me had been discovered in the old trunk. We were back in the hallway at the Holiday Inn, when he asked, "Why did you ask me about disappearances?"

My heart jumped, settling into a hard rhythm against my sternum. The lock on my hotel room door blinked red at me. I waved the keycard in front of the reader again, praying for the green signal that would let me in. It came.

I expected accusation when I turned around. Suspicion. But instead there was only concern—a shard of helplessness emanating from the cerulean sea of his eyes.

"It was nothing." I shrugged, trying to ward off the familiar slice of panic that slit through my chest.

Ridge cocked his head. "Why don't you let me decide that?"

It was the look in his eyes that convinced me—hurt, mixed

with uncertainty. I nodded, swallowing the knot that inhibited speech.

"A couple months ago, I received a phone call...at work... Someone I didn't know. He..." I choked on the words. Was I ready for this? The answer to that was a definite, no. But I needed help. I couldn't do this on my own. "He told me a girl disappeared in the woods at Sullivan Farm. I chalked it up to a prank. We get those sometimes."

I waited for Ridge's reaction. His face showed a calm understanding I didn't expect.

"After the break-in, I thought it was worth checking."

The burn of tears threatened the backs of my eyes. Not again. I wouldn't cry again.

"Any other details?"

I shook my head, afraid to trust my voice.

"I'll check into it." Ridge's tone was soft–smooth caramel. He reached for my chin, tilting my face so I had nowhere to look but at him. "I'm sorry about tonight. It's not how I wanted us to spend our time."

"No apology necessary. You have a job to do."

His brow arched–surprise. "Can we try this again? Another night?"

Heat pulsed through me. It may not have been the romantic evening I'd hoped for, but I couldn't face the silent walls of the hotel room. Not after what happened at the farm. And I'd done my part, I'd told him about the girl from the call. *Hardly*, my inner critic refuted. I silenced her and stepped toward Ridge, fingering the lapels of his jacket. "Tonight's not over yet."

The words hung between us for a moment, and I cringed under their absurdity. For God's sake, a dead woman's body was stuffed in my grandparents' steamer trunk. I'd like to claim inebriation for the temporary lapse of sanity, but the Guinness I'd had with dinner had long since evacuated my system.

Regardless, my body buzzed. Every nerve ending on high alert. Ridge wet his lips and cradled my face in his hands, giving me ample opportunity to change my mind. Instead, I rose on tiptoe to meet him halfway, sinking into our kiss. His lips were soft, gentle. His tongue warm, probing. I'd forgotten how good that spiral of warm connection could be. That seed of growing want melted into longing as he drew away. His eyes focused on mine.

"In spite of everything, I had a great time with you tonight, Liv." His voice was soft, airy–how I imagined he might sound if he woke up in my bed. His hand still cradled my chin, almost as if he didn't want to let go. My body ached for the pressure of his lips on mine again.

"Me, too," I breathed.

Ridge planted a kiss on my forehead before pulling away. He strode down the hallway of the Holiday Inn and disappeared into the stairwell, leaving me hungry and alone.

14

RIDGE

Adam poked his head around the corner of the kitchen when Ridge arrived back at Sullivan Farm.

"What are the odds, huh?"

"Of what?" Ridge asked as he pulled on his nitrile gloves to head back into the crime scene. He was not in the mood for Adam's sense of humor.

"That you'd be on a date with the owner of this farm when a body was discovered in a trunk on her patio?"

"This is her Grandmother's farm, Adam. Liv has nothing to do with this."

"Right." Adam stretched the word out as Ridge shouldered by him. "I forgot. Hot chicks can't be murderers."

Ridge ignored his partner's poorly planned comment and refocused. The writing on the top of the trunk was still clear. The childlike letters sent a chill down his spine as he reread the warning, *"She's not who you think she is."*

"How'd you know there was something inside?" he asked Shana as she finished up some final notes on the scene.

"We didn't at first. Brought out the luminol and that's when we saw the trail. Blood led from the door to the trunk. There was a pool at the base." She pointed out a darkened area in front of the trunk. "Whoever dumped her in here tried to clean up. But it's not Jane Doe's blood in the message. The precipitin test proves it."

"The blood is animal?"

Shana nodded. "The lab will confirm species, but it's definitely not human."

Ridge opened the now-empty trunk. "Did the ME have any idea on cause of death?"

"Not at this point. Too much soft tissue decomp to tell. But this was found with the body." Shana held up a vintage skeleton style key, not big enough for a door. Ridge took the evidence bag in his hand.

"How long has she been in there?"

"A day, two days—not long. There's fresh dirt in there with her. She was stashed somewhere else long enough for full decomp," Shana said over her shoulder, turning and exiting the porch out the side door. The techs would return to remove the trunk, haul it to BCI for testing.

"Shit." Ridge spat the curse under his breath. He was hoping the remains had been in the trunk much longer than that. So long that Liv wouldn't have to be involved in any kind of interrogation about a dead girl on her grandmother's farm. So much for that stroke of luck.

Right now, all he wanted to think about was the way she felt in his arms. How her body molded to his, her curves fitting him in all the right places. How her lips had melted into his, sweet and soft—hungry.

"Sowards is going to want to know about this."

Ridge hadn't heard his partner creep out onto the porch. Or

maybe, he'd been too engrossed in his memories of Liv. Either way, he didn't like it. It meant he was losing his edge.

"I'll take care of Sowards," Ridge said. "Any news on missing persons?" He wanted to change the subject.

"Nothing here in Cascade Hills. I've got calls in to neighboring precincts, but so far, nothing. Our Jane Doe is a ghost."

15

LIV

My grandmother and the little girl visited me again that night. Both of them stood in a fog of blue haze at the edge of the woods at Sullivan farm.

"Who was she?" I asked, determined to gain at least a little clarity if I was going to lose a chunk of sleep.

Neither of the apparitions answered. My juvenile doppelgänger still imploring me with those big green eyes while my grandmother stayed stoic, determined to make me work for whatever it was she needed me to discover.

"If you want me here, you have to let me know why," I bargained. A corpse on the patio was not exactly the sign I needed if her plan was for me to carry out her legacy of taking over Sullivan farm. I felt my own frustration creep in. The vision wobbled in front of me.

The little girl stepped forward, this time carrying something in her hands. As she drew closer, the details solidified. She clutched a small mahogany box against the front of her smocked dress. For the first time she came close enough for me to touch.

I reached out a hand. "Who are you?" I whispered, careful not to disrupt the flow of energy that brought her to me.

"We need you. Please. You're the only one who can help." Her voice was young and fragile–scared, even. She opened the box in front of her as rays of light danced from inside–nothing decipherable.

"But I don't understand. Tell me what you need from me."

"Freedom." The ribbons in the little girl's hair fluttered in an otherworldly breeze. The box slammed closed in her tiny hands. "You need to find the key."

Contrary to logic, I slept more soundly after that than I had in a very long time, waking only when my phone's ringtone jarred me from sleep around 9:30. The little girl's words flitted in the back of my mind, as my mother's name stretched across the screen.

"Did you forget?" No hello, how are you, take a hike, anything... I sighed. Guess the honeymoon was over.

"Forget what?"

"We are supposed to meet your grandma's lawyer today to go over her will."

"Today?" I'd been known to forget things, but this was something I was sure I would've remembered had it been conveyed in conversation.

"You need to get here. Jack Reynolds' office, 27 North Main Street. He's waiting, says he can't go over anything until you're here. I'm not sure why, but we're waiting for you."

Ahh... it made sense now. This was intended to be a private little pow-wow between my mother and Grandma's lawyer. Kudos to Grandma and Jack for including me.

"I'll be right over."

I'd met Jack Reynolds on a few occasions when I was running errands with my grandmother. Even in line at the grocery store, he exuded confidence. Always impeccably dressed in an expensive suit and tie, his silver hair and athletic build gave him that self-assured sexiness older men sometimes possess. It was no secret my grandmother thought he was the best thing since sliced bread. I'd suspected the feeling was mutual.

I ran up the steps and into the posh offices of Reynolds and Reynolds, Attorneys at Law. The secretary was absent from her post at the front desk and several lights were darkened, making me wonder if I was in the right place. Jack saw me from his open office door and smiled, motioning for me to come inside.

"Olivia, I'm so glad you are able to join us today. Your mother said that you might not be able to make it."

We shook hands before I sat in one of the oversized leather chairs opposite his desk. My mother perched on the edge of the chair next to mine, ignoring my entrance. A familiar pang of disappointment cut through my chest—our recent mother daughter moment, long lost. Lyle sat next to her, as he had at Foster's, holding and stroking her hand. He smiled a greeting.

"I'm sorry I wasn't here on time, Mr. Reynolds."

"Jack. Please, call me Jack."

"Okay, Jack. I must not have heard the date correctly. It's been a bit of a whirlwind since I've been back." I glanced at my mother, hoping for some recognition. But her face remained stoic.

"Oh, it's no problem, Olivia. Why don't we get started?"

I watched and listened carefully as Jack explained how this process worked. He would read the last will and testament aloud and then, after answering any questions we had, we would fill out the necessary legal paperwork to initiate the transfer of my grandmother's assets to the named beneficiaries.

Jack's long silver letter opener slit the manila envelope open with a whoosh of pent up energy. He scanned the one-page document briefly before declaring, "This should be short and sweet. As all of you know, Grace was a smart lady. Always clear on her intentions."

He cleared his throat and leaned back in his chair before continuing. "I, Grace Moira Callaghan Sullivan, decree that my entire residual estate be transferred to the property of my granddaughter, Olivia Grace Sullivan, to be used as she sees fit."

The silence of the room was deafening. My pulse thumped in my ears and for a brief moment the possibility that I could be in the midst of an uncomfortable dream sent a wave of anxiety crashing over me. I waited for what would come next.

"That can't be," my mother said... way too calmly.

"Actually, Mrs. Sullivan, she put Olivia's name on the real estate some time ago."

My mother turned to glare at me. "Did you know about this?"

"No. I actually found out about the farm last night, but before that, I had no idea. She never told me."

Tears began to prick the backs of my eyes. I yearned for my mother's gentle touch, the shared moment of, *I'm glad you're here,* from three days before. Realization joined the ranks of disappointment, racing through my chest with the speed of a tornado and leaving just as much damage in its wake.

My grandmother had already given me so much, not in title or estate, but in love—in trust. And I'd done nothing to repay the favor. I could count on one hand the number of times I'd visited since she'd been at New Horizons. And she died alone. My skin on the tips of my fingers tingled, the back of my scalp prickling. She loved that farm. After her family, it was her most prized possession, passed down through generations before her.

She'd told stories about our ancestors and how hard they worked to get that piece of land. How that property was their redemption after years of suffering and share-cropping in Ireland. Visions of Irish men and women chucking rocks from over-farmed fields invaded my thoughts.

"She was senile." Mom broke the silence. "We'll contest the will." She shot a look at me. "That's what we'll do." Panic clipped the tone in Mom's voice.

Jack answered simply, "I think we both know, Mrs. Sullivan, that Grace was far from senile."

Mom sat a moment longer, saying nothing. But when Lyle stood, she followed his lead toward the door. The look on her face now, I recognized–shock. I'd never seen my mother ruffled like that. The woman who always had it together in public was fighting a battle of emotions. One anger. The other, unmistakable fear.

I reached for her arm as she passed, but she pulled away, retreating through the doorway without another word.

Jack's voice pulled me back to the present. "I knew this wouldn't be easy. Are you okay?"

"Of course. Do I have a choice? I mean, of course I am." I attempted a smile, but instead, a choked sob escaped my lips. Jack came around from behind his massive desk and folded me into a hug. The embraces my father and I once shared crept into memory, deconstructing the dam of tears into steady streams down my cheeks.

"This is a lot to take in." Jack handed me a few tissues. "There are some details we need to take care of. If you think you're up to it, I can walk you through it now."

After signing what felt like hundreds of papers littered with legal mumbo jumbo I had no hope of understanding, Jack asked, "Olivia, do you have a financial planner?"

I laughed at the ridiculousness of his question. "No."

"You're going to need one. He slid a folded piece of paper toward me. This is the amount that will be transferred to an account we'll set up in your name. It usually takes a week or so, but you need to be prepared. I have a friend who I trust implicitly. I'll set up an appointment with him. Of course, this is cash only and doesn't include the stocks, bonds, and real estate. My secretary is on vacation this week, but I'll have her draw up a list of those for your reference when she returns."

I unfolded the paper. I grew up knowing that my grandparents had never wanted for anything, but I was a child. They both worked outside the home and I didn't understand the specifics. I never asked. I counted the digits–all seven of them—on the page like a teenager being handed a particularly generous graduation check.

"I... don't... I..." I couldn't form a coherent sentence.

"You don't have to say anything. I just wanted you to be prepared." He began packing up the paperwork. "So, do you plan to move back–live at the farm?" Jack thankfully changed the subject as he finished stacking the files.

"I don't know. Yes, I guess? Maybe?"

I loved that farm, but managing it alone? Even with the financial assistance of my grandmother's money, I wasn't sure I was ready to move back to Cascade Hills permanently. I hadn't heard from Celeste. Maybe I had a job to go back to after all.

Confusion blurred my thoughts. The image of a little girl, hand tucked firmly into my grandmother's, flitted through my brain. Followed by the blue eyes, I'd seen just yesterday, lifeless. I knew then, Grandma didn't leave everything to me in generosity. She left it to me because the farm was the key. Both girls, whoever they were, in life or in death, were undoubtedly connected to Sullivan Farm. Connected to me.

Jack assured me he'd be in touch. But after a lonely walk back to the rental, all I really wanted was someone to talk to.

Someone who would listen as I poured my heart out about my grandmother's apparent faith in me. *Ridge.* His name popped up unbidden. *One date doesn't constitute friendship, Olivia.* I pulled away from the curb. I only had one option left–my grandmother.

The deep, rich, brown of mounded dirt, freshly piled in front of the elaborate Sullivan headstone stuck out against the frosty grey ground. I shut off the engine and kneeled on the frozen earth beside the hunk of speckled granite. My fingers traced the names on the stone, first my grandfather's, and then my grandmother's, her death date still empty, waiting for the engraver to complete his work.

"Thank you, Grandma... for trusting me. I will find out who they are. I'll make you proud. I promise."

My breath puffed in clouds that drifted away on the bitter breeze. I sat on my heels, legs folded at the knee. The iciness of the ground seeped into my kneecaps and spread from there. I was wiping away the cooling trickle of tears when I heard the crunch of footsteps behind me.

"I thought I might find you here." The warmth of Ridge's voice pierced the cold atmosphere.

"How did you know where I was?"

"I was tying up some loose ends at the farmhouse, so I knew you weren't there. The hotel said they thought you'd gone out. This was my last resort before issuing an APB." He smiled down at me and reached out a gloved hand to help me up. He was dressed in khakis and a button down, his leather jacket open.

"Why didn't you just call my cell?"

"I tried. It went to voicemail every time." He hesitated, wiping the lingering tears from my cheeks. "I started to worry."

I patted my empty coat pocket.

"I must have left it at the hotel. Are you still on duty?"

"Yes. On call, anyway, but it's my dinner break. I hoped maybe you'd join me. I know a great little café down the road." His eyebrows arched as he eyed me.

"I'd love to." Even the side of my brain that was against these little interactions with Ridge couldn't argue that talking with a live person in a warm café was better than one-sided conversations with dead people in a cold cemetery.

The restaurant was cozy and inviting, definitely family owned. Once again, the waitress knew Ridge, but I wasn't as concerned about the grandmotherly influence of this server as she showed us to a booth in the back.

"So, what did you get into today?" Ridge asked as he hung our coats on the rack next to the booth.

"I had a meeting with my grandmother's attorney. It didn't go well. Mom was there with her new beau." I tried not to let the snark seep into my voice but failed miserably.

"Ah." He smiled that genuine grin before probing for more. "So, I take it they didn't know about the farm?"

"No, they didn't... how did you know about that, anyway?"

"It's all a matter of public record. I found it when I checked out your information."

"Right." My eyes glanced to the lanyard that was strung around Ridge's neck. His picture on a card, name lettered in black underneath. I couldn't help but focus on the DET. emblazoned before his name.

"I suppose that's what detectives do, huh?"

He smoothed the card against his shirt. "It's in the job description."

"They call detectives out for trespassing reports now?" I attempted to keep the accusation from my voice, but it was there, alive and well.

A chuckle erupted from Ridge's chest. "You watch too much TV." He smiled at me before explaining. "This is small-town PD. We have to be a jack-of-all-trades around here."

"Seems like it's been a busy week for Cascade Hills PD."

Ridge laughed and his blue eyes sparkled. "Definitely."

Dinner consisted of traditional comfort foods and the best hot chocolate I'd ever tasted. Ridge recommended the pie for dessert, but after meatloaf, mashed potatoes, and three cups of hot chocolate, there was no room left. I was amazed at how someone could eat as much as he did and still look so good. Good genes, I guessed.

He drove me back to my car at the cemetery and escorted me to the driver's side, all in silence, which worried me. I finally got up the nerve to comment, "You're quiet again. Historically, that's not a good sign."

"I don't want to scare you off. And I know how crazy it is that I tracked you down, but I needed to see you." Ridge slid his bare hands down my arms, watching as his fingers wrapped around my own.

I bit back the surge of electricity that spiked through all ten digits. It was all I could do not to pull away. Like the buzz of tissue cut off from circulation, the skin on my hands tingled. The numbness of a vision without the accompanying picture.

"I needed to make sure you were okay."

"Believe it or not, Detective McCaffrey, I'm a big girl." I pulled my hands from his, calming my breath. "I promise not to end up at the bottom of a box." The words slipped out before I could catch them.

He smiled as if what I'd said was no big deal, and I blew out a breath. I guessed the discovery of a corpse at Sullivan farm wasn't likely to stay a secret for long. I slid behind the steering wheel of the rental, checking for that smile. But it didn't reach his eyes. Tension filled the space between us.

I had to be honest, his overprotectiveness was weirding me

out just a bit. As attracted as I was to him, I couldn't make sense of what I felt when he touched me, or why he was paying so much attention to me. We'd been on one date. Admittedly, it was a good one, but still. I watched in my rear-view mirror as his Shelby pulled out behind me, following for several blocks before veering off down a side street.

16

LIV

I t had been three days since our impromptu dinner at the diner, and Ridge still hadn't called. Mom wasn't talking to me and Jason was out of the question, so my only human interaction was with Jack Reynolds and his financial planner. It was Jack who finally started making some sense.

"He can't keep you from the farm, Olivia. The longer you stay away the harder it will be to go back. I read the report. It's a tragedy, but not one you're responsible for." Jack twirled spaghetti onto his fork with the aid of a too-big spoon.

I could feel my lips twist into an uneasy frown. Jack was a local, my grandmother's confidante. He knew my history. And he was the only one, as far as I could tell, that still treated me like a normal person.

"I saw her. In the woods. I know how she died."

Jack slipped his napkin from his lap and dabbed at the corners of his mouth. "A vision?"

I nodded, picking at the piece of garlic bread at the edge of my plate.

"Did you tell the police?"

"No." I gave in to the truth of the words itching to meet air. "But I want to. Maybe they can find out who she is. Notify her family. Bring them some closure."

"Have you thought about what that decision would mean for you?"

His eyes latched onto mine. "Look, Liv, I can't tell you what to do. In the end you're the one who has to live with your decisions. But I can tell you this, your grandmother spent her life trying to make sure you had some choice in who you were. Living with gifts like yours is no easy feat. Grace knew that. Just remember, whether you decide to go to the police or not, it won't change the past. A girl will still be dead. You'll still have to live with that ghost."

I chewed my bottom lip, forcing down the questions that rose up like a geyser from within. I could tell Jack I'd seen Grandma. Ask him about the mysterious little girl. Maybe he knew who she was. Maybe there was no literal key, maybe Jack was the key. Instead, I shifted gears.

"Grandma saw them, too, didn't she?"

Jack nodded.

"I was never quite sure." The words were an afterthought, a whisper in the chatter of the busy restaurant. "Thank you, Jack, for everything," I managed, piling my napkin across my plate and pulling a twenty out of my purse, before sliding out of the booth and toward the door. He didn't try to stop me.

Crime scene tape still draped the doorway of the farmhouse, and the air was the coldest it had been since I'd been home, so I decided not to stay. Instead, I made a mental note to get the gas and electric turned back on as soon as possible. All I needed were busted pipes to make the job of cleaning the place up even worse.

I slipped around the back of the house and entered through the broken patio door. There was a distinct chemical odor hanging in the nearly empty space. The trunk was gone and with it, the vengeful image of a murdered young woman. I sucked in the rancid air and kneeled on the floor, tracing my fingertips over the faded bloodstain darkening the boards beneath. Again, nothing. Was she done with me? Had I played my part?

Confusion muddied my thoughts, and instead of nosing around the farm, I reverted to my high school routine of driving around Cascade Hills, snapping photographs in little known nooks and crannies of town. Back then I did it to get away from my mother. Now, it was to escape the chaos of my own mind. Jack was right. The cops would think I was crazy, Ridge included.

I found my way back to Murphy's, but instead of tucking myself away in a booth, I chose a seat at the bar instead. I wasn't the only person sitting there. The place was doing good business for a small-town Thursday evening. A handsome bartender stood at the other end of the bar talking with a patron as I selected a stool. As soon as I was seated, he walked over with a smile.

"What can I get you this evening, Miss?" he asked cheerfully.

"Guinness, please," I answered. I wasn't exactly the kind of girl that hung out in bars alone and it must have shown. When the bartender returned with my drink, he spoke.

"You must be new in town." His eyes twinkled under a mop of dark brown hair that matched the stubble on his chin.

"Not exactly, but it's been a while since I've been back."

"I'm glad you stopped in. Make yourself at home."

I took a swig of the dark beer, wiping away the trace of foam that clung to my lips. Two seats down, one of the customers climbed down off his perch and I overheard him say, "Catch you later, Brian. Thanks again," before heading past me toward the door.

I gauged whether or not to ask if he was the same Brian Ridge had mentioned. Instead, I sat nursing my Guinness for quite a while before noticing Melanie, the waitress from the other night, talking with Brian and gesturing toward me. He glanced in my direction once before giving her a tray of glassware to take back to the kitchen.

"Can I get you anything else?" he asked. "Maybe a bite to eat?"

"I could eat something. Any chance you have the pork loin tonight?"

"Of course. It's a crowd favorite. Why don't you make yourself comfortable in one of the booths and I'll be out with it shortly? Another pint, too?"

"Sure," I decided, before heading to the booth Ridge and I had occupied less than a week ago. It seemed so much longer. I noticed that Melanie was tending bar now, and before long, Brian sidled up to my booth with a fresh Guinness and slid in opposite me.

"I'm Brian, by the way. Melanie tells me this isn't your first time at Murphy's."

I glanced at the pretty blonde behind the bar.

"True. I was here the other night with a friend."

Brian studied me carefully. His eyes were as deep as Ridge's were vibrant, and the comparison intensified the ache of loneliness.

"That must make you Liv Sullivan."

"Guilty. Do you make it a habit to keep track of all your

patron's names?" I teased, certain Melanie told him who I was, but his next comment jarred me off my game.

"Ridge has mentioned you."

Now I was intrigued. Butterflies took flight in my belly as I waited for Brian to say more.

"Ridge is like a brother to me."

"Everyone needs someone in their life like that." I smiled, but it must not have been as convincing as I'd hoped.

Brian's head cocked to the side and he studied me. "He's a good guy. He hasn't stopped talking about you."

I considered what I was about to admit. "I wish he'd share some of those thoughts with me."

Brian smiled and patted my hand before he stood to leave. "Looks like your dinner is here. I'll let you eat in peace." Melanie came to the table with the pork loin perched on a tray.

"Brian?" I stopped him before he could step away. "I wouldn't mind a little company, if you're not too busy."

He chuckled. "I suppose I gotta eat sometime." He told Melanie to bring him the fish and chips, and she scurried away, never acknowledging my existence.

"So, what do you want to know?" he asked. "I know you didn't invite me to stay for my rugged good looks."

I laughed. He was right. Although he definitely fell into the handsome category, my thoughts were too wrapped up in Ridge to notice.

"I just thought it might be nice to get to know Ridge's friends. I think friends tell a lot about a person, don't you?" I realized as I made the comment that my lack of friends spoke volumes as well. Suddenly, I wished I could take my question back.

"Hmm... I'm not sure he'd want you to judge him based on me. I'm not exactly a saint. Ridge and I differ in a lot of ways."

"Like?" I pressed.

"I've been in my fair share of trouble. Ridge is kind enough to look past that."

"What kind of trouble?" It felt so good to be having a conversation with someone other than my inner voice that I found myself delving deeper than any normal person should in a first conversation.

He surveyed me carefully before completely changing the subject. I'd gone too far.

"I hear you're a photographer."

"Kind of," I responded. "I enjoy it."

"Are you any good?"

"Absolutely." I tried to sound more confident than I felt.

"Good. I need someone to take pictures of the pub for advertising. How much would you charge for something like that?"

"It depends on exactly what you need, but I'm sure I could cut a friend of Ridge's a pretty good deal." A bubble of excitement expanded in my chest. Did I just book a paying photography job here in Cascade Hills?

"Great. Come by sometime in the next few days. We can talk about what I need and your fee. We can watch the weather. Maybe you can even take the pictures then."

The rest of the conversation consisted of friendly small talk. Brian had a great sense of humor and I laughed more that night than I had since coming home. It felt good. For at least a couple hours, I was able to forget about the scared eyes of a dead girl, my grandmother's legacy, my own secrets, and Ridge's apparent refusal to keep that second date.

Before Brian excused himself to tend bar as the dinner rush hit, he leaned over and answered a question I'd been too afraid to voice.

"Don't let him scare you off, Liv. He can be pretty intense

when he..." Brian's voice trailed off, as if he thought better of his admission.

"When he, what?" I pried.

"...when he cares. He can be quiet, overprotective. It's a fault, but just bear with him, okay? He's been through a lot."

I watched Brian head back to the bar while Melanie served the growing crowd. I desperately wanted to know more. If silent overprotectiveness was Ridge's worst fault, I would gladly take it on. Even though I barely knew this man, I was quickly realizing that he was way more than fling material, and I couldn't resist the urge to wonder what happened to make him the way he was.

17

RIDGE

Ridge and Adam sifted through every recent missing persons report they could find. Nothing matched their Jane Doe.

Wallace flung a folder on Ridge's desk. "DNA came back on our Jane Doe."

"And?" Ridge and Adam exchanged glances. Ignoring the choral request for more information.

"She's not in the system. We'd run dental records, but whoever killed her or shoved her in that case, pulled her teeth out before they did it," Wallace said. "This has cold case written all over it. Make sure to check records in neighboring precincts. See if you can get anywhere."

The two men waited for Wallace to stalk back to his office before heading for the lounge.

"You know you'll have to pull Liv in for questioning," Adam said. "It's all a little too perfect. No one even knows about this girl until Liv shows up and in a matter of days she's dug up and dumped in Grace Sullivan's farmhouse?"

"I need some time, Adam. If there is a connection to Liv, I

need to be able to tell the brass it's a coincidence. We already know someone's been creeping around the old place. What reason would Liv have to plant a body in her grandmother's trunk?"

"None."

Ridge and Adam both swiveled toward Liv's unexpected voice.

"Sorry to interrupt. Shana said I could find you in the lounge."

A sliver of icy dread threaded through Ridge's heart. He saw the proof in Liv's eyes. The pain of betrayal. It was an expression he'd become familiar with–one he'd found in his own reflection before Liv washed it away. Now he was the cause of her pain.

"Good to see you," Adam smiled at Liv, waited for the tumble of the Coke machine to deliver his beverage, then slipped out into the hallway. *Coward,* Ridge couldn't keep the thought from bubbling up.

"I understand your suspicion," she started, working her hands into a nervous knot. "I just gave my statement to Shana. But if there are questions you need me to answer, just ask." Liv spoke quietly, every word slicing into Ridge's chest. "I've got nothing to hide."

Ridge stepped toward her, close enough to feel the heat of her body. He twisted a curl around his index finger and watched her eyes droop closed. Every part of him was alive, buzzing with an energy he hadn't felt in years. Damn Sowards for making this so complicated. Liv's hand grazed his bicep, her breath slow and deliberate. He tugged her hair, gently, just enough to tip her head back, exposing her lips to him.

"I'm sorry I fell off the grid and I know you had nothing to do with this, Liv. I just need an alternate theory."

"I want the same thing you do." She looked up at him with

jade green eyes, lips parted. "Whatever you need me to do, Ridge, I'll say yes."

His name on her lips sent him crashing into her, pushing past the table to pin her lightly against the cinder block wall. Her lips were as soft as he remembered, her scent as sweet, her tongue as intoxicating. Why had he waited so long? The thought charged through his brain. But he knew exactly why... Sowards. He pushed against her, their bodies melded together, letting her know how much he wanted her.

Footsteps from the hall forced space between them, and Ridge released her, lowering into the closest chair as Shana entered the lounge.

"Told ya he was back here," Shana said with at least feigned obliviousness.

"Yeah. Thanks, Shana. I appreciate it."

How the hell could she be so damned composed? He was still working to quell the storm she'd initiated.

Shana grabbed a soda and said a quick good-bye before leaving them alone again.

"Probably not the best place for this," Liv said, a smile tugging at her lips. "Maybe we could talk over dinner?"

Liv backed toward the door.

"Yes. Dinner." What was he, a Neandertal? *Speak, idiot!*

"Tomorrow night? Seven o'clock?" she asked.

He nodded. "Tomorrow. Seven."

She took one last look at him before slipping through the door and out of sight. Ridge groaned, giving in to the frustration before checking his watch for the time. Still enough time to catch someone at the Bureau who could shed some light on Liv's sealed juvenile record.

THE BUREAU's federal court liaison was happy to oblige when Ridge called them to chat about Liv's expunged records.

"This one was interesting," the woman said from the other end of the line. "Family must have some clout to keep this one off the books." She waited for a response but gave up after a few beats.

"Seems she was collared for manslaughter about fifteen years ago. Apparent suicide in a small town in Ohio called Cascade Hills. A classmate, girl by the name of Andrea Chase, was found dead in a lake. Olivia Sullivan claimed she committed suicide, but she was the last to be seen with the victim, apparently fighting."

"About what?"

"That part's not clear. The Sullivan girl's interview is full of..."

Ridge sighed, rubbing his temple. "Craziness?" he offered.

The woman on the other end of the line let out a strained chuckle. "Good word, Agent McCaffrey."

"The Sullivan girl never went to trial. Spent six months in a psychiatric facility."

Ridge ran a hand through his hair, rubbing the tension from the back of his neck. "Anything else?"

Ridge heard the suck of her breath on the other end of the line. "I hope I'm not overstepping here, but is she?"

"Is she what?"

"The records indicate she claimed to be ... psychic?"

Ridge cringed at the way she stretched out the word. He could almost hear the air quotes punctuating the line–as if it wasn't a real phenomenon. He shook his head. In another time, with another suspect, he and this agent would have gotten along just fine.

"Just send me what you've got. I'll take a look at it and see if it's anything I can use."

"Will do, you'll have it within the hour." She sounded disappointed Ridge wasn't divulging more.

Ridge tossed his cell onto his desk and leaned back in his chair, scoping out the precinct. There were enough old-timers here to remember a dead teenager fifteen years ago. How was it he'd been working the Sullivan family since setting foot in this town and not one officer had mentioned Liv's history? A girl's apparent suicide seemingly obliterated from Cascade Hills history.

18

LIV

I woke up in my bed at the Holiday Inn surrounded by smoke. The heat of it threatened to singe my lungs. A fit of coughs doubled me over and I clung to the duvet, clutching its realness, as the dream intensified around me. A family huddled under a wool blanket outside a burning house. A middle-aged man, a young girl (about seven or eight years old), and a teenage boy looked on as flames licked at the two-story in front of them.

Firefighters sprayed the home from three sides, stopping momentarily as a figure dressed in full fire regalia exited the front door of the home. Although none of his features were visible behind the protective mask, the unmistakable form of a body draped limp and lifeless from his arms.

The family surged toward the fireman just as flames exploded forward, consuming the entire front porch of the home. Paramedics rushed to meet the firefighter, helping him stretch the body of a teenage girl on the grass near the ambulance. I knew without hesitation that the girl was dead. The teenage boy pitched himself toward her, ripping himself from the older man's grasp.

The dream smoke began to dissipate, snaking away as the fiery backdrop disintegrated, leaving only the teenage boy and girl in focus. His head rose from its position on the girl's shoulder just long enough for me to gasp in recognition. *Ridge.* I would recognize those eyes anywhere. His face was streaked with smudges of soot and his clothes were wet, sticking to a gangly frame. But it was him. A girl's voice broke into the dream, repeating the same phrase until the vision disappeared entirely.

I sat up in bed trying to make sense of what I'd just seen. The girl's words, *"Don't let him blame himself,"* echoed through my mind, suddenly joined by Brian's voice, *"He's been through a lot."*

Unable to lure sleep back, I spent the early morning hours soaking in the jetted tub, sorting through the vignettes playing out in my mind. A woman dead in Sullivan woods. My grandmother and her hauntingly familiar companion. A painful secret I wasn't yet meant to know. The guilt of betrayal bubbled in my gut.

I'd given up on the girl in the woods. Refused to come back to Cascade Hills when she first came up. Funny thing was, she hadn't visited since that call several months ago. But now that I was home, didn't I owe it to her to at least look her up?

I swirled the washcloth in the cooling tub. I once thought every apparition that came was in search of truth, a way to connect to the loved ones they'd lost. But if the past had taught me anything, it was that the needs of the living far outweigh the whims of the dead. I swallowed against the memory of my best friend, teetering on the edge of the dam at the other end of Cascade Lake. If I'd never told her what I knew, she'd be alive today. Of that much, I was sure.

As far as my grandmother was concerned, I'd need to get back to the farm to work out whatever it was she and the little girl needed from me. The electric was supposed to be live by tomorrow morning, so it would have to wait until then. My thoughts circled back to Ridge. Was I betraying him in some way by knowing what happened to his sister? It wasn't like I could just bring it up. *Oh, by the way, I had a dream about your house burning down. Was the girl who died your sister?* That would go over well.

I sighed and dried myself, studying my reflection in the bathroom mirror. *This is who you are,* my inner critic reminded. *This is why your relationships don't work. People are made to have secrets, Olivia, both the living and the dead.* I shook away the nagging in my brain.

Maybe Brian could confirm my suspicions without Ridge ever knowing what I'd seen. That was my best bet at this point. If the fire had claimed Ridge's sister, the intermittent pain that flickered through his expression now and again made sense. Surely that was what Brian meant when he said Ridge had been through a lot.

I slid into a pair of jeans and a sweater and checked my hair in the mirror before heading out of the hotel room. There was one stop I had to make before heading to Murphy's to take the photos I'd promised Brian.

THE CASCADE HILLS PUBLIC LIBRARY sat on a corner, tucked two streets behind the main drag of town. The last time I'd been here, I was seventeen-years-old. Young and naïve enough to believe that everything a ghost said should be relayed to whomever they left behind. The basement was a treasure trove of newspaper and magazine articles, formerly on microfiche. As I parked the Civic in the quiet lot, I hoped they'd been converted to digital. It sure would make the search less cumbersome.

"Good morning." The clerk behind the desk greeted me as I walked in, still focused on the paperwork in front of her.

"Morning," I returned. Color drained from her face as she looked up, removing her reading glasses. I pretended not to recognize the now aged librarian who'd assisted me fifteen years ago. "I was hoping to use your archive room for a little research this morning. Is it available?"

"Olivia Sullivan, I had no idea you were back in town."

"Just for a visit, my grandmother passed away."

"Yes, that's right, I heard. I'm so sorry, my dear." She smiled. The genuine tug of her lips sending a spike of hurt through my core. "So you need the archives, then?"

I nodded, a building knot of emotion clogging my throat. She led me through the stacks to a stairwell and we descended together, into the basement. The archive room hadn't changed much, with the blessed exception of four microfiche machines now replaced by desktop computers. Only one relic of the past remained on a desk in the corner.

"As you can see, we're about ninety-seven percent digital at this point. If there's anything you need from that other three percent, you let me know and I'll get you set up with old Betsy over there." She nodded toward the last remaining microfiche machine. "Still better than newsprint all over your fingers."

She held up all ten digits and smiled at me. A blossom of warmth opened up in my chest as a laugh escaped. Maybe checking out visions had been a ruse just to hang out with someone who oozed warmth and compassion. Lord knows I needed it back then. Who was I kidding? I needed it today.

"I'll be upstairs if you need anything, Liv." She hesitated at the door. "It is really good to see you."

I smiled and thanked the librarian before pulling a chair up to the farthest computer. The database was already pulled up on the screen, so I started typing. Homicides in Cascade Hills. I scanned the list of results, looking for a female victim to narrow down my options.

I drug a notebook out of my bag and made some notes: years, methods of death, that sort of thing, forcing my eyes past any record that included the name, Andrea Chase.

By the time the librarian came to check on me, two hours later, I'd narrowed the identity of the girl in Sullivan woods down to two possible candidates.

"Finding everything you need?" she asked, popping her round head around the doorframe so fast she nearly startled me.

"Great. I've almost got what I need," I offered, waiting for her to disappear from the hall before scanning the next newspaper article.

October 27, 1993, the *Cascade Hills Gazette*:

A young foreign exchange student for Sullivan & Roarke was reported missing by her loved ones when she didn't return home to Ireland as scheduled. Attorney Stephen Sullivan was questioned by authorities and is not a suspect in the disappearance, offering his support to the family and prayers for a safe return.

"Jennifer Tipton was a model student at our firm and an important part of the team at Sullivan & Roarke. We wish nothing but the best for her and hope she chooses to return home to her loved ones very soon."

Authorities in Ireland are looking into the possibility she may have chosen not to return home and at this time no wrongdoing is suspected.

I leaned back against my chair and reread the snippet over and over again. Her name echoed in my mind, *Jennifer Tipton*, and her eyes flooded my memory. I queued up the document to print and reached for the nearby printer, pulling the warm page from the tray and skimming it for the thousandth time.

The timing of the article was too perfect, three days after my birthday. A coincidence? Maybe. But life is rarely riddled with true quirks of chance. More often than not, our twists align with purpose.

19

LIV

After lunch I drove to Murphy's to take the photos I'd promised Brian. I planned to stay most of the day, but Brian had asked for some sunset shots. And since sunset in March across ice glazed trees is a photographer's dream, I stayed. I could still run home when we were done in time for my date with Ridge.

Just thinking about the evening sent a whorl of butterflies loose in my gut. I was glad to have the distraction of this job. Who knows how I'd manage if I had to stare at the four walls of my hotel room all day, inventing scenarios to attach what I learned at the library to what I saw in my dream.

I snapped all the interior shots and waited with Brian in the parking lot for the sun to recede behind the adjacent tree line, casting a sparkling orange glow over the pub. I was working up the courage to ask Brian more about Ridge's past when a familiar black Shelby pulled in.

"I told him just to meet you here," Brian confessed. "I hope that's okay."

"It's your pub." I shrugged and snapped a few frames, hiding my giddiness behind the lens of my Nikon. Brian's lips turned into a satisfied smile as he watched the grin take over my face.

"Hey, Brian!" Ridge greeted, giving Brian a brotherly handshake and pat on the back. "Thanks for letting me know about your visitor."

"Anytime," Brian said, winking at me.

The three of us engaged in bare bones small talk about the weather and work before Brian declared, "I've gotta get inside. Who knows what they're doing in there without me. Let me know if you need anything, Liv."

"Will do," I called after him.

"How are the pictures coming?" Ridge sidled up next to me as I perched on a cross rail fence waiting for decent lighting.

"Great." I slid off the rail as the sun fell perfectly behind the pub, clicking the shutter in rapid succession. "I think I'm just about done for the day." I slung my camera over my shoulder. "I've got a date tonight."

He smiled at me. "Well, it's not quite seven yet, but wanna go inside and get a drink?"

I popped my head into the kitchen to let Brian know I was finished for the night.

"I was afraid you were going to tell me you had to work." I slid into the booth across from Ridge.

"I just got off. Seven seemed too far away."

Knowing he had questions about my role in the crimes at the farm did little to stem the rush of pleasure thrumming through my core. There was something about being with him that made me feel whole. And I failed to hide the smile turning the corners of my lips.

Our conversation flowed like it always did, easy and fun. I

learned a bit about his family back in Bishop's Hollow. His little sister was now a junior at the University of Virginia. Which would line up with the age of the younger girl I'd seen huddled under the blanket during the fire. I pushed recent revelations to the outskirts, focusing instead on controlling the butterflies that erupted with his every touch. Every smile, every glimmer of hope that rooted inside, gave me a sense of the life I'd been missing. The life that was possible.

I managed to nurse two Guinnesses, trying to extend our time together while ensuring I could make it home without his help. It was nearly midnight by the time I forced myself away from the booth.

He walked me out of the pub, the electricity between our bodies building with every step. His fingers entwined around mine, igniting sparks that sizzled from my extremities down into my core. He tugged at our clasped hands, turning me to face him before pressing his body hungrily against mine.

I leaned back against the door of the Civic, the iciness of the metal a stark contrast to his heat. Desire pulsed through me, stronger than the buzz of alcohol, as he leaned into me, hand coiled in my hair, lips consuming mine.

Our bodies fit together like matched puzzle pieces. And before long, I found myself grasping at the lapels of his leather jacket, silently begging him to push harder, probe deeper, explore further. His strong hands were gentle as they traveled from my hips, heightening my senses as his thumbs worked under the hem of my jacket. The heat of his touch against the soft skin of my belly clashed against the cold March air, igniting a wave of gooseflesh from head to toe.

My mounting need forced me to suck in a breath, his scent filling my senses, nearly tipping me over the edge. Part spice, all man, it lit into my soul, sparking an insatiable craving. The sweetness of his breath grazed the top of my ear as his arms wrapped around my midsection.

I longed to touch him, to feel his muscles contract against me. Giving in to the urge, I pressed my hands down his torso. Need burned like an inferno as my fingers explored every hard edge of muscle. I watched his eyes close to my caress, his breath hitch. I didn't expect him to catch my wrist and pull me away, his crystal eyes suddenly serious.

He exhaled a shaky breath. His clash of emotion palpable against my flesh. His jaw clenched and released in succession before he freed my wrist.

"I need to ask you a question, Liv. Before this goes any further." He ran a hand through my hair, twisting the curls around his fingertips.

That's right. The case. We hadn't even broached the subject since he arrived.

"Do you want to go somewhere to talk? Back inside?"

Ridge shook his head. "I read the report you gave Shana. How did you know what was in the trunk?"

"I didn't know for sure," I lied. "I saw the writing–the blood. It wasn't too far a stretch. Did you find out who she was?"

A pulse of energy sparked in the air between us–surprise, verging on anger.

"I never told you the victim was female." His eyes darkened.

The image of the girl in the woods flooded back. Her fingers digging against roughened skin. A stranger's unyielding grip around her delicate neck. My overactive imagination replaced the attacker with Ridge. I stepped away, pulling my hands into the sleeves of my coat for protection against the heat nipping at me from Ridge. Carnal hunger replaced by betrayal.

His jaw twitched in the glow of the streetlight. "I need to know everything you know. How you know it."

"I'm observant, I guess." It was a lame excuse, even by my standards. Part of me wanted to come clean, but Jack's words whistled back, *"You're the one who has to live with your decisions."*

"Too much has happened out there since you've been back, Liv. It's suspicious. If you tell me you're not involved, I'll believe you, but..."

"But, you think I am." I backed away another step. Ridge's gaze drifted up to meet mine.

"I don't know what to think." His features softened. "You had access to the house."

A ribbon of fear streaked through my core, raising goose-flesh. This had happened before. I was no stranger to the skepticism of law enforcement.

"I put a call in to LAPD. Your name came up in several investigations over the past few years. Most of them connected to homicides."

Ridge waited for me to respond. With what, I had no idea.

"You knew things, about the victims." Another stagnant pause. "How?"

I sucked in a breath and pulled my jacket tighter across my midsection. I shivered, but not because of the nip in the air. This was no different than high school. It's what I got for trying to help, trying to make peace for forgotten spirits.

"I should go." I turned toward the Civic and popped the lock.

"You have a juvenile record." Ridge let the revelation hang in the air. "Who's Andrea Chase?"

"That was a misunderstanding." I had no desire to revisit that nightmare, especially with Ridge, but my body tingled with the memory, cool skin under my fingers, gripping, clawing to bring her closer, to make her understand. She'd been my best friend. My only friend as far as high school was concerned, and I'd let her go. Asked her to believe too much. Pushed her too far. Maybe not literally as town gossip would have you believe. But her death was on my hands.

Ridge could have pressed, forced me to relive the night my best friend took her own life. The ensuing arrest. But he didn't. Instead, he reached for me. The gentle warmth of his hands through my coat broke the spell of memory. "Tell me what you know, Liv."

Panic set in. How much he already knew, I wasn't sure. But I wasn't ready. "I know someone broke into my grandmother's empty house. I know a woman was killed and stuffed in a box on the back porch. I don't know why. You're the one with the badge, Ridge. Do what you need to do."

Ridge scuffed his shoe back and forth over the loose pebbles peppering the perimeter of the parking lot. He lifted his gaze. "Did you see her?"

My lungs clenched. "What?" The word was barely audible.

"You heard me. The cases in Los Angeles, the girl at the farm. Did you see them?"

"I didn't know any of them, Ridge. They were strangers."

"That's not what I mean." His voice was soft, patient.

He'd read Andrea's case file. I was sure of it. So much for sealed records.

"Did you..." He was searching for the right words. A bubble of emotion worked its way into my chest.

"I'm not crazy," I managed. My grandmother's words echoed in my skull as I escaped into the Civic. *Don't ever be ashamed of who you are.* "I'm sorry," I said, slamming the door and cocooning myself from Ridge's questions.

I pulled the rental out of its spot and revved through the gravel toward the main road. I watched in the rearview mirror as Ridge's form got smaller, blurred by the slow procession of uncontrolled tears. The whole drive back to the Holiday Inn I couldn't tell if I was crying over the lies I'd been forced to tell Ridge, my grandmother's unrealized expectations of me, the innocent girl found stuffed in my grandparents' trunk, or the blast from the past reminder of why women like me were too scarred to deserve love.

20

RIDGE

Glen Helen was busier than it had been when he'd met Sowards just over a week ago. Who comes to the park in the middle of March? He argued with himself as he pulled his Shelby in next to Sowards' grey sedan. Too close, his supervisor would tell him later. But to hell with what Sowards had to say.

Ridge opened the passenger door of Sowards' car and tossed Liv's file into his lap.

"You need to find someone else for this job."

"Get in," Sowards growled at him.

Ridge slid inside and shut the door. The car reeked of cigarette smoke. Ridge could almost feel the tar and stench sticking to him, seeping into his pants and coat. He'd have to burn these clothes later, for sure.

"What's the problem?" Sowards asked.

"I'm not the man for this job, Marc. I don't believe in this shit. I didn't believe it when Grace was spouting stories of ghosts and visions, and I don't believe it now that..." He cut himself short.

"Sounds like you already did the most important part of your job."

Ridge watched out the passenger window as a woman three cars down unloaded a husky from the back of her SUV. He missed those days. Normal days. Dog walking, grocery shopping, all the minute details of life that most people chalk up to trivial time sucks. He missed being ordinary.

"She didn't admit it. But somehow she knows more than she should. Consider this my formal request to be taken out of the field, off this case. I don't care where you put me. I know Virginia's out. Columbus, Cincinnati, Timbuktu–anywhere but Cascade Hills."

"And who would you suggest as your replacement?"

Ridge shrugged. "Miller?"

Sowards sucked in a lungful of the stale smoke air. Ridge stuffed the urge to roll down the window and lean out for a clean breath of his own.

"You'd be surprised how much research and thought is put into the choices we make for assignments like these. These past two assignments–Grace, and now Olivia–you were selected for a reason, Ridge. Replacing you is not as easy as you might think."

"Enlighten me, Marc. Why me? It doesn't make sense. For one, I'm a skeptic. You're asking me to believe the shit they're telling me is true?"

"Being skeptical is what makes you good at your job, Ridge. We need someone who can see all the facets–truth, lies, omissions–all of it. It's your job to categorize it. Choose which facets are most likely to put the program–her–at risk."

"What risk? She's got a record. Far as I can tell, it's the people around her that are taking their chances."

"What is it you're not telling me?" Sowards asked.

Exasperation crept into Ridge's voice. "We found the

corpse of a dead girl at Sullivan farm. Long dead, but recently moved. Which is odd enough, but I pulled reports from LAPD. Liv was involved in several homicide cases out there. Never could pin anything on her, but she knew too much. Details only someone at the scene would have. I put the interview transcripts in her file."

Sowards rifled through the folder in his lap, drawing out the few stapled pages of dictated transcript. "Five homicides. All women." Sowards skimmed the transcript. "Do you think she's involved?"

"No." The truth felt good. "That's the problem. I don't think she's capable. But everything points to her. If she didn't do it, she knows who did."

Sowards shook his head slowly, considering. "Maybe." He tucked the pages back into the file, thumbing the corner. "Your work here isn't done, McCaffrey. If you want that job in Virginia, you'll find out what she knows."

His supervisor chucked the folder against Ridge's chest, holding it there until Ridge grasped the edges and took it from him.

"You have your orders, McCaffrey. Find out if she's psychic. Find out if she knows how that girl ended up dead at Sullivan Farm." Steel had returned to Sowards' voice. He turned the key in the ignition. Nodding a silent dismissal to Ridge.

The word psychic grated against his nerves. Liv's face was not the face he saw when he pictured a self-proclaimed psychic. In fact, to this day he still saw the image of the Zoltar machine from the movie "Big" when the word entered conversation.

Ridge's chest tightened as he climbed out of the sedan. He'd known it was a long shot, asking Sowards for an escape route. But how could he face Liv after last night? At the worst, he'd accused her of murder. At the least, she now thought he pegged her as crazy. He could still see the hurt in her eyes when he brought up her record. If she was what Sowards' thought, how could he blame her for lying? He tried to imagine what it would be like to live with a secret like that, to see the unseen and have no way to process through that horror. Liv's juvenile record held a key, he was sure of that now.

He sucked in a breath of the heavy March air as the first shards of icy rain pelted him from the sky. Going back to face her was going to take a heavy apology, a dose of imagination, and, possibly, some alcohol.

21

LIV

I tore what was left of the yellow tape from the entrances of the farmhouse. Crime scene, my ass. This was about to become my home. It took several gallons of bleach to clean up what was left of the mess on the patio. I'd spent a few hours Googling the best way to get rid of blood stains, and short of replacing the patio flooring, bleach was looking like my best option.

The utilities had been on for a couple days, long enough to warm the place up a bit before I checked out of the Holiday Inn. Didn't take long to suck all the heat away after opening every downstairs window, trying my best not to suffocate on toxic fumes.

By the time I'd finished repainting the walls in the living room, bleaching the patio, and cleaning up the mess from the spilled secretary, it was Thursday—five days since I'd talked to Ridge and almost two weeks since my grandmother's death.

I sat on the living room couch, a fire in the fireplace, and a glass of Moscato on the end table, listening as ice pellets spattered against the windows. My muscles ached and my eyes were heavy with the weight of sleep I'd missed over the past several days. I heard the voice before the accompanying dull ache penetrated my skull.

"You've forgotten about us." My eyes fluttered open, the little girl standing within arm's reach.

"I haven't," I refuted, but the hurt in her eyes was proof she remained unconvinced. No wonder Ridge ran the other direction. I may have lied to him, but how could I blame him? Here I was bargaining with ghosts.

"You need him, you know."

"Need who?" I rubbed my fingers against my forehead, pressing against the dull slice of pain.

"Ridge." The curve of the little girl's lips around Ridge's name sent prickles along my spine.

"We'll see," I said, sloughing off the spookiness to regain control. "Can I see what's in your box?"

The little girl took a step away, clutching the box with tight, white fingers.

"Find us," she turned her head toward the open door of my grandfather's office. Bedraggled bows fluttered gently in a nonexistent breeze. *"Please, Olivia. We're running out of time."*

The vision dissipated, leaving only the patter of ice peppering the silence.

It took me less than fifteen minutes to find the box in my grandfather's old study. As soon as the little girl had looked that direction, I recognized where I'd seen it before. My grandmother had bought the box during one of her trips to Ireland, and my grandfather had stored his most precious cigars inside. A hand-carved humidor, with an ornate Celtic shield knot on its top, and woven patterns along the sides, it held a place of honor in my grandfather's locked bookcase behind his desk.

Dust had crept in along the shelves, but for someone who knew exactly where to look, it wasn't hard to find. A few more minutes to locate the key to the shelf and I was in business. It was only when I had it cradled in my arms, sitting back on the sofa, that I realized it was locked.

"It's got to be here somewhere." I said, rifling through every drawer and cupboard in my grandfather's old office.

By the time I finished, the room resembled the foyer after the break-in. Ancient papers littered the floor like leaves in the woods. I'd emptied the entire desk and every bookshelf. All for nothing but ancient papers and an old revolver with a mother-of-pearl handle.

"I can't do this tonight." I said, shoving the gun back into the desk drawer. The little girl's eyes still haunted my memory. "Just a little sleep, first."

The last thing I remember was restoking the fire before curling up under my grandmother's quilt, box tucked safely under the skirt of the sofa beneath me.

THE NEXT MORNING, I searched the kitchen and my grandmother's bedroom for the key before frustration got the better of me. I left the house, walking tentatively toward the hulking barn, a box of trash bags in one hand and a bucket of cleaning supplies in the other. It was the only structure on the property I had yet to scour.

Somehow, the act of disinfecting seemed to cleanse away some of the frustration and loneliness that had become constant companions. It was cathartic, and right now I was in desperate need of therapy.

The main floor of the barn was an easy job. Consisting of eight stalls, a feed room, and a tack room, (all long empty) there wasn't much to do, other than sweep and dust. My fear of possible human barn occupants subsided with each thrust of the broom, aided in part by the discovery of a mother cat and a litter of kittens. A few photographs of maternal nature at its best and I was back to work.

I was in the haymow, a trash bag in one hand and empty Corona bottle in the other when I realized without question that Ridge's instincts had been right. Someone was using the barn as his or her own personal campground. Old hay bales were stacked around the expansive space in neat formations. Some looked like they served as decent couches, while others must have been used as beds. It was eerie to be up there alone. With each passing moment the regret I felt about choosing to clean the barn became stronger. Regret turned to fear when the sense that someone was watching me became tougher to ignore.

I scanned the empty room for the hundredth time and gave myself a confidence-building pep talk before going back to work on the piles of trash strewn about the floor. Just as I was settling back in, a group of pigeons roosting peacefully in the rafters screeched a warning and flew off in rapid succession. I had to stifle a scream when Ridge's voice penetrated the eerie silence of the musty barn.

"You really should use gloves, you know?"

"You really shouldn't sneak up on people like that." I paused for a moment, allowing my heart rate to return to normal. Looking down at the empty bottle in my hands, I suddenly cringed at the thought of dirty lips around the nickel-sized opening. I tossed it disgustedly into the bag as I mustered up the courage to sound indignant. "What are you doing here, Ridge?"

He shoved his hands in his pockets as he strode across the wood planks toward me. My breath caught as he answered. *Damn it.* Even in the wake of his interrogation the other night, my body still vibrated with anticipation when he was around.

"I'm sorry. I wanted to see you...apologize."

I glanced up at him, gauging his honesty. What I wouldn't give to be able to read thoughts.

"I went to the hotel, but they said you checked out. I figured you were either here or..." he stopped short.

"You thought I went back to L.A.?"

I studied his face as I rose from the floor. There was a look I couldn't quite place in his eyes—hurt, maybe. He was definitely guarded.

"I'm just trying to clean the place up," I said. "I'd say I've got proof of those uninvited guests."

"I'd say so," Ridge agreed as his eyes scanned the haymow. "Come on, I've got some gloves in the car. Let me help you with the mess."

I worked up the courage to send him away, to leave him as hurt as he'd left me. But I doubted I'd ever manage that. Besides, the thought of some stranger lurking around penetrated my resolve.

"Okay." I hesitated before reaching for his outstretched hand and clasping my fingers through his. He tucked me into the crook of his arm as we walked, and my skin buzzed. Every step was an exercise in denial. Blocking the spread of warmth—a hum of attraction I wish had disappeared into the darkness like the taillights of his car—took every ounce of effort I had. I hated what he'd done to me, but denial only gave the energy more power.

His car was parked and running just outside the barn. Checking the barn must have been an afterthought when he got no answer at the house. He opened the car door to kill the ignition and popped the trunk, every movement carried out with precision and finality. I focused on tamping down the school girl wave of attraction. *Stupid,* I told myself. *You're just asking to get hurt again.*

Ridge closed the trunk, coming back with two pairs of blue gloves.

"They'll probably be a bit big on you, but it's better than nothing," he offered.

An awkward silence passed between us as we made our way back up the stairs to the haymow. We were cleaning silently when he spoke.

"I should have handled myself differently."

I laughed, nervousness taking control. Was this an apology?

He stopped what he was doing and looked carefully at me, his voice not much more than a whisper. "I led you on."

Wait, what? He said the words, but his eyes deceived him.

"That was wrong of me."

Anger hissed through me, settling at the base of my skull in a dull throb.

"Then why are you here?" I folded my legs under me and sat on the dusty planks. I aimed a snake stare at the man who I'd once thought might accept me.

"There's still the matter of a corpse on your property. There's been a development." He shrugged and tossed a greasy Big Mac container into the trash bag. "And I was worried about you."

"You could have called."

"I didn't know what to say to you."

"You seem to be stringing sentences together without any trouble now. What's the development?"

"The prescription bottle we found in the box came from your grandmother's nursing home. There's a partial print, so we're running it through the database to see if there are any hits. I just thought I'd come by, see if you could think of any reason why it was there. If maybe you'd touched it for any reason."

"You think *I* stole my grandmother's medication?"

"That's not what I..."

"Get out, Ridge. Unless you're prepared to arrest me for something, I think I can manage this on my own."

"Liv..."

"Please." I don't think he had a follow up. A sliver of victory slid through my gut as I stood and took the trash bag from his hand.

"I'm sorry," he said in breathy words. "I never wanted it to turn out this way."

I kept my eyes averted for as long as I could, knowing I would melt into his. I stared down at my gloved hand, the light blue now almost black with grime. I held my breath as some ball of cupids and hearts inside me cracked open. I ached to touch him. To tell him the truth, tell him how I knew about the girl in the trunk. How I'd been named an accomplice in my best friend's suicide. And then prove I was more than a freak of nature.

That breath burned in my lungs until he started down the stairs. His shoes clamping against old boards. This was it. The end. Was I ready for it?

He hesitated at the bottom of the stairs. Tugged off the gloves before glancing up at me. "Are you sure you'll be okay out here? Alone, I mean?"

"I've been fine all week, Ridge." *Arrogant ass.* "I'll be fine tonight," *and every other night without you.* Odd when even the lies we tell ourselves become second nature.

I watched through the loft window as Ridge strode toward the waiting Shelby. He'd made it halfway up the driveway before I let loose, chucking the broom to the other side of the loft with a vindictive curse.

22

RIDGE

"How'd it go?" Brian asked as Ridge settled onto a stool at the bar.

"About like you might expect." Ridge turned his lips into a fake smile and aimed it at his friend. "She kicked me out."

"Remind me again why you're doing this?"

"She doesn't deserve this life, Brian."

"Hate to break it to you, but it's not up to you to decide what she does and doesn't deserve."

Ridge ran a hand through his hair, scratching at the back of his head. It was ridiculously simple advice, yet somehow clarifying.

"You like her, right?"

"Right," Ridge answered. Brian Murphy was the one person he'd never been able to lie to. At least not successfully.

"But you can't have her because of the case you're working on, right?"

Ridge nodded. Keeping his lips closed meant he couldn't divulge anything that might get him in trouble later.

Brian swiped at the bar with a clean white cloth. "There's this little thing some of us know about. It's called honesty. You might try it sometime."

"Still waiting on the Guinness," Ridge said, ignoring Brian's lesson in morals.

Brian slid the pint glass in front of his friend and continued, "Look, I've seen you at your best and I've seen you at your worst, Ridge. This girl, the way you talk about her. Your eyes when you're with her. She brings out your best. I don't understand why it has to be an either or situation."

"Let me put it this way, if you fell in love with an alcoholic, would you give up your job–the pub?"

Brian narrowed his eyes at Ridge. "You're saying you think Liv's a criminal?"

"Just, answer the question, Brian."

Brian leaned back against the counter behind him, arms crossed across his chest. "I don't know. I guess, if she wanted me to. But here's the thing, Ridge. People who love each other don't ask their significant other to give up their dreams. Besides, I'm too busy running a pub to date, so it shouldn't be an issue." Brian went back to work with the towel.

He was right. Ridge knew that. And seeing her today only solidified the fact that he wanted her in his life. When she'd kicked him out–the venom in her eyes–it cut into his core. He hadn't felt that kind of hurt in years.

"I barely know her." Ridge attempted to bolster his argument. "She's hiding something."

"Get to know her, Ridge. She's good. Something special about that one."

Ridge shook his head, a smile tickling the corner of his lip.

"Hell, if you don't date her, I will," Brian teased, pulling his phone out of his pocket. "What's her number again?"

The pub door swung open and deposited two rain-soaked

travelers into the restaurant. Melanie met them at the hostess stand.

"Didn't know it was supposed to rain tonight," Ridge said absently.

"Yeah, another ice storm, I think. Better finish up so you can get home before the worst of it hits."

Ridge nodded and polished off the remainder of his Guinness.

"Think about what I said, right?" Brian added, pulling a pint for the customers that had just come in.

Ridge nodded. Brian knew him, probably better than anyone. What he said made sense. If Liv was psychic, maybe it didn't have to be a deal breaker. Everyone has a quirk, right? He didn't have to love the quirk, just the woman behind it. And after this afternoon, he was fairly certain he already did.

23

———

LIV

That night, I curled up in one of my grandmother's quilts in front of the blazing fireplace, replaying the afternoon encounter with Ridge. I was already into my third glass of Moscato. The first two had successfully obliterated my anger, the third had me yearning for a do-over. I turned my phone over and over in my hand. I could call, tell him everything. Tell him why I came back to Cascade Hills, the truth about the vision of the girl in the woods, the mysterious cigar box with a missing key.

I'd tell him I knew about his sister's death in the fire. He'd wrap his arms around me, tell me I was doing the right thing by staying in Cascade Hills. Except–I dropped my phone to the carpet below–he didn't care about any of it.

I woke to the sound of ice pelting the windows. It was pitch black outside and my fire had burned down to nothing more than glowing embers. I spun the roller switch on the table lamp beside me, but the lamp stayed dark. I uncovered myself, padding across the floor in stocking feet, to try the hall switch. I flipped it up and down several times without luck.

The ice storm must have knocked out the power. A glint of movement out the corner of my left eye, sent a ribbon of fear into my core. I turned to get a better look just as a blow landed hard against my temple. Panic clutched at my lungs. I staggered to stay upright, the room spinning. I grabbed at the wall, then the couch. A lamp hit the floor before I felt the hands from behind.

All my breath escaped in a surge. Gloved fingers clasped my arms and jerked them behind my back. My body lurched sideways, out of my control. My shoulder grazed the corner of the end table as I fought the strong fingers holding tight to my wrists. With a heave, my knees slammed into the thin wool of the living room area rug.

I struggled to see through the darkened room, as it spun. My breath came in short spasms. An intense burn took hold in my shoulders as thin hardness bit against the skin on my wrists. I pulled and tugged while it threatened to tear into my flesh with every effort I made.

A knee thrust into my lower spine caused my legs to buckle, my upper body forced against the floor. The thick warmness of blood oozed over my cheekbone as an angry voice sneered in my ear.

"You are in over your head!"

"Get off me!" I screamed, but my words erupted weak and slurred.

He was masculine, strong. And smelled of hay. The scent filled my nostrils tickling the back of my throat into a cough. Secure against the floor, I dared again to open my eyes. Boots. The heavy-duty hiking kind. Dusty dark wash jeans. A leather strap just below the knee. My lungs seized in panic. A knife.

Sense began to return, memories of the self-defense class I'd taken in college trickled back. I kicked and screamed and bit. I lashed out in any way I could, ignoring the pain from my shoulders, wrist, and body. But what they don't tell you in class is that all of that is ineffective when you've been hit on the head and are hogtied in the middle of your living room floor. My attacker's wicked laugh was the only response. And finally, I lay still, listening to his heavy footsteps as he explored every room.

"Where is it?"

"What?" My voice was rough, sandpapery. The throbbing in my head, merciless.

"Don't play dumb, Princess!" It had been years since anyone had called me by that name. "I know you're smarter than that."

His voice came closer. I tensed. Every muscle on alert. The push of something cold and hard against the back of my skull. Gun. That's when a light flickered outside the living room window. Not the light of day, but headlights.

My attacker must have noticed it too, because he threw his weight into my back once more. A slice of pain against the back of my head drove my face into the carpet. Twinkles flirted on the outskirts of my vision as he growled, "This isn't over." The double thump of the patio door followed him.

Three hard knocks pounded the front door.

"Liv?" His voice.

I willed my legs to move, to push myself toward the sound, but my efforts went unanswered, my legs useless. I screamed, but it sounded small, even to my own ears. I heard a crack, heavy against the door. The squeak as it swung open.

"This is McCaffrey," His voice again. Calm. Steady. "I need a bus, asap, 7667 Sullivan Road." Relief pulsed through me as I felt his hand against my shoulder. Noise. Was he talking to me? I couldn't tell. Blackness crept into the edges of my consciousness.

I awoke to voices, not his. EMTs, as they arranged my body

on a stretcher and carted me off into a waiting ambulance. I don't remember their faces, only their voices, "BP 158 over 101, patient is stable."

Their methodical speech made me feel safe. I could feel them tending to my wounds. Pressure and release. My wrists were free, but my arms were heavy, useless. I must have drifted in and out of consciousness for several hours before the fuzziness finally gave way.

RIDGE'S PARTNER took my statement. I couldn't tell him much. The storm had stopped and the trees outside the hospital window glistened in the morning sunshine. I stared out the window, aching to take a picture.

"I think that's all I need for now," Adam Miller said as he put away his notebook. "I'll let you get some rest. Is there anything you need? Anyone you want me to call?"

"No." My tongue still felt thick in my mouth. I reconsidered. "Wait."

A tear trickled involuntarily down my cheek as I whispered his name. "Detective McCaffrey."

The corner of Adam's mouth turned up in a small smile. "He's waiting outside. I'll let him know you're awake."

I smiled, and thanked him, becoming aware for the first time of the bandage covering the left side of my face, stretching from just above my eye to my ear. The knot on the back of my head was cushioned by the pillow.

Ridge's face said it all as he strode to the side of my bed. He pulled a chair over, the scrape of the legs against the floor setting off a thunder of pain in my skull. He stopped. Apologized. Settled into the chair.

Worry and pain were etched in his brilliant blue eyes. He

leaned toward me and nestled my hand carefully between his palms, his eyes searching my face.

Tears choked my throat, spilling out onto my cheeks. All I could do was nod when he asked if I was okay. My head felt too large for my body, heavy and cumbersome.

He wiped away my tears with the pad of his thumb.

"I didn't mean anything I said today," he whispered. "I'm so sorry I hurt you."

I closed my eyes. Bliss from his apology trickled through my bloodstream like a drug.

He kissed me on the unbandaged side of my forehead. "Get some rest."

"Don't leave," I pleaded sleepily, reaching for his hand.

He wrapped my hand in his, his reply coming just as slumber won the duel.

"I'm not going anywhere."

24

RIDGE

Liv was exhausted when the doctors finally discharged her the following evening. Ridge could see it in her eyes. She'd had twenty-four hours to rest, but the nurses woke her up every hour on the hour, asking who she was, where she was, and why she was there. A pang of guilt sliced through his gut every time they entered and interrupted her sleep. This was his fault. He should have been there. He was responsible for her protection, and he'd failed. He'd seen the evidence in the barn with his own eyes. It wasn't safe for her there. If he believed Sowards, it wasn't safe for her anywhere. Besides, Brian was right. She was good. And he needed more good in his life.

After a half day of hourly checking, the last three of which she'd stayed awake, talking and laughing with Ridge as though he hadn't been a colossal jerk just eighteen hours before, the doctors decided it was safe to send her home as long as someone would be there with her. The look on her face as they'd said those words broke his heart.

He saw the pain as clear as day. Heard her start to tell them she lived alone, before he cut in.

"I'll stay with her." He didn't think about what it meant. Just seemed like the right thing to do. But her eyes, wide and clear as she looked at him in that moment, were souvenir worthy. Forgiveness, apprehension, and gratitude all wrapped up in neat green packages. He might be saving her from another overnight stay in the hospital, but she was saving him from himself.

Ridge didn't say much on the way back to the farm. What could he say? He was bringing her back to the scene of her own assault. But the officers had checked every nook and cranny. There was no way anyone could be in the place, waiting for her to return. In fact, when Ridge pulled to a stop in front of the house, there were still two police cars parked in the driveway.

"Let's go in the back," Ridge said as he helped Liv out of the car. "We're going to need to stay out of the living room for a while. Looks like they're still working the scene."

Liv balked. "He went out through the patio door. Have they checked that yet?" she asked, her voice small.

"They're done back there. It's okay."

She hesitated at the base of the back porch.

"You don't have to stay here. I can get you a room some-where." His voice softened. He cradled Liv's head in his hand, caressing her cheek. "You could stay at my place."

This was a big step. No woman had been in Ridge's house since his ex-wife. Ridge bit back the urge to reconsider. *She deserves this.* Her eyes scanned the cruisers parked in the driveway.

Ridge followed her gaze. The officers' silhouettes were visible through the living room windows. She glanced up toward the darkened second and third stories, her grip on Ridge's hand tightening. *She needed this.*

Ridge's eyes settled on Liv's, those eyes that revealed every emotion, the eyes he'd walked away from twice. Eyes he promised he'd never walk away from again.

"Let's go." Ridge ushered Liv away from the house. "Where to, m'lady?" He offered a butler's bow in her direction. Anything to lighten the mood.

"Your place?" A tentative question.

Ridge sucked in a breath and nodded. "Sure. I'll run in and get you a few things, okay? Anything in particular?"

She glanced down at the borrowed scrubs she'd worn from the hospital as he helped her back into the car.

"Anything is better than this."

Ridge's lips curved into a relieved smile before he turned toward the house.

"Ridge..." she called. "There's a box, under the sofa. And my phone is in there somewhere. Could you bring them?"

He stared at Liv for a beat before nodding and heading inside.

Ridge returned about five or ten minutes later with a grocery bag full of clothes and toiletries tucked under one arm, and a mahogany box tucked under the other. Ridge gave some last minute instructions to the officers before tucking the items in the back seat of his Shelby.

"What's with the box?" he asked as he maneuvered up the driveway.

"It's an old cigar box of my grandfather's. I thought maybe you could help me figure out how to get it open without breaking it."

Ridge kept his eyes on the road, sliding his right hand from the wheel to Liv's thigh.

"I'll do what I can," he said as Liv laced her fingers between his. The warmth of want sparked in his core, winding its way through his extremities. How could he ever think he could just walk away from this woman? It was the most ridiculous notion he'd ever had, and he was damn lucky he was getting another chance.

Anxiety that hadn't fully subsided slipped away as heat from her hand flowed into him, radiating throughout his body. When he looked over, she was asleep, head tipped back against the headrest, lips parted. Peaceful.

25

LIV

The jostle of Ridge's Shelby winding its way down a residential street woke me. The drive we pulled into led to a small white Cape Cod style home. It was the second house on a cul-de-sac and had a nice sized yard on either side, providing just enough distance between neighbors. He paused in the driveway, staring at the house, as I yawned the remainder of sleep away.

"I could get you a hotel room, you know. I'd be happy to stay with you."

"If you don't want me to stay here, just say so. It's fine." I tried to sound convincing, but the constriction in my throat was bound to give me away.

"Liv, it's not..." I tried to read his expression, to figure out why he would prefer I didn't stay here, but time ran out before his face changed, his eyes widening and jaw relaxing. "Forget it," he said. "Let's go."

He threw open the driver's side door and grabbed the bag and box from the back seat before joining me on the passenger side. The equilibrium issues hadn't yet subsided, and it took me a minute to get my feet under me. I gratefully took Ridge's arm and he escorted me to the side door.

As soon as I was inside, I knew exactly why Ridge didn't want me here. Floral drapes accented a mauve sofa in the living room. A wallpaper border sprinkled roses around the perimeter, and even the walls seemed to emit a soft pink glow. This wasn't his home. This was his wife's home. That thought must have been apparent in my expression.

"As you can see, I haven't really done anything to the place since ..." His eyes roamed the room. "I don't really spend much time in this part of the house anyway. Come on, I'll show you where you can sleep."

Ridge led me down the hall toward what I only assumed was a cluster of three bedrooms. He opened the last door on the right. This room, although still decidedly girly, was more toned down than the living room. Sunny yellow walls were the canvas for sunflower curtains and bedding.

"Make yourself at home. Can I get you something to drink?"

"Do you have any tea?"

He nodded, "Chamomile okay?"

"That sounds good." I smiled at the idea of Ridge McCaffrey drinking chamomile tea. "I'll be out in a minute."

I looked through the bag Ridge left on the bed. He'd actually done pretty well picking out supplies for me, a product of his years as a married man, no doubt. He had my cosmetic case complete with cleanser and moisturizer and had packed a comfortable button-down shirt and my favorite pair of jeans.

I put the clothes and toiletries on the dresser and turned my attention to the box. I was exhausted, but I needed to know what was inside this box, now more than ever. Whoever had attacked me was after something. What if this was it?

I tucked the humidor under one arm and headed to the

kitchen, dragging my fingers along the wall for support. The teakettle blared as I rounded the corner, causing a stab of pain to slice through my skull before Ridge could pull the kettle from the burner. I slid the box onto the table. He glanced down at the Celtic knot as he pulled the kettle off the stove and filled a mug.

"What do you expect to find in there?" he asked.

I shrugged. "I really have no idea. But whoever attacked me last night was looking for something. I thought this might be it."

I held my breath, hoping he wouldn't ask what made me think that. I didn't want a replay of the other night, that was for sure.

Ridge examined the lock on the box.

"I can get it open, but the tools are at the precinct. Can it wait until tomorrow?"

"Of course," I answered, only slightly disappointed as the throb in my skull roared back.

26

RIDGE

"How's she doing?" Adam asked Ridge from the other side of the kitchen island.

Ridge slid a full cup of coffee toward his partner.

"She's okay. Got a good night's sleep at least."

"I told Wallace I was coming over. He wants you to take a couple days if you need to. The Sullivan case is dead in the water right now. There's nothing that can't wait."

Ridge eyed his partner, "Except finding out who did this to her."

Adam twirled his mug on the countertop between them. "You think this has something to do with the threat Sowards mentioned?"

Ridge shrugged. "I wish I knew."

"This the box?" Adam turned toward the kitchen table. "You're right, Ridge. Looks like it'll fit for sure." He rummaged in his pocket and withdrew an envelope, dropping it onto Ridge's open palm. "Soon as you get it open, let me know.

Wallace will have a stroke if he finds out I'm smuggling evidence."

Ridge laughed. "This is hardly smuggling. You're doing this for the good of the investigation."

"Right," Adam scoffed. He started to sit until he caught a glimpse of Liv peeking from around the corner of the hall.

"There she is," Ridge announced, sliding the envelope below countertop level and stuffing it into the silverware drawer.

"I hope I'm not interrupting anything." Her smile was forced. Ridge wondered how long she'd been standing there.

"Just talking about you." Adam plunked himself down on the stool, swiveling to look at Liv.

"Sounds dangerous." The corner of Liv's mouth curved into a pseudo-smile. Long enough. She'd heard something.

"How's your head?" Adam asked.

Liv glanced at Ridge before answering. "Oh, it's okay." Her hand shot up toward the bandage. "Thanks for asking."

Ridge let his eyes comb over her. Sleep-mussed hair, arms crossed over his wrinkled Eagles t-shirt, pale legs under too big boxers. The craving started low, working its way into his chest and lungs. He swallowed the urge to pull her into his arms, glad to have this island to hide behind.

"Liv, you remember Adam from the precinct."

I nodded as Adam cut in. "Just wanted you to know they're finished at the farm. Already took care of cleaning everything up. You've done a great job out there. The place looks great."

Liv thanked Adam and joined them in the kitchen, sitting carefully on a nearby kitchen chair.

"Guess that means you could go back tonight," Ridge said, adjusting himself before venturing beyond the veil of cabinetry.

"Good. Thanks." Liv nodded toward Ridge and Adam. Some unreadable expression stretched across her face. Ridge lowered into the kitchen chair beside her, pulling her hand into his. But she tugged away.

"Don't want to make you late, Adam. You probably need to get back to the station." Ridge prompted, but Adam didn't bite.

"So, Liv, did you know your boyfriend here makes the finest French toast this side of the Mississippi?" He relocated to the table as Liv's cheeks flushed, the corners of her mouth tipping into a smile. Ridge would take that over the blanch of suspicion any day.

"Maybe I'll get to try them someday, Adam."

"Today's as good a day as any, don't you think?"

Adam winked at Liv and Ridge groaned, returning to the breakfast bar. Why his partner, a trained FBI agent, couldn't take a hint was a secret of the universe he'd never understand. Ridge pulled ingredients from the cabinets around him.

"Ha! I knew I could get him to make 'em!" He landed a light punch on Liv's shoulder, which prompted a sharp intake of breath from Liv.

"Sorry, Liv. I didn't mean ..."

"No, it's okay. Just a little sore."

Adam glanced at Ridge, a silent apology. Awkward calm enveloped the space.

"You know, I probably should get going. No need to give Wallace another reason to come down on me, right?"

Liv smiled at Adam and looked away. She was uncomfortable. A thread of irritation crept into Ridge's chest, he felt the clench of his jaw, the tightness in his chest. He blew out a silent stream of air as Adam excused himself.

The front door clicked behind Adam as Ridge gathered ingredients. "You don't need to make them for me." Liv said, her voice a whisper.

Ridge broke an egg into a bowl. "You've got to eat something," he managed, tamping down bubbling frustration and whisking the milk and egg mixture as if his life depended on it.

Liv picked a mug from the carousel next to the coffee maker and poured a cup of coffee before returning to her spot at the table.

"Thanks for letting me stay last night, Ridge. I appreciate it."

There was an air of finality to her words that Ridge didn't like. But he accepted her thanks and moved to the stove, garnishing the first order of French toast with butter and syrup before sliding the plate in front of Liv. His mind raced. He'd love nothing more than to start this whole operation over. Make his intentions clear from the start.

"Adam was right, they're delicious." Liv said as Ridge slid into the opposite chair with his own plate of eggy goodness.

They ate in silence, exchanging glances until there was nothing but tell-tale puddles of syrup on their plates.

Ridge smiled and took Liv's plate to the sink.

"Here, I can help," Liv slipped around the island to the sink, squeezing a dollop of dish soap into the filling basin. Ridge pulled her in front of him, sandwiching her between the sink and himself. He pushed her hair off the back of her neck, giving into the urge to kiss her sweet, soft skin.

Her breath was his reward. Deeper and faster, punctuated by short huffs when he found a particularly sensitive spot. He knew she could feel how much he wanted her. Her softness molded against him as he turned her around, soapsuds sprinkling from her hands onto his jeans.

Another kiss, deeper this time, her hands warm against his chest. His name on her lips. She was pushing him away.

Ridge stepped out of the embrace, his eyes found the flush on her cheeks, the bedroom droop of her eyelids, the corner of her lip tucked behind a front tooth. Nothing that indicated she wanted him to stop.

"Are you okay?"

She nodded, pulling open the nearby drawer and wrapping her hand around the envelope inside. "But I need to know where this came from."

27

LIV

So we were both keeping secrets. Damn it if he hadn't been standing there in a fitted white t-shirt and tattered button-fly blue jeans. I wrapped my hand around the contents in the envelope. The hard curl of metal filigree against my palm waged war with carnal desire. I sucked in a breath. Metal would win this time around.

"Where did you get the key, Ridge?" My head pulsed with every heartbeat. My hand reached involuntarily for my temple, and he noticed.

"I'll tell you," he promised. "But take this first." He moved for the prescription pain killers the doctors had prescribed. Why was he always so perceptive? It was starting to get under my skin. Who was I kidding? He'd already crawled in and set up camp. Ridge stood over the sink, reading the label like an uncertain parent.

"Just give me one," I demanded, my palm outstretched.

Ridge did as I asked, and I sucked the pill down with a gulp of lukewarm coffee. He watched as I dropped the key into the palm of my hand. I clenched against the immediate stab to my brain. The image coming fully formed, the girl's eyes, wide, scared. The panic that squeezed her chest, the hands that gripped her throat. I ignored the shaking of my fingers, squinting through the vision. My left hand splayed against the table, anything to keep myself rooted—real. My fingers wobbled as I held the key up to the lock, knocking against the brass guard twice before finagling it inside. It turned easily, clicking the internal tumblers into the unlocked position.

The ache started in my jaw. Tension creeping its way from my cheek to the base of my skull. I gripped the table harder, my knuckles white against the honey oak. I closed my eyes, as if that would make her go away. Tears would be next. I could already feel their sting against the back of my eyes.

"Liv." Ridge's voice was quiet, but it was enough to pull me back, the spark of an internal flame. "Stop. Let me explain."

I unhanded the key. It's brass curlicue of a handle stuck out at me—mocking.

"I'm listening." And I was, but my eyes weren't leaving the box. I had no idea what to expect inside. There'd been a corpse in the always locked trunk on my grandparents' patio, what body part might I discover in a cigar box? The first tear trickled down my cheek as Ridge pulled a chair up behind me, tugging downward on my—his—shirt.

"It's from the crime scene—the corpse we found in the trunk. The key was inside—with her." I slid the assaulting hunk of hand-forged metal out of the lock. The image clawed at me, nausea creeping up from someplace low and dark. I returned the key to its envelope and handed it back to Ridge. I wouldn't need it anymore. And I never wanted to see it again.

"Did he put it there?" I asked.

"Who?" Ridge scooted a chair next to mine. The heat of his arm blanketed my shoulders.

"The guy who attacked me."

"Is that what you think?"

"I know she had the key. Around her neck." The words tumbled out. The result of the knock on the head or just the need to end the charade, I wasn't sure. My own fingers clawed at the bare skin at the base of my neck. "It was on a string."

"Liv…" A note of warning. A reminder that the truth I was about to spill was irreversible. There was no tangible proof. The police didn't know who she was. All I had was a vague newspaper article from twenty-some years ago. I might not know a lot about Ridge, but if I knew nothing else, it was that he needed real life proof.

"You once asked me if I saw them." My voice wavered in the air between us. "I saw her." I couldn't look, but I heard the sharp intake of air. The reaction that signaled the end.

"When?" he asked.

"In L.A., a colleague routed the call to me. There was a man on the other end of the line. But it was her. I watched her die while he talked to me."

"Liv, I–" Ridge took my hand. Guilt bubbled beneath the surface of his skin, tingling through my fingertips as he laced his fingers through mine.

"The caller told me they'd come after me next." The gentle ebb and flow of guilt ceased, replaced by a wall I couldn't interpret. "I watched him strangle the life from her. And just now, when I touched the key."

Ridge turned me to face him. His thumb brushing away another tear as it toppled onto my cheek. "Look at me."

His eyes–part fear, part disbelief–emotions overshadowed by something darker. A choked sob rose from my chest. I couldn't do it anymore. Couldn't keep anymore secrets. I'd reached my quota. Logically, I knew this was a result of the concussion. But it didn't matter. There was freedom in the truth. No matter how hard it might be. Prickles marched along my scalp and I sucked in a breath, preparing for the fallout from the admission I was about to make.

"A few nights ago, I saw your sister."

The silence that followed was deafening. The only sound the thump of blood pulsing in my ears. His grip on my arms loosened, skin against skin as his hands dropped from mine. I stared at the floor, counting the taupe flowers that marched the perimeter of the kitchen tile.

When I finally gathered the courage to look in his direction, he was staring at me. His palm covered his mouth and his eyes were wide.

"That's not possible."

"I'm sorry. I wanted to tell you before, but after the other night in the parking lot, I–"

Ridge stopped me. "What did you see?"

"Fire. A family huddled outside a burning house. Firemen trying to put out the blaze." I paused, gauging Ridge's reaction before continuing. "One of the fireman came out through the flames. He was carrying a girl."

"Riley..." Ridge choked out. "Her name was Riley."

"Riley," I repeated. "That's a pretty name." I flinched at my own words. *What a stupid thing to say.* The man I cared for was trying to comprehend how I saw his dead sister from beyond the grave and here I was telling him she had a pretty name. Ugh. The dead were easier to deal with than the living.

"Did she say anything?" Hope climbed alongside disbelief in his eyes.

I nodded, pulling him closer. I ran my hands down his face as I relayed the message I'd been saving for him.

"She said to tell you to stop blaming yourself."

"Holy, Christ." It was more choked sob than distinct curse. Ridge stood as quickly as he'd spewed the words, knocking the chair to the floor and turning his back to me.

I turned toward the box, giving him time to process. Regret welled inside me, roiling and receding like active lava flows.

"I'm sorry, Ridge," I whispered, standing. I tucked the box under my arm and headed toward the hall. Grief choked me, squeezing like an iron corset. I tried to rationalize why what I'd done was a good thing as I opened the door to the guest room. I slid the box onto the foot of the bed, careful to keep it closed. I wasn't ready.

"It's my fault she's dead." His voice filtered into the room from the doorway. I turned to find him watching me.

"We'd been in a fight. One of many. She was mad because I'd been–" Ridge glanced at me, searching for the right words. "–experimenting with drugs." A sad smile tickled the corner of his lips. "She was eighteen months younger than me, but she was always more responsible."

I lowered onto the bed, resting my hands on my knees, careful not to touch him.

"I figured I'd show her, you know? So, I lit up a joint in my bedroom and put my headphones on. The last thing I remember is Green Day blasting through my headset speakers. I woke up in a smoke-filled room." He looked around as if he could see it himself. "Flames were already eating the wall between our rooms. I panicked. I should have gone in to get her, but I didn't. I thought she was already out."

Ridge paused. Arms crossed across his chest, he leaned against the doorframe focusing on anything but me. His brows stitched together into an angry line and pain infiltrated his voice. "It was me. My stupidity started the fire. And my cowardice killed her."

"It was an accident, Ridge. She doesn't blame you."

"How can you be so sure?" He squinted in scrutiny, finally meeting my gaze.

"I only know what they want me to know. I have to trust them."

Ridge was silent as he reached for his phone, pulling it from his back pocket.

"I know this is a lot to take. I understand if you need some time to process." I said carefully, readying myself for whatever his response might be.

"Liv." His voice was quiet, resolute. "I have a job to do. I need you to tell me what you know about the girl in the trunk."

The blinking red light of his phone's voice memo feature taunted me from the top of the dresser as he touched the record button.

I nodded, the knot in my throat inhibiting speech.

"Please state your name, for the record."

"My name's Liv Sullivan."

"How did you come by the information we're about to discuss?" The caramel of his voice morphed from liquid to harsh right angles, but his face remained unchanged. Soft and concerned.

I sunk my fingers into the comforter on either side of me. Accusations from a decade ago sparked in my memory. The detective's relentless quest for the truth he'd invented in his mind. But this wasn't Detective Carson. This was Ridge. I sucked in a balancing breath.

"Sometimes I can see..." How long had it been since I'd said the words aloud? "...dead people."

28

RIDGE

Ridge spent the majority of his adult life coercing information out of people who didn't want to give it up. But this was the first time he'd ever had to fight the urge to shut the recorder off, take the interviewee in his arms and run away. His gut churned with the impulse to forget Sowards, forget the evidence, leave a decomposing corpse in the past where it belonged and move on.

In any other situation he'd swear she was crazy, some media whore looking for her fifteen minutes of fame, or more likely, a certifiable nut job. He'd experienced both in his time with the Bureau. The fallout from what she was saying turned in his mind as she talked, relaying the last moments of a frightened young woman against the backdrop of the Sullivan woods. Her details were too accurate, he realized, even for someone who'd grown up at the farm. She could tell him the weather, the scent of leaves in the air, the whistle of wind in the trees. And maybe she'd made those up. But the grip of the man's hands around the girl's throat—that was real, proven by the medical examiner's detailed report, the broken hyoid bone at the base of the victim's throat. No, there were two options, Liv actually possessed the power to communicate with dead people, or she'd been there the night this girl was murdered, the latter of which was impossible if he believed the M.E.'s time of death estimate of somewhere in the late 1980's.

Liv fell silent, clasping her hands in her lap, forcing the pad of her thumb over the knuckles of her opposite hand. They reddened under the pressure. There was more she wasn't telling him.

"You never saw her attacker, though?" he asked.

"It doesn't work like that. I never see them."

Ridge wanted to ask why, but he knew she didn't have an answer. "How do you know the body we found in the trunk belongs to the same woman you saw in your..." He stopped short, wrapping his tongue around the word, "...vision?"

"Her name's Jennifer Tipton. She worked for my father as an intern back in the early nineties. I found a newspaper article at the library."

Ridge swallowed the burn of suspicion. Instinct was not his best asset in this case.

"I can't prove it's her if that's what you're thinking." Liv lifted her eyes to meet Ridge for the first time since he'd been grilling her. "Call it intuition, psychic phenomenon, sixth sense, whatever you want. I've just learned through the years to trust them."

Trust. God, he needed more of that in his life. Instead, here he was lying to the one person he wanted most to be honest with, treating her like a common suspect.

"When did the visions start?" Ridge moved from his stance in the doorway and sat next to her, reaching for her hands to stop her from rubbing her knuckles raw. This question wasn't meant for Sowards. This one was for him.

"I think there was something different about me from the beginning. But they started out as dreams, you know? I was ten when I realized what I saw actually happened in real life."

"So you can see the future?"

Liv laughed, a hard sandpaper chuckle. "No. Everything I see has already happened. I'm not your go-to girl for lottery numbers."

Ridge processed the implications. The woman next to him, who claimed to see death, but had no way to stop it, no way to intervene...no way to make a difference. Living life with Riley's death on his conscience was hard enough, he couldn't fathom waking every day knowing there was someone else out there he hadn't been able to help. No one would make that shit up. He reached toward the dresser and pressed the stop button on his phone.

"The man on the phone, did he tell you what he meant by saying they'd come after you next?"

"No. I don't know who he was talking about. I never gave it much thought until the attack at the farm."

Ridge swallowed. This was on him. Sowards told him she needed to be protected. He'd let his emotions run the operation and Liv suffered for it. "I'm sorry."

Liv shrugged.

"How do you..." he didn't know how to end the question. Cope? Survive?

"Manage?" Liv saved him. "I try to help the ones I can. Figure out what they need. Sometimes that's easier said than done."

"And Jennifer Tipton, what does she need?"

"I wish I knew. Maybe she's just like all of us, wants to be remembered for who she was, not some decomposing corpse with no name."

Ridge picked up on the trickle of accusation in Liv's voice.

She was right. Even now, the dead girl didn't rank as a priority at the station. There were no cold cases from the right time frame. Why this girl? Why the Sullivan farmhouse? If he wanted answers he was going to have to open up to the possibility that Liv was the only one capable of getting them.

His sister's face, soot-blackened and fire scorched singed his memory. Liv admitted she'd been to the library. She could've gotten those details from public record. But why bother?

"You have to understand how difficult this is for me to believe."

"I understand."

"But can I offer you a truth of my own?"

Ridge waited for Liv to look at him, to recognize the honesty behind his eyes.

"I've known since the night we met that something about you was different. I felt it, that spark of...something...I've never experienced that before."

Ridge combed his eyes over the woman next to him. The curve of her jaw, the silky curl of her hair, he shouldn't care this much. It was dangerous, for both of them. But he did. Ridge picked up a stray curl and wound it around his finger. Liv looked away, tucking her lower lip under her front tooth, a habit that sparked a ribbon of desire deep in Ridge's core. He cleared his throat and leaned closer, not quite touching, but close enough to feel her warmth, catch a whiff of the strawberries and cream shampoo.

"So what happens next?" she asked.

"We dig into that box you brought. Figure out what's inside. Lay all the cards on the table."

Her eyes locked on his, searching, heating his core. "What do we have to lose?"

Everything. The word came unbidden and Ridge clenched

his jaw against the threat. Focused instead on the woman in front of him as she picked up the humidor and clasped it to her chest.

"Ready when you are."

29

LIV

A choke rose in my throat as he stood, equal parts fear and relief. The hard edges of the box dug into my chest reminding me of secrets yet discovered and truths left untold. I couldn't tell him about Grandma, about the ghostly little girl. If he didn't think I was crazy now, he would then.

I inhaled sharply as he stepped forward, his fingers trailing my jawline. The memory of his lips on mine kicked my heart into high gear. I closed my eyes as he leaned down, lips trailing my collarbone, his hand at the small of my back, pushing the soft fabric of an over-washed t-shirt out of his path. I bit back the urge to reciprocate, losing myself in the heat of his lips before the trill of my ringtone interrupted us.

My mother's name, Beth Sullivan, stretched across the screen. I tossed it away toward the foot of the mattress. That's what I got for leaving the ringtone on in the first place.

"You should talk to her," Ridge urged, pulling his arms from around my waist. He tapped the box. "A few minutes won't matter. I'll be in the kitchen if you need me."

He closed the door behind him with a gentle click. Maybe if I waited long enough the call would go to voicemail. She hadn't bothered to leave a message any of the other times she rang, why would today be any different?

Ridge popped his head back into the room, a smile playing on his lips. "Answer her."

I waved him away, but he didn't close the door this time. I tapped the line open with a too jovial, "Hello, Mom."

"Liv, I'm so glad I finally got through to you. I heard about the accident the other night. You hadn't called. I was worried about you."

I set the cigar box aside and fiddled with the corner of the unmade bedspread, trying my hardest to ignore the sincerity of controlled panic in her voice. "I'm fine, just a bump on the head."

"Good." There was a stagnant pause on the other end. I was just about to toss the standard, "What have you been up to," line out when her voice broke back in. "I was hoping we could get together. Talk things through, about the farm?"

I swallowed the urge to tell her to mind her own damn business.

"Are you free tonight?"

I looked at Ridge who'd peeked back around the doorjamb. So much for privacy. I smiled and shook my head, mustering the most malicious stare I could. Failing miserably, he just shrugged and smiled innocently.

"Would it be okay if I brought someone?" I asked, deciding Ridge deserved to be pulled into this particular nightmare.

My mother hesitated a beat before answering. "This is family business, Liv, but if that's what you're comfortable with, I guess it would be okay." Her words were hesitant, and I didn't believe for a moment that she was really okay with the idea. However, she'd dragged Lyle to meetings where he'd had no business, so it seemed fair. I caught myself diving into old patterns of teenage me, blaming Mom for my own bad behavior.

"It's someone I'd like you to meet," I managed, working to hide the smile that kept creeping onto my lips with every thought of Ridge and our last moments together.

"Jason?" Hopefulness permeated her voice. My smile disappeared.

"No, Mom. It's not." Back to picking at the bedspread.

"Okay." She was waiting for more information. "Well anyway, I look forward to meeting this illustrious stranger soon enough. We'll have an early dinner. The Hunter at five o'clock? Will that work for you and, uh –" Jesus, she was a pro at this.

"Ridge, Mom. His name is Ridge." I eyed Ridge in the doorway. He cocked his head to the side upon hearing his name, obviously wondering what I'd roped him into.

"Fine. Ridge. I look forward to meeting him." Her voice was tight. "See you this evening, Olivia."

"Bye, Mom."

I lay my phone on the dresser and joined Ridge in the hallway, wrapping my arms around his torso. His thumb traced my jawline before he leaned down to kiss me.

I pulled away as he said, "I figured you were going to owe me that one, considering you've roped me into who-knows-what."

His teasing smile urged me up for another kiss.

"You have the honor of accompanying me to dinner with my mother and her boyfriend, Lyle, tonight at The Hunter, where they will relentlessly try to talk me into selling the farm."

A shadow passed over Ridge's eyes, sending a seed of panic into my core, but he recovered quickly. Wrapping his arms around me he admitted, "Then I suppose I might be an asset since the last thing I want is for you to leave Cascade Hills."

"It's not quite that simple," I said. Tensing, I pulled away a bit.

At this point I wasn't sure I'd ever be able to live there, at least not alone. A tickle of memory sent prickles marching along my spine, raising gooseflesh on my naked arms and legs. As a girl I'd never been afraid to be there alone, but something had changed. Even after my cleaning purge, the air was different there. The sanctity of the place, violated.

"I know," Ridge agreed before freeing me. "So, about that box..."

I reached my hand up to his face, trailing my palm down his jawline. How did I ever get so lucky? I watched his eyes close as he leaned into my touch.

"I'm not ready to go there just yet."

I traced his lower lip with my thumb, pushing the hard edges of what awaited me in that cigar box away. I tipped up onto my toes, kissing him. Right now, I wanted to live in the moment he'd created for me. Forget about the what-ifs. Replace the pain–the visions of death–with pleasure. He leaned into my kiss. His breath hitched as he pulled me in close.

The taste of him was enough to obliterate the visions of dead women and ghostly little girls. His lips enveloped mine hungrily, his tongue probing, insistent. The heat of his touch, even through the t-shirt, sent pulses of electricity through me that I'd never felt, even with Jason. He wrapped me tighter. His jeans did little to mask his desire, and I ached to touch him–feel him. His breath, hot against my skin, urged for more. Warmth spread from my core through my extremities, and I tangled my fists in his shirt, straining for control. There was no question I'd do something we both might regret if I let it go much longer.

I knew exactly how to break the spell. "I should get back to the farm this evening." Hardly more than a whisper, but it was enough.

He shook his head. "You can't stay out there alone."

"Okay," I answered. Surprised eyes met mine. "Will you stay with me?"

His lips parted silently, and he nodded.

"I have some packing to do."

"Packing?" Ridge didn't look at me, just leaned back against the door frame, bracing against my response.

"You knew this was coming, Ridge. I've got to go back to L.A. There's business I need to take care of."

"I thought," he started, but couldn't finish.

"You thought I'd come home, cash in and just stay here?" I bit the inside of my cheek to keep the teasing smile at bay.

"That's not what I mean, I just. Your mom. This dinner. What are you going to tell them?" There was an edge in his voice as he gathered his thoughts. "Look, I know your life isn't here. And after what happened at the farm, I don't blame you for wanting to go back. I just..."

"What?" I asked, coaxing.

"We need more time."

I shrugged. Time to end this game. I didn't have the stamina for it. "Come with me."

"Liv, I can't just take off and leave. We're in the middle of an investigation. You just identified a dead girl. Too many people depend on me here."

"Okay," I said, hoping he'd reconsider. The fact remained that I had to go back. He stood silently, calling my bluff. He narrowed his eyes, a wall of protection slid into place between us.

"I've never driven a moving truck, but I'm sure I could manage." I tried appealing to his chivalrous nature.

"Moving truck?"

"I have to be moved out of my apartment by Friday. The

new tenants were supposed to be able to move in the first of April. I had to get an extension. I've got until the fifth."

"So, you're moving? Back to Cascade Hills?" Ridge's voice was careful, exacting.

"There's nothing for me to go back to." I smiled at Ridge as his eyes searched mine. I'd already committed to the truth. I had to trust he'd be able to protect me when the vultures of skepticism reared their ugly heads. Which, as history had proven, they were prone to do.

Ridge reached for me, wrapping me in his arms he swung me off my feet in a tight circle.

"Whoa! Girl with concussion, here," I said as the room began to spin.

He put me down gently before bending to kiss me more passionately than I thought possible. Our tongues intertwined, exploring each other, as insatiable hunger took over my body. I could only assume the same desire was affecting Ridge as he swung my legs up, supporting me effortlessly and carried me, not to the Sunflower bed, but to his own muted master suite. He laid me gently on the mattress. His morning stubble softly chafed my cheek as he pulled away and nestled next to me, the muscles in his shoulders taut, easily supporting his weight.

"I've always been a skeptic, Liv. In Murphy's parking lot, when I asked if you saw ghosts, I wanted you to say yes. I wanted you to say yes so I had a reason to pull away. But it was too late. I'd already fallen for you."

"And what I told you today?" Breath clung in my chest, refusing to break free until he answered.

"Those days without you were the longest days of my life. I can't pretend to understand how your mind works. But I want to."

He pushed a hair out of my eyes.

"When you were lying on the floor at the farmhouse, there was so much blood. You were so still. I thought I'd never get the chance to show you what you mean to me."

I turned toward Ridge and pulled him closer.

"Show me now," I urged.

30

RIDGE

Ridge waited outside the bathroom for Liv to get settled into the shower before heading for the kitchen. Over the rush of water, the buzz of his ringtone sounded from the guest bedroom. He trotted the last few steps to snatch it off the dresser where he'd left it a couple hours before.

"McCaffrey," he said into the speaker.

"This is the third time I've tried to call. I was about to get off my ass and come over there."

Ridge laughed and exhaled a relieved breath. "Brian. Sorry. It's been a rough forty-eight hours."

"So, I've heard. All I got was snippets of gossip until Adam came in. Is Liv okay?"

"She's..." He wasn't sure how to finish. Excellent, amazing, phenomenal, confusing, inconceivable—all those words would be a perfect fit, but that's not what Brian meant, and Ridge wasn't about to go into the events of the morning. "She's doing really well. Took a pretty nasty bump to the head. Doctors are treating her for a concussion. I think she's more scared than hurt."

"Sure would scare the shit out of me. Tell her not to worry about the publicity pics. Whenever she gets to them is fine. No stress on my end."

"Thanks, Brian. For everything." Ridge disconnected. He had Brian to thank for the morning he'd just spent with Liv. He could be hard-headed sometimes, and Brian knew just when to tell him to soften up, even if it did mean navigating a web of lies Ridge would rather avoid.

"Everything okay?" Ridge spun toward Liv's voice, tossing his cell onto the kitchen island, ignoring the half-dialed number of Sowards hanging across the screen.

"How was the shower?"

"Refreshing." Liv tilted up on tiptoe to reach his lips. Ridge skimmed a finger along the now-exposed bruise on Liv's temple. The bits of dried blood had been washed away, but the sight of the sutures in her delicate skin turned the vise on his lungs.

It was his fault she'd been hurt. His fault for ignoring Sowards' warning. Pushing her away and leaving her alone in an unsecured house. Mistakes he couldn't afford. Mistakes that, if Sowards was right, could take Liv from him forever.

He fought against the practical side of his brain, the drill sergeant insisting that her knowledge of Riley was somehow a fluke. It had been in the papers. She'd had time to do her research. Her livelihood in California relied on superior observation skills. This was nothing more. But his heart knew better.

"You ready?" he asked, glancing at the mahogany box tucked under her arm.

"If you don't mind."

Ridge took Liv's hand and led her down the hall toward the den.

"I like this room." She smiled.

He surveyed the room around them. A large screen television decked one wall, and a comfortable looking taupe sofa was at home opposite the TV. A brown rocker-recliner sat off to the side of the couch. There was not one flower in sight.

"Thanks. I had it redone right after Bridget... that was my wife... right after she left."

"Good choice."

Ridge smiled, ushering Liv onto the sofa. He removed the box from under her arm and set it carefully on the coffee table.

Tension built like tight coils at the base of his neck. Suddenly, this small task felt insurmountable. The possibilities of what could be lurking inside, waiting to destroy the fragile foundation they'd built, were overwhelming. He blew out a jagged breath before turning his attention back to Liv, hoping for a few more moments of peace.

"There's just one thing I'd like to do before we open that box."

"What's that?" She gazed up at him with innocent eyes. Forget research. What she'd known about Riley came from her core. She wasn't conniving. She had nothing to gain by using that information against him. At least, nothing he could see.

Ridge released his pent up breath and knelt in front of Liv. Cupping her head in his hands, he stroked her cheek, careful not to touch the bruise.

"I owe you an apology, Liv. I never should have left you alone." He bent to meet her lips, inhaling the sweet scent of her fresh shampoo.

"That's ridiculous, Ridge. You had no way of knowing what would happen."

Yet he did. Plain as the ink in her file. He may not know who, or why, but he'd known there was a risk. He planted a soft, tender kiss on her cheek and leaned into her, hungry lips a welcome distraction from the task at hand.

She arched into him, memories of their morning in his bedroom sparked insatiable need as he trailed his lips along her jaw, working his way southward. She closed her eyes to his touch, a light moan escaping as he slid his hand under the hem of her t-shirt. Her skin soft and warm against his palm. Another moan, a hint of desperation this time. He sank back onto his feet, finding her eyes just as she squinted, raising a hand to her injured skull.

"Liv, baby... Are you okay?" He released her, eyes scouring her face for clues.

"I'm fine." She said, the grimace of pain fading from her cheeks. "Maybe a little too much excitement for one morning."

She grinned at Ridge, running a finger across his lips. "So... I'm baby now?"

The name had slipped out–some carnal instinct. "I guess so. If that's okay with you."

He grabbed her hand and kissed the tip of her teasing finger. She nodded, pulling her eyes from him and onto the ornate box to his left. Remnants of pleasure clashed with bubbling anxiety as he pulled the box from the table and sat on the couch, arranging the hand-carved humidor between them.

He let her take the lead. This was her box. Her mystery. He'd only provided the key.

31

LIV

Ridge and I sat on the sofa in his den going through the contents of the box piece by piece. I tried to control the breath of relief when he'd opened the lid onto nothing more than a pile of papers. No Grimm's Fairy Tale endings after all, at least not today.

Topping the neat pile were several photographs. I recognized my grandmother in two of the three. In the first, a woman I didn't know, holding a newborn in her arms, smiled down at the infant as my grandmother stood off to the side. Names and dates were scrawled in my grandmother's unmistakable hand across the back of each one. My own name stared back at me partnered with a name I had never before seen, Aimee Callaghan. The date was listed as October 27th, same as the newspaper clipping, and just three days after I was born. I passed the first two, nearly identical, photos to Ridge.

"Do you know these women?" he asked examining each snapshot.

"Just my grandmother." I pointed her out.

I clutched the third picture tightly in my hand. My scalp prickled as a knot of insecurity climbed into my chest.

"These don't look like they were taken around here. Look in the background." Ridge was still laser focused on the first two photographs. He pointed toward the window in the background of the two pictures. I didn't need to look. I had each photograph memorized. Even the tiniest details were seared into my mind.

I knew the land in the background was green and rolling, a wrought iron bench, empty, not far beyond the window. A low stone fence meandered along the hills in the field beyond.

"They weren't," I said. "They were taken in Ireland. In my Grandmother's cottage near Lough Dan." I shrugged, qualifying my remark. "At least as far as I can tell."

"So, this is you, right?" Ridge flipped over one of the pics and scooted closer on the couch, pointing out my bald head in one of the pictures. I worked to forget about the third picture. Maybe he wouldn't ask.

"But this... this doesn't look like your mom." Ridge squinted at the grainy photo. "Is it?"

"No. The back says her name is Aimee Callaghan. The same woman from that picture." I pointed. "Except that's not me."

Ridge peered into the second photo. Almost exactly the same as the first, he flipped it over and read the inscribed names, "Aimee and Ashlyn Callaghan." He swallowed hard and didn't ask any more questions.

I tucked the third photo under my thigh and reached into the box for the next paper. My fingers skimmed the embossed seal as I reread the text over and over, working to make sense of it all.

"Aimee's my birth mother." The words felt foreign to me.

"Birth mother?" Ridge repeated.

My tongue felt swollen–thick and heavy in my mouth. So instead of answering, I shoved the certificate toward him. My eyes lingered on the embossed harp at the top of the page.

"I guess I was adopted."

He took the document carefully out of my hand, eyes riveted on my face the whole time.

"A birth certificate..." His eyes flicked expertly over the paper, gleaning the information effortlessly. "I take it this is something you didn't know. Who's Ashlyn?"

I shook my head slowly as betrayal flooded my veins, threatening to spur my tear ducts into action. I clenched my jaw and stared down at my hands, fingering the edge of the photo I'd hidden under my leg.

Once I was certain I'd staved off the threat of tears, I shifted my gaze to watch Ridge scan the document for a second time. The furrow in his brow gave away his confusion.

"Why would your parents choose to adopt a child from Ireland? Why not just find a baby in the States? I mean, I've heard of couples adopting internationally... but it's usually China, Korea, even. But, Ireland?"

I had no answer for that, so I did the only thing I could think of to stop the barrage of questions about the evidence of my birth. I passed the hidden picture his way. "This one was taken here."

Ridge was silent as he studied the third image. He turned it over, read the inscription aloud, "Jennifer Tipton and Stephen Sullivan, 1992, Sullivan Farm."

I grasped a stack of letters from the box, tied with an aged blue ribbon, similar to the ones I'd seen on the pigtails of a ghostly little girl. I couldn't watch him connect the dots I'd already connected in my own mind. But the buzz in my fingers as I pulled the ribbon free, stopped me cold.

"This is her, isn't it?" Ridge's wide eyes met mine, the

picture still pinched between his thumb and forefinger. "This was your grandfather's box, you said?"

"My grandmother gave it to him as a gift. It was in the book case in his office." I sucked in a regulatory breath. I knew where this would go from here. An investigation. My life torn apart. Everything I'd tried to avoid by leaving Cascade Hills a decade ago.

"You know I have to report this."

"I know." I tried to avoid it, but my voice betrayed me, hitting the air small and scared.

"What about the letters?" He nodded down at the stack I'd left untied in the box.

"I don't want them. I know enough. I can't take anymore."

32

LIV

The Hunter Grille was a happening place for five o'clock on a Sunday. Ridge walked me to the door, leaving his car blocking the valet zone far longer than the attendants would have liked.

"I'm sorry I can't come. I need to be at the farm in case the dogs hit on something. Text me when you're done. I can be here in fifteen minutes."

The dogs had been dispatched a little over an hour ago. Ridge had explained how unlikely it was for a cadaver dog to find evidence of a body after almost three decades, but if someone had churned up the soil, left a scent of his own while doing it, the likelihood ratcheted up a few notches. Seemed worth a shot considering the newest revelations. Jennifer Tipton had been alive at some point at Sullivan farm. No longer the vision of a crazy person, there was photographic evidence to prove it. I tried to think of happier things, but the image of a dog sniffing through the dirt, braying at the scent of a stranger on the land I loved, polluted my efforts.

I enjoyed the heat of one final kiss, ignoring the penetrating frustration emanating from the valet attendants as they glared from the bottom of the steps.

I barely got to the hostess stand before I heard my name from the rear of the main dining area. I nodded at the hostess and wove my way between busy tables to the back of the room.

"Liv, I'm glad you made it," Lyle said as he stood, my mother nowhere in sight. "Your mom's been worried about you since the accident."

"Where is she?" I asked.

"Ladies room," Lyle answered before looking around me. "I thought you were bringing a friend."

"I was, Ridge McCaffrey, but he was called in for work at the last minute. He's sorry to miss meeting you.

An odd look flickered across Lyle's face. Recognition? Maybe. Mom came out of the restroom before I could sit, so I repeated Ridge's excuse for her benefit.

My mom reached over and took my chin in her hand, twisting my face to get a better look at the damage caused two nights before.

"Oh, Olivia. You can't stay in that old place. It's not safe."

I wished I had a way to refute that statement. But she was right. It wasn't. And, if I was honest with myself, I wasn't sure I wanted to stay there.

Lyle stepped in, taking the lead in the conversation, a role for which he was astoundingly unqualified considering the subject matter. After the initial, "I'm glad you're okay," chitchat, he delved right in.

"Your mother just wants what is best for you, Liv."

"And what is that exactly?" I felt hostility creeping along my spine. At this moment, I was a child again—being told what I could and couldn't do with my life. And I resented it now, just as I had back then.

"We think it's best to just sell the old place. Think about it,

Liv. It's a wreck. Vines are taking over and it's not even spring yet. Imagine what that place will look like when they start growing again." Lyle's lilt grated against my nerves.

"I've been cleaning it up," I chimed in. "I've repainted three rooms so far, cleaned up the barn. It already looks better."

"Liv, I'm sure it does, but that's not the point. I..."

"I'm perfectly capable of taking care of it," I cut off my mother's next statement. "Grandma wouldn't want Sullivan farm sold. Besides, you'd never be able to find someone to purchase the house and all that acreage."

I was just as doubtful as Lyle and my mom were about my ability to care for 400 acres, but I refused to admit it. Not now. Not to them. I slid my phone out of my purse, hiding it under the white tablecloth as I tapped a text to Ridge. I needed him here. I needed to get out of here. Now.

"That's true." Lyle said, glancing at my mother who had become uncharacteristically mute. I watched him take her hand and anger welled up in my core. The throb of tension at the base of my skull started pounding out a rhythm.

"We, your mom and I, think it would be best to split it up. We have a buyer interested. You should talk to him."

"Who is it?"

"That's not really important right now, is it?"

"If you want me to talk to him it is."

Lyle stayed silent for a moment before answering. "Sheridan Homes."

My heart thundered in my chest. *No. This couldn't be.* Breathe, Liv, just breathe, I coached.

"You want to sell the Sullivan land so that it can become a housing development?"

I said the words carefully, making sure not to stumble over them in anger.

"They're going to keep the name. Call it Sullivan Estates.

Your grandmother's name will live on forever. Liv, think of what an honor, what a legacy, that would be for your grandparents."

That's when it hit me. Mom and Lyle had this plan all but finalized. They'd simply been waiting on Grandma to die so they could sell off the farm chunk by chunk. Who knew how much they were going to get for it? Sheridan Homes was one of the premier homebuilders in the area.

I knew they'd pay an obscene amount for that land. The image of identical, vinyl sided two-story homes, with tiny front porches and two-car garages plunked down over my grandparents' beautiful farm unleashed a knot of nausea in my gut. But then, logic kicked in. A sense of relief washed away the sick as it dawned on me that they couldn't touch it. Not now, not ever.

I painted a satisfied smirk on my lips and took a sip of water.

"The land belongs to me. I intend to live there, just as my grandmother wanted. I will do whatever it takes to make a life for myself here in Cascade Hills. I'm sorry it interferes with your business interests."

"Your life is in California, Olivia." My mother finally spoke up, but she didn't look at me.

"What is there to go back to?" I asked. "I've got no job, no friends. Do you know about some portion of my life of which I'm unaware?"

Mom glanced at Lyle, then straight at me. "What about Jason?"

"What are you talking about, Mom? Jason's been out of my life for years."

"He came to see us, Liv. He wants to try again."

"He told you that?" I stood on instinct. My voice too loud for the decorum of the restaurant. "When did you see him?"

"Just a couple days ago. He said he saw you at Flanagan's.

He's getting ready to go back to L.A. and he wants you to go with him."

"Mom, it's over between Jason and me. Done. Besides, even if it weren't, I wouldn't go all the way back to L.A. just for him. I can't explain right now, but Grandma needs me here."

"Grace is dead, Olivia." Lyle's voice cut through the tension.

I glared at him, gathering my purse and coat, unable to come up with a suitable response. I looked to my mother who nodded without meeting my gaze and watched as Lyle studied me with what appeared to be a satisfied smile playing on his lips.

"I don't think you realize what you're getting yourself into, Liv."

"I'm a big girl, Lyle." I spat back. "I'll take my chances."

Ridge was at my side by the time I reached the hostess stand. He slipped his arm around my waist as we walked. I was impressed that he only looked toward the back table once.

I was furious. Furious at myself for buying into my mother's invitation. Furious for bothering to come. Furious at my mother for dredging up ancient history. And furious at Ridge for not being there to back me up. Although, even I knew that last one was the anger talking.

33

—————

RIDGE

That drive back to Sullivan Road was a quiet one. Ridge asked about the dinner once, but Liv brushed him off. "Just the usual," she'd said. After that, he kept his thoughts to himself. Google had been a friend over the course of the last couple hours. He'd stayed out of the team's way, watching from the front porch of the Sullivan farmhouse as beams of light skimmed methodically around the woods beyond the barn.

His research had only led to more questions, and as he sat next to Liv in the closeness of the Shelby, he couldn't help but wonder if she could tell what he was thinking. Wikipedia had provided a list of almost thirty different types of psychic abilities. From there, he'd picked the ones that seemed to fit with what Liv had told him so far. He ran through the front runners. Mediumship, ability to communicate with spirits, and retrocognition, the supernatural perception of past events, were his top two, but telepathy and psychometry ran close behind.

Of the four, telepathy and psychometry scared him the most. He'd never heard of psychometry before tonight–the ability to touch an object to gain insight into either a person or the object itself. He'd heard of intelligence agencies, both here and abroad, using it in cold cases, but he'd never actually seen the process with his own eyes.

Telepathy–the ability to read someone's thoughts–just weirded him out, especially considering some of the thoughts he was having right now.

He glanced at Liv. She was staring out the passenger window into the fields beyond. She didn't act like she knew what he'd been rehashing in his mind since he picked her up. He forced a breath out through tight lips.

One thing he had learned is that psychics usually have a trigger of some kind, a way to open themselves to psychic energy. Skilled ones can manipulate that trigger to close themselves off. He had no idea what Liv's trigger was, or how well she could manipulate it.

"Who's here?" Liv asked as they pulled down the driveway. A BCI van had arrived since he left to pick her up, a sure sign of what he already knew–they'd found the shallow grave where Jennifer Tipton's remains spent the better part of three decades.

Ridge killed the engine and turned to face Liv. "They found her grave. Not far from where you described. It was freshly unearthed. Techs are sure the soil samples will match the dirt we found in the trunk with her remains."

Liv's chest rose, the glow from the Mercury light in the barn lot reflected off the bare skin visible above the low-cut neckline of her dress. Ridge cleared his throat, shoving the thoughts of what he wanted to do with that dress as far away as possible. This wasn't the time.

"Good," Liv managed. She popped the passenger door open without waiting for Ridge, and he scrambled to get out of his own side before she got too far. "Do they need to talk to me?"

Ridge reached her just in time to hear her question. "They will. Tomorrow we'll go to the precinct and you can give your statement."

She swallowed, still looking out toward the woods. Her chest rose with another deliberate breath. Anxiety.

Ridge slipped his arm around her waist and pulled her against him. He kissed the crown of her head as she leaned into him.

"Guess this means L.A. is out of the picture."

"I made some calls. I'm having a moving company head over to your place. They'll pack everything up and bring it all back here. I hope that's okay."

She laced her fingers over his and closed her eyes. His heart kicked up a notch in his chest.

"The investigators won't believe me, Ridge. They never do."

He wrapped his arms around her and swiveled her to face him, choking back his own uncertainty. "Just tell them the truth, Liv. They'll believe you. I promise."

It wasn't the worst lie he'd told in the course of their short relationship, but it was undoubtedly the most dangerous.

34

LIV

The only thing that made walking into the empty house bearable, was the heat that seeped from Ridge's body into mine. I couldn't explain it, but whenever we were together, I felt it. The life in him—the love I wanted desperately to return.

Each step brought a fresh wave of panic. And as Ridge fidgeted with the lock on the front door, my temple began to throb. The urge to turn around intensified, away from the anger and loneliness of the farm and back to the sunshine and flowers of Ridge's house.

"You okay?" he asked as the door opened wide. I nodded. I had to sleep in the house tonight. Otherwise, I might never be able to force myself to go back, giving my mom and Lyle exactly what they needed to unload the property to Sheridan Homes. I stepped over the threshold, bracing myself against a wave of fear that never materialized.

"It's like nothing ever happened," the words came out in a relieved rush.

"We had the place cleaned after the attack. Carpet, couch, everything."

It wasn't what I meant, but there was no point in trying to explain.

"They did take the lamp into evidence. The base was cracked anyway." A smiled tickled the corner of his lips. "You have a harder head than we thought."

I elbowed him, I had no memory of being hit with the lamp, but the smile came anyway. "Thank you."

Ridge spent most of the evening on the phone, pacing back and forth in my grandfather's office. I curled on a chair at the dining room table just off the kitchen, my laptop propped in front of me, alternating between editing photos of Murphy's, and tracking Ridge's every move, afraid to let him out of my sight.

When Ridge ended his call, he stayed in the office a few more minutes before joining me at the other end of the house.

"Can I get you something to drink?" he asked, pulling a Guinness for himself from the refrigerator.

"Just tea, I think." I hadn't had a sip of alcohol since the night of the attack, and I wasn't sure I wanted to start again tonight.

Within a few moments Ridge was handing me a steaming cup of Celestial Seasonings Sleepytime tea, my favorite, and the only one available in the barren cupboards of the still-vacant kitchen.

"What are you working on?"

"Just finishing up the proofs for Brian."

"Speaking of Brian. I was talking to him the other day... He was impressed with the raw files you've shown him so far. He thinks you're really talented."

"That's nice of him to say." That sounded ridiculous, but I wasn't used to accepting compliments.

"When things calm down, he wants you to stop out. I think he has a bit of a business proposition for you."

"Really?" I pulled my gaze up to meet his. Ridge's eyes sparkled, dulling just a bit when he caught me staring. I looked away, pulling up another group of photos on my laptop. "What's the proposition?"

Ridge spun the bottle of Guinness between his thumb and forefinger, grinning mysteriously. "Good things come to those who wait."

"Give me a break," I teased. "I guess I should have enforced that virtue this morning."

Ridge paused, his voice quiet–thoughtful–as he said, "I'm glad you didn't."

A pang of desire flickered through my belly. I changed course. "I hear you helped Brian fund his business venture."

Ridge cocked his head. "I'm surprised he'd mention that." A shadow passed over Ridge's expression. "But, yeah, I guess I did. Brian went through some rough patches, but he got himself together. If anyone deserved a second chance, it was him."

I sipped the tea noisily as Ridge leaned over to kiss my neck. His hand reached up to the fresh bandage spread above my eye. "How is it?"

"About like you'd expect. It's starting to take on a beautiful purplish hue. Your friends at the precinct tomorrow will think you beat me."

Ridge laughed, "Good thing they know better. By the way, I called a security company. They'll be out in the next day or so to install a system in the house. I also think we should replace the locks on the doors, but I figured I'd run that by you, first."

"Sure." I agreed. It would make me feel better if there was 24/7 monitoring. But the conversation spiked a fresh wave of panic I wasn't prepared for. Or maybe it was the photograph in full resolution on my computer screen. I leaned closer.

"What is it?" Ridge slid his chair closer. A memory locked in my healing brain worked itself free.

"He said something else to me," I mumbled.

"Who?"

It felt weird to say, "my attacker," so I didn't say anything at all. Ridge stroked my hair, tugging gently at the waves of curl. His touch was electric. I reached up and removed his hand from my hair, holding it in my lap and stroking his long, capable fingers.

"He told me not to play dumb, that I was smarter than that." I paused. Suddenly certain of the image on my computer screen. "He called me Princess."

"Princess?"

I shook my head, trying to get the sound of Ridge's voice saying that name out of my head. "Please don't," I begged. "Only one person in my life has ever called me Princess."

There was a long pause, so long that I thought maybe he wouldn't ask me to explain any further. I looked over as he stood, running a palm through his hair.

"You have to tell me who, Liv. Who called you that?" Realization dawned across his face. "The guy from the bar?"

I nodded, "Jason Abbott. He wasn't just a guy I had drinks with. We were engaged in college."

Ridge stared at me. Slowly he returned to his chair. "Go on."

I gave Ridge the abbreviated version of how I'd met Jason, how we'd been virtually joined at the hip for two years, and how he'd left me shortly after we moved in together.

After I finished the synopsis I said, "But, I shot this."

The blood in my veins charged as I swiveled my laptop toward Ridge. A hum of electric current just under my skin, impossible to shake.

I pointed to what, on first glance, looked like nothing more than a shadow in the trees behind the barn. I enlarged the image as much as possible, so much so that it became grainy and unfocused in the process.

"Is that him?" Ridge asked, jaw set. I could feel the anger in him, bubbling just beneath the surface.

"I think so."

"When did you take this?" Ridge's detective instincts kicked in as he reached for the computer to get a better look. I checked the date to be sure, even though I already knew exactly when I took the shot.

"Last Friday, before I started working on the barn. I was all over the property that day, taking pictures. I took this from the front porch."

Without a word, Ridge sent the .jpg image to Adam's email account at the precinct. Within five minutes Adam was on the phone to get his instructions. I listened as Ridge spoke.

"I want to see his face." His words sent a chill down my spine. The picture was grainy, but I'd know him anywhere. It was Jason.

"Adam," Ridge lowered his voice, returning to my grandfather's study. "I need to know everything there is to know about Jason Abbott. Previous residence would be Los Angeles. See if you can get a facial recognition match to the man in the picture."

Ridge pocketed his cell phone and strode to the front window, gazing out toward the barn.

"When he asked me out for drinks, I never should have gone." I was saying the words for my benefit as much as Ridge's.

Ridge crossed the room and took a seat next to me. His fingertips, no longer pulsing with anger, traced my thigh.

"I wasn't going to go," I choked back a sob. "But I was at the stupid hotel–alone. It was suffocating. So I met him at that bar on Lane Avenue. I knew as soon as I saw him there that it was a bad idea. I told him it was over."

Ridge sighed lightly. I couldn't tell if it was out of frustration or relief. "And that's where I stepped in, right?"

I nodded. "He wanted another chance and I shot him down. You think that's why he did this?" I searched Ridge's face for confirmation of what I already knew in my core was true.

"Liv, this isn't your fault. Anything could have set him off. Do you know where he was staying?"

I shook my head quietly before he pulled me from the chair, wrapping his arms around me.

"We'll find him," Ridge promised. I pressed myself against him, bathing in the warmth and security emanating from his body.

"I won't let anyone hurt you, Liv. Never again."

35

RIDGE

The call came in the middle of the night. Ridge's body molded to Liv's sleeping frame, his skin hot where her body met his. He skimmed his hand along the sheets, his fingers climbing for the nightstand just out of reach. He gave one last lurch for the phone, peeling himself from the warmth of her form, holding his breath as she sighed lightly in sleep.

"McCaffrey," he whispered. Padding softly to the bathroom, he locked himself inside.

"It's Miller," Captain Wallace's voice was tight, angry. "He's been shot. We need you down here, McCaffrey, now."

Ridge dressed with lightning speed and was fastening his belt when he leaned toward Liv's sleeping face.

"Liv, baby. Wake up." There was that light moan again, like a siren's call. Under normal circumstances he'd climb in bed and take her right there, but nothing was normal right now.

Her eyes fluttered open, the intense green forcing him back a step. "I need you to get dressed, baby. We've got to leave."

Liv's brows pinched together. "What's going on?" Her voice sleepy, not yet understanding.

"It's Adam. He's hurt. I've got to go. I'm taking you to a hotel. You'll be safer there while I'm gone."

She sat up on the edge of the bed. He could almost see her thoughts kicking into gear. Before he knew it, she was brushing past him and into the bathroom, coming out seconds later fully dressed. He snatched a duffle bag he'd packed for her from the floor and grabbed her hand in his, leading down the stairs and into the dark of the living room below.

The cold night air sucked the breath from his lungs as he swung the front door open. The night was quiet. Still. Too still. He paused to scan the barn lot and the woods beyond. He tucked Liv into his side and ventured on, shielding her from any possible threat.

The growl of the Mustang roared into him, amplifying the flow of adrenalin through his veins. Wallace had been intentionally vague, and it pissed him off. The more he knew, the better prepared he'd be for whatever waited for him.

"Is Adam okay?" Liv asked, her hand sliding from the console onto his thigh.

"He's in surgery. I don't know any more than that." Ridge rocked his fist against the steering wheel. "He should have waited for me. What the hell was he thinking going after him alone?"

The eruption made an impact on Liv. One he never intended to make. She drew away, sidling closer to the passenger door.

"I'm sorry, Ridge. I never should have..." Liv didn't finish her thought. She didn't need to.

Ridge just shook his head, angry with himself. She'd been through enough. She didn't need him playing the blame game.

"It was Jason, wasn't it?"

Ridge veered into the Marriott parking lot as she asked. He didn't answer. He'd be damned if he'd make her feel like an accomplice to Adam's injury.

"Not sure yet," Ridge lied. "But Adam got a shot off before the perp ran."

Ridge waited for Liv to look at him, exonerate him for jerking her out of bed in the middle of the night and erupting in an angry outburst with her a prisoner in the car.

"Damn it, Adam," Ridge muttered under his breath as he strode around the Shelby to help Liv out. He tucked her just inside the door with the bellhop, keeping his eye on her while he rummaged through his trunk. He couldn't help but notice her eyes widen as he strapped the Kevlar vest around his midsection. He switched firearms, exchanging his Sig P226 for his Glock .45. He closed the trunk and shrugged into his navy-blue field jacket.

He ushered Liv from the entrance to the front desk. He'd called ahead, and they had the key ready, the eyes of the front desk clerks bulged when they saw him in his gear. He gave Liv's hand a squeeze, trying for a silent reassurance that this was no big deal. Everything would be fine. He was sure she wasn't buying it.

"When will you be back?" she asked after he'd checked every crevice of the corner room. She stood at the foot of the bed, watching as he went from space to space, checking windows, vents, and closets.

He let his eyes rake over her. Even with sleep-mussed hair and no makeup she was perfect. He held her face between his palms, careful to avoid the bruise. "As soon as I can," he answered. "Don't open that door until I come back, okay?"

She nodded.

He leaned down and kissed her, her scent calming the

storm that raged in his gut. As he pulled away, her eyes latched onto his.

"Ridge, what happens if you don't come back?"

The words stabbed into his heart as his cell buzzed from his jacket pocket.

"I'll be back," he assured. He skimmed his fingers along the length of her arm and pulled the door closed behind him. After tonight, he was determined, there'd be no more secrets. He'd get Abbott to come clean. Sowards could find another effing agent if that's what he needed to do. But he wouldn't keep lying to Liv.

36

LIV

The hotel was nice. The lobby brightly lit and cheery, even at two A.M., the exact opposite of the emotions that churned inside. The kiss we shared before he left my room was perfect. Everything about it encompassed how I felt about him. Which is why I had to ask what would happen if he didn't return. I watched from the window of the twelfth-floor room as Ridge's Shelby sped away. The cruiser that had joined him in the parking lot turned on their siren. The rise and fall of the sound cut into my eardrums while worry twisted my stomach into knots.

There weren't enough channels on the hotel cable system to keep my mind from drifting into the realm of the horribly possible. I had visions of Ridge being hurt, or worse, trying to hunt down Adam's attacker. And no matter how I tried to avoid it, I couldn't help but picture Jason in that role. It was after six when a knock sounded on my door. It was so soft I almost thought I'd imagined it, but it came again, louder this time. I threw the covers back and rushed to the door, swinging it open wide, ready to launch myself into the arms of the man I loved.

Instead, a rough gloved hand covered my mouth. I shoved against the door, trying to push him out, but he was too strong. He gripped me to his chest, his hand pressed against my lips as he twisted the deadbolt, locking us inside the room.

The familiarity of his face warred with fear. The stench of sweat and hay filled my nostrils, sucking at my breath. I fought at the hand covering my mouth and nose, but his grip was too tight. I watched the reflection of our struggle in the nearby mirror.

He was dressed in a brown Carhartt jacket and blue jeans. Mud covered hiking boots protected his feet and the knife I remembered from the other night still hung securely strapped below his left knee.

He turned me around, slamming me against the mirrored closet in the entryway. The glass splintered behind my skull, shards raining down past my shoulders to the floor below. His hand planted hard against my mouth. The oversized t-shirt I wore was no buffer from the cold circle of metal stabbing at the skin over my ribs, sending a shiver through me.

"You scream, you die."

I believed him. I had no reason to think he wouldn't hurt me. He'd proven that he would. He'd shot a police officer, for God's sake. That's when it hit me. If he was here, where was Ridge? Panic flooded my lungs, squeezing, as Jason slowly removed his hand from my mouth, keeping it close in case I decided to disobey his command.

"What are you doing here?" I fought against the vise constricting my lungs. I stared at his boots, working to keep my voice steady. To combat the panic, I made a concerted effort to breathe in slow, balanced breaths. How had he known where to find me?

"Sit on the bed." He motioned me over with the barrel of the gun. I obeyed.

"I'm here to finish what I started." His face twisted into an evil sneer. "You know too much, Princess." He stood over me, the smell of him overpowering my senses. He was filthy. Pungent days-old sweat intermingled with the decay of decades-old hay. I breathed through my mouth to avoid the stench. Only then did I notice the rag wound tightly around his upper thigh. Bloodstained and filthy, I couldn't take my eyes off it. He noticed.

"Oh, this? Your friend did this. What's his name?" He tapped his head with the steel of the barrel. "Oh, yes. Officer Miller. Adam, is it? How's he doing anyway?"

I swallowed hard as he cocked his head to the side, a slight smirk spread across dry, cracked lips. I didn't answer. This was not the same man I'd had drinks with two weeks ago.

"That good, huh?" Jason lowered himself to the bed beside me. Too close. I shifted away and he grabbed my leg, hard fingers digging into thinly veiled flesh. Goose bumps rose in protest under my leggings. I couldn't stop the squeak that escaped my lips. My hands flew to his as his fingers probed higher against my inner thigh.

"No!" I yelled through gritted teeth. "Jason, stop!"

I glanced at the door, willing Ridge to come storming through to save me, but it didn't happen. Instead, Jason lunged over me, flattening me against the mattress before laying the chrome-plated revolver on the nightstand. My body tensed against his. My eyes drifted to the gun. I could almost reach it.

Jason's chuckle distracted me. "Oh, now. We wouldn't want anyone to get shot by accident, now would we?"

He grasped the gun again, tucking it in the back of his pants.

Stupid. I scolded myself for not being more discreet.

He eyed me as he unsheathed the hunting knife from his leg. Jason's arms and legs on either side of my body pinned me down. I pushed against the muscles in his chest, my fists beating against him as the knife grazed my temple. The pointed tip of the blade tugged at my sutures, sending a stab of pain into my skull.

"I'm sorry I had to do that to you," he said, almost an apology.

The razor sharp edge traced the curve of my neck as he pushed my shirt upward. He leaned back, studying newly exposed flesh.

"Hmm...you really haven't changed, have you? Still my sexy little princess." He lunged forward, breath hot against my face. "Still afraid of knives?"

He raised the knife and stabbed it toward my head, narrowly missing my ear as it tore through the fitted sheet, slicing into the pillow top mattress.

I clenched my eyes closed, fighting to contain a reactionary scream. Giving him the moment he needed, he snatched my hands off his chest and held them tight against the headboard.

"You were always game for a little bondage, right Princess?"

I opened my eyes. His hazel irises glared back at me. They were wild, dark, and desperate. The pupils constricted beyond what they should have been, especially in the low light of the hotel room.

"Please don't do this," I hissed through clenched teeth. "Think about what you're doing, Jason."

"Oh, now, Princess. We gave you a chance to avoid this. You're the one making this happen, not me." He leaned down, the open zipper of his jacket cold against oversensitive flesh. "You should have said yes at Flanagan's, Liv."

His breath hit my ear, hot and heavy, singeing my flesh. I jerked my head to the side. Fighting the realization of what was coming. I squinted my eyes and kicked. But he was too strong, too methodical. Nothing panicked him. It was as if he had all the time in the world. Another wave of terror ricocheted through me. *Ridge.*

I squeezed my eyes shut, holding onto an image of Ridge, anything to distance myself from the situation. The screech of duct tape being unwound from its roll brought me back to reality. It tightened across my lips first, then around my wrists and, finally, my ankles.

My breath came in short huffs now, my head buzzing from oxygen deprivation. I fought to slow my breathing. But each of Jason's movements ignited a fresh wave of panic.

I heard his zipper, felt the tug of my yoga pants. His fingers looped around the fabric at my waist. He leaned against me, growing hard, the thin layer of Lycra the only barrier between us. I shook my head, throaty whimpers of protest my only defense. I struggled away from him, but the knife poised under my jawbone grew sharper, more insistent.

The zipper of his jeans scuffed the soft skin on my thighs, chafing with each grind. I held my breath and closed my eyes, praying to any deity who would listen to just let me survive.

He shifted position—forced my leggings out of the way. I braced against the expected attack. One moment stretched into two. Motion ceased. In place of anticipated pain and violent thrust, I felt my leggings being tugged back into place. Heard the ragged sounds of his breath.

The cold steel of the knife continued to bite against my throat. I opened my eyes slowly, afraid of what I'd see. My heart thumped wildly in my chest as I forced my eyes toward my attacker. His free hand covered his face as he straddled me, pants unzipped. He shook his head slowly from side to side. The first tear dripped from his lowered head onto my stomach, its heat scorching hypersensitive flesh.

"That son of a bitch can't make me do this. Not this." His ragged breaths turned to sobs.

He left me bound as he went to the bathroom and washed up. I watched from the bed as he splashed water on his face and stared at his reflection. His lips moved in a silent monologue. He noticed me watching and kicked the door closed. He was there less than a minute or two before returning to the bed. I lay still, working to slow my racing heart and make sense of what was happening.

He pulled the gun from his jeans and pointed it at my head as he bent to slice through the tape securing my legs.

"Keep your mouth shut," he insisted.

I nodded my head in answer, the reduced adrenalin in my system finally allowing a full breath to deliver oxygen to my carbon dioxide riddled brain. He ripped the tape from around my ankles, leaving raw red rectangles.

Next, he yanked the strip from my lips, the sensation spiraling into a wave of pain as tender flesh began to sting and throb. I tasted blood, my tongue instinctively working to provide relief.

Covering my bare midsection with the comforter was his last act before heading toward the door, leaving my wrists bound together.

"I have the letters," he said casually, as if the past ten minutes had been a figment of my imagination. He paused. "I need to know how much you've put together." He stared at my face, his eyes softening before reaching over to wipe an escaped tear. I wiggled away before his fingers could make contact.

I sat against the headboard, my knees drawn up to my chin, wrists bound. The coverlet wound around me, a buffer of protection. Jason sat on the edge of the bed like an old friend as he asked again, "What do you know, Liv?"

"Nothing, Jason. I know I'm adopted. That the girl in the trunk was Jennifer Tipton. That's all I know."

"What about the name on the other picture?" Jason asked.

I'd read it, like the others, had it memorized. "Ashlyn Callaghan?"

"Who is she?"

I shrugged. I didn't know.

"What about your cop boyfriend?"

"He doesn't know any more than I do. Please, Jason... why are you doing this?"

Jason shook his head. The glisten of tears returned to his eyes. "It wasn't supposed to happen this way, Princess. It was never supposed to go this far, but you just couldn't play along, could you? This should have ended at Flanagan's."

"What are you talking about?" I asked as he rose from the mattress and strode to the door, pulling the handle to exit. My ears picked up a faraway siren. The rise and fall came closer.

"I just couldn't do it, Liv. I tried. I really did love you, you know? But then..." He pointed the gun directly at my head and released the safety. I held my breath as he took aim. Just as his finger tensed on the trigger, he lowered the weapon, adding helplessly, "He'll have to clean up his own mess."

He stared at me one final moment before limping toward the door, launching into a crippled run down the hallway.

37

LIV

Shana Collins was the next person I saw. The last time I'd seen her was at the precinct when she'd interrupted Ridge and me. Her chocolate eyes had sparkled then. Now they were flooded with empathy as she glanced into the room, spotted me huddled on the bed.

The hotel manager had let her in. I'd heard them in the hall, Shana encouraging him to unlock the door. He trailed close behind until Shana got a better look. I sat in the center of the bed, surrounded by sheets bloodied slightly by Jason's leg wound, the coverlet still wound around me. She turned on her heel, ushering the manager outside and sealing us in the room–alone.

Before I could stem the flow of tears enough to say anything, she was on her radio.

"I have a signal 31, sexual assault, at 357 Latham Avenue, Room 1214." Shana was calm as she spoke into the radio.

I wiped repeatedly at my eyes in a futile attempt to clear my vision. I swung my legs to the side of the bed. The muscles twitched, felt overused, and I wobbled as I attempted to stand.

"Oh, honey." That was all she said. And although we were nearly strangers, her voice comforted me.

Blubbering like an idiot as another wave of tears cut loose, I blurted out, "It's not what you think, Shana."

"Collins, where is she?" Ridge's voice permeated the mumble of activity in the hallway.

"Ridge is okay." The breath of relief gave way to a shudder of dread. Every muscle inside me tensed. He couldn't see me like this. But I wanted his arms around me. Needed to hear him tell me everything was okay. The conflicting emotions were too much to take.

Shana studied me for a beat before rushing into the hallway, her boot propping the door open just a crack so she could get back in.

"Ridge, you can't go in there. Not yet."

"Let me through, Shana." He tried shouting around her through the door, "Liv!" But Shana blocked his attempt.

I watched a sliver of Ridge through the crack in the doorway as he grasped the lapels of Shana's jacket.

"Jesus Christ, Shana, please just tell me she's okay." Panic broke his voice.

"Shana, it's okay, please." I choked back the tears and hollered meekly toward the partially closed door. I couldn't watch Ridge in agony any longer. I lunged for the door to let him in, tripping on the coverlet and landing hard on my knees.

"Liv..." He released Shana and swung the door open wide in one lithe movement. Wrapping his arms around me, he picked me up off the floor and carried me to an empty chair in the corner of the room. Shana stayed outside, leaving the two of us alone.

His eyes scanned me from head to toe, panicked and desperate. "Jason?"

I nodded and tried to explain. "It's not what you think."

Ridge studied me, taking in my bloodied lips and still-bound wrists. The patches of red at my ankles were his next target. He pulled a small knife from his pocket and I winced. He slowed, carefully slicing through the leftover silver tape. His eyes darkened. Panic turned to anger.

"Did he touch you?"

All I could do was shake my head, tears choking my throat. It wasn't as bad as it could have been. I heard the involuntary bubble of relief in Ridge's throat as he exhaled into my hair and clutched me to his chest, safe and protected.

At that moment two officers I'd never met invaded the room. I watched Ridge shift from concerned boyfriend to cop, intercepting them before they got to me. Ridge explained the situation and once I'd answered a few questions to their satisfaction, they left.

I refused a trip to the ER, and Shana ended up taking my official statement. I was thankful she was the one asking the cold, clinical questions and not Ridge. I kept telling myself that no real damage had been done. But the fact remained that I'd allowed it to happen.

I watched Ridge pace the hallway just out of earshot and was relieved when Shana put her notebook away. Speaking had become laborious. The parts of my body that had been taped were swathed in crimson, and my lips were no exception.

It was around 10:00 A.M. before we checked out of the hotel. Ridge drove us back to the farm. My ears ached from the silence. I was glad not to have to talk, but at the same time I needed desperately to know what was going through Ridge's head.

I needed him to tell me that this wouldn't change things for us. Give me a reason to shut up the inner critic buzzing through my skull. Ridge had reasons to be angry with me. I opened the door without checking to see who it was. I let Jason leave without trying to get anyone to stop him. I feared Ridge's silence marked the end of the relationship we'd started to build.

"How's Adam?" I needed to break the silence.

"Fine–good. They'll probably discharge him within the next couple of days. Jason caught him in the shoulder, but he's out of surgery. Captain says he's doing really well."

"Good." I willed Ridge to look at me. Without making eye contact, he slid his hand over to my knee.

"Are you sure you're okay?" His voice softened.

"I'll be fine, Ridge." I couldn't get Jason's voice out of my head, confessing his love for me. Every time I closed my eyes, I saw his wild desperate eyes scouring me hungrily. I didn't understand what motivation he could have had for the attack or who would have put him up to it. Confusion and hurt clouded my brain.

Ridge's gentle fingers gave my thigh a reassuring squeeze, causing Jason's angry groping to flash through my brain. I pulled away as a shiver shimmied down my spine.

"I'm sorry," escaped my lips as he glanced over before returning his hand to the steering wheel.

"I told myself I didn't want to listen, when you were giving Shana your statement. But I was wrong. I need to know what he did to you." Ridge's voice was quiet, hesitant, laced with barely controlled anger.

I grasped his hand in mine, trying to siphon some warmth and security from him. Instead, all I got was frustration.

"He forced me onto the bed, grabbed my leg."

I watched Ridge's profile as he nodded slowly. The half-honesty of my statement nagged at me. *Full disclosure.* My inner voice finally said something reasonable for once.

"He..." Ridge's jaw tensed as I began. "He started to." I admitted. "He pushed my pants down." I wasn't sure I could go on. The tick of anger in Ridge's jaw scared me. But he was bound to find out the details eventually. All he had to do was ask Shana or read her report. It would be better if it came from me. "He stopped, Ridge. He didn't go through with it. He didn't hurt me."

If white lies are what we tell to protect the ones we love, then I'd just told the little white lie of the century.

Ridge drove silently for a few moments. "Okay." His voice was barely a whisper, his eyes focused on the road ahead.

38

RIDGE

"You owe me an explanation," Ridge demanded, staring through the windshield of Sowards' car, rivulets of rain obscuring his view of the trees beyond. "Who's Jason Abbott, and what does he want with Liv?"

"Liv?" Marcus Sowards cocked an eyebrow at Ridge. "Maybe you should be asking why *Liv* was involved with Abbott in the first place."

Ridge ignored Sowards' sarcastic drawl of Liv's name. He was treading in dangerous territory. He didn't need Sowards to remind him.

"She knows more than you think she does," his superior said. "The Bureau is sure of it. We just don't know to what extent."

"What about Abbott?"

"He's been on the radar for a while now. That's actually how we tracked her down. Seems it's hard to snuff out an old flame. I never thought he'd end up trying something like this."

"So, he's not the threat the Bureau is worried about?"

Sowards shook his head. "Until now, he's been harmless."

Ridge examined his hands. "Not sure I'd classify two attacks in the span of less than three days, harmless."

Sowards sighed and shifted in his seat.

"I'm sorry. You know if we'd thought he was a threat we would have taken care of it. In the meantime, I'll have the boys in the office scrounge up anything we can find on Abbott."

Ridge nodded. "What about Liv?"

Sowards shifted in his seat to face Ridge. A concerned crease appeared between his steely grey eyes. "Meaning?"

Ridge had to ask. It was why he was here. "Is she harmless?"

"That's the part we don't yet know. You said she'd never known about the adoption, right?" He waited for Ridge's nod. "She has reasons to lie, though."

This is where it was starting to get fuzzy for Ridge. He'd lost objectivity. Sowards should have removed him from the case when he'd asked. For the life of him, Ridge couldn't see why Liv would lie. "Care to enlighten me?"

"She's not going to want any of this out. She wants to protect her family's name, the Sullivan legacy."

That part, Ridge could understand.

"She's been physically attacked twice, Sowards. I'm supposed to be protecting her and I'm doing a damn poor job. Problem is, I have no idea what I'm protecting her from."

"Did you read the letters?"

Ridge nodded, the stack of correspondence that Liv had refused to touch made for good reading. Real daytime drama fodder. Stephen Sullivan's affairs, first with Jennifer Tipton and later with Liv's birthmother, Aimee Callaghan, were on full display. At the bottom of the stack was a newspaper clipping from *The Irish Times*, reporting Ashlyn and Aimee Callaghan's death in Ireland. Of course, all of it ended with

Stephen Sullivan's suicide less than a month after receipt of the clipping.

"Abbott took copies from the precinct the night he shot Miller. But we'd already entered them into evidence."

"Then you know how damaging that information could be to the Sullivan legacy."

Ridge looked back down at his hands. "I'm not the right person for this assignment, Marcus."

"Yes, you've mentioned that. But it seems to me you're exactly the person we need. She trusts you. We don't have time to send someone else in and try to start over. Not after all that's happened. Use that trust, Ridge. Find out what she's hiding."

"How do you know she's hiding anything?"

Sowards narrowed his eyes. "Grace Sullivan knew her way around a cover up. Those letters prove she kept the ruse going even after Stephen Sullivan's mistress threatened to go public. For God's sake, Ridge, she paid her off. Keeping everything, even the existence of Olivia's own twin sister, tied up in a neat little package three thousand miles across the Atlantic where no one could find them. You said yourself Olivia has been there with her grandmother. Do you really think all of this will be news to her?"

Ridge wanted it to be. He needed Liv to be innocent. But if she was psychic, then how could she not know? Evidence was piling up faster than he could make half-assed excuses. The fact that she wouldn't go to the hospital after the encounter with Jason was a huge red flag. How did he know she was there? Was she covering up for him? The questions filed through Ridge's brain like soldiers, each one shooting a round through his heart that he couldn't take.

"You said she's in danger. That someone's tracking her. We already know about Abbott. If it's not him, then who else is there?"

Rain tapped on the metal roof, punctuating the silence. "That's classified, Ridge."

Ridge clenched his fist, bit back the temptation to rock the dash with a well-placed right hook.

"How can I protect her if I don't know what the threat is?" He spoke the words carefully. Spitting each one at his supervisor. "And if I'm going to do this right, I need to know more about her record. She spent six months in a psych facility. Did you know that?"

Sowards nodded, his thumbs tapping the steering wheel. "It's not pertinent to this case, McCaffrey."

"Bullshit," Ridge spat back. "Everything's pertinent, Marcus. I'm the one in the trenches, let me decide what is and isn't important from now on. Right?"

"It's not my decision, Ridge. But I'll see what I can do. For now, secure the property. Tell her what you know. Show her the letters. You've built the foundation. She told you about the visions, now find out what she plans to do with them."

39

LIV

Iwoke in the dream disoriented and confused. A woman screamed, the sound reverberating in the tight space around her. I fought to figure out where she was. She struggled with a chromed door handle before I knew. A car. The windows darkened.

An eerie green glow pulsed around them before blackness enveloped the vehicle. I heard the slosh and gurgle as air escaped the car's interior. Water. The screams of the woman became dull, useless. She pounded her fists against the unyielding glass of the driver's side window. Her strawberry blonde hair flowed up around her head, and the bubbles cascading from her mouth and nose began to slow. Her emerald eyes fixed on me. Palms pressed helplessly on the glass before the dream dissipated, giving way to the soft neutral hues of my freshly painted bedroom.

I coughed. Lurching forward I gasped air into aching lungs, a remnant of visions I'd yet to discover how to shake. I couldn't place her face, but something about her eyes was familiar. *As green as the hills of Éire.* The echo of my grandmother's voice broke into my thoughts before the Tylenol PM kicked in and pulled me back into slumber.

IT WAS ALMOST noon two days after the attack before Ridge re-opened the subject. I was sitting with him on the couch in the living room, listening as the ADT technicians skirted the house like ants, drilling and poking wires into various corners of the farmhouse.

We hadn't had a decent conversation since the Marriott. He'd spent yesterday at the police station, and it was obvious something was eating him up inside.

"What do you think Jason wants from you?" he asked.

"I'm not sure. I think the first time he wanted the box, or whatever was inside. The letters I guess, but he has those now."

"Why didn't you want to read the letters?"

Ridge's question surprised me.

"I just found out I'm not my parents' biological child and probably have a twin sister. I guess I needed a moment before I tried to process any other big news." I tried to keep the note of indignance out of my voice, but I was sure he could hear it. There was no way I was going to mention the fact that the ribbon around the letters matched a ghostly little girl's pigtails. Even a psychic can only take so much. I changed the subject.

"As far as Jason is concerned, someone is putting him up to these things. He's not doing this by himself."

"How do you know that?" Suspicion. Clear as day. I pulled out from under Ridge's arm, sat up straight.

"Before Jason left the hotel he said, '*he* would have to clean up his own mess'."

"You mean someone wanted him to assault you?"

I shrugged, ignoring the note of distrust.

Ridge's eyes found mine, searching–no, hunting–for truth. I didn't know how else to convince him that I'd told him all there was to tell.

"We should go, we're supposed to pick Adam up at one." I swallowed against the burn of skepticism and rose from the couch, happy to step away from the moment.

Adam sat up in the hospital bed, his sandy hair disheveled and two days of beard growth obscuring his face. He was pushing rather soggy looking mashed potatoes around on a hospital food tray with a rather disgusted look on his face. The expression disappeared the minute he noticed Ridge and I enter the room.

"Ridge! Liv! God, it's so good to see you guys!"

"Likewise," I replied, trying hard to hide the incredible guilt I felt over his hospitalization. "How are you feeling?"

I eyed the sling that supported his left arm, the shoulder bandaged tightly.

"Oh, I'm good. They tell me I get to blow this joint today. I can't wait to get back to some decent food!"

Although I didn't know much about Adam Miller, one thing I had picked up on was his fondness for food. Luckily for his sake, he was built like a beanpole and could probably eat whatever he wanted and not see a single ill effect.

"I've got some French toast with your name on it, Adam," Ridge said. "Liv and I are here to take you home."

"All right!" Adam gestured a little too forcefully with his forkful of potatoes, wincing before carefully placing the utensil back on his plate.

"Take it easy there, champ," Ridge teased as he moved the tray out of the way. "Let's get you ready to get out of here."

I waited in the hall while Ridge helped Adam change and get his stuff together to leave. The nurse finally brought the signed discharge papers and the three of us hightailed it to Adam's house.

Adam lived in one of the few apartment buildings in the city of Cascade Hills. It was a newer place, built to accommodate the throngs of suburbanites desperate to get away from the city. As a confirmed bachelor, Adam loved the lifestyle. He got to enjoy the amenities available to the residents of the complex, like a gym and swimming pool, without ever venturing much farther than his front door.

I had to hand it to Adam, he kept his place neat as a pin. I think he was the first proud single man that I knew who made sure to make his bed and wash the dishes before going to work each day. This was a new side of Adam, and I was impressed.

"How do you like it, Liv? Are you ready to trade in that drafty old farmhouse for the apartment life, yet?" he chuckled.

"I think I'll leave the cramped two-bedroom existence to you, Adam." I said, hesitating before saying the words I had to get off my chest, "I'm so sorry about what happened. I never meant for you to get hurt."

Adam's jaw tensed as he sat carefully on the sofa. "Liv, that was not your fault. We had no idea that maniac would make a play at the station." He reached out for my hand, eyes roaming over the still red swath around my wrist before I pulled away, embarrassment heating my face.

"Besides, I'm just glad it was me and not you."

I could tell by his eyes he was being sincere. I was suddenly floored by the caliber of Ridge's friends. Each one of them had special qualities that made them completely endearing and utterly unforgettable. I thought about Cee, wondering why I seemed to be incapable of forming friendships, as an emptiness settled in the pit of my stomach.

"You still want that French toast?" Ridge's question interrupted my thoughts.

"You bet! You can't promise me something like that and then renege. You heard him offer. Right, Liv? No weaseling your way out of this one, McCaffrey!"

The three of us laughed and talked throughout the French toast and well into the evening. The conversation was winding down when Adam turned serious, "Did they catch the bastard, yet?"

"Not yet," Ridge answered, glancing at me and taking my hand. I let myself enjoy the warm pulses of affection that hummed through my fingers. I hadn't realized how much I'd missed his touch.

"He found Liv later that morning."

"What are you talking about?" Adam asked, looking me up and down.

"I left Liv at the Marriott to help Shana run down your perp. He assaulted her in the room at the Marriott."

Adam scoured me with a dark look. "That explains the wrists. Lips, too?" I'd tried to cover the tracks of red with makeup, but Adam was too observant to be fooled. His voice dripped with contempt. "What did he do?"

"Just shook her up a bit," Ridge answered vaguely. "He said some interesting things, though. There's got to be more to all this. We think someone else is behind him. Jason's the puppet."

We, it was the first time Ridge had gone back to the solidarity of "We," since the attack.

"That's something I wanted to tell you. I checked up on your Jason Abbott. He's had a couple DUI's out in L.A. since you two parted ways, a rather interesting set of employment skills, but nothing too crazy that I can find."

Ridge scanned me before asking, "So he's a bit of a drinker?"

"He likes his Corona," I offered. "I think he might've been on something the other night."

"Why do you say that?" Adam asked.

"His eyes, they were different, wild, I guess."

Adam and Ridge exchanged looks.

"I talked on the phone with the consulting firm he worked for out in L.A. He was fired about eighteen months ago. Seems our boy has quite a bit of technical knowledge. Might be time to dump your phone, Liv."

"What do you mean?"

"Did you tell anyone you were going to be at the Marriott?" Adam asked.

"Who would I tell?" I watched as Adam and Ridge traded glances again.

"Adam thinks maybe he's got a tracker on your phone. It would explain how he knew to go there to look for you."

I sat looking out at the trees beginning to show the faintest signs of spring blossoms as we rode home in the Shelby. I'd missed the change of seasons. The perpetual sunshine of Los Angeles was nice, but the renewal of the seasons somehow seemed more natural, a time for rebirth, to start fresh. Which was exactly what I needed.

40

RIDGE

Ridge stopped at his place on his way home from work the following day. He grabbed another stash of clothes before heading back to the farm. In spite of the skepticism that started brewing in his gut the night of the attack at the Marriott, Ridge couldn't deny his feelings for Liv. He tried to tell himself that it wasn't love, infatuation, maybe. But something inside refuted that argument. On the surface, he told himself he was staying with her out of obligation to the operation. But underneath it all, he knew it was more than that. Regardless, with Jason still on the loose, spending nights at the farm had become his new norm.

He saw Liv as he pulled to a stop in the barn lot.

The new high-tech security system gave him comfort when he was away, and he could see Liv's own trepidation slowly lifting. Now, she was outside, aiming her Nikon toward a small grove of peach trees, just beginning to bud out.

Ridge approached silently, staying out of her way when she paused to snap a photo. A sliver of heat wound its way through him. The desire to push her against the tree, make her forget about Jason hovering over top of her, seized him. It was the first time since the attack he'd had the impulse.

"This is really a great place, Liv." He piped up as she checked the camera display. "I'm glad you're staying."

She met his gaze, surprise in her eyes. His reservations had been obvious, after all.

"So am I. No matter what's happened the past few weeks, I've got too many good memories to let it be auctioned off to the highest bidder."

Ridge looked off into the distance. The sun was setting just beyond the trees on the other side of Cascade Lake, sending hues of oranges, reds, and pinks across the silvery surface of the water. He stepped close, pulling her in, turning her to take in the sunset in silence.

"What's your favorite memory?" His breath skimmed the top of her ear. "You said you had a lot of good memories of this place. Which one is your favorite?"

She paused. "Fourth of July."

When she turned, her eyes were soft, welcoming.

"They used to set off fireworks just past that tree line." She pointed toward the sunset. "It seemed like the whole town came. Everyone would sit in boats or on the pier and watch the fireworks. I have pictures somewhere." Ridge felt her sigh against him. "Mom even used to come, but I don't remember that. I only remember Dad and Grandma and Grandpa. We'd have a picnic and then all the kids would play until the fireworks started." Another thoughtful pause. "I can't remember when they stopped doing that. Sometime when I was in middle school, I think."

Ridge tangled his fingers in hers as she resituated, leaning against the nearest tree as the sun sunk lower.

"What about you? Do you have a favorite childhood memory?"

Ridge turned toward her, using his hands to tame Liv's wind-blown curls. "It's not my childhood, but...this is it," he said, meaning it. "This is my favorite memory."

He pulled Liv to him, gently tasting her still tender lips. He soothed the coppery remnants of her encounter with his hungry mouth. Her hands slid up his biceps and around his back, her fingers teased the nape of his neck before sliding south and coming to rest at his waist.

He grasped the hem of Liv's blouse and pulled it free of her waistband. She closed her eyes and sucked in a breath as his hands explored her soft skin, her breasts, supple beneath his fingers, molded against the palm of his hand. She sighed, bedroom eyes skimming to meet his, and he no longer cared about the Bureau's operation, their insecurity in her loyalty. No longer wondered why she'd opened the door to Jason. He only wanted her, to feel her, be with her, love her.

A loud vibration from Ridge's jacket pocket interrupted the moment. He tried to ignore the disappointment in her eyes as he reached to retrieve his cell. She pulled herself free, a tickle of disappointment playing on her lips as he answered the call.

He listened to Wallace's words, "We found him, I need you in the field."

"I'll be right there." He pocketed his phone and reached for Liv's hand.

"I've got to go," he said, waiting for her response.

"I know," she said, silently taking his hand. They walked back to the house. Ridge still didn't like the thought of Liv in the big house alone, but the security system was done, new outdoor lighting installed, she was as protected there as she was anywhere else.

"Call me. If you hear anything, or if something just doesn't feel right. Call, okay?"

"I will," she promised, glancing at the phone she'd left on

the end table. If Adam was right, this device meant to provide comfort and security was now nothing more than a homing device for an unpredictable maniac.

"We'll go first thing in the morning and get you a new phone. I'll be home as soon as I can."

"Home?" He caught the glint of playfulness in her eyes and couldn't resist calling her bluff.

He grabbed Liv around the waist, pulling her tight against him. A shot of adrenaline sparked through his veins as he kissed her. Her tongue sweet and salty against his own. Ridge trailed his lips down the curve of her neck. Pulling away to look into Liv's eyes. All teasing aside.

"Anywhere you are is home, Liv."

Ridge pulled the door closed behind him, allowing one more surge of attraction to wash over him before he headed for the Shelby. The promise of retaliation replacing unsatisfied desire.

41

LIV

I woke on the living room couch alone, sunlight streaming through the windows. The grandfather clock in the entryway ticked, chiming the nine o'clock hour, and ushering in the realization that Ridge had never returned.

Fear crept like ants along my arms and legs as I called his cell, only to hear his recorded voice. I would have driven to the station house myself if I'd had access to transportation, but since Ridge had convinced me to return the rental on our way to pick up Adam, I was stranded. I made a mental note to buy myself a car as soon as I figured out why Ridge wasn't back.

I tried Brian first. He hadn't heard from Ridge but said he'd keep his eyes and ears open and let me know if he heard anything. Adam was next on my list. He wasn't due to go back to work for at least another week, and then he'd be on desk duty, but I knew he had a scanner and could at least tell me where Ridge had been dispatched. He answered on the third ring, sounding tired, "Hello?"

"Adam? It's Liv. Ridge got called in last night and I haven't heard…"

"Liv," Adam cut me off. "Everything's okay. I'm here at the station. Ridge brought Jason in just about an hour ago."

"Ridge is okay?"

"He's a little scuffed up, but otherwise fine. They're going to want to talk to you again after they finish the preliminary interrogation. Can you come down?"

"I don't have a car, Adam. You're sure Ridge is okay?" It was all I cared about.

"I'll send a car for you. We'll see you soon."

I hung up and flicked nearly every light switch in the house to the on position, before locking the front door. The last thing I wanted was to return to a dark, empty house. I paced the porch, waiting for the cruiser to pick me up. It seemed like an eternity before Shana arrived in a shiny black sedan.

"They found him?" I asked sliding into the passenger seat.

"Yes, they did, honey. You won't need to worry about him anymore." Shana smiled a comforting grin and patted my hand as we sped toward the city.

Shana led me to the farthest of the three offices at the back of the building and told me to have a seat. She brought me a Styrofoam cup of coffee a few minutes later and I pushed it away, remembering the insipidness of the first cup I'd tried several weeks ago. Had it really only been a few weeks? It seemed like so much longer. I took in the sparse walls surrounding me. The top of the faux wood desk was empty, making the already unwelcoming room even colder and more uninviting.

The commotion from outside caught my attention and I craned my neck to see what the noise was about. Across the expanse of workstations, I noticed movement in one of the interrogation rooms. I stood and went to the office window for a better look. Gooseflesh rose on my arms and legs as I watched the scene.

Jason sat at a table similar to the one in the office I was in. His hands were cuffed and resting on top of the table. His eyes were averted as an officer stood over him, shouting the question that had been torturing me. I recognized the timbre of the voice, even though I'd never heard him use it so angrily.

"You're not doing yourself any favors by protecting him. Who is putting you up to this?"

Ridge's hand came down loudly on the table beside Jason who gave a reflexive jump in time with my own. Jason's response was too soft to hear, but whatever he said silenced Ridge, sending him back a step to sit in the chair across from Jason. I watched helplessly as Ridge studied his prisoner, listening intently to every word that he uttered.

At that point, a man with a sport coat knocked on what I assumed was a one-way mirror. At least, I hoped it was. I didn't want Jason to be able to see me watching, even from the safety of the glass office.

Ridge gave a nod and excused himself from the tiny interrogation room. The man in the sport coat was older than Ridge, shorter and balding. He spoke to Ridge in hushed tones before gesturing toward Ridge's temple. I noticed a thin stream of blood oozing from just above his eye. My chest ached with the urge to go take care of him.

Ridge's arm shrugged off the man's obvious concern, but when he took Ridge by the shoulder and led him to a doorway, Ridge reluctantly obeyed. Once the balding man had successfully delivered Ridge through the door, he turned his attention to the office I was in, walking confidently in my direction and producing a tiny smile when he noticed me watching through the glass.

"You must be Olivia Sullivan," he said with a firm but gentle voice. He entered the office and clicked the door closed behind him, his arm extended for a handshake. "I'm Captain Frank Wallace."

"It's nice to meet you." I took his hand. A barely perceptible buzz filtered through my fingers.

"Please, have a seat." He gestured toward the uncomfortable wooden chair as he sat in the tall leather one behind the desk.

"Olivia, I'd like to ask you a few questions if you don't mind."

"No, of course not. Please, call me Liv."

He smiled, confirming my request. "Liv, can you tell me how you met Jason Abbott?"

I relayed the story with as much detail as possible, trying to think of anything that might help the police discover who was putting Jason up to the break-ins and attacks. I finished by adding, "I don't think Jason is really a horrible person. Someone is making him do these things, Captain Wallace."

The Captain averted his gaze as he nodded, asking, "Do you have any idea who it could be?"

"No. I can't think of anyone that would hate me that much." I shivered with the thought of what might have happened at the Marriott if Jason had followed through on his assignment.

"Tell me about your relationship with your grandmother, Liv."

"My grandmother?" What did she have to do with any of this?

"It was great," I admitted. "My mom and I never really developed that mother daughter bond, you know? So, my grandmother kind of filled that role, I guess."

"Hmm..." He nodded thoughtfully before continuing. "Did you come to visit her very often?"

A pang of guilt hit me from the pit of my stomach. "Not as often as I should have."

"What can you tell me about her medical condition, Liv?"

"She had some kind of episode with her heart not long after my dad died. The doctors attributed it to stress. My grandmother was always a very active person. It was hard to watch her decline so quickly. I helped her move to the nursing home a few years ago."

"That must have been very difficult for you." Captain Wallace looked down at a file in front of him. "Give me a moment, will you?"

The captain excused himself and went out to speak with Ridge, who had returned from the doorway with a small bandage above his left eye. Captain Wallace came back just a few moments later with a new line of questioning.

"Liv, do you take any prescription medication on a daily basis?"

"No." I didn't know where he was going with this.

"Were you prescribed any pain killers after the break in at the farm house?"

"Yes, Vicodin, I think. I didn't take very many of them. They made me feel a little loopy." I struggled to keep an impudent nervous giggle at bay.

"Yes, Vicodin has that effect on some people. Do you recognize the pills in these pictures?"

Captain Wallace slid two pictures out of the file and over to me. The pills in the photographs were in small plastic Ziploc baggies. There were three bags, each with about ten small, pink, perfectly round pills. On one side of the tablet was printed the number 20 and on the other were the letters OC.

"No." Fear was beginning to creep back up my spine.

"We found these in your overnight bag, in the room at the

Marriott. Can you tell me why these would be in your possession?"

Before I could answer, I noticed the captain looking past me through the glass before he excused himself again, leaving me to banter with my thoughts. When I turned around, I noticed that Ridge had returned to the cell with Jason and was seated across from him. His arms were crossed across his chest and he was listening intently as Jason spoke.

Captain Wallace walked over and stood next to Adam, who was watching the discussion through the one-way mirror. The two men exchanged some words. Adam glanced quickly over his shoulder toward me before Captain Wallace began his walk back across the room.

When he came back into the office several minutes later, the only words I could utter were, "What did Jason tell you?"

42

RIDGE

Ridge wanted to punch the wise-ass smirk right off Jason Abbott's face. But everything in here was filmed, and he'd already roughed the guy up enough at the Motel 6.

"This whole thing was her idea," Abbott claimed. "I can prove it."

"I'm listening," Ridge said, sitting across from Abbott in the interrogation room.

"I ran into Liv a couple months back. She was coming out of the Starbucks in Von's near 3rd and Vermont. I'd run in for a couple groceries and there she was, like a blast from the past, you know?"

Ridge scribbled in his notebook. "And..."

"We just chatted at first. I asked her if she'd want to grab dinner and she agreed. So we started seeing each other, just casually, you know?

He was getting tired of the scum saying, "You know?" like they were friends or something. Besides the fact that he couldn't imagine any relationship with Liv being anything less than all-consuming.

"Let's just pretend I don't know, from here on out. Tell me what happened." Ridge clicked his pen, waiting for the next revelation.

"She gave me this sob story, about how she was having trouble making ends meet. She was working for a psychic hotline." Jason's eyes darted around the room, landing on Ridge. "She said her mom was going to axe her out of Grace's will. She wanted to make sure Beth didn't get the chance."

"What are you implying?" Ridge forced the words through the clench in his jaw.

"Liv killed her grandmother. I never thought she'd go through with it. But she had it all planned out, laced Grace's heart medication with Oxycontin. The doctors had been treating Grace for some kind of arrhythmia ever since Mr. Sullivan died. Over time, I suppose the oxy had the opposite effect. You'd have to ask her about the details, but over time the oxy won out."

Ridge licked his lips, processing Abbott's claim.

"She didn't come back to Cascade Hills until after Grace's death."

Jason paused, tracing an invisible line on the tabletop with his index finger. "She made it worth my while."

"So you're admitting to being an accomplice in Liv's plan to murder her grandmother?"

Jason nodded. Ridge tapped his pen on the slick surface. The night he'd met Liv flashed through his brain. The slam of the back door, the woman standing in darkness. Fury heated his veins. Had he been set up from the beginning? He forced away the heat of betrayal.

"Liv didn't need to kill Grace. She was already sole inheritor of the estate."

"Yeah, but Liv didn't know that at the time. That's where Jennifer Tipton came into the picture."

Ridge leaned back in his chair, listened as Abbott confessed to digging up the girl's corpse, on Liv's direction, of course. She was the one who'd told him where it was, how to get it into the farmhouse, where to put it and what to write on the top.

"She's not who you think she is." Ridge repeated the words scrawled across the antique trunk, rising to pace the tiny room. "Why those words?"

"She wanted it to look like someone was after her." Abbott cocked his head. His hazel eyes bored into Ridge as he leaned across the table. "It worked, didn't it?"

A spike of hate drove through Ridge's core. He could kill Abbott. Here. Now. The weight of the gun on his hip taunted him. But his bare hands would provide more satisfaction. Ridge ran a hand through his hair, refocused.

"Why was the Tipton girl's body in the woods? She tell you that?"

Jason shrugged. "I never asked." He paused, the air thickening between them. "I get it, though. Liv's something. Roped me into this, didn't she? It's not much of a stretch to believe she fucked her way under a cop's skin, too."

Ridge launched across the table, his left hand closing around the collar of Abbott's shirt. "You're out of line," he seethed.

Thump-thump-thump, a knock on the glass signaled relief.

"You need a break," Wallace said, slipping inside the interrogation room. It was an order, not a question. Ridge unhanded Abbott. The fingers of his dominant hand still clenched in a ready fist.

"You alright?" Ridge shrugged away Adam's grip on his shoulder. Holding his palms up in defense before stalking off down the hall. He felt her eyes on him before he saw her standing on the other side of the office glass. He met her stare.

Eyes wide, with what? He wondered. Fear, but of being caught, or of Abbott's lies? He couldn't tell. She placed her palm against the glass and an IV drip of hurt trickled into his system, dulling the knife of hate.

43

LIV

I was the girl who never got in trouble in school. I sat quietly, followed directions, and avoided confrontation at all costs, especially with authority figures. Until prom night my senior year.

Eight years later, as I rode home that night with Ridge, all I could think about was how everything had come full circle. How inherently unprepared I was to be blamed for something that I didn't do. And how this time my father couldn't save me.

The muscle in Ridge's jaw worked through a jawbreaker of frustration. I wracked my brain for something to say that might ease the tension between us. Wondered what he knew about Andrea. Did it make a difference? Or was Jason's testimony the sole reason behind Ridge's silence. Captain Wallace had tried to have another officer drive me home, but Ridge wouldn't have it. Insisting he be the one to take me back to Sullivan Farm.

When he pulled up to the farmhouse, his eyes didn't even meet mine. "I can't stay here tonight. Make sure you arm the system when you go inside." His voice was raw, hurt.

"Please, just tell me. What did Jason say?" His were the

only words that mattered right now. Jason had done this, pulled us apart.

"I need some time, Liv." The engine of the Shelby grumbled idly as I stared at him, willing him to look at me, to say these things to my face. He never did. "Time to process what Abbott said."

I opened the door, jerking my legs out of the car before I gathered the nerve to respond.

"I don't know what he told you, but whatever it is, don't I get a chance to tell my side of the story?" I exhaled, forcing a threatening wave of tears aside.

I didn't wait for an answer—exiting the car and slamming the door behind me. I took the porch steps two at a time toward the empty house I'd lit up like a Christmas tree.

I was fumbling with the new lock on the front door when the car's engine went quiet. Boots slowly ascended the stairs behind me. Angry tears streamed down my cheeks at that point, and the last thing I wanted was for Ridge to see me cry. The new burglar-proof lock was sticky, hard to manipulate. They should add emotional idiot-proof to the packaging, too. Maybe they'd be able to charge even more.

By the time I persuaded the key to turn the tumblers inside, I heard him speak.

"Liv, wait."

The velvety smoothness of his voice ran like honey through me, relaunching another wave of hurt and frustration. At that moment I would have given anything just to get back on a plane to Los Angeles. I had no job. The array of freshly delivered moving boxes on the front porch was proof my apartment was gone as well. My life in L.A. neatly boxed into three giant moving boxes. But at least LAPD didn't have a morally compromised witness or physical evidence against me. *Why was I still here?*

"Please." He caught my elbow to keep me from escaping inside. I finally faced him, tears and all. My only prize, the expression of hurt that washed over his face.

"What Jason said...I can't..." He took a step back, blew a breath through his lips. "It's an ongoing investigation. Talking to you about his statement could jeopardize the case."

"But whatever it is, you believe him?" The sparking energy in the air between us was enough. Jason's story hurt Ridge deeply. That much was clear. And now, hours later, he still carried the energy of that pain. I shrunk back against the house, away from the heat of his emotion.

"I don't want to leave things like this. Please try to understand."

"What is it you want me to understand?" I shot back, the power of Ridge's energy fusing with mine. "I understand perfectly well. You trust a man—a stranger to you—who attacked me twice, more than you trust me. You don't even have enough faith in me to tell me what he said so that I can defend myself."

Ridge stared, eyes wide, the pulse of his pain simmering to a more manageable flow. "It's not that simple."

"Nothing ever is, Ridge. Good-night." I stepped inside and closed the door behind me, leaving the grip of Ridge's energy out there with him. This was the worst the sensation had ever been. Prickles of energy turned into hot spikes of rage. I'd take a vision over this any day. "Why are you doing this?" I whispered to the silence, knowing full well I'd never get an answer.

I watched through the sheer curtains on the bay window as Ridge sat in the rocker on the porch, elbows on his knees, running his hands through his hair. He reapproached the door twice, but never actually committed to knocking.

It was what he did on the way back to the Shelby that made me want to run to him. He trotted down the steps, stopping to deliver a frustrated right hook to the brick façade. I heard the crunch of contact. The impact sending a startled yelp from my lips.

I slid down the inside of the door, listening to the distinct grumble of the V8 as it roared to life, diminishing as it pulled away from the house. Guilt enveloped me, tentacles of blame wrapping me in a blanket of remorse. I should have told him everything. Should have told him about the little girl in my dream, my grandmother's demands. I should have been the one to tell him about Andrea. In the midst of secrets, he was bound to find a lie.

THE SLEEPLESS NIGHT gave me ample opportunity to make a list of the things I needed to accomplish the next day, and I wasted no time checking things off after a quick shower and breakfast. The associate at the local Verizon store was no help in trying to determine if my phone had a tracker on it.

Chad, according to his name tag, told me that technically it would be "virtually impossible" to tell just by looking. He even used quotey fingers when he said it. So, erring on the side of caution, I bought a new iPhone and stuffed the old one in the donation box at the store. *"Let whoever is tracing me come after the poor soul who ends up with it next,"* I thought angrily as I strode back to the waiting taxi and asked him to drop me off at the nearby Ford dealership.

I spent the rest of the morning purchasing my very first brand new car. The car of my dreams, really—an emerald green Mustang GT. It was an occasion I should have been celebrating, but instead, anger and loneliness overpowered glee.

I kept wishing Ridge was there with me. Not that I needed a man to help me buy a car. I wasn't *that* girl. But it was lonely not to have someone to bounce pros and cons around with.

Once the deal was done, though, it felt good to be driving. Even as a teenager, being behind the wheel was something that brought me a sense of peace. I drove well out of my way across quiet country roads to return to the farmhouse.

I didn't recognize the car when I pulled in behind it. A bright yellow vintage Dodge Charger, one that would be hard to miss under any circumstances, was parked in the driveway, just short of the front sidewalk. As I slid from behind the wheel of my own car, the Charger's door popped open and Brian stepped out.

"Hey, Brian!" A breath of relief escaped as I waved in greeting, trying to sound chipper and welcoming. "What brings you all the way out here?" He didn't answer my question.

"Nice ride." Brian nodded toward my Mustang. "New?"

"Brand spanking," I said, continuing the upbeat façade as I patted the front quarter panel of the coupe, pretending to buff a nonexistent smudge from the paint. "1978?" I nodded toward his Charger.

"Ridge said you know your cars." Brian smiled before looking toward the house. "You've been cleaning the old place up. Looks great."

"Thanks. You want to come in? I've got some iced tea in the kitchen."

"Sure," he said. I led him into the kitchen and gestured for him to sit while I poured two tall glasses of tea.

"So, what's up?"

"I was gonna ask you the same thing," he said solemnly. "He's a wreck, you know."

It surprised me that Brian already knew about the rift between Ridge and me. I wanted him to understand that the way we left things between us was not working for me either.

"He's not the only one."

"Look, I don't know how I'd react to the situation you two

are in, but I know for a fact that Ridge is miserable with the way things are. He might be too proud to admit it, but trust me, I know him."

I studied Brian carefully. "How's his hand?"

Brian cocked his head to the side, probably wondering how in the world I knew about the right hook.

"Pretty banged up, a couple broken bones. He successfully earned desk duty for the next few weeks, I think." Brian took a swig of his tea. "He needs you, Liv."

There was something about Brian I trusted. I could talk to him, and what I needed more than anything right now was someone to talk to.

"He's the one pushing me away. What am I supposed to do?"

A suppressed sob began a slow climb in my throat and I made every attempt to choke it back.

"I'm sorry, Liv." I welcomed the warmth of Brian's arms as he enveloped me in a hug.

Silence engulfed us as I regained composure and pulled away from Brian's embrace. It took a beat before Brian asked, "Did you do it, Liv?"

"Do what?" Exasperation took over. "I don't even know what Jason told him." I searched Brian's eyes. He knew. "What was it, Brian? Ridge told you, didn't he?"

"Just bits and pieces. He claims you planned all of this. Roped him into being your accomplice to lace your grandmother's heart medication. Put the body in the trunk. He told Ridge the two of you are a couple. Claims you called him from the Marriott to let him know where you were." Brian took a deep breath before adding, "That he slept with you that night–consensually."

"What?" Shock permeated my veins. Everything Brian had said was so far from the truth I didn't even know how to begin.

Thoughts jumbled in my mind. The pictures of the pills Captain Wallace showed me danced in my memory. "I'd never hurt my grandmother." My voice broke, but I had to force the words out. "And I'd never use Ridge like that."

"I don't know all the details, Liv. I just know that whatever Jason said, they've been able to corroborate." Brian didn't look at me, his eyes fixed on the iced tea in front of him.

"Like the drugs they found in my bag at the Marriott?"

Brian nodded. "And the calls from you to him in your phone records."

"But I never–" I was doing everything I could not to raise my voice, but the revelation was incomprehensible to me. "I had nothing to do with any of this, Brian. I need to talk to Ridge. He needs to know the truth." Frustration bubbled in my voice.

"Look, Liv. Ridge has been burned, badly. When his ex-wife left I didn't think he was going to make it."

"He never told me what happened between them."

Brian paused. "They were high school sweethearts. Found out she was pregnant when Ridge was just into his first tour with the Marines."

Brian studied me then, gauging my reaction. I tried not to look as shocked as I felt. Marines wasn't a shocker, but Ridge as a father? That was one I'd never have guessed.

"They lost the baby four or five months into the pregnancy."

The pain and hurt I'd seen so many times in Ridge's eyes suddenly started to make sense.

"Ridge was never really the same after that. I guess Bridget wasn't either. She went on to finish school and he finished his commitment. After graduation she was offered a job at an advertising agency in Columbus, so they relocated from Virginia.

Ridge seemed excited. I think he thought it would be a fresh start for them both. They bought that house. Long story short, Ridge found her in their bedroom with one of her co-workers. It happened right after I moved up here. I think they'd been in Cascade Hills less than two years."

Silence strung between us. "I didn't know."

"I figured. Not many people do. He should have told you, though. You deserve to know. Trust is a big issue for him."

"What am I supposed to do?" My voice was barely a whisper.

"Look, I just wanted to come out here and check in on you. I know how hard this must be. I've heard Ridge's side of the story. I wanted to give you a chance to tell yours."

"Thanks, Brian," I said, and I meant it. At least someone believed I wasn't a cheating murderer.

"It's Jason's word against yours right now, Liv. Unfortunately, he's the one with proof." Brian strode to the door, "Call me if you need anything. I'm on your side."

I was into my second ill-advised bottle of wine. I'd downed the first before finding my grandmother's leather-bound photo album, the one I'd last seen in my dream, tucked in the drawer of a living room end table. I broke the seal on the second bottle before scouring the album pages for the little girl she swore to me had all the answers. I was almost to the end of the book and the only faces staring up at me were ones I'd already seen.

Wisps of accusation filtered like smoke into my brain. I'd done nothing of value since I'd been back in Cascade Hills. My grandmother had been counting on me and all I'd managed was a half-baked fling with a too-hot cop and soon to be official police reports. The shame of betrayal was clouding my brain when a soft knock on the front door broke the silence. I stumbled to the foyer and glanced through the curtains to see Ridge's black Shelby parked in the driveway. Alcohol removing any inhibition, I swung the door open wide.

His demeanor was cautious. A muted blue button-down shirt un-tucked over charcoal grey jeans. A tiny butterfly bandage closed the gash above his left eye. The urge to reach out and touch him nagged at me. I caught myself looking him up and down hungrily, suddenly conscious of the mistake I'd made with the wine.

"You've been drinking."

I might have seen a smile playing on his lips as he said the words, but if it was there it was fleeting.

"Yes, I have," I replied a little too loudly. Gripping his hand, I drew him farther into the room, my eyes settling on the thick white bandage stretched around his right hand. The wrap secured a hard splint that ran up the underside of his wrist. Another twinge of guilt toyed with my inebriated conscience.

"Has the alarm been working like it's supposed to?" he asked, pulling his arm out of reach and glancing toward the control panel on the wall.

"Yes, it has." I stifled an involuntary giggle. His face grew serious as I urged him toward the living room sofa.

"Liv, maybe I should go. I have some things I want to talk to you about, but I'd rather you be sober." He picked up an empty bottle of Moscato off the end table, studying the label before setting it back down.

I tried to clear my mind, to focus on the conversation he wanted to have, but instead, all I could think about were his hands. I needed them to help me forget the events that were outside of my control. I craved the sensation of his skin on mine, that light spark that accompanied every touch. I could imagine the strength of his hands—well, one of them anyway—

on the small of my back. I ached for the softness of his lips caressing the curve of my neck. I was completely and unreservedly in the throes of inebriated fantasy.

"Wait," I breathed, but he got up anyway. "Don't go."

"I'm not." He studied me for a moment. "I'm going to make you some coffee." He didn't wait for a response before heading toward the kitchen, I cocked my head to study the view as he walked away. He glanced over his shoulder before turning the corner down the hall.

I groaned softly on the couch, struggling to gain some focus on reality. A couple cups of coffee while I hungrily watched Ridge pace around the room, checking the alarm sensors, helped–slightly.

"What is it you want to talk about?" I began, after the coffee started winning the battle between booze and caffeine. It would have something to do with Jason, I knew, and I welcomed that conversation. Maybe we could finally get back to normal. Maybe I could convince Ridge that I had nothing to do with any of Jason's lies. The thought of normalcy made my stomach lurch.

"Let's start with what happened the other night," he said, his gaze lowered–evasive. But he joined me on the sofa.

"Okay." I watched his eyes as they lifted to meet mine, his brows arched in curiosity. He was waiting for me to say something. "I'm not sure what you want me to say," I admitted.

"I didn't want to leave it that way, Liv."

"You needed time to figure out that whatever Jason told you was a boldface lie."

I stared at him. Daring him to tell me that wasn't the case. His eyes bored into my soul. The desire I felt before crept up, overwhelming me once again. I don't think he expected what happened next. Hell, *I* didn't expect it. I lunged toward him, supporting my weight on my arms before grazing my lips hungrily over his. He responded, hesitantly at first, but each moment our lips were together increased his own commitment. His gentle kisses grew hard and forceful, his frustration coming to fruition in our kiss.

What I read as a moan of pleasure escaped his lips, his hand reaching up, fingers winding through my curls, pulling my face away from his to stare into my eyes.

"Don't do this, Liv. I can't do this." His words hit me like a wall. Every effect of the alcohol evaporated in that one nanosecond. I pushed away, refusing to show the disappointment streaking across my face. I failed miserably.

"Why?" was all I could muster as I sat back on my heels.

"I can't. You…"

There it was, the beginning of an accusation. "I, what?" Venom dripped from the words.

"I thought I knew what was going on between us. But then…"

I pulled away from the sofa and retreated toward the window, gazing out toward the barn. He followed, placing his hands on my shoulders and letting his palms trail down my arms, the gauze of his bandaged hand like fine sandpaper against my skin. His breath on my neck produced an unwelcome surge of desire.

"I'm sorry, I know I'm not making any sense, but everything's all twisted. You're keeping secrets, Liv."

"I'm not your ex-wife, Ridge. I'd never do that to you." I hadn't meant to blurt it out like that, but I panicked. I was tired of guilt, blame. It was time to turn it around on someone else this time. I shifted to face him as he stepped back. Shock streaked across his face.

"I see you've been talking to Brian." He sighed. "My history has nothing to do with what happened at the precinct." Ridge walked over to the mantle, rubbing his hand absently over a century old nick. "You said Jason left you, right?"

"Yes, he did."

"Then why did you call him from the Marriott, Liv?"

"I didn't call him, Ridge."

"You did. I heard the message with my own ears." Ridge's voice got louder, the air between us charged. "Your voice, Liv. You told him to come. That you *wanted* him."

I shook my head, a chill sliding down my spine and lifting the hairs on the back of my neck. "I can't explain how those calls were made, but I swear to you, I *never* called Jason."

Ridge stared at me for a beat. Shaking his head as if ridding himself of a thought, he strode to the couch for his jacket.

"What about Andrea Chase? You lied to me about that."

"I didn't lie. You never asked." The words were a whisper.

"Look, Liv. Captain Wallace is going to call you in for more questioning tomorrow. They've taken me off the case. I guess they think my objectivity might be compromised." I could hear the sneer in his voice. He grabbed his jacket off the back of the couch. "I wanted you to be prepared."

"Thanks for the heads up." I didn't mean for it to come out the way it did, abrasive and sarcastic.

Ridge turned to me, sadness reflected in his eyes. He shrugged into his coat and walked toward the door.

"I just need to know one thing, Liv."

"Anything," I tried to make up for the nastiness of my last comment.

"How far were you going to let it go, between us, I mean?"

"What are you talking about? I'm sorry for keeping secrets, Ridge. It's how I learned to survive. But how I feel about you is real. Don't let what Jason said change that."

Ridge shook his head. "Why did you pull me into this? Did I just happen to show up here at the wrong time? Interrupt whatever was going on between you two that night? Was that it? You needed to keep tabs on me?" Anger and resentment built in his voice, emotions I'd never before heard directed at me.

"No." Tears welled in the back of my eyes. "Jason and I aren't together. I don't know why he's saying that we are. Whatever his plans were, I was never a part of it."

I crossed the room toward Ridge, an effort to soothe both my panic and his anger, but he pulled away at my touch, swinging the front door open.

"Good luck tomorrow, Liv. You'll need it."

Those were the last words Ridge said before the engine of the Shelby revved and drowned out my pleas for him to stop, propelling the car up the driveway and away from me.

44

RIDGE

Ridge sat at his workstation, watching as Captain Wallace and Detective Carson, the lead who had taken over Liv's case, ushered her into the interrogation room. It was the same room where Ridge had questioned Abbott two days before. She looked small between them, Carson's height and Wallace's stocky build dwarfing her petite frame.

She glanced his direction when she came in, but he'd avoided her, staring down at a file, instead. *Coward.* He'd spent his morning with Sowards, trying to make some sense of it all. He left feeling as if he'd asked the same questions a thousand times and gotten a thousand different answers.

Ridge slid a hand through his hair and leaned back in his chair, fingering the scrap of newspaper Sowards had scrawled a number on. No name, just a number. "Call him. He's apprised of the situation. He can help you," was the only instruction he'd received. He was just getting ready to dial the international number when Adam slipped into the chair on the other side of his desk.

"I knew you'd be here."

"You're not supposed to be here for another week," Ridge reminded his partner.

"Yeah, well." Adam's eyes drifted to the interrogation room. "They're getting ready to start."

"I know."

"How can you just sit there. You're not curious about what she's going to say?"

Ridge brought his eyes up to meet Adam's. "Of course I'm curious." Curious was an understatement. "It's being recorded," Ridge said.

"You were the one who taught me that the one thing audio/video can't always catch, is a tell. Come on, I'll stand with you."

Ridge had been partnered with Adam Miller long enough to know that he wasn't going to give up easily. And, frankly, Ridge had lied to himself long enough. He did want to know how Liv was going to refute the claims Abbott made. He did want to see the expression on her face when they asked about her relationship with Abbott. Deep down, he hoped she had something–anything–that could exonerate her from what they'd found. He wanted the struggle between truth and lies to end.

Adam stood, eyes on Ridge, and Ridge lifted himself from the desk. The two of them walked side by side to the glass. Adam gave Ridge's shoulder a couple pats. Ridge appreciated the gesture, one last way to show that no matter how this turned out, he'd be there for him.

Ridge hesitated. Blowing out the breath he'd been holding. Liv's hair hung in ringlets down her shoulders. They'd brought her a can of Dr. Pepper, which she just stared at, pinching the aluminum between her thumb and forefinger, before twisting it in semi-circles on the table. He saw

Wallace's lips start moving, his cue to turn on the outside audio.

"State your full name for the record."

"Olivia Grace Sullivan." Her name, in that small voice drove into him like a spike through the heart. He wasn't sure he could watch this.

"Good morning, Olivia," Carson started. "Tell us, how do you know Jason Abbott?"

Ridge caught her stiffen before she launched into the same explanation he'd already heard. Consistency. Good. Consistency was her friend, right now.

"When was the last time you saw Mr. Abbott?"

"Early morning, April first, at the Latham Avenue Marriott."

"Can you explain what happened when you saw him?"

Liv sucked in an unsteady breath. She glanced toward the one-way mirror before focusing again on Carson and Wallace.

"He forced his way into my hotel room."

"How was he able to gain access to a locked door?" Carson cut her off.

Liv narrowed her eyes at him. Defiance. "I thought he was someone else."

"Who?"

"Detective McCaffrey," Regret laced her voice now. Ridge felt his hands ball into fists at his sides. "Ridge dropped me off at the hotel. I thought it was him coming back."

"Even though he told you not to open the door for anyone?" Carson was taunting her. "What else do you remember from that night."

Liv shifted in her seat. "You have the police report, right?"

"I wasn't on the case at that time, Miss Sullivan. It would be helpful if you could tell us again."

Ridge paced a tight circle, rubbing the coils of tension from the back of his neck. But he didn't leave.

"Jason pushed his way in. I tried to shut him out when I realized it wasn't Ridge, but he was armed." Liv was doing a good job sounding detached, but Ridge could hear her voice wobble under the pressure.

"I see. Did anything else happen?"

Ridge watched as her chest rose and fell, her breath increasing.

"We played a game of Scrabble, what do you think happened?" She shot the words at Carson. Venom dripped from every syllable, coaxing the corner of Ridge's mouth into a half-smile. Damn if he didn't love that side of her.

"Liv, I know how hard this is for you, but we really need you to answer so we have your side of the story." Thank God for Wallace.

"He taped my mouth, wrists, and ankles. He was on top of me. Held a knife to my throat. I thought he was going to rape me."

Silence hung heavy in the room. Anger replaced Ridge's fleeting smile. He'd known all this, but to hear her forced to relive it, to tell complete strangers, made his gut churn.

"But he didn't."

Liv shook her head.

"And this encounter, it occurred without your consent?"

"Yes," Liv asserted.

"So, your claim is that you did not engage in consensual intercourse with Mr. Abbott the morning in question?" Carson just wouldn't let it go.

"No, I did not." Liv insisted. She swallowed, willing away emotion.

Detective Carson pulled out a small .mp3 player and

pushed the play button. Ridge kept his eyes glued on Liv's reaction. He'd already heard the audio. Jason's voice fuzzed through the speaker. "You always did like a little bondage, didn't you?" Liv's voice followed, "Absolutely."

"Where did that come from?" Liv shot at Carson. "That's not." Ridge tried to read her. Shock. Anger. Betrayal. Each presented the same way.

"Can you identify the voices on this recording Miss Sullivan?" Carson asked, unruffled by Liv's outburst.

"Yes, but."

"Is one of them yours, Miss Sullivan?"

Liv nodded, "But I never said that. Not to him. Not then."

"Do you recognize the other voice as Jason Abbott?"

"Yes." Liv fell back against the chair with another glance toward the one-way glass. Defeat.

"Why did you refuse medical treatment the morning of April first?" Carson cocked his head to the side, a look of feigned ignorance spread across his face.

"I didn't need medical treatment. Jason stopped before anything happened."

"You see, we think we know why you refused treatment, Olivia. Could it be because they would have found proof of your tryst with Mr. Abbott?" Before Liv could answer, Carson continued, "Weren't you engaged in an intimate relationship with Detective Ridge McCaffrey at the time this incident occurred?"

Liv didn't answer, and Ridge's heart squeezed.

"Let me ask you this, Miss Sullivan, did you meet Mr. Abbott at Flanagan's pub on March 16th?"

"I did." Liv spoke slowly, cautiously.

"What did the two of you discuss at that meeting?"

"Not much. Work. I told him about my photography."

"You mean, you lied about your photography."

Liv paused, studying the detective on the other side of the table. "At the time, yes. I guess it was a lie."

"Trying to impress him?"

"No," Liv shot at Carson. "I didn't want to talk about my real job, Detective. So I made something up. Is that against the law?"

"Of course not, unless it proves a pattern of behavior. What is your real job, Miss Sullivan?"

Silence took over again as detective and suspect stared each other down.

"At that time I worked for Celestial Spirit, a psychic hotline in Los Angeles."

"And are you? Psychic?"

Liv gulped, her throat bobbing. She wasn't prepared to answer this. Ridge's chest clenched. He wanted to bust in and save her, but she was on her own. There was nothing he could do.

Liv snorted, recovering. "Of course not."

Carson leaned back in his chair, a smile curling his lips. Ridge knew that look. Satisfaction.

"But you made a career of lying to people, assuming the role of medium in order to gain monetary reward, is that right?"

"I wouldn't call it a career." Liv's voice was quiet.

"I'd say that establishes a pattern of behavior, wouldn't you Captain Wallace?"

"Noted," Wallace said. "Move on, Carson."

Carson's mouth curved into a wicked sneer as he slid a paper across the table toward Liv. "Do you recognize this?"

Liv leaned forward to scan the document, her eyes lifting to meet Carson's as she swallowed, nodded.

"Can you state for the record what it is?"

"It's my release form."

Ridge glanced at Adam. "What's he up to?"

"Hell if I know," Adam said.

"Can you be more specific?" Carson urged.

"My release from Los Angeles Mental Health Center."

"Can you read the diagnosis for us?"

Liv's jaw twitched. Her focus drifting toward the glass before she answered. "Paranoid Psychosis."

"And are you still taking your medications as prescribed by the doctors at LAMH?"

"No." The word cut into Ridge's chest.

"Get me those records," he breathed toward Adam.

"Thank you for that, Miss Sullivan. Now, I'm going to need you to be more specific about your conversation with Mr. Abbott at Flanagan's."

"Um...I don't know what you want me to say. He followed me out to my car and asked if I thought we could give it another try. I told him, no."

"So *he* wanted the two of you to get together–romantically?"

"Yes, *he* did." Liv shot back.

"Is that why you called him several times the day after meeting him at Flanagan's?"

"I didn't."

"And consistently, it seems, every couple days or so." Carson checked some paperwork. Raising his eyebrows in expectation. "Until the day after the incident at the Marriott."

Carson slid another document across the table toward Liv. "Is that your phone number?" He tapped the top of the page.

"It is," Liv confirmed, "But I never made those calls."

"Do you recognize this number?" Carson jabbed a finger at one of the highlighted lines.

"No."

"Perhaps being off your meds has impacted your recollection of events. Let me refresh your memory, Miss Sullivan. That number belongs to Mr. Jason Abbott."

For the third time, Ridge wanted to open the door, swoop in and save her. But he knew it wouldn't solve anything. He'd still be the one without answers. The one she'd used if Abbott's story was true. At the very least, he'd be the one who suffered from her relapse into a paranoid psychosis. The words rocked through him.

He watched the color drain from Liv's face. Her breaths became shallow. Her hands shook as she brought the Dr. Pepper to her lips. The can slid from her grasp, tumbling to the table and onto the floor below. Liv whimpered, gripping the table like a vise.

"I need..." she started, struggling for deeper breaths. Ridge pounded on the window, exhaling a breath of his own when Wallace tapped on the window in response, pantomiming someone drinking. Ridge disappeared around the corner, out of view when Wallace opened the door, Adam was ready with a cup of water.

"Take a sip of water, Liv. Calm your nerves." Wallace spoke low to her, soothing.

Ridge watched as Liv downed the whole cup before launching into a meager effort to defend herself.

"I just don't understand, Detective. You are implying that Jason didn't attack me at the hotel, that we had –" She couldn't say the word. "You think I've been making calls to him–for what purpose?"

Carson leaned forward. Liv jerked away.

"That's not what I *think*, Miss Sullivan. That's what I *know*." His voice was an accusatory whisper. "Your story doesn't add up now, just like it didn't add up eight years ago. Jason Abbott is cooperating with this investigation. We have the evidence we need to hold you on drug charges. Is that what you want?"

The asshole was threatening her now. Adam tapped Ridge on the shoulder, handing him the Bureau file on Liv's juvenile record. Mouthing the words, "She'll be okay."

"Are you saying that if I had agreed to medical treatment the night of the attack, you could prove Jason was lying, and we wouldn't be sitting here today?"

"I'm saying it would change the narrative, now wouldn't it?" The detective locked eyes with Liv. "Remind us for the record, Miss Sullivan, who was Andrea Chase?"

"She was a friend, in high school." Liv's voice was barely audible.

"And what happened to Miss Chase?"

"Jesus," Ridge seethed under his breath. "How'd he get all this?"

"Same way we did," Adam answered. "She's a suspect, it's fair game."

Ridge watched Liv chew on her bottom lip as Carson pressed on. "Let me refresh your memory. Miss Chase's body was pulled from Cascade Lake the night of your senior prom, is that right?"

Liv nodded.

"You were the only one in the vicinity, if I'm not mistaken." Carson pulled a sheet of paper from the file. Ridge knew what was coming next. "Sentenced to six months in a psychiatric facility in lieu of prosecution, is that right?"

"I served my time."

Carson cocked an eyebrow at Liv. "But now, you're off your meds. Seems to me that might be a pertinent detail in this case, Miss Sullivan."

Ridge stalked back to his workstation. Carson was a dick. What was happening to Liv was out of his control. Maybe she was a part of the plot, and maybe not, but he couldn't stand there and watch Carson make her out to be crazy. He picked up the phone, calling in a much-needed favor from the one person that could help.

45

LIV

Carson's stare bored into me. The walls of the interrogation room seemed to shrink, growing smaller with every breath I took.

"I never hurt Andrea," I refuted stupidly. "And I'm not crazy."

Carson leaned back in his chair. "Let's leave the past in the past for now, shall we? Why did you ask Jason Abbott to help you lace your grandmother's heart medication with OxyContin?"

That accusation sucked the remaining air from the room.

"Let me ask this a different way. Why did you have OxyContin in your possession on April first?"

A knock on the door pulled the detective's eyes off of me for a blessed moment of reprieve. I was out of my element here.

"Miss Sullivan," the stranger walked up to me, introducing himself as my brain fought for function. "My name is Rodney Clark, I'm an attorney with Clark and Associates. I've been called in to help resolve this misunderstanding as soon as possible."

Mr. Clark nodded at Wallace and Carson. "You'll give me a moment with my client, won't you?"

The two men exited, a satisfied smirk playing on Detective Carson's lips.

"Who called you?" My voice sounded small and weak, even to my own ears.

He reached down and pushed the stop button on the recorder before answering, "Detective McCaffrey." He laid his briefcase on the table, sitting in Detective Carson's recently vacated chair. "It's not often I get a call from a detective to come help someone who's being interrogated." He studied me for a moment, his warm eyes softened. "You must be important to him." Mr. Clark waited for a response.

"I'm not so sure anymore."

Mr. Clark flicked open the brass clasps on his shiny black briefcase and pulled out a legal pad before asking me my version of events for the night of the Marriott attack and the meeting at Flanagan's. He also asked questions I wasn't ready for. How long had I known Ridge? What was I doing at the house the night I met Ridge? It was at least an hour before we were done.

"I have to be honest with you, Miss Sullivan. They have enough to hold you on a drug possessions charge, and enough to convict on filing a false report. They're close on manslaughter charges.

Once they have you in custody they will tear your world apart piece by piece until they find whatever it is they think they're looking for. If there is anything, and I do mean *anything*, that you think I should know, now is the time to tell me."

"My world has already been torn apart, Mr. Clark. I don't know what they're trying to find. Those drugs were not mine. I did *not* sleep with Jason Abbott. I don't know where that audio or those phone calls came from." I looked down, attempting to swallow the pent up tears that began falling into my lap. "I did not kill my grandmother." Mr. Clark patted my hand sweetly.

"I'll do everything I can to make this as easy as I can for you. You will be arrested today. Someone will be in shortly to read you your rights. I'll try to have you home by late this evening. They'll most likely keep you in the holding cell here in the station until I get the arraignment scheduled and then we'll get you home."

"They're going to arrest me?" Repeating the words left a sour taste in my mouth. My stomach was in knots when Detective Carson returned to the interrogation room. He seemed disappointed that he wouldn't get the chance to continue his line of questioning.

He read my Miranda rights and roughly cuffed my hands behind my back, gleaning a little too much enjoyment from the act. He shoved me out of the interrogation room toward the cells along the opposite wall. I was focused on forward movement, trying not to trip as Carson shoved me from behind, but out the corner of my eye, I saw him. Ridge stood with Adam, just a few feet away. He turned away as I exited, head lowered and arms crossed in front of his chest.

Adam spoke to Detective Carson as he led me by. "Are the cuffs really necessary?"

Carson didn't answer but shoved me forcefully from behind, causing me to stumble. Adam's good arm reached out in an effort to break my fall just before I regained my balance.

Carson maneuvered me toward a desk where they took my fingerprints. I watched helplessly as the car keys, Chap-Stik, and cell phone I carried to the station were catalogued and stowed. A hint of gratitude at not having my purse with me crept into the fray of already convoluted thoughts.

Thankful to be the only occupant in the cell, I surveyed my

surroundings. The walls were the same cinderblock as the interrogation room, except painted white. There was a small pedestal sink and toilet tucked in one corner. Even though there was a short partition, I couldn't imagine using it. I immediately resolved to hold it under any circumstances, at least until Mr. Clark could get me out of here, which my bladder was telling me needed to be sooner rather than later.

A small cot with a thin, dirty looking mattress lined the opposite wall. I swallowed my pride and took a seat on the mattress, hoping lice and bed bugs didn't inhabit tiny holding cells, realizing those were the least of my worries.

46

LIV

After several excruciatingly long hours, I saw Mr. Clark talking to Adam and Ridge in the main room outside. Ridge was standing stoically in the same position I'd seen before, his arms crossed and his head down as the lawyer spoke. As far as I could tell he wasn't speaking. Adam was nodding and conversing, but I couldn't hear the words. It wasn't long before Adam led Mr. Clark toward my cell.

"Liv," Adam started, "Mr. Clark wants a minute with you before your arraignment." He unlocked the cell and gestured for Rodney to enter. Adam stood in the doorway as Mr. Clark grasped my elbow and led me just out of Adam's earshot.

"They'll be bringing you over for your arraignment shortly. I'm sure we'll be able to get you home on bail. This is just a misdemeanor right now. Will you be able to meet a bond stipulation?"

"Yes," I nodded, sending a silent *"Thank you,"* up to my grandmother.

"Good. I'll see you soon," Mr. Clark nodded to Adam who gave me a sad smile before locking the door.

I remembered the first time I was ever in a courtroom. In my mind's eye I'd pictured a grand room, like what you see in *Law & Order*, jury and all. I'd almost been disappointed after Andrea's death to find myself in an average sized room that reminded me more of a classroom than a courtroom. The same was true today. Plastic chairs instead of the wooden benches I'd anticipated, made up the gallery. There were no chairs where I imagined the jury would be sitting, and an oversized wooden desk was the judge's station. The walls were dark mustard yellow, making the room seem dingier than necessary. In eight years, it hadn't changed a bit.

Adam led me in and seated me behind a table in the first row of plastic chairs. My eyes followed him as he took a seat in the row just behind me. A uniformed officer announced a case number, and I watched as Mr. Clark rose from his orange plastic chair, causing a scuffing sound to reverberate from the tile floor. We stood as the judge entered and asked for my plea, at which point it took all my strength to muster the words, "Not guilty."

I listened as the judge read the official charges of misdemeanor drug possession and filing a false complaint. The opposing attorney, a tall wiry fellow with sand colored hair, spoke up.

"Judge, we expect further charges to be forthcoming and would like the defendant remanded to custody. She is a resident of California and as such, a flight risk."

I watched as the judge, a middle aged man with a kind face, snorted a chuckle before addressing me.

"Miss Sullivan, your father was Stephen Sullivan, correct?"

"Yes," I replied tentatively.

"He was a good man. You've got good representation." The

judge's eyes were soft, sincere. "This is her hometown, Counselor. Bail is set at five thousand."

The sound of the gavel made me jump as the participants in the courtroom began milling about. Adam tugged on my arm and led me quietly back to the holding cell.

"I'm sure Clark will be here soon to get you," he said before leaving me alone.

Less than fifteen minutes later I saw Rodney's tall form through the window.

He entered the cell and said, "Officer Miller has asked to drive you home."

"I have a car here."

"It's in impound. Could be morning before I can get it out."

"Okay, sure," I said, wishing I'd held off a day before buying a brand new car that was now sitting in an impound lot. I guessed the impound workers weren't as conscientious as valet drivers.

"Are you sure that's something you're comfortable with?"

"Yes, that's fine." I pushed a breath of satisfaction out to convince Rodney I was fine. I trusted Adam. Mr. Clark must have noticed because he pulled me aside and leaned in, forcing me to take his next advice seriously.

"As your lawyer, I'm instructing you not to talk about anything to do with the case on the way home, Liv. You can't be too careful. I know you have personal relationships with some of the officers here, but none of these people should be trusted right now. Do you understand?"

I studied him carefully before answering. He knew more than he was telling me, I was sure. Although I wanted nothing more than to share my predicament with those strangers who I now considered friends, I knew Mr. Clark was right. After all this, I didn't know who I should trust.

"I understand."

"Good. I'd like you to come to my office tomorrow morning, at ten o'clock so we can discuss your case further." He handed me a business card, complete with address.

"Of course."

"I'll see if I can have someone deliver your car, so you don't have to worry about catching a ride."

I thanked him and watched him walk away, down the corridor toward the exit. I was still staring after him when I felt Adam standing next to me.

"Are you ready?"

I nodded, glancing over his shoulder at Ridge who was standing across the room. I caught his gaze before he looked down and strode away into Captain Wallace's office. The man I cared for more than anything could no longer stand to look at me. That understanding triggered a suffocating sob as Adam led me out a back door to his pick-up truck.

The ride home was mostly silent. I don't think either one of us knew what to say to each other. Adam's usually boisterous personality had been shelved in favor of a more subdued side. As we wound down the long driveway of Sullivan farm, Adam spoke.

"Liv, I hate that all this is happening to you. But I need to know, and please, be honest. Is any of Jason's story true?"

I looked squarely at Adam as I answered. "Not a word, Adam."

Adam nodded. "And what about the paranoid psychosis?"

"That was a long time ago." How could I explain a diagnosis that even I didn't fully understand? The six months at LAMH had been horrible. The meds made me fuzzy. As far as my family had been concerned commitment had been a means to an end, a way to keep me out of jail after Andrea died. But looking back, it was a terrible plan. No wonder Ridge couldn't believe me.

I watched Adam as he sat quietly with his good hand at twelve on the black leather steering wheel, the engine idling in front of the house.

"Thanks, Adam. For everything. I appreciate it."

He looked carefully at me before speaking again. "This is going to get worse before it gets better. You deserve to know that."

"Rodney mentioned that might be the case." I turned toward the door, but Adam's words stopped me.

"They have more evidence, Liv. Abbott turned over more recordings and voicemail messages this afternoon."

"What else are they trying to pin on me, Adam?" I wasn't stunned to hear that there were more audio clips like the one I'd heard. I wracked my brain trying to figure out how that was possible but dwelling on it wasn't going to make it go away. I needed motive. What was Jason trying to accomplish?

Adam looked down, his hand falling from the steering wheel and into his lap.

"Rodney told me about the manslaughter charges."

"Tox results came back today." His tone was somber, sad.

I stared at Adam's profile. "They did an autopsy?"

Adam shook his head, "Not a full one. Just standard post-mortem blood work."

The weight of Adam's comments kept me rooted to the seat. Finally, I pulled myself together enough to ask, "Ridge believes I did these things? That I cheated on him. Killed my own grandmother?"

Adam's hesitation was too lengthy. "He's a detective, Liv. His job is to base his perception of truth on the evidence. He doesn't know what to think. Right now, he's hurt–angry."

Adam reached into his jacket pocket, pulling out a stack of folded, photocopied pages. "He's been poring over these since this started. I think he's hoping there's some proof in there.

Something that will help your case. I haven't read them, yet. But I thought you should have a copy."

I unfolded the stack–letters from the wooden box. I managed to nod to Adam and thank him for the ride home without letting loose the flood of emotion that dammed up inside. I ran up the front porch stairs and into the empty house.

Images of Ridge refusing to look at me at the station interspersed with Detective Carson's hateful stare filled every thought. Complete frustration and panic washed over me. The constant ebb and flow forced me to the floor behind the closed front door, as I read the first letter. Ashlyn Callaghan, my sister, was dead. I sucked in a sob and read every letter, my father's affairs, my grandmother's attempt to sweep an unwanted pregnancy under the rug. I didn't try to stem the flow of tears as I sat on the floor of my grandmother's living room, awash in a tsunami of helplessness with nothing but lies to show for it.

47

RIDGE

The call from Sowards came about midnight. Ridge sat at Murphy's bar, swirling what was left of his Macallan. The dim lights of the space flickered through the amber liquid, shining prisms onto the bar top beneath his glass.

"McCaffrey," he answered without checking the number.

"You didn't make the call." Sowards said matter-of-factly from the other end of the line. Ridge slipped a hand into his jacket pocket, feeling for the scrap of newspaper Sowards had torn from The Columbus Dispatch two days ago. Ridge crunched it in his fist.

"Why bother?" Ridge heard the slur of his own words. Shook his head to rid himself of the buzz. It didn't work. The bar spun. He caught Brian's attention, miming for a glass of water.

"Damn it, McCaffrey. Aren't the Marines known for training the insubordination out of their soldiers?"

Ridge slugged a gulp of water, slamming it onto the lacquered wood a touch too hard.

"The Marines are known for never leaving a man behind, Sowards. If Liv is so important to the bureau, why are you treating her like a sacrificial lamb?"

Sowards sighed. "You need to learn to trust, McCaffrey. I see the big picture, you're responsible for the boots on the ground shit, got it?"

Ridge sunk back onto the bar stool. Trust had never been his forte. He understood he was at the bottom of the chain of command as far as Sowards was concerned, but that didn't make him hate it any less.

"Make the call. Identify yourself. Tell him you located Olivia Sullivan. Then, damn it McCaffrey, shut up and listen."

The line clicked closed. Ridge listened to the silence against his ear for a moment before dragging the phone down his cheek, scratching at day-old stubble.

"Everything okay?" Brian drifted to his end of the bar.

"Fine," Ridge slurred, using his arms to steady the sway of the room. "I gotta get home." He jerked his keys from his jacket pocket, unable to hold on as they skittered across the bar, landing with a clink against his empty Macallan glass.

"Yeah, I don't think so, brother. Hate to break it to you, but you're sleeping it off on my couch tonight.

"I'm good," Ridge refuted, reaching as Brian pocketed Ridge's keys.

"Melanie," Brian hollered over his shoulder. "Take Ridge up to the apartment, make up the couch for him, get him some water."

Brian's sister laced her arm through Ridge's guiding him through the kitchen and up the back stairway of Murphy's Pub. A trickle of humiliation might have filtered through him, but he was too drunk to notice. It had been a long time since he'd gone this far, let his emotions get the better of him.

Ridge watched from the doorway as Mel made up the pull-out couch. It wasn't the first time he'd stayed here. But it might have been the first time he'd been quite this fucked up. And he was gonna drive. Shame hit him with full-force. *Jesus.*

Mel waved him over and helped him sit, kneeling in front of him as she unlaced his boots, pulling off each one before pairing them up at the foot of the bed.

"Thanks," Ridge managed when she finished. His hand reached for Mel's shoulder to steady himself. Brian's little sister had always been pretty. Not his type, but when you're three sheets to the wind, Ridge wasn't sure anyone had a type. "Tell me something."

"What is it?" Blue eyes looked up at him through long lashes, her hair piled in a cute messy bun on top of her head. He resisted the urge to boop it.

"What is it with women and secrets, huh?" Ridge groaned as she guided him down to his back, sliding his legs under the sheet.

"Not all women keep secrets, Ridge."

"All the ones that want me, do." His eyelids flickered closed. The words barely intelligible.

He sensed Mel standing there, watching him. He could have sworn the heat of her lips brushed his, but he was too hurt, too tired, and too drunk to decide whether or not to reciprocate. It was better that way.

"Night, Ridge." Mel's voice was soft and smooth, a lullaby of its own. Ushering in the silence of sleep.

48

LIV

Rodney Clark was a man of his word. The next morning, my Mustang was parked in the barn lot, the keys in an envelope taped to the front door. I dressed, gathered the notebook I'd filled the night before, attempting to make some sense of what had happened, and tucked the letters under one arm. I left Sullivan farm with the first blip of optimism I'd felt since Ridge left me alone three nights ago.

The offices of Clark and Associates were easy to find, situated in one of the older buildings in downtown Cascade Hills. Located on the top floor of the four-story building, it had a pretty good view of surrounding downtown. It was meticulously decorated, much like Jack's offices were, with the addition of a perky blonde sitting at a desk just outside the bank of elevators.

After asking me which partner I was in to see, she led me down a generous hallway toward a corner office. I'd done a little research on Rodney Clark since yesterday, and it pleased me to know Ridge had selected an attorney who obviously made a good living defending would-be criminals. His list of successes was extensive. I hoped my name could be added to that list.

"Liv, it's good to see you." He motioned for me to sit in a leather swivel chair, next to a large rectangular table. He strode from around his desk to join me, giving me the impression that I was an equal, rather than just another case number. Even though I knew it was a calculated move, I appreciated the effort.

"How did you sleep last night?"

"I didn't," I replied honestly.

He smiled before opening the case file on the table. It wasn't very thick, and I couldn't help wondering if that was a good sign or bad.

"Well, Liv, I must admit, with the exception of that expunged juvenile record–inadmissible in court, I might add– I've found you to be the perfect client. Other than being pulled in as a witness a few times in Los Angeles, you're a defense attorney's dream. Gainfully employed, until recently of course. Not even an unpaid parking ticket."

I attempted to return Mr. Clark's smile, but my lips wouldn't cooperate. He noticed.

"We'll get right down to it," he started, "your arraignment on the drug charges went well. Your family name will definitely be an advantage for us."

"I hope so," I hedged. I assumed my father's infidelity was not common knowledge among his colleagues. I wasn't sure about his efforts to protect me.

"The first thing we need to do is figure out how those calls were made to Mr. Abbott. Let's brainstorm all the possibilities." Mr. Clark turned to a whiteboard behind him.

I pulled my notebook out of my bag and set it on the table, noticing a flicker of appreciation in Mr. Clark's thin smile.

"Do you mind if I ask you a question, Mr. Clark?" I needed to know how much he knew before we submerged ourselves in the plethora of possibility.

"Of course, what is it?"

"I've been told this is likely to get worse before it gets better," I ventured. "What is it that Jason and the police are really trying to pin on me? I know they think I hurt my grandmother. Is there more?"

Mr. Clark's expression grew dark and withdrawn as he capped his whiteboard marker and sat back in the chair. I watched him pop and recap the marker several times, his lips open just enough to let a thin stream of air pass deliberately through.

"I'm not sure, Liv. They're poking around, looking into Jennifer Tipton's death. At present, they've got enough to hold you on manslaughter charges. The fact they haven't moved on that makes me think they're close to something bigger. Murder, maybe."

"Because of the oxy the coroner found in my grandmother's bloodstream?"

His gray eyes locked on mine. Every muscle in my body tensed, pangs of anger and betrayal roiled inside.

"How did you know about that?"

"Adam Miller told me," I admitted.

Rodney licked his lips and leaned forward on his forearms. "Your grandmother's medical records indicate she suffered from SVT, supraventricular tachycardia. The Oxy in her bloodstream would be contraindicated with the Diltiazem she took to control the SVT. I petitioned to have the blood retested last night when I learned about that tidbit of evidence. The independent lab has the sample now." He checked his watch. "It's on a rush. I hope to know something one way or another by evening."

Tears shot to the back of my eyes—relief. I clenched my jaw tight against them, hissing my rebuttal, "Mr. Clark, just so we're clear—I have *never* taken Oxycontin in my life. I've never so much as smoked weed. I didn't know that Jason had ever taken Oxy before this all came about. But I assure you, I have never *stolen* it. I never put it in that overnight bag. And I had *nothing* to do with my grandmother's death."

He nodded gravely. "Who packed your bag for the Marriott?"

I stopped. Suddenly acutely aware of what Mr. Clark was implying. "Ridge, packed it."

Mr. Clark hesitated, making a note on his legal pad and giving the revelation time to sink in.

"He wouldn't do that. He'd have no reason." My voice rose a few notes with the strain of betrayal.

"Who else had access to your bag, Liv?"

"Just me." I let my mind wander back to the night at the hotel. "Jason," I said the name too loud. "He was in the bathroom for a couple minutes. He shut the door. He must have planted them then. It wasn't Ridge. It couldn't have been."

I fought back the tears as Mr. Clark changed course. But the seed of doubt that he planted had already begun to grow roots.

It was late in the evening when we finally called it a night. I felt as prepared as I could be under the circumstances. The only possible explanation for the telephone calls we came up with sounded like something out of a sci-fi flick and would require proof of Jason breaking into my hotel room to steal my phone. My attorney and I were none too confident in the story's ability to persuade either law enforcement or a jury.

Leftovers of the Chinese take-out we ordered for dinner still sat in tidy white boxes on the massive office table. Mr.

Clark no longer looked like his well-pressed suited self. He had long ago lost the tie and the sleeves of his button down were rolled up to his elbows, revealing astonishingly muscular forearms for a man of his stature. His dark brown hair was not meticulously brushed and parted. His hand had been through it too many times for the style to stay, and many hours earlier he had become Rod instead of Mr. Clark.

I divulged every tiny detail of my life to this man. Yes, even the existence of my dreams. He listened carefully to everything and asked thorough questions. He seemed particularly interested in why Jason would come to Cascade Hills, well before Grandma's death, for a mysterious consulting job that surely could have been filled by a company with closer headquarters. I had to admit it was a mystery. One I felt could only have to do with his intentions with me, whatever those were.

In contrast, I still knew remarkably little about Rod. I'd determined he was divorced with a teenage daughter who only stayed with him every other weekend, but other than that, the focus remained on me. And it hit me. Here I was again, putting complete trust in someone I knew very little about. But, what choice did I have? I made a mental note to be more discerning in my future relationships. The old wall that used to separate me from the rest of the world rose a foot or two higher.

As I drove home from Rod's office I said a silent prayer. It was a foreign concept to me. I hadn't actually been to a church service, other than weddings, since high school. Having accepted a pact with my parents as a child that if I would go to weekly mass without argument, they would allow me the choice once I turned sixteen.

Once I crossed that threshold, I opted out of organized religion, preferring instead to keep my sectarian practices off the public radar—quite unlike the rest of the Sullivan clan. But tonight, it felt natural. I didn't ask for all of my problems magically to disappear, as you might expect. I simply asked that whatever was thrown at me over the next weeks or months, that I be able to handle it like the Sullivan women before me—with grace and dignity. Under the circumstances, that seemed to me the best outcome.

49

LIV

The sun rose and set every day on the stagnation that had become my life. The independent lab confirmed the death of my grandmother due to fatal drug contraindication. The only question the police had yet to answer was how the Oxy in my duffle bag connected to the Oxy in Grandma's death. Rodney said until they determined chain of possession, there was nothing they could do. I was free on bond, awaiting trial for a misdemeanor possessions charge.

Other than that, no news was good news. The prosecution stopped asking for continuances, which Rod said was due to the fact they'd given up the complicity charges. He didn't mention anything more about theft with intent to distribute. I could only hope that had gone by the wayside, too. Unfortunately, neither of us had been able to prove my cell had been tampered with. Rod was able to track down my old one thanks to Chad at the Verizon store. As it turns out, those old phones you donate don't always make it to the hands of charity.

The trial was still five days away and my mind was still swimming. I hadn't heard from or seen Ridge since that day at the precinct. And with each sun that set, the possibility of pulling whatever we had back from the brink of ruin grew less and less likely. Some days I'd come to terms with that. Other days, his loss overwhelmed me. Today was one of those days.

It was April 17th, my grandmother's birthday, and I'd gone to the cemetery to put some flowers on her grave. As I trudged up the embankment leading to the Sullivan plot, I saw him. A figure kneeling in front of Grandma's headstone, carefully placing a large bouquet of white roses in the offset marble vase.

I almost turned and walked away, but if the past couple weeks had taught me anything it was that strength and determination were necessities in life. And I'd grown in both those areas since my indictment.

"Mr. Reynolds?" I said, approaching him from behind. He sprang to his feet, visibly flustered.

"Olivia—you surprised me. I didn't think anyone would be out here this time of day."

"Those are beautiful flowers, Jack. It's nice of you to think of my grandmother," I commented, grateful for human interaction.

He glanced back at the immaculate roses before returning his gaze to me. "Your grandmother—she meant a great deal to me, Liv. She was a special lady." Jack's chest rose and fell under his coat. "I miss her."

"Yes, she was." I watched him carefully, ignoring the voice in my head telling me to keep my mouth shut. "You were in love with her, weren't you?"

He twisted his hat in his hands. An expression of relief passed behind his eyes. "I was." "She never mentioned it to me."

Jack's face visibly crumpled.

"I'm sorry, I didn't mean it like that. I'm sure she felt the same about you."

Open mouth, insert foot. I sucked in a breath. Locking myself up alone in that big old house over the past week hadn't helped my interpersonal skills, that was for sure.

We sat on a nearby bench as he confessed the secret affair he'd had with Grandma. It started several years after my grandfather's death and continued until her recent departure. I asked Jack why they kept it a secret, what difference would it make for people to know? His answer was one I already knew.

"Grace was a woman of secrets, Liv."

He told me about vacations to Ireland, the only place where they openly shared time together. A woman of secrets or not, I still couldn't understand the need for secrecy in Cascade Hills. She was a widow. No one would fault her for trying her hand at love again. So much about my grandmother was foreign to me. Jack was silent, staring off over the headstones.

"I found pictures." My voice was barely a whisper. "My grandmother with a woman holding a baby. She'd written on the photos." I smoothed my hand over the plastic wrapped flowers in my lap. "Did you know my father had an affair?"

His eyes met mine, all grief and understanding. "I did. Grace did everything in her power to keep that from you."

"Is Ashlyn Callaghan my twin sister?" Her name scraped against my tongue.

"Yes, Liv. Grace kept in contact with her over the years."

Jack's admission took the air from my lungs. I thought I'd known my grandmother. That she and I shared secrets only the two of us knew. But I was beginning to understand that my memories of her were only one facet of the actual woman. In the short time I'd been home, I'd learned that virtually everything about my life, and hers, was a lie.

I sucked in a wobbly breath. "What about Jennifer Tipton? What happened to her?"

"I'm sorry, Liv. But that's a piece of history best left buried." Jack patted my knee and excused himself.

"Wait," I called after him. "Just answer one thing. Did my father hurt her?"

Jack reapproached, tugging his hat onto his head. "Emotionally, I think he did. But she was fragile, Liv. She lost both parents that summer she was away. Losing your father to her best friend was too much to take."

Jack left me speechless, making his way around headstones toward a Lincoln parked at the other end of the cemetery.

It all seemed so absurd, like a plot twist ripped right out of a daytime drama. A secret love affair between my father and two young college students. If the dates on the pictures were right, my parents would have only been married about four years before the other women came between them.

A wind kicked up, blowing one of Jack's roses from the container, cartwheeling it away. Why had my father done it? And if he wasn't the one responsible for her death, then who was? More importantly, if Aimee Callaghan had two babies, why did only one of us end up in Cascade Hills? None of it made sense.

I stood, tucking my own bouquet next to Jack's. I blew a kiss toward my grandmother's monument and walked away. The first wave of true desperation hit as I headed down the hill toward my Mustang. For the old me, a life of self-imposed isolation would be fine. But Ridge had changed me, shown me what it was like to be loved. I wasn't ready to give that up. Not yet.

IT WAS past two A.M. before I wound down enough to entice sleep. Grandma sat on the edge of my bed, that same dressing gown fluttering gently in an otherworldly breeze. Her hand skimmed my leg in a rhythmic caress before her voice broke into my dreams.

"*I'm sorry I never told you about Jack. I never intended to keep that secret from you. I almost told you when we were in Ireland, but I'd kept it to myself for so long by then, I couldn't bring myself to say anything. I was afraid opening up would feel too good–would lead to too many other revelations. I hope you can forgive me when all of this is over, Sweetie.*"

Tears pooled in my grandmother's eyes, spilling out over onto rosy cheeks.

"I still don't understand, Grandma. Jennifer Tipton's body lay in the woods for two decades. Who killed her? Why?" I was desperate for answers. Desperate to exonerate myself from this tangled web of lies. "What does Jason have to do with any of this?"

"*Jason was desperate in his own way, Liv. Desperation makes for poor choices. Talk to Ridge, Sweetie. Jennifer's death was a tragic accident.*"

"How can I believe that after everything that's happened?" The accusation cut my tongue.

"*Stay focused, Olivia. Ashlyn is the key. You can't wait any longer.*"

50

RIDGE

Marcus Sowards approached Ridge in the hall outside the courtroom the day of the trial. From the third floor of the courthouse, Ridge could see all the way to the tracks on the other side of town. He leaned against the stone wall, inches from the glass, gazing toward Sullivan farm. He grazed his left thumb absently over the scar running along the knuckles of his freshly unbandaged right hand.

"Still waiting for the verdict?" Sowards asked.

Ridge nodded and looked away.

"Heard you made the call." Ridge's jaw tightened. "That help clear anything up for you?"

Ridge ran a hand through his hair. His call to Michael Donaghey had been more than insightful, it had been down-right hard to take. "Why are you doing this to her?"

"I'm not sure I know what you mean." Sowards crossed his arms, unfazed.

"You knew who she was before she came back to Cascade

Hills. You roped me in under the guise of some bogus protective detail. Why?"

Sowards glanced out over the town. "We needed to make sure she stayed here long enough to get a good read on her. You did your job, McCaffrey. It's time to move on." Sowards pulled a slip of paper from his lapel pocket. "Looks like you're getting what you wanted."

Ridge took the paper. "You're reassigning me?"

"Charlottesville." He clapped Ridge on the back. "Congratulations. You should be happy." Sowards turned on his heel and walked away.

Ridge caught up to him, seething. "What about Liv? This isn't over for her."

"It is over. Look, we needed to know if she could be trusted before we took her on. I'd say that's pretty questionable right now, wouldn't you? Let it go."

"Why'd you have me call Donaghey if you were planning to cut her loose?"

"Donaghey needed to know she was alive, that she existed. That's all. Whether or not to bring her in is my call."

"Her sister is there, Marcus. She knows Liv's alive. She's going to want to see her."

"Maybe," Sowards admitted. "But Michael Donaghey and Ashlyn Callaghan are trained assets, Ridge. Unlike you, they know their place."

"Fuck you," Ridge spat, fury boiling over already frayed nerves.

"They'll do what's in the best interest of the program as a whole. Grace Sullivan devoted her life to making the GenLink program a success. You know that." Ridge stepped away, remembering all the conversations he'd shared with Grace over the past few years. She was a good woman. She wanted Liv cared for, safe.

Sowards droned on, "Liv, whether or not she's an active asset, is proof that GenLink protégés can be sustained with minimal intervention. That was the goal of your op, McCaffrey." Sowards stabbed his finger into Ridge's chest. "Go back to Charlottesville. Your family needs you."

The doors to the courtroom opened and a tide of people filed out. Ridge looked over heads, hoping to see Brian, Adam, or Shana, all three of whom stayed inside for the whole trial. Brian was the first to notice him. Ridge scoured his face, trying to glean a hint from his expression.

"Guilty." As Brian said the word, Ridge's whole body caved in on itself. "They had nothing but theories to refute the cell phone records. Jury didn't buy it. But the judge was lenient. A hefty fine plus time served. She's walking out today with a drug conviction on her record, but she'll sleep in her own bed tonight. That's something."

"Right." It was the only word Ridge could produce. The effort it took to push it from his lungs overwhelming. He'd seen the evidence, he knew the backstory, but he'd continued to hold out hope that what he'd heard on those recordings was manufactured. Maybe Sowards had been right. Liv couldn't be trusted.

Ridge turned and trotted down the hall. Brian called after him, but Ridge held up a backwards wave and kept going, the heat of defiance gripping his chest. The air in the courthouse suffocated him. He'd been used. He'd let that happen once before and he'd be damned if he'd allow it to happen again. Trust only ended in pain.

51

LIV

I stayed at Murphy's that night until Brian closed the place down at two A.M. I couldn't stand the thought of going home alone to an empty house. And let's face it, Brian was good company. He finally got around to asking me about the business proposition Ridge had mentioned in passing. So many things had happened since Ridge left that I'd forgotten about it until Brian brought it up as we cleaned the bar.

"So, I was thinking," he started. "There's empty square footage next door. I thought it might make a good studio space for you. It would be great to have a neighbor like you close by."

I took a moment, scouring my damp rag over the nearby bistro table, processing the magnitude of his offer.

"Thanks, Brian, really. But I don't think I can justify a studio space just yet." I was flattered, but right now I was uncertain how much longer Cascade Hills would be my city of residence. Turns out, small towns are the worst places to hide.

"I could hang some of your work in here. It would be good advertising. To sweeten the deal, how about I don't charge you rent until you start showing a profit. What do you think?"

"I think you're insane," I admitted. "You own the space?"

"Yes. Ridge found this building for me. It used to be an old factory of some kind—soap, if you can believe that. You wouldn't believe how stinky the process of making soap can be." Brian smiled. "Took forever to get the smell out. When it rains heavy, you can still smell it sometimes. Like ghosts from the past are coming back to remind me of its roots."

He looked around the building with an expression akin to awe. If only he knew how much I could relate.

"Anyway, I live upstairs. It gives me room for expansion if I need it in the future."

"Sounds like good business." I moved on to another table.

"Ridge's decision. I told him he was crazy for wanting the whole thing. But now, I'm glad he pushed for it. He's actually got a pretty good head for business. Helped me out a lot in the beginning."

A knot of loss tangled in my chest.

"So, Liv, what do you think?"

"I don't know, Brian. It's a great offer, I just need some time to think about it." I finished with the last table and scooted behind the bar to drop the rag in the sink. I clenched my jaw against the words, but they came out anyway, soft and deliberate. "How is he?"

Brian shrugged, carrying a tub of dirty rags to the kitchen. I followed.

"Same as you, I guess. He's surviving." Brian leaned with his back against the stainless countertop, his hands gripping the curved edge.

"Remember when I told you about Bridget?" He waited for me to nod. "What I didn't tell you was the reason behind her miscarriage. She was an addict. It started in high school—before that probably. The two of them would party pretty hard on weekends. Nothing major, marijuana, ecstasy, a few scrips somebody stole from their parents' medicine cabinet. But when Ridge's sister died, he fell off the deep end. She dove in right along with him. Somehow, he clawed his way out. She never did."

Brian was quiet for a minute, grabbing a nearby mop and bucket he started in on the spots missed by the kitchen crew.

"I shouldn't be telling you this."

I stayed silent. He was right. He shouldn't. But I wanted to know. My heart yearned for connection. Some way to feel closer to the man I'd lost. I thought if I held my breath long enough–didn't disrupt the silence–maybe he'd keep talking.

"Ridge felt like it was his responsibility to keep her habit in check. And when he was home, he did a pretty good job. But once he joined up, Bridget had too much alone time. She'd be strung out anytime he came home on leave. He'd spend his entire time off base drying her out."

Brian rang the mop out and emptied the bucket, stowing it in a nearby closet. When he looked at me, I knew what was coming.

"The drugs caused her to lose the baby?"

Brian swallowed, his Adam's apple bobbing in his throat. "Yes. I mean, the pregnancy was an accident. But Ridge had made peace with it. Wanted a family. I don't think Bridget ever did." He hesitated. "I think she knew what she was doing. I think she wanted the baby to die."

"Brian." My hand flew to my mouth in shock. No matter how bad this woman was, I never thought I'd hear an accusation like that come from Brian's lips.

"You never knew her, Liv. You..."

"What?"

"You're the antithesis of Bridget." He laughed, a single forced chuckle. "She was beautiful–a Greek goddess as far as Ridge was concerned."

"Gee, thanks." I tried to lighten the mood, swinging my legs so they tapped the metal rungs of the stool. But hurt tugged at the corner of my mouth.

"God, no, that's not what I meant, Liv." Brian's voice dipped, "You're beautiful. It's just–that's *all* she was. You are *so* much more than that. And Ridge knows it, Liv, just like I do."

Brian pulled me from the stool, my hands clasped in his.

"Don't give up on him yet, okay? Promise me?"

I managed to get out of the kitchen and back to my car without crying, which was a miracle in itself. I chewed my lip on the way home. Brian never meant to offend, but his words assaulted me–pinched and poked at the little girl inside who'd never been good enough, who'd always been a disappointment. I didn't know who I was anymore–what place I held in this world. But the one thing I knew I'd never be, was a Greek goddess.

I drove home on the back roads, wasting as much time as humanly possible. I wasn't ready for the ear pounding silence of the farmhouse. But as I drove back the isolated driveway in the wee hours of the morning, a flicker of light filtered through the cracks in the barn siding.

A fist of fear clutched my chest as I sat in my car, watching shadows dance through the holes in the century-old barn. Helplessness churned deep in my belly, but frustration at family secrets and the loss of Ridge superseded the emotion.

My first instinct was to call Ridge. I had the phone in my hand, even. But I stopped short–an image flooding my brain, Greek god and goddess, together again. Instead, I shakily opened the glove box, pulling out the 9mm from my grandfather's office that I'd been carrying off and on since Ridge stopped staying at the farm. I pushed the car door closed with a click and started for the barn. I might not be a goddess, but I was done being the victim.

52

LIV

I slipped off my hard-soled boots at the bottom of the stairs, tiptoeing up the flight of well-worn risers to the haymow. I'd done enough sneaking around this old farm to know stepping on the outer edges of the boards in my stocking feet would be the quietest way to approach.

I don't know what I thought I would do when I got up there. My life was falling apart, cracked and crumbling in broken shards around me. So, in that moment, it didn't really matter. I was halfway up the stairs before I could poke my head above the open railing enough to see into the expanse of the loft.

I clamped my molars on the fleshy interior of my jaw to keep the shocked squeak from escaping. At the far end of the room a man paced back and forth. A kerosene lantern burnt high and bright near his feet, shadows dancing on the walls around him.

I recognized Jason right away, but his demeanor told me that this was not the Jason from my past. This was the Jason from the Marriott. His pacing and angry fisted gestures proved his altered mental state. I watched from the safety of the stairway as he stopped pacing to crouch near the heater, tapping something into a spoon before thrusting the spoon into the flame.

I watched him use a syringe to shoot whatever he'd heated into his arm. He rose, dropping the spoon on the floorboards and began pacing again. But it only took a moment for the pacing to stop. He stood lethargically, his head tilted back toward the ceiling and fell to his knees. A moan—relief, pleasure—I wasn't sure, escaped his lips.

I climbed the next step, a creak ricocheted off walls and echoed against the roof. I closed my eyes and held my breath. My hand squeezed the checkerboard grip of the gun, doubt surging. Would I be able to use it if I needed to? On him? I clicked the safety off, silent proof, and prayed I wouldn't be seen.

"Liv?" Jason swung his head in my direction.

My grandmother's voice slipped into my head. *"Desperation makes for poor choices. Stay focused. Ashlyn is the key."* The truth of my grandmother's words dawned on me in that moment. Grace Sullivan had made a desperate choice, when she chose me over Ashlyn. But the dreams I'd had weren't proof of anything, they were only words. Excuses for the lies she kept in life. I bit back the surge of defiance that rolled through me. But my grandmother was right about one thing. Desperation does make for poor choices. And Jason was guilty of the most desperate decision so far.

I sucked in a deep breath, bolstering my waning courage, before climbing the rest of the stairs. If I ever hoped to make a life for myself in Cascade Hills, it involved earning one more chance with Ridge. If it didn't work out between us, so be it. But I deserved the shot. And the only way to get it was to uncover the truth, whole tangible truth. Who better to get that from than the liar himself?

"What are you doing here, Jason?" I held the revolver behind my back, not wanting to invoke a violent outburst. Chances were good he was armed, too.

"Liv?" his voice sounded hurt and puzzled. "Where have you been?"

"I was out. Have you been looking for me?"

Jason rose from the floor and strode straight toward me. His hands wrapped around my shoulders, embracing me in a hug. It was all I could do to stay still, focused.

"I need to talk to you, Princess."

"Don't call me that, Jason. I'm not your Princess. Tell me why you're here. Why are you doing this?" I stepped out of his hold.

"Doing what?" He looked genuinely confused as he reached for me again.

"Spreading lies about me? About us? Where did you get those audio clips? Who told you to go to the Marriott?" The questions eating away at my core spewed forth with rapid fire.

Hostility and rage replaced fear. This man had stolen the one thing I wanted more than anything else—not once, but twice. Half a decade ago he'd disappeared from my life, sending me into a downward spiral. Now he'd managed to snuff out any hope of a relationship with Ridge.

Tonight was my chance to retaliate. I stepped toward Jason, easing him backward toward a bank of hay bales. That's when I noticed the syringes lying on the ground. Not just one, but a good half-dozen littered the floor around the lantern.

Jason followed my gaze. "Don't worry, Princess. They're not all from tonight."

I studied Jason's eyes. His irises were nothing more than pinpoints, smaller even than I remembered from the Marriott.

"What are you on right now?"

He hesitated before answering. "Oxy. Have you ever shot it Liv? You've got to try it." He staggered from the bale, taking a couple steps before falling back into it. His eyes rolled back into his head for just a moment.

"I made a new friend," he said, the words thick and slow. He reached into a hole between two nearby bales and pulled out a kitten. They'd grown in the weeks since I cleaned out the barn. He held the little grey ball of fur toward me. "I named him Jasper."

I scratched the kitten on the head.

"How much did you take?" I asked, surprised at my own concern for Jason's well-being.

"I dunno," he slurred. He pulled the kitten to his chest and closed his eyes. Desperation clawed through me. His consciousness was fleeting. And I needed answers. To hell with his well-being.

"Talk to me, Jason." I tucked the gun into the back of my jeans, sliding my hands onto his shoulders. He sighed against my touch. The kitten purred, content in the arms of a junkie.

"I never touched a dead body before." His eyes fluttered open. The words a quiet admission.

I fought the image of Jason struggling through the woods with Jennifer's corpse.

"Why did you?"

"He said I needed to do something to prove I still loved you. He said you came back to find her. I never meant to hurt you, Liv."

"How would planting a body at the farm prove anything but hate, Jason?" My voice rose with growing frustration.

He shook his head. "I was desperate. I loved you when we were at USC, Liv. And I love you now. I never should have left you."

"You made that choice." It didn't matter–and I didn't care–but he hadn't answered my question, and it seemed like a good reminder, for both of us.

"I couldn't live the lie anymore, Liv. I didn't know when I agreed to go to USC what would happen. But, how could I say no?" He looked down at the kitten curled against his chest. His eyes drifting closed. "I never could have gone if it wasn't for him."

"Who are you talking about?" The bundle of fur on his chest slipped as his grip loosened. I grabbed the displaced and disoriented kitten and tucked him back with his siblings in the hay tunnel.

"He paid for me to go so I could keep tabs on you. I wasn't supposed to fall in love with you."

A quiet moan escaped Jason before he fell silent.

A pulse of panic threaded through me.

"Who? Who paid for you to go?" I wobbled his shoulders back a forth until long eyelashes fluttered open.

Jason looked up at me as if I was stupid, "Your dad, Liv."

His words knocked the wind out of me, and I dropped my arms from his shoulders, sliding onto the bale next to him.

"I saw the look on that cop's face when he listened to those recordings." Jason started. "When I told him we slept together. He was not happy." The last sentence was garbled. An airy laugh puffed from Jason's lips before his eyes reopened, focused on me.

"He loves you, you know. I could tell." He waved a finger at me. "The cop loves you."

Jason's eyes closed to a slit and he gave me a little salute. "Good for you Liv. That's nice." His voice trailed off.

"Jason!" I shoved him into consciousness.

"Wha-?" Hazel eyes, glazed and unfocused, fought to stay open.

"That's ancient history, Jason. You didn't do this on your own. Dad is dead, so no matter what he had to do with USC, you can't blame this on him. You're lying for someone, Jason, who?" Fury shook my voice.

Jason remained silent.

"Did you kill my grandmother?" The words sliced my tongue like razor blades.

Jason shrugged, gave a half nod. "He promised you'd never find out. He promised me you."

"Who?" I yelled again with another shake of his shoulders.

His finger rose to his lips in an ill-timed hush signal. "I stole your phone from the Holiday Inn and planted those calls. It's not hard to forge audio. Amazing what you can do with third party apps." Jason chuckled and took a wheezy breath. "But that wasn't enough."

"But you didn't have to do any of this."

A sad look passed over Jason's face, clouding his expression. "Murder." The word was a breath. "It's always about money—greed—isn't that what they say?"

I shook my head, fighting against the tears threatened to spill over onto my cheeks. "You've never been that guy, Jason. Who I was never mattered to you. Why now?"

But Jason didn't answer, diving off on a tangent instead. "How much do you think a person deserves when their sister is murdered by the man who was supposed to take care of her?"

Jason looked at me, color fading from his face. "You always thought your dad was so good. What if he's the reason we're here? What if it's not greed at all? What if it's revenge?"

The word slid like ice over my skin while anger simmered in my gut, bubbling like lava through my core.

"Lyle was right." The name smacked me backward. The course itchiness of old hay against the palm of my hand the only thing rooting me in reality. "He deserved compensation."

"What are you trying to say?" The words escaped the clench of my lungs.

"Your dad was no better than Lyle. Jennifer Tipton got in the way, the same way you're in Lyle's way now."

The realization sliced me open. My breath ragged with panic. "He's the one who called the hotline, isn't he?"

The image rushed at me, distancing me from the man slumped against the bales in the loft. Hot tears stung my face just as they'd stung Jennifer's. Her voice, *"Please don't do this,"* ringing in my ears. What had my father done?

"Dad killed Jennifer," I forced the words through uncooperative lips. Squinting against the vision that threatened to consume me.

Jason nodded, clawing at my jacket. His body lurched with the first sob, giving way to thick rivers of tears, choking his every breath. He pulled me closer and I gave in, contact pushing the image farther away. I let him hold me as he cried.

If I'd come back after that first call, Grandma might still be alive. I couldn't stem the runaway train of guilty thoughts. Whether in the eyes of the law or not, my actions were responsible for her death.

"I can't live like this anymore, Princess. I can't. Knowing how much I've hurt you. How much I've lost by leaving you— using you." He removed a hand from around my midsection, reaching up to my face to gently stroke the fading scar from the attack at the farmhouse. "And Grace, I always liked your grandma. She didn't deserve to die. But Lyle was right. It was so easy. Pretending to consult in their IT department. Slipping one pill in every time a new prescription came. No one even noticed. I'm so sorry."

The storm of hatred that festered since I'd discovered Jason's lie calmed as I studied him. Guilt. That's what opened him up to become the person I saw today. I stroked his forehead and he grew silent, drifting in and out of consciousness. The Jason of today was not the same man I loved in California. This man was helpless, a slave to a habit that gave him relief, but sunk its claws in deep. I had no doubt Lyle was responsible for that, too.

My heart pounded in my chest. The same heart that had pumped hurt, pain, and betrayal, now pumped illogical understanding through my system. Jason's eyelids flickered, ushering rational thoughts back into my brain.

"Jason?" I shook him, but he didn't wake. I tried again—louder this time.

Reality struck. Without Jason, there would be no exoneration for me. No justice for my grandmother or Jennifer. No revelation of truth. I jerked my phone out of my back pocket and dialed 911.

"This is Liv Sullivan, 7667 Sullivan Road. I need an ambulance at this address for a possible drug overdose." My voice was calm, steady, the first time I'd felt sure of anything in weeks.

I stayed with Jason while I waited for the ambulance, checking his erratic pulse every minute or so as he lay sprawled on the bales in front of me. When I finally heard the sirens, I stood, whispering to Jason. "I've got to go meet the EMT's. Show them where you are. They'll help you."

Jason eyelids fluttered but he didn't respond. I was a few steps from the bottom of the stairs when I realized the weight of the gun against the waistband of my jeans was missing. I turned around, feeling for the bulge at the small of my back. Gone. I turned to run back up to the loft just as the echo of gunfire rang through my ears.

I stood frozen on the stairway, flattening myself against the wall as Ridge and Adam ran in with sidearms drawn. Ridge motioned for the paramedics behind them to stay back. Adam passed me on his way up the stairs without so much as a look. I swung my eyes back down the steps toward Ridge. He stopped in silence and studied me, suspicion dripping from his gaze.

Adam shouted from the loft. "We're clear, male Caucasian DOA. Looks like a 10-56. It's Abbott."

Ridge stepped close enough for me to feel his heat. I sucked in a ragged breath as he grasped my chin, tilting my head back to get a good look at my eyes. I choked on the understanding that, to him, my guilt was never in question. The thought made me sick to my stomach and I wrenched my head away from his grip.

"You're okay?" Ridge asked. His voice distant, detached.

I nodded, crumpling to the stairs while Ridge holstered his gun and continued up to the loft. The rest of the night was a blur of red and blue lights and carefully orchestrated chaos as officers and detectives descended on the farm.

It was nearly five o'clock in the morning when I called Brian to tell him what happened. I hated to wake him, but I desperately needed someone to listen. And he was the closest thing I had to a friend right now. Brian was at the farm within thirty minutes, looking sleepy but concerned.

I retreated with Brian away from the commotion and into the house when an officer I'd never met asked for my clothes. "Why?" I asked.

"They'll be entered into evidence, Ma'am. Tested for gun residue." The numbness and shock of Jason's suicide dwindled, replaced by hot spikes of despair.

I changed in my room, staving off a moment of desperation, while Brian kept the cop occupied. When I came out, the officer bagged the clothes and carried them out through the front door. I doubted I'd ever see them again.

Brian stood next to me, rubbing circles onto my back, as we watched the activity from the living room window.

"It was my gun."

Brian put his arm around me, calming the quake of the tremor that shimmied down my spine.

"It's my fault."

"He did this to himself, Liv. If he didn't have your gun, he would have OD'd. You can't blame yourself."

"He forged the audio," I said, ignoring Brian's assurances.

"He said that?"

I nodded. "Not that I can prove it."

"Jesus, Liv." Brian turned and folded me into a hug. "Did you tell Ridge?"

"No. I haven't talked to him. He asked if I was okay when he found me on the steps–after he checked my eyes to see if I was high."

Pity seeped from Brian's skin into mine–heated pulses of sadness that scorched my skin. We talked for a while longer, but sleep must have overpowered the surge of adrenalin at some point during the morning hours. My last memory was being curled up on the couch next to Brian, the warmth of his body inducing sleep.

53

LIV

I woke up alone, covered by one of my grandmother's quilts. Muted voices wafted from the kitchen. I recognized Ridge immediately. His unmistakable timbre sunk into me, warming me from the inside out until reality broke through the fuzz of sleep. Brian's voice played tenor harmony to Ridge's baritone. I crept to the hall in my stocking feet, shamelessly eavesdropping on their conversation.

"How can you possibly know that, Brian? Every shred of evidence points at her. The drugs they found in the box the first night we met. Again after the incident at the Marriott, and then tonight? I can't ignore tangible proof. After this, she'll be lucky if they don't revisit manslaughter charges."

"That shit is like heroine, Ridge. You'd know if she was using."

"I made that mistake once. I won't make it again." Ridge's voice was calm but laced with regret and pain.

"Talk to her, Ridge. That's all I'm asking. Hear her out." A long moment of silence followed before Brian added, "You owe her that much."

I heard the footsteps just as Ridge came into the hallway, almost crashing into me as he rounded the corner. He paused just long enough for me to catch the scent of him before pushing past into the living room.

Brian rounded the corner as Ridge reached for the door.

"Ridge." The word was a plea.

Ridge focused his brilliant eyes on Brian. I stood against the wall where he left me, still wrapped in my grandmother's quilt, looking down at my stocking feet, willing him not to walk through that door.

"Fine," Ridge said finally. He stepped to the side of the door and motioned for Brian to exit.

"Call me if you need anything," Brian said to me, giving Ridge a pointed glance before pulling the door closed behind him.

Ridge had never looked at me the way he looked at me then. His glare was accusatory, almost hateful. Unbidden tears sprang to my eyes and I wiped at them angrily with the binding of the quilt. *Pull it together, Olivia.* Now was not the time for tears. We stood there feet from each other for what seemed an eternity before he spoke.

"Let me see your arms." It was a command.

"What?"

"Your arms," he repeated. "Let me see them."

I obeyed, dropping the quilt from around my shoulders, leaving me standing there in yoga pants and a t-shirt. I swallowed hard as he closed the distance between us. He grabbed an arm, examining the length of it before dropping it roughly and moving on to the other one. The same hands that had so gently enticed pulses of desire were now harsh tools of malice.

"I don't do drugs, Ridge." I breathed quietly as he dropped the second arm. I was afraid to look at him, afraid to see that hate directed at me.

"Sit," he ordered, pointing to the sofa.

This was a Ridge I'd never seen before, full of hostility, not at all the dimpled gentleman I'd fallen for. I tucked a leg under and perched on the closest cushion. Instead of sitting beside me, he chose to stand, pacing in front of the couch. Interrogation mode, I thought. I felt a sudden camaraderie with the criminals he arrested.

"What were you doing in the barn?"

"When I got home from helping Brian at Murphy's I noticed a light. I went in to check it out."

"Stupid," Ridge said under his breath. I wasn't sure if he was referring to me, or the action of going in alone. It was an accusation regardless. And a pang of grief rose into my chest.

"The gun was from my grandfather's study. I had it in my glovebox. I tried to be quiet, so he wouldn't hear me coming." I waited for what would come next, but when Ridge stayed silent, I compensated. "I don't know what I thought I'd do with it. It just made me feel safe, I guess."

"What happened? When you went in, what did you see?"

"Jason—at the far end of the loft, pacing back and forth, like he was angry—like you are now." I ventured.

Ridge stopped pacing. His eyes bored into me. I refused to return his stare. As it was, I was going to have trouble getting the image of this Ridge out of my mind, I didn't want to make it worse with confirmation of uncontrolled hate directed at me.

"What did you do?"

"Confronted him, asked him why he was here."

"And?"

"He said he was looking for me. Told me he loved me. That he was sorry for hurting me. That he couldn't live with himself."

Ridge said nothing.

"He said that Lyle was behind everything. That he's after

the Sullivan money," *as compensation for his sister's murder,* I wanted to add. But I was still processing that tidbit of information.

Still no response, so I continued. "I watched him shoot up. He was completely strung out, Ridge." His name on my lips lit an unwelcome ember of desire in my core. I made a mental note not to repeat his name. "But," I paused. "He admitted to forging the audio."

Every movement in the room ceased. Even the air seemed to hold its breath. Finally, Ridge kneeled in front of me.

"What else did he say?" His voice was softer, less angry.

I closed my eyes before answering, my voice not more than a whisper. "He said he could tell that you loved me."

Ridge remained silent. After a moment he stood and retrieved the quilt from the floor of the room placing it gently around my shoulders. I shrugged it tighter around me as Ridge sunk onto the cushion next to mine.

"We've got nothing that can corroborate that story."

"I know," I admitted, allowing my eyes to wander up the side of his face. His head was bent, focused on his hands in his lap. All his anger was gone. He looked as defeated as I felt. I watched him rub the fresh scars on the knuckles of his right hand.

"Why should I believe you?"

I wasn't sure how to answer, so I said the only thing that came to mind. "Because I would never hurt you. I'm not your ex-wife."

Shock replaced defeat as he scanned me with an unreadable stare. He sat for a minute before he stood and retreated toward the door.

"Seems you and Brian have been spending too much time together." The words hit the air with a singe of hatred. "Goodbye, Liv," he managed before disappearing through the slab of mahogany and out of my life forever.

54

———

RIDGE

Two things happened to Ridge once he closed the door on the Sullivan farmhouse that morning. The first was the overwhelming wave of panic that permeated every cell in his body. A whole body vise, suffocating him to the point he had to stop for air on his march back to his car. He paused. His hand rested on Liv's car, the curve where hood met front quarter panel. He drew in a breath of spring-fresh air.

The second didn't happen until two days later. He'd followed Sowards' command, asking for a leave of absence from Wallace before heading to Virginia. He stood next to his new desk at the FBI Field Station in Charlottesville, Virginia, unpacking a few things he'd brought from Cascade Hills, when he caught a woman standing in the doorway, watching him.

Strawberry blonde hair hung just past her shoulders in waves. The green blouse against the porcelain of her skin drove a spike of recognition through his core.

"Can I help you?" he asked.

"I do hope." The accent was thick, even in just those three words. She smiled, dragging a pair of oversized sunglasses off her face. His heart seized when he saw her eyes. Those eyes that stared into his soul and broke down every wall he had. He sucked in a breath, unable to force speech.

She extended her hand. "Special Agent, Ridge McCaffrey?" she asked. He nodded, shook her hand. "Ashlyn Callaghan," she provided. "We spoke on the phone a week or so ago?" She said it as if he could forget.

"I never expected–," he started, but changed course, motioning her into the office. "Please, come in."

As an undercover agent, Ridge was used to lies. After all, it was part of the job. But this case had been full of so many of them Ridge was having a hard time keeping them all straight. He came to Cascade Hills with one mission, find out what Grace knew about the Bureau's plans for the future of the GenLink program, and what, if anything, she'd divulged to others.

Grace had been involved since the beginning. Worked as a civilian liaison between GenLink assets and the program's predecessor, a "room mom" of sorts. What had her vision been for the GenLink program? What claim did her children, or grandchildren in this case, have? Did they know about her involvement with the Bureau? In other words, Ridge's sole responsibility was to find out what loose ends needed to be tied up in order for the Bureau to move forward without a Sullivan association.

Ridge had been more than skeptical. But he'd done his job, probing Grace for answers during lazy afternoon visits to the nursing home. He knew what GenLink was, had known since his training at Quantico. But until Liv, he'd never truly believed it. Did he think the military could train assets in psychological and profiling techniques? Absolutely. But as far as psychic abilities were concerned, he was more than skeptical. Even Liv's visions–glimpses into moments in time–didn't prepare him for Ashlyn Callaghan, and proof in action.

"I just flew in from Dublin. Sowards mentioned you were here. Thought I'd introduce myself in person."

Ridge shifted the cardboard box from the chair in his office to the floor, rubbing the palms of his hands down his jeans, suddenly feeling the grime of a morning spent moving. She thanked him and settled onto the black cloth seat.

"Michael and I were glad to take your call." Ridge watched as she spoke. Her lips moved in the same way as Liv's, twitching up at the corners. Her cheeks and nose sprinkled with the same light smattering of freckles. Her hair color, a few shades lighter than Liv's, the only defining asset all her own. "Michael's been hoping Liv would turn up." She hesitated, cocking her head. "I was surprised to learn you'd been excused from the Sullivan case."

Ridge wished for something on his desk to occupy his fingers. He rubbed the side of his forefinger across the pad of his thumb, relieving the need to fidget. "It was for the best."

"Hmm." It wasn't much more than a breath, really. But he felt the judgment. She glanced toward the doorway, using the toe of her black pump to urge it closed. "Permission to be candid, Agent?"

He had a feeling if he said, "No," she'd do it anyway. Another noted difference between Ashlyn and Liv. Ashlyn possessed fierce determination, undoubtedly forged by honed skill and expertise. Liv was softer, more delicate, unsure of the woman she was.

"She belongs in this program, Ridge. She was made for it. Quite literally, in fact."

"I'm not sure what you mean."

"Grace. GenLink. My mother was Aimee Callaghan. She was an empath. Selected by Grace to perpetuate the Sullivan legacy." Ashlyn air-quoted "Sullivan." "Liv's grandmother bred us, Ridge. Hand-picked my mother for an affair with her son. All for the purposes of this program."

Ridge thought back to his last conversation with Sowards. Liv was out. Untrustable.

"Do you really believe that?"

Ridge narrowed his eyes at the woman across the desk. "Believe that she was bred for the program?"

Ashlyn shook her head, strawberry waves cascading over her shoulders. "That Liv is untrustable."

Ridge stumbled back, reaching for his chair.

"You're a man who needs proof, aye?"

Ridge swallowed. *She was fucking reading his mind.*

"Can Liv do what you're doing right now?" *God, he hoped not.*

Ashlyn laughed, her smile, so similar to Liv's, squeezed at his heart. "Relax, Ridge. This comes with training. Training that Sowards, for whatever reason, is attempting to keep from her."

"She has a history of mental health issues."

Ashlyn's eyes narrowed. Her head tipped to the side. "Aren't we all a little mad, Agent McCaffrey?"

Ridge felt the suck of anxiety in his lungs. This woman in front of him who knew too much was hitting too close to home. "You don't think Liv was working with Jason Abbott?"

Ashlyn shook her head, as if the question didn't deserve an answer. She changed the subject. "I came over to try to convince Sowards to pull her into GenLink."

"And?"

"He's a lot like you, Ridge. To him GenLink is all about intelligence—the creation of information soldiers. And good soldiers don't question authority, do they? Sowards wants proof she'll fall in line. His words, not mine."

I just want proof she'll love me. The thought flitted through his mind before he could censor it.

One corner of Ashlyn's mouth tipped up. "I think you're about to get exactly what you want, Special Agent McCaffrey." She pulled a manila envelope out of her shoulder bag and slid it across the desk toward Ridge.

"What's this?"

Ashlyn lifted her shoulder in a familiar shrug. Ridge's chest clenched with regret.

"Loose ends." A shadow passed over her expression. "I just hope we're not too late."

With that, she stood and opened the door, leaving as suddenly as she'd arrived. "We'll be in touch," she tossed over her shoulder. He followed her to the hall, envelope clutched tight in his fingers, watching her disappear behind the closing door of the elevator.

55

LIV

At first, I thought the pounding was coming from inside my head. My body ached with exhaustion. Every muscle sapped of any strength it may have once possessed. I was useless. Had been for the past two days. But the pounding continued–louder.

I groaned, slapping a pillow over my head to drown out the sound. "Go away," I yelled to no one in particular. Finally giving in to the fact that someone was actually at the front door, and they weren't going to leave of their own accord.

I rolled my head out from under the pillow and checked the bedside clock, 2:59 P.M. I'd spent every hour since Jason's death either crying, throwing things, drinking, or leaving inappropriate voicemail messages on Ridge's phone. I considered it a success that my own suicide only crossed my mind once.

I wasn't sure which stage of grief this was, but about three o'clock that morning I'd graduated from angry, drunken tirades, to depression sleeping. I rubbed my eyes and reached for my robe, mounded in a pile on the floor, and padded down the stairs.

I saw Brian through the window before I ever opened the door.

"I've got it," Brian said, pushing past me into the living room.

"Got what?" I asked, "A death wish?"

"Ha, ha, Liv, that's funny." Brian deadpanned. "No, I'm serious. You wouldn't answer my calls, so I had to come out here." He paused, his eyes skimming me from head to toe. "You look like shit, Liv."

"First, no Greek goddess, now shit, welcome to my humble abode, Brian."

He glanced around the room. I knew it was a mess. Strewn papers, broken figurines, top sided lamps. His gaze hung on my phone, smashed into shards of plastic and innards on the bricks of the hearth. I did that after one of my soon-to-become infamous voicemail tirades. I picked up the claw hammer laying nearby and stowed it carefully on the mantle.

"I'm worried about you, Liv. That's all." He moved to pick up shrapnel from one of my grandmother's broken Hummel figurines. I swallowed the bubble of guilt that rose in my throat. "I've been thinking," he piled the handful of broken ceramic on the end table. "I figured out how we can prove what Jason told you."

I blinked through sleep and embarrassment, ensuring he was really standing in my living room. The sudden urge to tell Brian to go to hell, to mind his own business and stay out of mine, surged. But then Ridge's eyes came back. The pain when I'd told him I wasn't like his ex. Betrayal. I never wanted to see that in him again.

"Okay, I'm listening. But I need coffee first."

Brian smiled and followed me to the kitchen, launching into his plan as we waited for the drip cycle to complete.

"What if you go talk to him," he blurted out.

"I tried that, remember? Ridge doesn't ever want to see my face again, Brian. He made that pretty clear."

"Not Ridge," Brian said. "Lyle."

For the first time in two days I felt clarity. My eyes met Brian's. There was no joke hiding behind those oceans of blue, only desperation–a friend helping a friend.

"He's the only one that can fix this, Liv. If you can get him to confess, that will prove to Ridge what really happened."

"Brian, I can't do that." I poured coffee into my cup while the maker dripped a sizzling puddle onto the burner below.

"Why not?"

That one took me a minute. "If what Jason said is true, my father murdered the girl we found in the trunk. Her name was Jennifer Tipton. I can't...I don't know how to do that to my family."

Brian paused as I pulled the first sip of caffeinated goodness to my lips. "I'm sorry. I didn't know."

"Yeah, well. Welcome to my world. I'm damned if I do and damned if I don't." I smiled a wry smile at Brian. "You ever think about the concept of nature versus nurture?"

"Once or twice, I guess. Why?"

I slid around the breakfast bar to the dining room table and took a seat. Brian followed. "What if that's really who I am? The daughter of a freak and a murderer." I didn't know if Brian knew about Aimee or not. But at the moment, I didn't care. "What if that's the way I'm wired? Maybe I'd be better off behind bars. In an institution, whatever."

"Liv, you know that's not true. We all have baggage. It doesn't make us bad people."

"Doesn't it?"

"Besides, what about your mom? She's living with him, with Lyle. Aren't you worried about what he might do? To her?"

A thread of panic wove its way from the base of my skull and into my chest. How could I be so selfish? Brian was right.

I stood. My arms and legs heavy, buzzing with fear at what a visit to my Mom's house might turn up.

"You're right. I'm sorry, but I've got to go."

"Liv, wait. Let me help you. Don't go over there alone."

I headed for the stairs. "I'll be fine Brian. Really. I'll come by the pub when I know she's okay."

Brian nodded. By the time I'd dressed and come back downstairs, he was gone.

56

LIV

Before I could grab the keys to my car and make out the front door, the land-line phone on the kitchen wall rang with a high-pitched wail. I couldn't remember the last time I'd heard the trill of that ancient phone. I had no idea it was still hooked up. But like most things of that era, it would be a long time before it died.

"Hello?" I answered.

"Liv," there was a sudden release of breath on the other end of the line. "I'm so glad to hear your voice. I heard about Jason."

The tension in my body relaxed as my mom's voice traveled through the receiver. She said she tried my cell, but we know how that worked out.

"Are you okay?" I asked. "Are you alone?"

"I am. Why?"

"Can you come over?" Something in me softened, dulling the knife edges of pain that had jabbed me for two days. I stood near the wall, handset held to my ear, and surveyed my destruction. I'd need at least two hours to clean the house up, but those were two hours I couldn't risk. I'd get thirty minutes, tops.

"Mom, I'm glad you're here." I wasn't lying when I swung the door open. "Come in." The look on my mother's face was disconcerting, guarded. Her raven hair, normally twisted up into a formal knot on her head, hung down past her shoulders. She looked younger, more innocent. Jeans and a t-shirt completed the casual look of Beth Sullivan. And for the first time I caught a glimpse of the woman my father fell in love with all those years ago. The memory of my father made my stomach squeeze as I led my mom into the living room.

"Liv, you've really done a lot with the place." It may have been the first real compliment my mother had ever bestowed on me. "It looks nice."

"Thank you," I said, holding back the "if you only knew" of my mad scramble to free the main living areas of debris. As long as she didn't open the door to Grandpa's old study, my secret would be safe.

"Thanks for having me. I'm glad you're okay." Her hazel eyes checked mine. I pushed strength, not sure if she bought it. "I was hoping for a chance to talk. Just us."

Uh-oh, why hadn't I considered this? Was I about to get a guilt trip for not selling the farm? Leaving her to her happy life and expanded wallet? *Focus.* This was about life or death, not capital gains.

As soon as she was seated, she took a long cleansing breath, letting it out through tight lips, a mannerism I'd mastered myself, I realized. Her eyes remained on the exposed hardwood floor where my grandmother's old Oriental rug once sat, before it was bloodied by the attack at the farm.

Before I could speak, she blurted out, "Lyle was extorting money from your father."

I sat stupefied. Looking, I imagined, like the cartoon character that's been foiled, jaw dropped to the floor.

"What?" I needed her to clarify, help me make sense of the fact that she already knew Lyle wasn't the man he made himself out to be.

"I've been reading the newspapers. They released the name of the girl who was found here at the farm, Jennifer Tipton?"

She was waiting for me to respond, so I nodded, not yet capable of speech.

"It got me thinking about some documents I found after your father's death. He had a safe deposit box at the bank. It was full of old newspaper clippings, canceled checks. I didn't think too much of it at the time. They were from a long time ago. A time I wanted to forget."

"When Dad had an affair with Aimee Callaghan?"

My mom looked surprised. "I wasn't sure if you knew."

"I didn't. Not until recently."

Mom nodded. "Anyway, I went back to the bank yesterday. Took everything out of the box."

She started pulling thick piles of checks, letters, and clippings from her purse. All secured into packs with hardened rubber bands. She laid everything out on the cushion between us.

"I never really looked at the checks when I found them. Your father kept everything. But I did remember the name from the article. Yesterday, I paid more attention. The checks are all made out to Lyle Tipton. He must have changed his name when he came to the States. Two checks a month for over twenty years."

I picked the first pile up, the band disintegrated into pieces in my hand as I removed it. I flipped through the checks. All to Lyle. All for at least three-thousand dollars. I set the checks aside when I got to the newspaper article, the same one I'd dug up at the local library.

"Lyle is her brother," I said the words under my breath, Jason's claims becoming clear. This was my father's restitution for killing Jennifer Tipton.

"When did the checks stop?"

"Not until your dad's death."

That's it. That's what spawned Lyle's urge to claim what was his. The portion of the Sullivan inheritance he thought was his.

"Did you know about Jennifer?" I asked.

Mom nodded. "And Aimee."

"You knew Dad..." I couldn't form the words. But my mother knew. I felt it in her skin as she gripped my hand and held tight. Panic, fear, hate, and love all rolled together to create a bundle of energy that prodded and poked at me, scorching one minute and soothing the next.

"I was so afraid you were going to find out what your father had done." Mom swiped at the first tear to spill onto her cheek. "It's why I took you to all those doctors. To you, Stephen Sullivan walked on water. I didn't know how I'd face you if you found out that he'd had those affairs...killed a girl."

"Weren't you scared? To be with him?"

Mom shook her head. "I don't know what happened in the woods that night, Liv. Your father never told me. And the affairs ended. We got counseling. But he was never violent, Olivia. Never."

I wrapped my mother in a hug, working to process this new vision of my father. His relationship with my mother, and my mother's willingness to forgive so easily. But it wasn't my job to judge. Right now, my job was to keep her safe from the one threat I knew was still out to take what was left of the Sullivans.

My mother's tears dripped onto my shoulder, soaking

through the cotton t-shirt and onto my skin. She pulled away, dried her eyes.

"When you were little we used to come to the farm for Fourth of July. Do you remember that?"

"Of course," I answered.

"Well, when you–" she paused, her eyes locked on mine, "–when you were five you went missing out there. One minute, I looked over and you were sitting on the pier with a sparkler in your hand, oohing and aahing over the fireworks. I can still remember the colors reflecting off your face. The next minute, I looked and all that was left of you was a spent sparkler. You were just–gone."

"But you found me."

My mother's lips tilted into a smile. "A full day later. In the woods, of all places. Claimed you followed a lady walking through the trees. Of course, no one believed you."

"Until the night I saw Curt die."

Mom nodded. "But that Independence Day was when your father and I realized it would take both of us to protect you. And your future was always more important to us than our history. Does that make sense?"

In some weird way, it did.

"You were the glue that held us together." Mom patted my hand. "Liv, I'm so sorry about Jason," she said, shifting gears.

My breath caught in my throat. It was the first time anyone had tried to console me about Jason's death. And I felt the effects of that emotion on my soul. The tears stung as they spilled onto my cheeks. Someone noticed that this man, a man I'd shared a chunk of my life with, a man who–for better or worse–had played a part in making me the woman I was today, was gone. Forever.

"Lyle's dangerous, Mom. You need to get away. Out of the house. At least for a while."

My mother listened, eyes wide, as I told her about Jason's admission. His lies to the police and how he'd admitted to manufacturing the evidence that convicted me, and left Ridge believing I'd betrayed him.

"We need to figure out what to do next. Is there anything else you found?" I asked.

"Just a newspaper article about Aimee and Ashlyn's deaths." My mom pulled the fragile yellow clipping from the bottom of her purse.

She held it toward me, but I refused to touch it. She skimmed it, reaching for my hand.

"What's it say?"

"It's a retraction from the original article, the one your grandmother had stashed in the Celtic box. I should have told you sooner, but I didn't think it would matter."

The two of us studied each other.

"Ashlyn wasn't in the car, Liv. Aimee's body was the only one they found."

My heart lurched in my chest as the thought of Ashlyn being out there, alive, buzzed through me.

A long silence grew between us before her cool hand raised my chin. "Can you ever forgive me?"

It was a question I wasn't expecting, but one I was now more than capable of answering. "None of this is your fault, Mom. There's nothing to forgive."

"For pushing you away, for hiding so much from you for so many long years. I'm sorry."

"I'm sorry, too, Mom. I wish I'd known all this before now. Maybe things could have turned out differently."

My mother nodded tearfully, enveloping me in her arms and hugging tightly. Sizzles of regret and shame pulsed from her body, clenching my lungs and forcing distance between us.

"Whatever else happens, whatever we find out from here,

remember, I love you," she whispered. Her hand clutched mine as I clenched my jaw against the intermittent throbs of energy. I didn't know what this was, or why it was happening. But it was getting worse, and I wanted it to stop.

Tears crept up the back of my throat as I choked out, "I love you, too, Mom," realizing for the first time, that I meant it.

57

LIV

"I have a plan," I said as I slid onto a stool at Murphy's Pub. Brian finished pulling a pint for Melanie to take to one of the tables before turning his full attention to me.

"Is your mom okay?" he asked.

"She's at the farm. I convinced her to stay there until I get this worked out, which means I'm going to need some help."

Brian scanned the empty bar area. "Anything you need, you know I'm here for you."

"You're right. I need to talk to him."

"Who? Lyle?"

I nodded. "But I need backup. Someone who knows where I am, can get help if..." Finishing that sentence meant putting ideas out into the universe. And I wasn't ready to fully contemplate the possibilities of what could happen if Lyle saw through my charade.

"Don't get mad," Brian started, his hands raised in self-defense. "But I talked to Adam. He's willing to wire you, monitor what goes on, make sure we can get in there before he tries anything stupid."

"Great, glad to know you're planning for the worst possible scenario." I smiled at Brian, picking at a stray napkin. "Have you talked to Ridge?"

"Adam said he went home to see his dad for a couple of days."

"Good." I liked the idea of Ridge not being in Cascade Hills when I confronted Lyle. I didn't want him finding out and trying to interfere with the meeting, which I knew he would do if given half a chance. If there was one thing Ridge McCaffrey couldn't stomach, it was standing by while someone else put their life on the line. "Let's do this while he's gone. Tomorrow?"

"I'll touch base with Adam. Come by in the morning and we'll go over the details."

"You really think we can pull this off, Brian?" I asked, a ribbon of anxiety climbing through my chest.

"Absolutely." And I saw the truth in his eyes. "I know his type. If he is a sociopath, he'll want to talk. You're doing the right thing. I'll be there for you. Adam, too. I promise you, if one thing–one wrong word–is said, we'll end it. Neither of us wants you to risk your life for this."

Silence strung between us.

"Thank you," I managed. "And for this morning. I needed someone to talk some sense into me. I appreciate it, Brian.

Brian smiled and pulled his cell from his pocket, calling Adam. I could almost imagine the *Mission: Impossible* theme rolling through the pub speakers as I headed toward the door and out into the cool evening.

THE LACK of restful sleep over the past few days made the next morning arrive too soon. I can't honestly say I was on my A game when I pulled my Mustang into the parking lot at The

Hunter late that afternoon. I glanced in my rear-view mirror, squelching a tickle of panic, and searched for the surveillance van hidden just out of sight.

I trusted Brian and Adam, but since that morning, when Adam taped the microphone wire to the skin beneath my shirt, I'd known they were keeping something from me. They kept exchanging glances, and there was a pulse in the air between them that I couldn't decipher. I sucked in a breath and exhaled. *You can't think about that now. Later, Liv. Now is about protecting what little you have left. Focus on Lyle.*

I glanced once more at the van as I walked into The Hunter and asked for a booth. I sat, sipping from a glass of water and scanning the menu, trying to calm frayed nerves and forget about the tiny device taped to the flesh under my blouse. My fingers fiddled absently with the top button of the cobalt button-down for a minute or two before I checked the nervous habit.

I forced my hand down to the bench seat and tucked it under my leg, waiting anxiously for the waitress to retrieve Lyle from the back. He had a smile on his face as he approached the booth, calming some of the tension.

"Liv, it's good to see you! It's been, oh my, over a month?"

"I think so. How are you, Lyle?" I tried to appear as nonchalant as possible.

"Excellent, I'm excellent. I heard you had a little run in with the police, lately. And that horrible scene at the barn with Jason. I'm sorry to hear about that, Liv. If there's anything I can do to help you, please don't hesitate to ask." As he spoke I worked to remember the voice from the call to the hotline. It was fuzzy, granular in my memory. Even with the suggestion that it was him, I couldn't be sure.

Clamminess worked its way onto my palms, and I wiped

them on my napkin before answering. "Actually Lyle. That's why I'm here."

"Go on," Lyle encouraged, making himself comfortable in the booth and pouring a glass of water from the pitcher on the table.

"It's just... well," I stammered. *Get it together, Olivia.* "The police have been asking me some questions since Jason died and I was hoping you might be able to shed some light on them since you and my mom are so close. I would ask her, but I just don't want to upset her. You understand."

Lyle peered at me over his reading glasses, encouraging me to continue.

"They keep asking me about the woman, the one they found in the trunk at the farm." I tried to look as perplexed as possible. "Jason showed me a newspaper article about her death," I lied. "Her name was Jennifer Tipton. They think she might have been connected to my father some way. Has my mom ever mentioned her?"

"Jennifer Tipton," Lyle repeated the name, fixing his eyes on mine. His sunny expression narrowed and turned dark. Fear prickled along my spine. I did my best to hold my ground, my face expressionless, as he leaned toward me, glancing both directions before whispering, "Why don't we talk about this in my office."

"Oh, sure," I tamped down another surge of panic. Glad for the long walk to the back of the restaurant, I straightened my shoulders and readied for my best dumb act. The heat of the kitchen blasted me as we made our way down a tiled hallway. The din of clanging pots and pans, sporadic yelling, as kitchen staff prepared food, swirled with the nervousness taking root in my belly. No one would hear us back here.

He ushered me into a small office and closed the door. The click of the engaging lock sounded harsh against my eardrums.

"I'd hate for someone to interrupt us." He smiled, but it didn't reach his eyes. They remained dark, distant, angry. He motioned for me to sit in the chair as he propped himself on the edge of the desk, hovering over me.

"You've heard Mom mention her, then?" I asked stupidly, working to get a handle on my nerves.

"She's mentioned a Jennifer, in passing," Lyle said vaguely. "If memory serves, Jennifer was an exchange student your father had an affair with before you were born." He crossed his arms and looked down at me. "You already knew that, though, didn't you?"

I swallowed.

"What is it you really came to ask me today, Olivia?"

"I... I..." I stuttered, unable to form a coherent sentence. I turned away from the man taking up my personal space. I clenched my jaw, squeezing my eyes shut tight for a moment, willing away rising fear. *Get it together, Liv.*

"You forget what I already know about you, Olivia. You know perfectly well who Jennifer is, my dear, Aimee too, for that matter. All that beautiful correspondence between two lovers."

Shit. Jason had told him I knew about the letters. Of course. *Stupid.*

"Seems you don't give Jason enough credit. He was very thorough...until the end, of course." Lyle leaned forward, whispering the last of the sentence directly into my ear before pulling away. By the time the shiver had completed its trek down my spine, he was sitting in the high-backed leather chair on the other side of the desk.

"Jennifer and Aimee were best friends once upon a time. Until Aimee betrayed Jennifer, of course." Lyle's accent seemed to intensify.

"Did you know either one of them?"

My vocal cords finally produced sound. Lyle cocked his head to the side, a smirk playing on his lips.

"I knew them both. Jennifer was my sister, of course."

"Your name is different."

Lyle hesitated. "Come now, Olivia, don't tell me you've never wished to trade the name that follows you for someone else's?"

The air in the room thickened.

"Why didn't you look for her?" I managed. "The police say she spent almost thirty years buried in the woods at the farm. Did you ever find out what happened to her?"

"I knew enough."

Enough to get paid, I wanted to say. "And Aimee?"

"Tragic. Driving too fast on wet roads." The sarcasm in his voice was palpable. "No one could understand why she never applied the brake, though. Pity." An image of the woman trapped in the sinking car shot to memory, ushering with it a surge of adrenalin.

Lyle fixed his stare on me. "I've told you how I know Jennifer and Aimee." He hesitated. "I think it's only fair that you answer a burning question of mine."

He leaned forward over the desk, his weight supported on his arms. The room was tiny, my chair already pushed up against the wall behind me. There was no escape as he reached out, clutching my wrist in his grip.

"What have your little ghosts been telling you about me?"

His voice ushered in a cascade of images, Lyle with Aimee, the two of them in Sullivan woods, Aimee resisting Lyle's advances. His fingers around her wrist as they were around mine now. His lips on hers as she struggled to break free.

"You were in love with her...Aimee," I clarified.

He jerked away. My skin stung, burning under the imprint of his fingers.

"She chose my father."

"She chose wrong."

The images kept coming, fast and furious. Aimee screaming for help. Jennifer appearing through the clearing, fighting against her brother's strength. Aimee's footfalls as she ran toward the house, screaming for help. The vignettes dissolved into one I knew well, hands around Jennifer's throat. Familiar fish gulps of air as her own brother snuffed the life from her lungs.

"We all make choices that come back to haunt us, do we not?"

"My father tried to protect you. Those weren't restitution checks, those were...what?" Anger started a slow march from deep inside. "He should have had you arrested when he had the chance."

"Paranoid psychosis, that was the official diagnosis, was it not?" Lyle tilted his head, unfazed by my outburst. A slow smirk spread across his face.

"I don't know what you're talking about, Lyle." *Just play stupid, Liv*, I coached myself.

"You know, it's much easier for a law enforcement officer to believe there's a mental health issue when the suspect claims to speak to the dead."

"I'm not crazy, Lyle. I wasn't then. I'm not now." Anger surged through my gut.

"Okay then," Lyle acquiesced. "Let's chat about history a little less ancient. Do you know what happened to Jason after the two of you broke up?"

My breath caught. I wasn't prepared to talk about my history with Jason. The existence of the mic on my chest felt suddenly oppressive.

Lyle's smirk grew. "Your father was quite a generous man, Olivia. Offered to pay for Jason's schooling if only he'd watch over his little girl. Of course, that was an agreement between your dad and I." Lyle paused, seemingly lost in a thought of his own. "But, your dad stopped footing the bill when he broke your heart. Poor boy was all on his own until I swooped in and saved him."

"But why? Why pay tuition for a boy you didn't know?" I forced the words through the knot in my throat. Not sure I wanted the answer.

Lyle drummed his fingertips on the edge of the wooden desk. "What's the one thing your dad and Jason had in common, Liv?"

I shook my head.

"Affection for you." He leaned close, the words slipping through the clench in his teeth. "You're the reason I didn't get my due, Olivia. Once Aimee and Ashlyn were gone, your father cut us all off."

Lyle pulled back with a sigh, like explaining this to me was an inconvenience. "Of course, social media made Jason easy to find. You, not so much. But it seems old flames are hard to snuff out. Jason had kept tabs on you. Knew exactly where you lived, worked. It was delicate, though. I needed him to reconnect. Little did I know the lengths a heartbroken, out-of-work filmmaker will go for a second chance with the one who got away."

"By attacking me?"

"By ridding you of your attachment to this place. I did you a favor."

"You tricked Jason into killing my grandmother. Into digging up a corpse. What about the drugs, did you do that, too?"

The little bit of a plan I'd started with was now obliterated by anger and resentment. Accusations flew, leaving no room for admission. I had to slow down.

"Quite a stroke of genius, don't you think?" Lyle smiled. His eyes brightened with a glow similar to pride.

"You turned him into an addict."

"He was already an addict, Liv, like most creatives with big dreams. He was addicted to this image of perfection in his mind–to possibility. I just helped him focus his drug of choice."

Lyle studied me for a moment, as if waiting for a response.

"Did you really think Jason was capable of all of those things on his own? Of course, we wouldn't be having this conversation right now if he had followed the instructions he was given."

My breath quickened. *It was working, he was coming clean.*

"What instructions were those?" I almost had him.

"Oh, now, Liv, don't tell me he left this world without telling you?" Lyle's voice dripped contempt as he pulled himself out of the chair, sliding around the desk toward me. He cocked his head to the side and leaned over me. He wasn't a big man, but he was tall. He pushed in closer. My chair banged against the wall, his arms on either side of my head. "The Sullivans ruined my family. Stole the woman I loved and changed our lives forever. I deserved compensation. But once Aimee and Ashlyn were gone, your father reneged on our arrangement. Now's my chance to compensate. Jason should have killed you. Spared you a life of secrets."

Even though it wasn't news, his words hit me like fire. I squinted, drawing away from the hot spikes of anger pulsing off his body. "What secrets?"

Lyle drew back, giving me a moment to gain some clarity before continuing. "Jason was easy to control, up until that night he visited you at the Marriott. Before that, he did exactly what I needed from him. Found you in a city of four million people. Told me about your little ghosts, your stay at Los Angeles Mental Health. Got the detective out of the picture by forging that audio. All it took was the promise of a blushing bride, bright future, and a rather brutal opioid addiction."

The fire of adrenalin surged as I realized it was over. He'd done it, admitted to everything, and I had it on tape.

"Everyone claims to want the truth, but the fact is, brutal truth is a hard thing to take. Are you sure you're ready?"

He didn't expect an answer. I could tell by the sneer on his face as he lunged toward me, toppling the chair backward. Lyle's weight as we hit the ground forced the air from my lungs in a panicked yelp. His voice hot and thick against my ear, "Aimee was carrying my child the night my sister was killed, Olivia."

I sucked in a breath, pushing against Lyle's body, as a pinch of heat radiated up my side.

"The Sullivan legacy is through," Lyle seethed. "It's time to reclaim what's mine."

Before I could fight, the office door thrust inward. Adam and Brian crashed into the room, jerking Lyle from the ground and knocking the serrated hunting knife from his grip.

Warmth I'd attributed to nerves as the door sprang open, began to spread, working its way from my ribcage and down my abdomen—all before true pain ever hit. I clasped my hand to my ribs, pulling it away to see a veil of deep red obscuring my palm. The metallic heat of blood rose in the back of my throat. An incessant urge to cough in its wake.

Heavy pressure descended along my side. Brian's deep blue eyes searched mine as he moved me from the tangle of the chair and flat onto the floor. He was speaking. I blinked. Once. Twice. No. Yelling. But the sound of rushing blood in my ears drowned him out. I tried to wrap my lips around a word, his name, but a wave of coughs interrupted. I gripped Brian's sleeve as my world fuzzed around the edges, dimming to darkness.

58

LIV

Grogginess surrounded me like a veil as I awoke. The stark walls of the hospital room looked foreign to me, the voices I heard, muffled, as if my ears were full of cotton. Finally, my blinking eyes began to adjust, and my ears seemed to open up, interpreting sound more clearly.

My mother sat on a small, built-in couch that lined a large picture window. Beside her was Brian. He was bent forward, elbows on his knees, studying his hands. Fear and worry streaked across Mom's face while a woman in a white doctor's coat talked to them.

Panic seized me as the memory returned. Blood. So much blood. The sudden thought that I might end up the product of someone else's psychic dream, shot through me. I struggled against the mattress, shifting to raise my body into a sitting position. But my muscles were heavy, uncooperative. I stopped only when excruciating pain tore through my side. An involuntary moan escaped me, the use of my abdominal muscles sending a streak of agony to every nerve ending.

When I opened my eyes again, the doctor stood closest,

using a small light to look into my eyes. She nodded to Mom and Brian and excused herself. Brian took her place.

"Liv, don't try to move, take it easy." His hand gently brushed a strand of hair out of my face, my eyes locking on his.

"Did we get him?" My voice was hoarse and dry, unrecognizable to me.

He smiled, eyes twinkling. "You did it, Liv. Lyle's in custody as we speak."

I worked to process what he'd just said, my brain still foggy. A nurse cleared her throat loudly before sidling up to the bed, followed by Adam who carried a cardboard tray of three coffees.

"I see our patient is back with us," she said. "You're a fortunate girl, Miss Sullivan. We rarely get the chance to repair wounds like that. Lucky these fine gentlemen were there when you needed them." She nodded toward Brian and Adam, both of whom looked embarrassed by the compliment.

"Don't let her appearance fool you," Adam refuted, handing a coffee to my mom. "Liv's stronger than she looks. She's the one who deserves the credit."

"Quite," the nurse agreed with a warm smile. "How are you feeling?"

"Fuzzy," I admitted. "Sore."

The nurse assured me the mental fuzziness would continue to wear off and showed me a button attached to an IV, allowing me to control pain medication that was already dripping slowly through my veins.

As the nurse left, I turned to Brian. "Ridge? Is he back?"

Brian's face fell as he looked at Adam, who shook his head slowly. "Not yet, Liv. I've left him messages, but he hasn't called me back." I expected the choke of tears, but they didn't come. Instead, loneliness settled into my gut.

Mom took my hand, kissed it. "I love you, Liv," she whispered before medicated sleep pulled me under.

The pleasant soundtrack of caring voices played against the backdrop of my hospital room. The image of my grandmother and the little girl materialized at my bedside. The cool of my grandmother's hand on mine. The seeping understanding that I'd achieved what she asked. The vault of secrets I had yet to understand now cracked and open.

When my eyes reopened, a perfect full moon had exchanged places with daylight. Why was it I never had my camera at moments like these? I heard the drone of conversation outside my room. But the pain in my side reminded me why I was here. The nurse had been right. The cotton-like fuzziness had worn away. I strained to listen as the voices continued in the hall.

"Any luck?" I recognized Brian's voice right away.

"No, nothing. Even Captain Wallace doesn't know where he is." It was Adam's voice that answered.

"If we don't hear anything by this afternoon, I'm calling his dad. This isn't like Ridge."

I pulled in a wobbly breath. I'd done what I could. Whether or not it brought Ridge back to me was out of my control. This was the life I'd forged for myself. At least it was one with answers.

The memory of Ridge crept in unannounced. I would have given anything in that moment to wrap my arms around him, to hear his honey baritone telling me what I'd done had been worth it. I couldn't stem the frustration gnawing at my gut, fueled by the knowledge that he was not only ignoring me, but his best friends, too. Guilt flooded, launching a wave of tears as the nurse bustled in for her morning rounds.

"How are we feeling to–" She stopped when I turned to face her, failing to compose myself in time for her arrival.

"Not so good today?" she ventured.

"Actually the fuzziness is gone, and the pain is a little better," I said, attempting a smile. She snagged a tissue from the nearby box and began wiping at my tear stained cheeks.

"I'm glad to hear that." She smiled. The doctor wants you up today, walking a bit. He thinks you might be able to go home tomorrow if you have someone that can assist you around the house. You'll need some help to get around, dress. Things like that. We'll talk more about restrictions before you leave."

I nodded, remembering the night Ridge stepped in as my nurse after the attack at the farm. That seemed like a lifetime ago. I returned the nurse's sad smile, wondering if I had someone to fill that role this time.

"But what about this?" she asked, gesturing to my puffy eyes and barely controlled tears.

"This..." I gestured to my face, "has nothing to do with this." I finished by gesturing to my midsection.

She smiled sadly at me. "The wounds we can't see often take the longest to heal."

She patted my hand, and I watched her bustle away toward her next patient.

My tears were under control and my face wiped clean by the time Adam and Brian entered a few minutes later. Neither of them looked particularly pleased, but they did a pretty good job faking it for my sake.

We sipped coffee, my reward after an excruciatingly long walk down the hall and back, until my mother bounded in.

"The doctor says you can go home tomorrow, Liv. Isn't that

wonderful? Do you want to stay at my house, or would you rather stay at the farm? I'm fine with whichever you choose."

She looked happily into my eyes and I couldn't help but grin in return. This was the mother I'd missed for twenty-six years, and no matter how the ache in my chest pounded with the reminder that Ridge was gone, my mother's love was infectious.

59

RIDGE

Ridge sat in his office at the FBI Field Station in Charlottesville twirling a pen from one finger to another, down the back of his knuckles and back up again. He didn't flinch when his supervisor approached from behind, flopping a file onto the table between them.

"You did the right thing."

The man fixed his steel grey eyes on Ridge. Watching, waiting, expecting him to show the remorse that bubbled in his gut. Ridge wouldn't give him that satisfaction. Instead, he bit back the urge to tell Special Agent-in-Charge, Marcus Sowards to fuck off. Walking away from Liv was the most difficult thing Ridge had ever done. The hole in his heart oozed like a gaping wound that refused to be sutured closed. And now, it was all he could do to keep from returning the tsunami of calls from Cascade Hills, each one invoking an image of Liv bleeding out on the floor of a madman's office.

"So now what?" Ridge asked.

"We wait." He slid the file toward Ridge, who stopped the pen midway through its descent down his hand. He checked the tab before opening the folder, Liv's name exchanged for code, GL Asset 32 - ACTIVE. The involuntary clench of Ridge's jaw sent a blade of pain through his temple. She was more than a number. So much more.

"You knew it would end like this." Sowards continued.

"With Liv fileted on the floor of Hunt's office? Sorry, Marc, that was a scenario I wasn't prepared for."

Sowards closed the door behind him, sliding into the chair across from Ridge. "I apologize for how things went down, Ridge. I know this was more than an operation for you. But Callaghan was right. Olivia proved her worth. We got Hunt."

"Why not tell me what this was all about from the start? Why send a civilian in to do our job?"

Sowards sighed, ran a hand through his wiry hair. "We didn't know exactly what Liv was capable of. You were kept in the dark to protect the operation. If she'd read something in you, the op would have been jeopardized. We needed her to trust you. The less you knew, the better."

"And now?"

"She did her job. Hunt's been transferred to Federal custody. He'll come clean, tell us who Grace was working with in Ireland."

"And if he doesn't?"

"Then we find another way in. Grace had an entire network working on the next generation of GenLink, Ridge. We'll find out who they were. One way or another." He paused. "Olivia did what she was bred to do, McCaffrey."

"Except she doesn't know that, yet."

Ridge set his eyes on Sowards, who gave a silent shrug of understanding.

"Callaghan's plan is solid. She thinks Olivia will go to Dublin willingly. At this point it's out of our hands. The most important thing right now is to keep your distance. There's no need to muddy the waters. We've got a team in place ready to train. It's a done deal, Ridge."

Ridge glanced down at the picture of Liv clipped to the first page in the file. Green eyes shone up at him. "I should be there. This was a mistake."

Sowards leaned forward, his voice a quiet threat. "We've got a program self-destructing from the inside, Ridge. Assets missing. Three in the last six months alone. You know as well as I do that Liv is on that hit list. The only hope we have of saving this program, and the assets involved, is to find out who Grace was working with and why. Hunt's obsession with the Sullivan family is the best chance we have to pinpoint the leak."

"She'll be safe?" Ridge questioned. "In Ireland, I mean."

"As safe as humanly possible." For some reason, that didn't soothe any of Ridge's worries. "The team info is in her file. If you have questions, you know where to find me."

"And me?"

"Officially, your post is here. But I want you back in Cascade Hills once Olivia leaves. That's where this all started. Chances are, it's where it will end." Sowards shrugged. "Your cover's intact. Tell Wallace you had family business to take care of. Keep your ear to the ground until you hear otherwise from me. Understood?"

Ridge nodded. Gathering his jacket, he stood. Sowards reciprocated, following him toward the office door.

"This whole op is fucked up, Sowards. You know it as well as I do. I didn't realize it before. But now..."

"Now?" Sowards cut in. His voice tightened, eyes blazing as he stood toe to toe with Ridge. "Now, you went too far. You made it personal, McCaffrey. The GenLink operation is a government intelligence initiative, not your own personal dating pool."

Ridge dropped his jacket and lunged, shoving his supervisor against the file cabinet behind him. Sowards showed no fear. Glancing up at the camera mounted in the corner of the room he whispered, "Watch yourself, McCaffrey. You can't help Liv from behind bars."

Ridge held firm, his fingers digging into the fabric of Sowards' sport coat. "Liv didn't choose this life." Ridge spat the words through clenched teeth. His frustration bubbled to the surface.

Sowards pulled away, resituating his jacket. "No, Ridge. This life chose her."

He opened the office door and motioned Ridge through. "Take a few days while we get things cleaned up. Go see your dad. The distance will do you good. I'll be in touch once the asset reaches Dublin."

Ridge knew it was pointless to respond. The operation was bigger than him. Bigger than Sowards, even. Psychic intelligence had been on the fringes of Bureau operations since the seventies. His personal involvement with an unwitting asset wasn't going to change the government's interest. All he could do was follow orders, keep tabs from afar, and hope for a chance to apologize for tearing her life apart.

60

LIV

Water lapped gently against the nearby shore of Cascade Lake as I sat on the screened-in porch with my eyes closed, soaking in the warm sunshine. Lost in the chatter of early Spring birds, it took a minute to notice when voices from the driveway pierced the peacefulness.

There'd been no sign of Ridge, not so much as a phone call, but each time the bubble of silence surrounding the farm was broken, a spiral of hope wound through me, squeezing my insides in a flux of excitement. My mind had invented all kinds of scenarios over the past week, most of which still left me alone and heartbroken.

I ran my right hand absently down my left side. My fingers tracing the bandage that covered a jagged line of stitches extending from the bottom of my ribcage through the soft skin of my abdomen almost all the way to my belly button. It would leave a horrible scar, no doubt. But I was alive.

Hurt crept into my chest and I pushed it away angrily. A seed of resentment had taken root deep inside me. I'd risked my life by confronting Lyle for one reason, to prove to Ridge that I was neither a lunatic nor an adulterer. Looking back, it all seemed so pointless. I sighed as deeply as my wound would allow, wondering how different my life would be if I hadn't confronted Lyle at all.

"You up for some company?" Mom leaned on the door-frame that separated the kitchen inside from the porch.

I nodded, expecting her to join me on the glider, but she turned and stepped to the side, allowing Jack Reynolds to step through.

"You're looking well," he said, taking a seat in the patio chair across from me. I smiled at Jack.

"The paperwork I sent to Ireland regarding your grand-mother's properties was returned today. I thought I'd bring them over."

Jack placed the manila folder he'd carried in on the table between us.

"Thanks, Jack. I appreciate everything you've done for me."

"My pleasure." He hesitated, as if he wanted to say some-thing more. "I received some information I think you might find interesting. It's in there as well." He pointed to the envelope.

I wasn't in the mood to go over the minutiae that remained regarding Grandma's estate, but since Jack had driven all the way over, it was the least I could do. I pulled the package closer and picked it up. Bending the brass clasps to their open posi-tion, I turned the envelope upside down and shook the contents out onto my lap.

A letter was on top, but the weight of the paper underneath gave it more momentum. Thick photography paper slid from under the typed document. Green eyes bored into me from their upside-down position. I righted the photograph, my breath catching in my chest. These weren't the eyes of a ghostly five-year-old girl, these were the eyes of a woman.

"It's your sister, Olivia. It's Ashlyn." Jack's voice was quiet, soothing. "The letter is from her, too."

I glanced back down at my lap, studying the beautiful face staring back at me. Words escaped me. The reality I'd been living abruptly shoved to the outskirts of importance.

"Thank you," I whispered. But thank you would never be enough.

"She wants to meet you."

My eyes flew open wide, focused on Jack. A long silence passed between us. How was I supposed to respond? I should want to meet her, right? I mean, she's my twin sister for God's sake. A flicker of panic embedded itself in my chest, wrapping around my heart. I pushed the photograph and letter back into the envelope. I stared at the sun-bleached floor of the porch.

"Olivia?" Jack's voice broke my trance. "If you're not ready, it's fine. She'll wait."

"No," I shot back. "I'm ready." I whispered.

SUNLIGHT STREAMED through the windows and warmed the early May air when we gathered to welcome Ashlyn Callaghan to Sullivan farm. I had so many unanswered questions, and so many years of life to learn about. I could almost feel my grandmother and father smiling down on me as the particles of sunshine glistened over the farm.

I stood on the front porch looking at the lot of cars spread near the barn. My mother's Mercedes and my Mustang sat side by side closest to the hulking structure. Adam's older model Silverado was next, flanked by Brian's Charger. Behind them sat another row that included two police cruisers, driven by Captain Wallace and Shana, who were both on duty.

Rod had parked his silver Jaguar away from the rest of the

pack, which I thought was appropriate given his intense lack of trust. The whole picture struck me funny, and I couldn't help but reach in the front door to grab my Nikon and capture a few frames. I had a feeling there would be lots of photo ops today.

"Any sign of them yet?" Mom stepped out onto the porch, offering me a freshly made glass of lemonade. "Here," she offered. "Adam said I make the best lemonade he's ever tasted."

Her smile made my barely contained excitement bubble over. I giggled softly before the painful reminder of Lyle crept along my side, subduing laughter.

"I didn't know you could boil water, let alone make lemonade," I teased.

"Oh, that hurts," Mom said, feigning offense. "But, for the record, lemonade is much easier. No boiling necessary." She started to disappear inside when the crunch of gravel caught our attention.

"I think it's them," I whispered. Nervousness wrapped around my vocal cords. I faced my mother to find the reflection of anxiety within her own wide hazel eyes.

I teetered down the stairs to meet Jack's car, favoring my bandaged side. What if we had nothing in common? What if we couldn't find anything to talk about? But Jack's beaming smile as he lifted himself from the car eased some of my concerns.

He walked around to the trunk to lift Ashlyn's bags from the back as the passenger door opened, revealing a tall, beautiful strawberry blonde. We studied each other a moment before a smile spread across her lips and she ran forward to meet me.

"Liv." She was just about to throw her arms around me when she noticed the bandage around my midsection. Instead, she grabbed both of my hands and bubbled, "You have no idea how lovely it is to finally meet you."

Light pulses of contentment pricked at me from Ashlyn's hands as we stood together on the porch. In awe of Ashlyn, I secretly wished I'd been the twin to win the battle of height. As far as twins go, we weren't identical, but we shared the same almond shaped green eyes and had the same prone-to-smiling mouth.

The lilt of Ashlyn's Irish accent had us all enchanted and her sense of humor soon became obvious as we chatted throughout the evening. We learned a great deal about her life in Ireland, and I was surprised to discover she worked for local police in the Republic as a crime consultant. Adam seemed enthralled by that tidbit of her life. He followed her around like a lap dog, bringing it up again and again over the course of the evening.

She never divulged too much about how she went about her work, but I was happy to see them getting along so well. I felt the first twinge of what I can only identify as envy as I watched Adam and Ashlyn talk from across the room, her eyes flicking in my direction every now and then. Missing Ridge now colored even the happiest moments of my life.

The plan was for Ashlyn to stay at Sullivan farm for the week. So as the party died down I showed her to the largest of the guest bedrooms. It was the first time we'd really had to ourselves all night. She asked me to stay as she unpacked a few items from the smaller of her two suitcases.

"Grace is really proud of you, you know?"

Her green eyes were locked on mine when I answered, "I know."

"Ridge said you have them." My knees buckled. My hand catching the dresser to keep me upright. She took a seat on the side of the bed, patting the empty space of mattress next to her. "The dreams," she clarified quietly.

"Yes," I answered. She waited for me to formulate the question. "You talked to Ridge?"

She smiled, her perfect white teeth gleaming. "Who do you think sent me here?"

"But he..." How could I finish that sentence–left me, abandoned me, sacrificed me, scarred me.

Ashlyn gripped my hand in hers, pulses of energy flowing from her skin into mine. Emotion swirled, nonsensical.

"He knows what you did for him. He wants to be here. He can't, Liv." Her eyes were locked on mine. She meant every word. Whatever was keeping him away was beyond his control.

"But why not?" I felt like a child asking the question, but I needed to know. I deserved to know. Ashlyn slipped her hand from mine.

"They're getting more intense aren't they?" she asked.

"My dreams?" She'd changed the topic, gone back to stowing her clothes. I couldn't restrain the nervous chuckle as dreams from the past few months flooded back. "I guess."

Ashlyn smiled. "Can you talk to the visitors?"

I nodded.

"What about the people around you? Can you feel them?"

I didn't answer.

"There's nothing to be afraid of, Liv. It's energy. The universe is made up of it. Embrace it. It's a gift, you know."

"It's never felt like a gift." Those were words I'd never spoken aloud. People who didn't have tendencies like mine couldn't understand. In my experience, they either thought it would be the best thing in the world or they looked at me like I was a freak. Frankly, even those that started out on the first side sooner or later converted to the second group. But this was Ashlyn. Of all people, she should appreciate my struggle.

"Mom had them, too, you know," she said.

I swung around to face my sister. Pain shot through my side

in opposition to the sudden movement. I was pretty certain that even the momentary grimace wouldn't hide the shock that streaked across my face.

Ashlyn shrugged. "Lyle knew about Mom's visions. I'm certain it's why he suspected you'd been talking to ghosts. Maybe he figured you'd been talking to Mom."

I swallowed a knot of unresolved panic, Lyle's last words seeping into my consciousness.

A mischievous grin spread across Ashlyn's lips as she rose to meet me. Her arms slid down my shoulders as her emerald eyes brightened, holding my gaze. "That's not true, you know."

"What's not?"

"What Lyle said to you, that Aimee was pregnant." Ashlyn watched me, gauging my reaction. "You're a Sullivan, Liv, through and through."

"I took a DNA test. My dad had a sample still on file. I'm just waiting for the results." Regardless, Ashlyn's assurance was comforting. Focusing on something real, scientific, felt good. My sister, this microcosm of metacognition, was more than I could take.

"Oh, Liv, you remind me so much of Mom. She didn't want the extra responsibility that comes with this gift. She fought it for years. Stuffed it away until Dad told her about your dreams–" Ashlyn's face fell.

While I was the one wondering why my mother chose to abandon me, Ashlyn had grown concerned by why her father had done the same. We'd both grown up with holes that needed to be filled. "I saw you. When you were little–four or five years old."

Ashlyn looked at me through the reflection in the dresser mirror.

"I thought you were dead."

"Our dreams are simply moments in time, energy captured

within the human consciousness. You've never been restricted to those who have passed. The only restrictions you have are those you place on yourself."

I stared at my sister. Eyes like mine. Lips curved in the same bow. A reflection of similitude. "Why did she let her best friend die?"

Ashlyn sighed. "She was scared. If she could have reached your father a few seconds sooner, maybe it would have turned out differently." My sister lowered onto the bed beside me. "She never forgave herself for what happened that night, Liv. I think the work she did helped her feel worthy. Every time she helped a family I think it hurt a little less, but her grief never went away. I think it's why she wanted to work for the Garda, to make up for letting Jennifer down."

I nodded. Regret was an emotion I knew well. A pang of guilt joined the dull throb of pain I'd grown accustomed to over the past several weeks.

"I know growing up for you was difficult. Perception in Ireland is a bit different, I think. I had Mom to help, but it wasn't like that for you. But you need to know, there is good in what we can do."

The single sarcastic chuckle erupted without permission.

"There is. I promise. But you have to believe. And it takes time. Patience ... training." Ashlyn raised an eyebrow, waiting.

Talk of goodness only conjured up one image–Ridge.

Ashlyn squeezed my free hand, the corners of her mouth turning up into a secretive smile.

"It's not over, Liv. Come visit me in Ireland. There's so much I can teach you."

Find out what happens next in the
Blood Secrets Saga

Keep reading for a sneak peek.

Inherent Lies

Blood Secrets

Book 2

ALICIA
ANTHONY

BLOOD SECRETS ✚ BOOK 2

INHERENT
LIES

CHAPTER 1
INHERENT LIES

LIV
Dublin, Ireland

I should have been three thousand miles away that night, not standing in the drizzle watching recovery units unearth the remains of a twelve-year-old girl. I shivered as the piercing caw of a crow sounded from the church steeple behind me.

"'Tis an omen, it is." Michael Donaghey's white hair lay plastered to his head, darkened by an afternoon spent in Irish mist. Although he now lived in Dublin, he'd grown up in County Cork and his accent was heavy even to native Irish. To an American like me, he sounded like what I'd always thought an Irish man should sound like, a mix between Darby O'Gill and a post-pubescent Lucky Charms leprechaun.

Michael had been with the Dublin Garda "since God was a young man," as he liked to say, and had taken me under his wing since the afternoon I'd mustered the courage to call the number on the scrap of paper I'd found in my grandmother's old cottage. That was almost six months ago. I'd never intended to stay this long.

The trip was planned. Head to Ireland, tie up some loose ends with my grandmother's estate, go home. I'd even factored in a little time with the sister I'd never known. All that, and it'd be time to go back to Cascade Hills. Time to pick up the pieces of my jigsaw puzzle of a life. But it was easier to stay. Easier to claim that life had gotten in the way. When the truth was, death had other ideas.

Michael's arm blanketed my shoulder in warmth as he joined me at the rock wall. Below us, the countryside opened, revealing lush hills and valleys just outside Dublin City. Behind us, across a narrow road, was Johnnie Fox's Pub, whose claim to fame was being the "highest" pub in all of Ireland.

I'd been there with Ashlyn my first night in Ireland. Beyond the quaint nooks and crannies of the pub, there'd been another draw. A sensation, greater than the cozy warmth of Guinness filtering through my veins. It was a sense of belonging.

Whispers of, *"Welcome home,"* wafted on the breeze. Maybe it was because I was with the sister I'd just recently learned existed, or the fact that I was in a country that held a special place in my grandmother's heart. Regardless, I felt safe and welcomed in the land of my ancestors, people who afforded magic and the unexplainable an air of importance I'd never before experienced.

Trust me, I know how cheesy that sounds. And now, as jacketed professionals sifted through a blanket of overgrown vegetation to haul the decomposing remains of an innocent little girl to the morgue, safe was the most remote emotion.

I pushed the memory of that first night at the pub away and leaned into Michael's side, the rainproof fabric of our navy blue Garda jackets sliding noisily against each other.

"It's unfair," I heard myself say, realizing too late that I was more distraught over the role I was forced to play versus the death of someone's daughter. I took a breath and tried to cover, scuffing my tennis shoe over a loose rock at the base of the wall. "She didn't do anything to deserve this."

"Oh, Liv, thirty years I've been watching these things happen, and thirty years later I still don't understand the evils of man." Michael paused, his voice getting quiet. "You, though, just like your ma, you see it."

"What if I don't want to see it anymore?" It was the first time I'd lent a voice to the frustration that nagged at me.

Michael sighed, his broad shoulders rose and fell as he gave my shoulder a squeeze. "We aren't always given the opportunity to choose our destiny."

Michael had become one of the few people I could confide in. Before the trip, I anticipated Ashlyn would have filled that role. I owed her a debt of gratitude for giving me reason enough to leave the heartache of Cascade Hills in my rear-view mirror. But since I'd been working with Michael, my relationship with my sister had changed.

We still got together for dinner and drinks at least once a week, but there was an air of inexplicable friction between us. The way my body buzzed with pent up energy when we were together proved she felt the rift as powerfully as I did. Even so, she never let on.

She was busy with her own caseload for the Garda, so our talks usually circled around the everyday minutiae of our jobs. Rarely did our conversations border on our personal relationship. I was thankful for that. I had a feeling I wouldn't like what she had to say.

"Perhaps it's time to take a break, my love." Michael had started calling me that the first day I met him, and the nickname had stuck.

I glanced over at him, grateful for a reason to stop watching as techs zipped what was left of the girl's blackened body into an oversized bag and lifted her onto a gurney.

Michael's blue eyes twinkled down at me, the skin crinkled at the corners above round rosy cheeks. His easy smile was what had first drawn me to him. Many officers in the Garda were so serious in their work. Michael tempered his professionalism with a good dose of Irish wit. It was obvious why my birthmother had chosen him as her partner some twenty years before.

No matter what case he was working, what horrific crime he was forced to solve, he never allowed the horrible parts of his job to cloud his psyche.

"The devil knocks on our door every day, lads. The key is, not to let him in." I'd heard that turn of phrase from Michael countless times. The younger generation of officers had taken to ignoring him. It was hard not to notice the sideways glances between them, the condescension of an old man teetering on the edge of senility, spouting nonsense. But from the beginning, I knew he was different.

"Donaghey, Sullivan! Over here!" One of the crime scene investigators motioned for us from the bottom of the hill. I followed Michael over the low rock wall. Picking my way down the embankment with care, I worked to keep a firm grip on the wet foliage beneath the rubber soles of my tennis shoes. Michael, by contrast, trotted easily down the incline, ignoring any threat the rain-glazed vegetation posed to a man of his age. I hurried to join him just as one of the investigators began to speak.

"Could be the murder weapon." The older of the two men pointed into the knee-high grass.

Michael glanced back at me, waiting for my input. I peered down into the weeds. A knife, about eight inches long with a curved blade glinted up at me. It was caked with mud, the ivory handle blackened by time and grime. I blew a silent stream of air through my lips as relief flooded me. The knife had nothing to do with the girl's death, sparing me from the impromptu vision that too often accompanied crime scene finds.

"It's not the murder weapon. She was strangled."

Two sets of eyes bored into me.

"Quite a coincidence, then, isn't it? How can you be sure?" The younger of the two crime scene investigators gave me a doubtful look, one eyebrow raised, voice ripe with skepticism.

"Has she been wrong before?" Michael shot back. "Give us a ring when the forensics come in. Sure, they'll be looking for ligatures."

And so it had been for the last several months, Michael cocooning me from skeptics while I re-opened cases long cold with ever intensifying visions. There was an obvious divide within the Garda. A good majority believed that psychic dreams held merit. Most still had grandmothers that swore by the call of the banshee. But not everyone was willing to admit those beliefs, at least not out loud.

Others asserted psychic mediums were nothing more than a spoof, a hoax meant to draw attention or money. I had a file full of newly closed cases to prove otherwise, so it didn't bother me, except when we were in the field and one of the investigators called me out.

Sometimes I think they just wanted me to go there, to tell them the gory details of the images that haunted me, rubber-necking their way into my own personal freak show. But there was only one person I wanted in the room when I was relaying a vision, and that was Michael.

I glanced up the hill toward Johnnie Fox's as we walked away from the scene. The setting sun peeked slowly from behind receding clouds, shooting rays of sunshine down onto the sheep field beyond the pub. In a moment the weeping skies would clear and there would be a rainbow, a meteorological phenomenon marking the predictable shift of the Irish sky that never ceased to amaze me.

A crow called again from the church as Michael and I approached the car. The steeple drew my attention once more just as the bird took flight, vacating the bell tower with a few strong flaps of blue-black wings. The girl had been found exactly where I'd said she would. Our job here was done.

The rain-streaked passenger window of the car brightened as the clouds drifted away. An arc of vibrant colors slid down behind Johnnie Fox's just as Michael pulled the car away from the side of the road, winding down the hill toward the city while the fear-widened eyes of a twelve-year-old girl shadowed my thoughts.

ACKNOWLEDGEMENTS

This book would not have been possible without the generous support of a whole slew of people I'm excited to name in print. My Spalding University MFA family, who were the first to lay eyes on this piece when it was called *The Girl in the Yellow Dress*, were instrumental in its development and of me as an author. From Louella Bryant's kind and careful encouragement to Nancy McCabe's critical eye, both helped this story gain legs. Special thanks to my many Spalding friends and traveling companions, particularly Diana Wilson and Mackenzie Jervis, without whom the journey wouldn't have been nearly as much fun.

Special thanks to the many friends I've made in this tight knit community of worldwide writers. To my Golden Heart® Persisters and Omegas, this is how the story starts. To Kandy Williams for talking me down off the ledge a few times when in the editing phase of this work. Our lunches are highlights for me. And to my Central Ohio Fiction Writers and Buckeye Crime Writers friends, who always make me feel welcome even when I've missed a bazillion meetings, thank you.

To my family, especially Doug and Jillian for making this dream possible. Without your sacrifice I could never have made it this far. Your belief in me helps me believe in myself. I am eternally grateful for your love and support.

My grandmother, Betty Alkire, was the initial inspiration for the Blood Secrets Series. Her creative spirit endures through her art and in the memory of those who knew and loved her. I penned the first scene following her death and am eternally grateful for the guidance she gave me both in life and beyond. I have no doubt she guides me still.

ABOUT THE AUTHOR

Alicia Anthony's first novels were illegible scribbles on the back of her truck driver father's logbook trip tickets. Having graduated from scribbles to laptop, she now pens novels of psychological suspense in the quiet of the wee morning hours. A full-time elementary school Literacy Specialist, Alicia hopes to pass on her passion for books and writing to the students she teaches.

A two time Golden Heart® finalist and Silver Quill Award winner, Alicia finds her inspiration in exploring the dark, dusty corners of the human experience. Alicia is a graduate of Spalding University's School of Creative & Professional Writing (MFA), Ashland University (M.Ed.) and THE Ohio State University (BA). Go Bucks! She lives in rural south-central Ohio with her amazingly patient and supportive husband, incredibly understanding teenage daughter, two dogs, three horses, a plethora of both visiting and resident barn cats, and some feral raccoons who have worn out their welcome.

When she's not writing or teaching, Alicia loves to travel and experience new places. Connect with her online at www.AliciaAnthonyBooks.com. She'd love to hear from you!